Reviews for "The Village Twins"

"In the spirit of Sholem Aleichem… These stories of identical twins, confused from birth, will charm with their simplicity and sincerity." – *AudioFile*

"…a good story very well told" – *The Jewish Independent*

"Wired Words/Electric Prose… Weekly installments… are short enough to read easily on the screen and they carry readers into an ongoing story." – *The Providence Phoenix*

"…it's clear from the start that there is nothing factual about this book, which traces the lives of the Schlemiel family and the community that surrounds them. [Readers] will really get the humor written between the lines…. the mix-ups are many and the potential for laughter abundant" – *Jewish Book World*

For "A Village Feasts"

"Abrahmson's prose savvily mixes the homey and the surreal, and he's a master…" –*Publishers Weekly*

"…wryly funny with dollops of heartwarming schmaltz." – *Kirkus Reviews*

For "Winter Blessings"

"…utterly charming…a large side order of whimsey… so right and so touching… This Chanukah, who could ask for anything more?" – *The Times of Israel*

For "A Village Romance"

"Abrahmson outdoes himself…" – *AudioFile*

"engaging tales… Village stories that deftly lift a curtain on a world of friendly humor and touching details of Jewish life." – *Kirkus Reviews*

THE VILLAGE TWINS

Izzy Abrahmson

Light Publications
Providence

The Village Twins
by Izzy Abrahmson (Unabridged and revised edition)
Copyright 2022 by Mark Binder

Versions of this book have been previously published as **The Brothers
Schlemiel** by Mark Binder. The weekly serialization began in February 2000
in *The Houston Jewish Herald-Voice*. One-hundred installments later, the novel
concluded on January 16, 2002. An abridged edition, illustrated by Zevi Blum,
was published by The Jewish Publication Society in 2008. A limited edition was
published by Light Publications in 2013.

Cover design by Lou Pop
Book design by Beth Hellman
Copy editing by Jessica Everett

Bulk discounts and licenses to reproduce excerpts from this book are available
for schools, churches, synagogues, mosques, book clubs, and other civic groups.
Please email: licensing@lightpublications.com

For information about author visits and story concerts by Izzy Abrahmson and
Mark Binder, please visit http://markbinder.com

Softcover Print ISBN: 978-1-940060-46-0
eBook ISBN: 978-1-940060-52-1
Library of Congress Control Number: 2021937778

Printed in the United States of America
Electronic edition originated in the USA
10 9 8 7 6 5 4 3 2 1

Light Publications
http://lightpublications.com
PO Box 2462 • Providence, RI 02906 • U. S. A.

<u>Dedication</u>

For Richard and Robert, the twins

Those who leave Chelm end up in Chelm.
Those who remain in Chelm are certainly in Chelm.
All roads lead to Chelm.
All the world is one big Chelm.
— I.B. Singer

Chapter One

Oy

"Oy!"

"Push!"

"Oy!"

"Push!"

"Jacob, stop that!" Rebecca Schlemiel snapped at her husband. "We're moving a table, not giving birth. Not yet anyway."

"I'm practicing," Jacob laughed. "It's going to happen any day now."

They both looked down at Rebecca's bulging belly. It was huge, the size of a boulder, and just as heavy.

"I can only wish," Rebecca said. She looked around the crowded kitchen, and not for the first time wondered how they were going to fit another person into their lives. The house was tiny. In fact, calling it a house at all was a gracious compliment. Two rooms – a bedroom and the kitchen, plus a privy out back. "Do you think the crib is really going to fit between the table and the cupboard?"

"Relax," Jacob said. "I measured it myself. The first knuckle of my thumb is exactly one inch long. The distance between the cupboard and the table is…" He began measuring again.

Rebecca looked at her husband, inching his thumb along the floor, shook her head, and put on a pot of water for tea. This was going to take a while.

Jacob and Rebecca Schlemiel lived in the village of Chelm, a tiny settlement of Jews known far and wide as the most concentrated collection of fools in the world. Chelm was celebrated in Yiddish jokes, shaggy dog stories, foolish songs, and the occasional ribald limerick. If someone in Moscow did something stupid, it was blamed on Chelm ancestry. A silly accident in Warsaw begged the question, "What part of Chelm did you come from?" And when a new politician promised revolutionary change, he was laughed down as "another wise man from Chelm."

Now, the villagers of Chelm did not think of themselves as doltish, stupid, slow, or otherwise mentally impaired. They kept to themselves, rarely traveling further than Smyrna for market day. If they were aware at all of the outside world's low opinion of them, they ignored it. Or perhaps they took it as a compliment.

After all, as the learned Rabbi Kibbitz once said, "Wisdom shmisdom. What good is knowing everything if you can't laugh?"

All of this is a roundabout way of saying that Rebecca Schlemiel didn't think it at all unusual for her husband to measure a four-foot space with his thumb. She saw it purely as an opportunity to rest her aching feet.

This pregnancy business was much more difficult than she'd bargained for. When she'd complained to her mother about back pains, swollen toes, and hair falling out, her mother had laughed. "You think you have problems? When I was pregnant with you, I couldn't get out of bed. Your father had to use the hay winch to hoist me up in the mornings. Three days before you were born, he had a hernia. He had to hire a horse to pull the winch to pick me up. Then the rope broke and the horse ran away! Now those were problems."

These were the kinds of things mothers rarely told their daughters about in advance. Or if they did, they were ignored as nonsense. This was probably for the best because otherwise the human species might never have reproduced. The youngest of seven sisters, Rebecca wondered what else her mother hadn't warned her about. For several months now, as her belly swelled, she found herself remembering the troubles she'd gotten into as a girl and shuddered at the faint echoes of her mother's shrill curse, "Just wait 'til you have children of your own!"

"Foo!" Jacob spat. "Rebecca, is my right thumb bigger than my left? You know, I'm not sure the crib is going to fit."

Rebecca nodded. "I told you that before, but you didn't believe me. No… We had to move the kitchen table to see. Even if it did fit, I wouldn't be able to open the silverware drawers."

Jacob was a wonderful carpenter, the best in all of Chelm. In the workshop that he rented from Reb Cantor, the merchant, he had built a beautiful crib of the finest polished oak. Unfortunately, he had forgotten to take measurements in their small house before construction. To be honest, he wasn't even sure the crib could fit in the front door. This he didn't dare tell Rebecca, especially not after moving the heavy table back and forth across the kitchen seventeen times.

"What about next to the stove?" Jacob asked.

"Wonderful," Rebecca said sarcastically. "I'll be making a pot of chicken soup, I'll sneeze, the pot will spill, and boiling water will pour on the baby…"

"Enough!" Jacob interrupted. "We could hang the crib from the ceiling. He'd be out of the way then."

Rebecca snorted. "I am not going to have my child suspended above me like a bird in a cage. Besides, how do you know it's going to be a boy? My mother had seven daughters and her mother had seven daughters. I'm the seventh daughter of the seventh daughter. You don't think that means something?"

"I need boys to help me in the shop."

"Boys are clumsy and slow," Rebecca said. "Girls are careful. Imagine what wonderful work you could do with seven lovely assistants."

"I'm sure they would do wonderful work," said Jacob, putting his hand to his heart. "All I know is that I am not going to have seven daughters. Not unless you let me hang five or six cribs from the ceiling."

Rebecca laughed. "Let's not talk about seven. I'm worried enough about this one. Do you think we're doing the right thing?

The world is cold. Nights are dark and long. People get sick, there are robbers…"

"Don't think of such things." Jacob stood, and put his hands on his wife's shoulders. He began rubbing them softly. "In the spring when the flowers come up, are they not the most beautiful and delicate things in the world? On a cold night a fire is warm. And as for robbers, what do we have to steal? I have you and you have me. A child is a blessing."

Rebecca sighed. "It's so quiet tonight. You know, after she is born, you and I will never be alone again."

"He," Jacob emphasized, "has to sleep some time." Rebecca looked so beautiful. He leaned down to kiss her forehead.

"Oy!" Rebecca said.

"You know, we don't have to move the table right away," Jacob said. "We can try again in the morning."

"Oy!" Rebecca moaned.

"All right," Jacob shrugged. "I'll push and you pull."

"OY!" Rebecca screamed.

"Oy?" Jacob said. His eyes widened. "Oy? Oy! Oyoyoyoyoyoy!"

And thus he ran shrieking out of the house to get the midwife.

The moment he was gone, Rebecca burst into laughter. She wasn't due for another week. It wasn't exactly nice to get Mrs. Chaipul out of bed to play a joke on Jacob, but Rebecca would make it up to her with a walnut strudel.

Rebecca looked at her nice neat kitchen. Even with the table wedged nearly against the far wall, it was clean and tidy and well kept – a good place for a daughter to grow up and learn how to cook.

The water on the stove came to a boil, and Rebecca began the slow process of hoisting herself up out of her chair.

"Oy," she muttered. Then her eyes widened. "Oh! OY!"

It seemed that Mrs. Chaipul wasn't going to be wasting a trip after all.

The Lost Father

Only in Chelm could a father get so lost going to fetch the midwife, that he misses the birth of his first child. Or perhaps only Jacob Schlemiel. If he'd turned right instead of left as he ran out of his house, who knows, perhaps his entire life would have been different. At the very least he never once would have heard his wife utter the complaint that would haunt him until the day he died, "And your father couldn't even bother to be present when you were born…"

He didn't do it on purpose. Who would do such a thing on purpose? He was on his way to the restaurant that Mrs. Chaipul, the midwife, owned. Her establishment, which served the finest chicken soup with the heaviest lead-ball knaidels, was less than two hundred yards from Jacob's house. He had been there hundreds of times – only last Thursday for corned beef on rye with a dab of mustard…

But Jacob Schlemiel was in such a panic at the thought of Rebecca giving birth that he decided to take a short cut. Never mind that his short cut was in exactly the wrong direction. At the moment he made the decision to turn left, he was certain – absolutely certain – that he was going the right way.

Even then, all could have been well. Chelm is not such a large village. There are fewer than eighty houses clustered around seven or twelve streets (depending on whom you believe and how you count). You could crawl from one end of Chelm to the other in fifteen minutes. Twenty if you got stuck in the mud. Thirty if you enjoyed playing in the mud, as most of the children of crawling age did. So, it was quite reasonable that after a moment of confusion, Jacob Schlemiel would have realized his mistake and looked over his shoulder to get his bearings.

Which is exactly what he was doing when he had the good misfortune to run full speed into Reb Shikker, the town drunk. The two men met, collided, rebounded, and sprawled into the mud.

Now, for many years Chelm did not have a town drunk. Every other village, town, and city had at least one, if not dozens. So naturally, the people of Chelm put an ad in the regional Yiddish newspaper, and in a matter of months the position was filled. Chelmites no longer felt excluded when a visitor from Smyrna boasted of their drunk's exploits. "Why that is nothing compared to our Reb Shikker…" they would answer, their voices trailing off mysteriously. For none of them were quite sure what it was that the town drunk was supposed to do.

Truth be told, it wasn't easy being a drunk in Chelm. No one else in the village imbibed, except on the Sabbath and holidays and festivals. No one made vodka, so Reb Shikker had to import his vodka from Moscow. And that was expensive, so he had to work. As it turned out, Reb Shikker was a skilled bookkeeper, but he couldn't keep his figures straight when his head was fuddled. And then there was his marriage to the Rebbe's niece, Deborah, who sneezed at the smell of alcohol. So, although he had been fully qualified for the position, it was now quite rare for Reb Shikker to take even a sip from his flask.

In fact, the first words he uttered after finding himself sitting and mud-splattered were, "I'm not drunk!"

"Nor am I. I'm sorry," answered Jacob Schlemiel. "It was my fault. My wife is about to give birth…"

"Mazel Tov!" said Reb Shikker.

They helped each other to their feet, and then Reb Shikker remembered his role in the village. "Nu? Would you like a drink to celebrate?"

"I'm about to become a father," said Jacob, dusting himself off.

"All the better," said Reb Shikker. He pulled out a steel flask and struggled to remove the cap. "Once you're a father, you can't drink around the children. Besides, vodka will steady your nerves. Ahh. Here."

Reluctantly, Jacob Schlemiel accepted the offer of the flask. He took a long pull and then gasped.

"Good, isn't it?" laughed Reb Shikker. "But it's not good to drink alone. You have a drink for me. Because, I can't. I have to go back to work."

"All right." Jacob took another. This time his face went as red as borscht.

"Oh! And to the health of your child!" said Reb Shikker.

Jacob took a swig for himself, and another for Reb Shikker. He coughed loudly.

"And the health of your wife!"

Again Jacob drank, and drank again. His eyes crossed.

"You, my friend," said Reb Shikker, taking his flask, "have had enough for both of us. I'm not about to lose my reputation."

With that, Reb Shikker clapped Jacob on the back and trotted off.

By now, on an empty stomach, Jacob Schlemiel was thoroughly kafratzed. He stumbled off and knocked on the first door he came to.

Esther Gold, the cobbler's wife, opened the door. Jacob started to explain that his wife was in labor, and that's as far as he got because Mrs. Gold had already been preparing a noodle kugel for just this occasion, and she only had to wrap it in a towel for Jacob to take home. Five minutes later, he was standing outside again with a warm kugel in his hands, still wondering which way to turn.

At every house it was the same. Reb Cohen, the tailor, gave Jacob a teeny tiny suit of clothes. Reb Cantor, the merchant, presented him with a live chicken tied to a string, like a dog on a leash. And so it went. Everyone was so cheerful and happy for him. Some gave him tea, others gave him bottles of wine. The baker gave him a challah. It was only when he arrived at the home of Rabbi Kibbitz, still struggling with boxes, bags, and the fussing chicken, that Jacob remembered that he was supposed to fetch Mrs. Chaipul.

"Rebbe, Rebecca is in labor and I'm looking for the midwife!" Jacob blurted.

"Isn't she at her restaurant?" asked the rabbi.

"I don't know," Jacob answered. "I forgot to go there."

"Well, then we'd better hurry."

The rabbi pulled on his coat, and the two men rushed back toward the center of Chelm.

On the way, they naturally passed right by the Schlemiels' small house, where they heard a peculiar mewling sound.

"Isn't that interesting?" said Rabbi Kibbitz. "That sounds just like a child crying."

"Yes," agreed Jacob Schlemiel. "And my wife is supposed to be having a baby any second now…"

Jacob stopped in his tracks. "She'll kill me."

"Nonsense," said the rabbi. "You're the father. If she killed you, she would probably be executed as a murderer and the last thing she wants is to give birth to an orphan."

"Come in with me," Jacob begged.

"Not a chance," said the wise old man, shaking his head. "You're on your own." He pushed Jacob through the door, and then backed away.

So, overburdened with packages and drink, Jacob stumbled into his house.

There was Mrs. Chaipul, in his kitchen, stirring the soup pot.

"I've been looking for you all over Chelm!" Jacob said. "Rebecca's gone into labor."

"I know. Go on back," Mrs. Chaipul said, nodding toward the bedroom. "Hurry."

Jacob dropped the kugel, challah, and the other various packages on the kitchen table. The chicken ran behind the stove.

Meekly, Jacob peeked his head into the bedroom. There he saw Rebecca, looking tired but beautiful. And wrapped in a blanket was the smallest and loudest creature he had ever seen.

"It's been six hours!" Rebecca said. "You couldn't even bother to be present?"

"I'm sorry. I got lost," Jacob answered. "Is it a boy?"

Rebecca smiled. "It's… AiEEEEEE!"

"What?" Jacob shouted. "What?"

"AIYEEEEEEE!"

Mrs. Chaipul came running. "Get out of the way!" she shouted, shoving Jacob into the kitchen. The door closed behind him.

"What?" he muttered. "I said I'm sorry."

<u>Sunset, Sunrise</u>

It was to be the longest night of Jacob Schlemiel's life, and it was just beginning.

A few moments later, Mrs. Chaipul returned with the newborn babe wrapped in a blanket.

"Here." She handed him the bundle. "Hold this."

Jacob stared at the package. He held it in front of him in both hands like it was a brisket on a platter. "What am I supposed to do with this?"

The midwife stared up at him. "What, you never held a baby before?"

Jacob shook his head. "No."

Jacob was an only child born to a thirty-nine-year-old mother. He had grown up without young cousins or nieces and nephews. Although he had carved rattles for every family in Chelm, this was the first time that he'd ever actually held a baby in his arms.

"Oy yoy yoy," Mrs. Chaipul chuckled. She showed him how to hold the infant close, how to support its head and neck. Then a shriek from the bedroom summoned her back to her patient.

And so, Jacob was left staring at the tiny red ball of a head cradled in his elbow. It was asleep. The whole face was sort of bent and smooshed in, as if someone had flattened it like a pancake.

"You are ugly," Jacob thought. He would never say such a thing aloud. "I hope you are a boy, because if you're a girl you're going to have some big problems finding a husband."

Outside, it was growing dark. The sun had just gone down, and the only lights in the house were from the stove and a single candle that Mrs. Chaipul had lit on the kitchen table. In the bedroom, Rebecca's cries subsided, and the small house was suddenly very quiet. Jacob could hear the crackling of logs in the stove and the occasional footsteps of Mrs. Chaipul in the bedroom.

Jacob looked at the little one. "So, you want to play cards?" he whispered. "I'll teach you canasta."

No answer. Of course not. The little one was asleep. Besides, if the face was so small, how tiny would the hands be? Canasta would keep.

Then there was a shriek from the bedroom. Jacob was so startled he nearly dropped the bundle. The scrunched-up face opened in a look of surprise, followed immediately by a bellowing yell that was surely heard all the way to Jerusalem.

The baby's screech was ear piercing. It stabbed through Jacob's skull like an ice pick into a summer melon. He had drunk too much vodka and not enough of anything else. Jacob lurched toward the bedroom to ask Mrs. Chaipul what he should do, but another shout from Rebecca stopped him cold.

"Make it stop!" his was wife shouting. "Please!"

Something was going wrong and that frightened him more than anything had in his whole life. Just that afternoon he and Rebecca had been happy and joking. Yes, they'd bickered a little about where to move the kitchen table in order to fit the crib. Now, with his child screaming in his arms and his wife screaming in the bedroom, Jacob Schlemiel came face to face with the idea of a life he couldn't bear to imagine. What if… Life without Rebecca? What if… His wife and his love? He stood frozen, suspended in fear.

It was the infant crying in his arms that brought Jacob back. The tiny life in his hand, red as a beet and bawling, reminded him that there were other things to do.

But what?

"What can I do for you?" he asked the yowling child, but he could barely hear his own words. "Are you hungry? You must be hungry."

Jacob's eyes darted toward the bedroom, but he was more afraid of interrupting Mrs. Chaipul than he was of the infant's cries.

So, he did the only thing he could think of. He began to pray. And as he prayed, he davened, rocking back and forth, and the baby started to calm a little. But it felt funny, awkward, as if he was going to fall forward or drop the baby by accident, so instead, he began to daven from side to side, the way Rabbi Kibbitz sometimes did. A moment later, the little one was asleep, relaxed in his arms.

The candle burned slowly. Cries from the bedroom rose and fell like the waves of an ocean. Sometimes all seemed calm, and sometimes the fear rose in Jacob's heart, but still he rocked and prayed. Somehow during the night, he managed to switch the baby to one arm long enough to take a drink of water. Then, inspired, he dipped the end of a clean napkin into his cup and watched in pleased surprise as the baby took the cloth and began to nurse.

As the red glow of morning rose from the east, Jacob noticed that his legs ached and his throat was hoarse from prayer. Still, the baby was quiet, sleeping and sucking on the tip of the napkin. Slowly, ever so slowly, he lowered himself down into a chair.

Suddenly, Jacob saw the baby's face twitch.

"No! Please don't cry," he whispered. "Hush, hush."

Then, in the dim light of dawn, Jacob saw the baby's blue eyes open for the very first time, and he fell in love. What a perfect child! How wonderful.

He barely noticed as Mrs. Chaipul put her hand on his shoulder.

"You have another boy," she said.

"A boy," Jacob nodded, smiling back at the tiny one. "So that is what you are."

Then a wrinkle passed over his face. He turned to Mrs. Chaipul. "Did you say, 'another?'"

The midwife nodded and held out another red-faced bundle. "Twins," she said. "As identical as I've ever seen."

And they were. Now, Jacob Schlemiel held two babies in his arms. When he looked from one to the other, the only difference that he could see was that the first one was a little bit cleaner and a little less smooshed.

The two brothers stared at each other for a moment, and then with one voice they began to howl to the heavens.

"Rebecca?" Jacob shouted over the din as he jumped to his feet to resume his side-to-side rocking. "How is my wife?"

"She's fine! She's asleep!"

"She's the lucky one!" Jacob grinned. "No, that's not true. We're all lucky!"

And with that, Jacob Schlemiel began to dance. He danced

until, exhausted with joy, he and his two boys crawled into bed with their mother.

The crib could wait another day.

Soon, everyone was asleep, and the Schlemiel house was quiet.

For about ten minutes.

Chapter Two

Bris

"You want what?" Rabbi Kibbitz stared at Jacob Schlemiel. Had he heard correctly? "You want me to perform the circumcisions differently?"

"Well, they're identical," Jacob said.

"Twins." The rabbi nodded. "Yes. They frequently look alike."

"No, Rabbi," Jacob said. "These two are exactly the same. I can't tell them apart. Their own mother can't tell them apart. There aren't any birthmarks. Their eyes are the same. They both have ten fingers and ten toes."

"That's good," said the rabbi.

"But I don't know which one is which."

"Why is this a problem? They can't be getting into much trouble yet."

"But when they do," Jacob said, "how will I know who to blame?"

"You're going to make them drop their pants?"

"I don't know, Rabbi." Jacob Schlemiel put his hands over his eyes. "I just don't know." Then he began to weep.

The rabbi sighed. The interview had gone relatively well up until then. When Jacob Schlemiel had knocked on the door to his study, the rabbi had given him warm congratulations and asked after the health of Rebecca and the new boys. Yes, Jacob had looked tired, but who wouldn't three days after the birth of one, let alone two, infants?

It was only when Rabbi Kibbitz drew out his paper and pencils to jot down the details for the bris that the confusion began.

Usually, it was just a matter of scheduling. According to Jewish tradition, the ritual circumcision celebrating God's covenant with

Abraham took place eight days after the child's birth. But, with one boy born just before sunset and the other born at sunrise… That was tricky. You might be able to say that they were both born the same day. But the local authorities never understood that the Jewish day didn't begin at midnight, but at sunset the day before. And even worse, Mrs. Chaipul wasn't totally certain whether the first one was born just before or just after sunset.

So, naturally, the rabbi had stalled by asking about the catering. It was clear that Jacob hadn't given it a thought, perhaps because he hadn't had time for more than a quick bite in days. Obviously, the rabbi had suggested that Mrs. Chaipul handle the whole thing. Jacob had nodded and shrugged.

"So, what are their names going to be?" Rabbi Kibbitz had asked.

"We thought we'd call the first Abraham," said Jacob, "after Rebecca's great uncle's cousin on her mother's side. And then we'll call the second one Adam, after my father's brother's father."

Rabbi Kibbitz scratched his head. "Your grandfather?"

Jacob nodded. "Yes."

"Why wouldn't you call the first one Adam, since he was the first human?" Rabbi Kibbitz asked. "Although I suppose Abraham was the first patriarch of the Jewish people…"

"Rebbe," Jacob said, "I would call the first one Adam, or I would call the second one Isaac. I would even call them One and Two. But who can be sure? When I first held them in my arms, I knew which was which. But the next morning, they both looked the same."

That was when Jacob had taken the rabbi's hand and asked if the rabbi could help them figure out which boy was which – surgically.

Rabbi Kibbitz rummaged through his pockets until he found a clean handkerchief, which he passed to the poor weeping carpenter.

"Listen, Jacob," he said, "what you're asking isn't so easy. All my life, ever since I was trained and certified as a mohel to perform circumcisions, I have striven for only one thing during a bris – consistency and perfection. Two things. It's not like building a table, where if one leg is a little short you saw off the other three to even things out. There's not a lot to work with. I perform the circumcision the way my teacher taught me, and it's not something you want to experiment with. Nu? You know?"

Jacob sobbed loudly.

"But wait!" said the chief and only rabbi of Chelm. "I have an idea. We'll bring in another rabbi! I'll do one boy, he'll do the other. Since we're not totally sure when either of them was born, we'll do them both exactly at midnight. And then it won't matter which was first. One will be Abraham, one will be Adam. And you should be able to tell the difference. Like a signature."

His cheeks still wet with tears, Jacob Schlemiel's face broadened into a smile. "Thank you," said Jacob. "Rabbi Kibbitz, you are wise like Solomon."

"Nonsense," the rabbi blushed. But when the carpenter left, he chuckled and admitted the possibility. "And Solomon had only one baby to cut!"

In a big city, rabbis are a dime a dozen, but in the tiny village of Chelm there was only Rabbi Kibbitz. He sent a note to his friend, Rabbi Sarnoff of Smyrna, but it seemed that there had been a baby boom in Smyrna, and the learned rabbi of that town would be unable to assist. So, Rabbi Kibbitz put a free advertisement in the Yiddish newspaper and hoped for the best.

Every day he went to the post office to see if there was an answer, but every day he was disappointed. He didn't dare tell the Schlemiels. Why worry them? They were busy with the babies. Besides, who knew what would happen at the last minute?

Finally, the appointed night arrived.[1]

The Schlemiel twins' bris was a strange event, even for Chelm. Usually, circumcisions were scheduled in the family's home

---

[1] It has been noted by scholars that the circumcision ceremony is traditionally performed during daylight. Furthermore, since the new Jewish day begins at sunset it would make better sense to perform one bris before sunset and the other just after. However, and this is an important point, word had reached Rabbi Kibbitz that, on the very day that the Schlemiels were born, the territory that included Chelm had been traded by the King of Poland to the Czar of Russia for fifteen pounds of caviar and two boxes of Cuban cigars. Ultimately, the rabbi thought that for legal reasons it was crucial that the boys be circumcised as close as possible to their birth dates on the Polish and the Russian calendars.

during the day when there was plenty of light, but in this case the ceremony would have to be performed by candlelight. Since the Schlemiels' house was so tiny, the rabbi had argued that with all the guests (the mother alone had six sisters, six aunts, and at least thirty-six cousins) the synagogue's social hall would be a better setting. Now, candles were expensive, but everyone in Chelm was glad to bring a candle or two with the promise of one of Mrs. Chaipul's delicious bris brunches. Chopped liver, corned beef, pastrami...

Rabbi Kibbitz wiped a speck of drool from his lips. He was hungry.

He was also nervous. So far, there was no spare rabbi. Perhaps at the last minute...

But it was not to be. Rabbi Kibbitz waited outside the shul until five minutes before midnight. At last, wearing his best and most confident smile, he went in to perform that most delicate of duties.

The two boys were held, one on each of their grandfather's knees. He gave them some wine to quell their cries and set his instruments on the table. Rebecca Schlemiel nearly fainted right then, but her mother propped her up.

"You know," Rabbi Kibbitz said to Jacob, "as the father, it is your duty to circumcise your sons, but you may delegate this duty to me. Under the circumstances, perhaps you could do one and I could do the other?"

Jacob Schlemiel nodded solemnly, then his eyes rolled up into his head and he fell to the ground with a crash.

"It was just an idea," said Rabbi Kibbitz. He shrugged and began the procedure as Jacob was quickly revived.

But which one should be done first? Which was Adam and which was Abraham? Did it even matter? He had to pick one to start, so he chose the one on his right.

A moment later, the baby began to scream, and the rabbi gave him another sip of wine.

Now, on to the second. Perhaps he could try something a little different...

"Oops!" the rabbi said.

The villagers of Chelm gasped.

Rebecca Schlemiel screamed, "Oops?"

Jacob collapsed to the ground again.

"Relax! Relax!" Rabbi Kibbitz shouted, quelling the near riot. "Nothing's wrong! They're both the same. That's what the 'Oops' was. I couldn't do it differently!"

Of course, in the chaos, the babies were switched once again, and not even Rabbi Kibbitz could tell which was who.

So, one was named Abraham and one was named Adam, but it would be many, many years before anyone in Chelm could tell the difference.

Chapter Three

Termites in the brain

To say that Jacob Schlemiel went temporarily insane after the birth of his twin boys might be overstating the matter. The poor man certainly had a breakdown. His spirit, which had been as strong and as straight as a nail, was bent. His caboose went around the bend, off the track, and into the river. It was as if the mule pulling his wagon down the road of life had suddenly kicked him in the head.

You couldn't really blame him. Jacob had been raised as an only child, which was a rare thing in those days. So, rather than growing up in an atmosphere of barely restrained chaos, he had grown up in a house that had been quiet and calm. His late father had been a great scholar, and Jacob's earliest memories of his mother were the soft hushing noises she made when he cried. In his parents' house, everyone spoke in a soft whisper.

It had, in fact, come as a complete surprise to Jacob's parents when he'd taken up carpentry. "How can you stand all the racket?" his father had asked after he had confiscated the wooden mallet five-year-old Jacob had borrowed from a childhood friend. Eventually, the clamor had gotten so bad (and Jacob's love of constant banging so great) that they'd been forced to send him away from Chelm for his apprenticeship.

Jacob couldn't explain that the noise was something that his heart and ears longed for. The pounding of nails into wood, the harsh rasp of the saw, the repetitive burr of the plane… They were as calming to Jacob as a page of Talmud was to his father. He especially loved early mornings, when he unlocked the quiet carpenter's shop, picked up a hammer, and began whacking away with unrestrained glee. The instant transition between silence and din was delightful.

Children, however, were another matter entirely. Hammering at least was under his control. He could stop it when he wanted. The inconsolable screams of two hungry babies with wet diapers were more than the poor man could stand. For one thing it never ended. No sooner was Abraham fed and cleaned than Adam was filthy and hungry. Jacob barely slept a wink at night. Even when the babies were calm, there were dishes to clean, laundry to do, and dinner to make.

Rebecca, bless her soul, was still flat on her back from the effort of twelve hours of childbirth. And of course she had to feed the twins herself, a task that took far more energy than Jacob could imagine.

You would have thought that one or two of her six sisters, six aunts, or dozens of cousins might have been able to lend a hand from time to time, but not all of them lived in Chelm, and the ones who did had families of their own to care for.

The grandmothers tried to help, but that was mostly during the day. He could see the feverish look of relief on their faces when he came home from work. The two of them were out the door almost as soon as he took off his coat. So, not only did the carpenter spend a good ten hours a day making the finest furniture for all of the villagers of Chelm, he spent an additional fourteen hours a day taking care of the boys.

"If I could fill the bags under my eyes with gold," he joked to a customer, "I could retire a rich man."

Actually, it was a wonder he survived those first weeks with all his fingers. One day, while hammering together the shelves of a bookcase, he actually dozed off in mid-blow. He only woke up when the hammer landed on his foot. He didn't dare use his largest two-handed saw for fear of lopping off an arm.

Jacob's day-to-day existence faded into a numbing blur. One morning he woke up, put his pants over his head, dumped a pan of scrambled eggs into his shoes, and didn't notice that he was still wearing his nightshirt until he got to work, and reached into his pocket for his keys. An ordinary man might scream in frustration at such an occurrence (or conclude that he must still be asleep, having a nightmare from which he'd soon wake up). Jacob Schlemiel shrugged, found the keys in the pants pocket next to his ear, and went into his shop as usual.

At first, his friends and customers didn't say anything. They knew that Jacob was suffering, but the transition between no children and children was something they'd all been through themselves. Yes, having children was difficult, one of the hardest adjustments of their lives. But you got over it. You got used to it. You muddled through.

It was when Jacob presented Reb Stein, the baker, with a brand new work table with only one leg that they began to worry. Even a two-legged table might have worked, if it could have been nailed into a wall. But the single leg was in the middle of the table. Reb Stein raised his eyebrows and started to object, but Jacob had fallen asleep on his way out the door. (As it turned out, the table actually worked quite well as a kneading board. Reb Stein gave his four apprentices a huge ball of dough, and they made quite a game of trying to prevent the table from tipping onto their side while pushing it over to somebody else's.)

But not all of Jacob's new creations were so successful. The milking stool with the legs sticking up from the seat, for instance, could only be used upside down. And the dowry chest he made for Reb Cantor's oldest daughter, Leah, had seven lids and no sides. Jacob tried to explain that he had intended it that way – so that it could be opened from any angle, but Reb Cantor knew that the poor man was blithering.

Still, the villagers of Chelm were nothing if not polite and patient. They knew that sooner or later Jacob Schlemiel would get the hang of living, and working, and taking care of himself and his newly expanded family. They could wait for their carpenter to return to normal.

But one afternoon, Reb Levitsky, the synagogue's caretaker, pushed on the door to Jacob's shop and was surprised to find it locked. He knocked and peered in the windows, but the shop was dark and silent. Perhaps one of the children was sick. He decided to stop by the Schlemiel house and try to cheer them up with a song.

It was a warm day, so the door to the house was slightly ajar when Reb Levitsky arrived. Inside the house he found Rebecca standing by the stove, stirring a pot of stew.

"Shh, the boys are asleep," she whispered.

"It's good to see you're feeling better," Reb Levitsky said. "Is Jacob napping also?"

"No," she said. "He should be at his shop."

"But I just came from there," said Reb Levitsky. "The door was locked."

"Didn't he leave a note?" Rebecca asked. "He always leaves a note. I wonder where he's gone…"

"He probably went for a walk," Reb Levitsky said.

"Of course," Rebecca agreed. She had to get the house in order and care for the boys. "He probably just needed some fresh air."

"That's it!" Reb Levitsky agreed. "Don't worry.

After Dark

Until it got dark, Rebecca Schlemiel hadn't really worried.

Yes, she was a young mother with newborn twins. True, Reb Levitsky said that her husband, Jacob, hadn't been seen at his carpenter's shop all day, and hadn't left a note, but perhaps the note had blown away.

During the warm light of day, it hadn't even occurred to her that something unfortunate might have happened to Jacob, that he might vanish forever into the foggy wilderness of the black forest that surrounded the small village of Chelm. No, after Reb Levitsky had gone, she had remained quite calm, stirring her stew and taking care of Abraham and Adam.

But then the sun went down. And Jacob was still nowhere to be found.

At night, when there is no moon and the sky is full of clouds, Chelm grows very dark. If you wandered away from the soft glow of hearth fires, lanterns, and candle lights the night became as black as the bottom of a dry well that has been sealed by a boulder. No one went out after dark without a lantern. If you did, you might trip over your own shadow. You could walk ten yards from your house and never find it again. And the only lantern the Schlemiels owned was at home with Rebecca and the boys.

When it was time to light that lantern, Rebecca started to panic. She had waited long enough! Now she couldn't escape the thought that her Jacob might be lost somewhere in the woods, hurt and helpless.

Chelm is not a very large village. In fact, the civilized portion is quite small. Surrounding the motley collection of well-kept houses, well-swept huts, and a few well-loved businesses is a thin ribbon of cleared farmland, and surrounding the farmland is the Schvartzvald. The ancient Black Forest made a wonderful setting for scary stories told in front of a warm fire on a midwinter's night, but in truth the forest was a fearful wilderness that a man could disappear into without a trace.

Perhaps Jacob had gone into the Schvartzvald to cut some wood. Usually he bought his wood from a woodcutter, but maybe he needed something special, a wide board for a table, or a particular length of branch for a chair. Such trips were rare, but not unheard of. If he had tripped over a tree root and dashed his head against a stone...

There were still bears in the woods. And wolves. Packs of wolves. Mothers told stories of those wolves to scare their children into behaving.

Rebecca had only to imagine Jacob lying unconscious on the forest's moss floor while one wolf sniffed at his feet and another licked at the small stream of blood oozing from his forehead! She gave a little shriek and immediately bundled the boys into warm blankets. She couldn't manage the boys and a lantern at the same time, so she left the lantern at home and carried one baby in each arm, feeling her way along the dark streets.

Chelm is not a rich city like Warsaw or even Smyrna, with streetlights at every intersection helping late-night travelers reach their homes safely. No, in Chelm there was only one streetlight, directly in front of the synagogue. It was a well-known fact that if you lost something at night, that was the place to look for it because everywhere else it was dark.

At last Rebecca saw the reassuring glow of the synagogue's streetlight. Someone was there, standing right next to the pole! She hurried closer, her heart lifting with every step.

"Jacob?" she said, a smile on her lips.

The man turned, and in an instant Rebecca's hopes vanished, like a candle snuffed in the wind. It was only Rabbi Kibbitz, who was smoking a cigarette, which he immediately dropped and began stubbing out with his shoe.

Thin wisps of panic began to float like smoke through Rebecca's mind.

"I was enjoying the night air," the rabbi hastened to explain, "but I'm a bit afraid of the dark."

"Jacob is missing," Rebecca said. Abraham (or was it Adam) began to cry. She bounced him gently against her hip.

"Nonsense," said the rabbi. "Misplaced, perhaps. Lost, possibly. But missing? No. How could that be?"

"If he isn't in his shop, and he isn't at home, and he isn't here in the light," Rebecca asked, "where could he be?"

"Jacob has his mother," the rabbi said, reassuringly. "He has friends. Perhaps he went to someone's house for a visit and has lost track of the time."

"But he didn't leave a note. He didn't tell me where he'd be."

"Child," the rabbi smiled sadly. "Sometimes a man needs to get away on his own."

"But whenever he leaves the house he always tells me where he's going and when he'll be back."

"Ahh," said the rabbi. "Then won't you feel foolish when you arrive back home to find him waiting and wondering where you've gone?"

"He's at home now?" Rebecca's face brightened.

"Of course," said Rabbi Kibbitz. "Have I ever been wrong?"

Actually, Rabbi Kibbitz was famous for being wrong, but no one in Chelm had the heart to tell him. And at that moment, Rebecca

was so eager to believe everything was all right that she accepted the
rabbi's statement at face value.

Together they hurried down the dark streets back to the
Schlemiels' house.

In Chelm, one small house looks much like the other. After
sunset, and without a lantern, who can tell one door from another?
So, of course, Rebecca and the rabbi walked into one wrong house
after another. It was a natural and common mistake, and the
surprised neighbors tried their best to make the frightened wife and
confused rabbi comfortable.

As was only polite, Rebecca and Rabbi Kibbitz accepted the
offers of tea and strudel at the Golds', of Turkish coffee and cake at
the Kimmelmans', and so on. In fact, so kind were the neighbors
that (after a snack) each and every one offered to help Rebecca find
her way home.

It was quite a parade that finally managed to find its way back to
the Schlemiels' house. By then, Rebecca's stew was done, perfectly
cooked and ready to be served. Since no one in Chelm could ever
refuse a free meal, the table was set and the feasting began.

In their later years, Adam and Abraham claimed that evening
was their first memory – the warmth of the fire, the laughter of the
villagers, the smell of their mother's rich stew, and the underlying
sense of terror and dread. Despite the false laughter and pretend
good cheer, everyone in the house was terribly frightened.

Jacob Schlemiel was still not home.

And, one by one, as the hour got late and the guests made their
apologies and got up to leave, each and every visitor had the same
unbidden notion.

"What a wonderful party," they thought. "It's too bad Jacob's not
here."

One good thing did come of the celebration. With all the
excitement, with so many neighbors taking a turn playing with
Adam or bouncing Abraham, the boys slept soundly.

Rebecca was not so fortunate. She stood by the window, looking
out into the dark night, and whispered prayers until the glow of the
morning sun began to rise.

Gossip

Three days passed, and there was still no sign of Jacob Schlemiel. Where was he? That question was on the lips of every man, woman, and child in Chelm. Of course Jacob had been late for the birth of his first child, so at first everyone had joked, "He's just gotten lost again. He probably turned left when he should have turned right." Now that he'd been missing for three days, it wasn't funny.

You see, in Chelm, nobody gets lost for very long. It's not a big place. When a child runs away from home, he usually gets only as far as Great Uncle Mordechai's house, where Tante Nora feeds him cookies and milk until he decides to go home for a nap. But Jacob Schlemiel's Tante Nora and Uncle Mordechai had emigrated to America long ago. So where was Jacob?

Chelm is nestled in a valley. To the north are two small round hills that are known on maps as West Hill and East Hill, which the townsfolk sometimes call Sunset and Sunrise. A small stream meanders west of Sunset, down the valley, and through the farmland, skirting the edge of the village. An offshoot of the great Bug River, this shallow brook makes a somewhat revolting gurgling and coughing sound that gives it the name Uherka.

Farms surrounded the village, and the Schvartzvald, the ancient dark forest, surrounded the farms on both sides of the river. Even though visitors to Chelm saw the Black Forest as a bleak and blighted place filled with wolves, bears, and snakes, at least during the daytime, most of the time, it wasn't really so bad. The Black Forest was an integral part of the community. Its wood was used to build houses and furniture and bowls. And from spring until the first snow of winter, the forest's dark moist ground was a glorious source of delicious wild mushrooms, which everyone in Chelm loved to eat. Besides, the Schvartzvald was not really so big. You could see as much on the map. If you walked for an hour or two in any one direction, you were bound to come to a road.

There are only two roads in Chelm. The Smyrna Road goes

north between Sunrise and Sunset, through the Schvartzvald, to
Smyrna. The Great Circular Road is more mysterious. It heads east
into the Schvartzvald, but it is such a long and twisted path that
no one in Chelm is certain where it ultimately leads. Anyone who
sets off on a journey down that road eventually gets disgusted with
the endless forest scenery, turns around, and comes back. Everyone
in Chelm knows that if you happen to be lost in the woods and
come to a road, all you need to do is take a left and keep walking.
Eventually you'll come back to the village.

Jacob Schlemiel ought to have been able to find his way home
by now.

While Jacob was missing, Rebecca Schlemiel showed her
neighbors what a strong and determined woman could do. Not
only was she feeding and caring for the boys; she had also taken
charge of the rescue parties.

The searchers had looked everywhere. They had gone to the
tops of Sunset and Sunrise. They had walked along the banks of
the Uherka. They had even formed a human chain and arm in arm
walked through the forests. If Jacob had been lying unconscious, as
Rebecca had feared, they would have found him.

Rabbi Kibbitz sent word to Rabbi Sarnoff of Smyrna, and Reb
Cantor, the merchant, inquired with his suppliers. Farmers talked
to the cart drivers. Even the wandering peddlers were asked if they'd
passed a lost carpenter. The world was not so big. Someone should
have seen him. But no one had.

The gossips in Mrs. Chaipul's restaurant talked of nothing else.

"He's not dead," said Reb Gold, the cobbler.

"How do you know that?" asked Reb Stein, the baker.

"Because," answered the cobbler, "you don't hide yourself under
a rock to die like a bug. Everyone I know who's dead, died in their
bed, walking to shul, or shoveling snow."

"That's the way most people go," agreed Reb Levitsky, the
synagogue's caretaker.

"You think he was kidnapped?" asked Reb Shikker, the town
drunk.

Everyone laughed. "What an idea!" "Ridiculous." "Who would

want to kidnap a poor carpenter?"

"Who would want to kidnap anyone?" retorted Reb Shikker. "I'll tell you. In Gdansk a gang of thugs kidnapped ordinary men right off the streets and stole their livers!"

"Their livers?" Reb Stein raised a skeptical eye.

"Yes," Reb Shikker continued. "I suppose they had a taste for human chopped liver…"

"That is repulsive!" shouted Mrs. Chaipul. "I'll have no talk like that in my restaurant."

The men, still giggling, quietly apologized.

"It could happen," Reb Shikker insisted at a whisper.

"Shh," hissed Reb Gold. "Do you want to get us all banned from the only restaurant in Chelm?"

Reb Shikker glanced nervously at Mrs. Chaipul. "Can she do that?"

"Oh yes. Some idiot from Smyrna once claimed her corned beef was too dry and she chased him out with a frying pan."

"Besides," said Reb Levitsky, "we're ignoring the obvious. If Jacob Schlemiel is not lost, injured, or dead, only one thing's left."

"What's that?" Reb Stein asked.

"He's run off."

"Run off?" laughed Reb Gold. "Like a dog or a bird?"

"Birds don't run," said the baker. "They fly away."

"Whatever," answered the cobbler. "Jacob is a man, not an animal. He is married to a woman he loves, has a thriving business, and a beautiful new family. Why would such a man run off?"

"I'll give you two reasons," smiled Reb Stein. "Twins."

"What's the second reason?"

"Twins," Reb Stein said. "That's two reasons."

"Twins is only one reason," Reb Gold said. "Twins and something else, now that would be two."

"There are two boys," Reb Stein insisted. He held up his fingers. "Adam and Abraham."

"If you could tell them apart," said Reb Gold, "that would be two. But they look the same. So, I still say it's only one reason."

Reb Stein's face started to get red.

Reb Levitsky calmly raised his palms. "Friends. It doesn't matter. One reason, two reasons. What matters is that Jacob has not been himself since the boys were born. I am afraid he's had a change of heart."

Everyone nodded, except Reb Gold.

"What do you mean? A lovely wife and two healthy boys. Why would you run from that?"

"Joshua, you don't have any children."

"Not for lack of trying!"

Everyone laughed. The cobbler and his wife had only been married for six months.

"No! Children are a blessing. Esther wants five. I say ten. Twelve!"

"Have you lost your mind?" asked Reb Shikker, who had eight of his own. Reb Stein laughed and shook his head in agreement.

"He doesn't know," said Mrs. Chaipul from behind the counter.

"I don't know what?" said Reb Gold.

"Children change everything," said Reb Levitsky. "A blessing or a curse, wonderful or horrible, that's all a question of luck and how you look at it. What is indisputable, however, is that from the day your first child is born your life isn't the same. It is never yours alone again. And that's not an easy thing to accept."

"Especially," concluded Reb Stein, "with twins."

Meanwhile, not far from the restaurant, Rabbi Kibbitz had just broken the news to Jacob Schlemiel's seventy-two-year-old mother, Ruth, that her son was missing. He explained that he hadn't wanted to tell her sooner because he didn't want her to worry, but…

"Oy, that silly little boy," laughed Ruth Schlemiel. "I know just where he is."

"You do?"

"Yes." The old woman nodded. "And if he's not dead, I'll kill him myself."

Found Father

Later that afternoon, Rabbi Kibbitz was eating a bowl of chicken soup and explaining the tale to everyone in Mrs. Chaipul's restaurant.

"She knows where he is?" Reb Shikker asked.

"So she says," the rabbi answered between slurps. "And no, she wouldn't tell me where. First she tells me she's going to kill him, and then she starts making him lunch. Seventy-two years old, she hops out of her chair like she's nineteen and begins cutting a salami."

"Ruth always was a good mother to Jacob," Mrs. Chaipul said.

"You think she really knows?" Reb Stein asked.

The rabbi shrugged. "I just hope she isn't deluding herself."

At that moment, Ruth Schlemiel was pushing open the door to her son's wood shop. "Jacob!" She shrieked. "Jaay-cob!"

In the tiny attic above the shop, Jacob Schlemiel's eyes popped open, and he sat up so suddenly that he smacked his head on a low rafter. "Ahh!" he yelped, muffling the sound by pressing his lips into his arm.

"I know you're up there!" his mother shouted.

Jacob, cowering in fear from the old woman, felt like he was ten again. Still, he kept quiet.

"Do you want me to come up there? I'm not so old I can't climb a ladder. Though my eyesight is not so good. I might miss a step and plunge to my death. Or even worse, I could lie on the dirty floor with a broken leg, screaming. But your shop is closed, so no one would hear me, so I would lie in sawdust and filth wondering if my every breath would be my last."

Jacob rolled his eyes, but said nothing.

"The rabbi came to me today," Ruth Schlemiel said.

She set down her wicker basket and, after wiping off a section of the worktable, took out a plate, a sandwich, and a slice of potato kugel. "He told me that my son hadn't been seen in three days."

As soon as the basket opened, Jacob began to smell the garlic from the salami and the sweet paprika scent of the still warm kugel. He'd been hiding in the attic for days now and had long ago eaten up the few scraps of food he'd found littered around the workshop.

"I remembered that when my Jacob was just a boy, a cute little boy, whenever he was upset he would hide in the attic and pretend he was dead." Ruth Schlemiel reached into the basket and found the jar of pickles she had packed at the bottom. "He was so quiet we never knew where he was until it was dinner time."

The sound of the pickle jar opening and the sour smell of the cucumbers in vinegar reminded Jacob of those days, so many years ago.

"Jacob," his mother said with a sigh, "am I really going to have to come up there and look? Risk my life just to be certain that my little boy isn't dead?"

It was all too much.

"All right. I'm coming, I'm coming."

"Did I hear a mouse?" the old woman said. "Or could it be a rat nibbling on my son's bones?"

"I said I'm coming!" Jacob shouted. He yanked open the trap door, leaned out to repeat, "I'm coming!" and then fell out of the attic, six and a half feet down onto a half-finished table, which collapsed with a crash.

"Are you all right?" his mother asked. "You fell."

"Ow!" he answered. She knew he was fine.

"Always with the dramatics," Ruth Schlemiel said, shaking her head but smiling inside. "Just this once you couldn't use the ladder?"

After Jacob had devoured the sandwich, the kugel, and the entire jar of pickles, he sighed and licked his lips.

"So?" his mother asked.

"Mama," Jacob answered.

"You still run away from your problems like when you were ten?"

The young man shook his head. "You don't know what it's like."

"I wasn't thirty-nine years old carrying a little baby named Jacob who screamed his head off for nineteen months with the colic?"

Jacob covered his face and rubbed his forehead. It was a story he had heard all his life. He was an unexpected child, born to a woman who had thought she would never have children. And he had been such a problem – crying, sickly – everyone thought he was going to die.

"Mother, I've got two," he said. "I know it was hard for you, but I've got two."

"You're only thirty-three. They're babies. They'll grow up. You can manage for a few years."

"It's not that," he said. "Yes, I was exhausted. One or the other was always crying. I didn't mind carrying them around. When they finally fell asleep it was such a good feeling."

"So?"

Jacob grew silent. His mother opened her mouth and then decided to wait. She looked around the shop and thought about putting on her apron and taking a broom to the floor. No. For once, she told herself, sit still and be quiet. She waited.

At last, she could wait no longer. "So?"

"I'm afraid," Jacob said at last. His voice was soft in the dim afternoon light. "I'm a carpenter. I make things out of wood." He shrugged. "There isn't enough money. When it was just Rebecca and myself, then I felt as if we could make do. But now I think about the boys… They're not eating much now, but in a few years it will be like living with voracious wolves. And what about school? And clothing? If you have two children in a row, then you can pass a jacket or shirt down from one to another, but we will need two of everything. And from what will the money come? Tables? Bookshelves? What can I make that everyone doesn't already have? How often does someone need a new table or a chair? Food. Clothes. Shelter. Those are things people need. If they have to, they'll sit on the floor, or roll a rock inside."

"Jacob," his mother whispered. She put her hand on his shoulder.

He shook her hand off, stood up and began pacing the room. "Already I hold the boys for eight hours, sleep for four, and work for twelve. Where can I get more money? And if I have that money, will I ever be able to rest? To catch a breath? To have a conversation with my wife?"

"So, you run away? You think that maybe you'll sneak out of your attic, go to Moscow, and forget about this family that you started?"

"I could go to America," Jacob retorted. "There is work there."

"Then you would never see your wife," Ruth said. "And you would miss the blessing of watching your two boys grow into manhood. You can run away if you want, but then you won't be able to see how good it is, enjoying the fine times and preparing for the difficult days to come. It's time for you to go back."

"Do I have to?"

"Yes."

"I know." Jacob nodded. "I know."

"Don't forget to say you're sorry. Then beg. If you're lucky, you'll only have to sleep under the table for a week."

Jacob smiled. "It wouldn't be any worse than sleeping in the attic." He wiped a tear from his mother's cheek and kissed her on the forehead. "Thank you, Mama."

Then he headed home.

Ruth Schlemiel smiled. Her seventy-two-year-old body felt warm and glowing. She looked around her son's shop and knew, difficult though it might be, he would do well.

Then her eyes fell on the debris of his lunch and she clucked her tongue.

"Just once you couldn't clean up before you run off?"

Coming Home

The sun was setting gloomy gray, with the promise of a late overnight frost, as Jacob arrived at the door to his house. His hand reached for the latch and stopped. What would he say to Rebecca? What could he say? For three days, he had vanished, hiding in the tiny crawl space of an attic above his wood shop. She must have been worried sick. How could he explain the panic he'd felt and the thoughts he'd had during the long hours crouched in the dark?

He rehearsed his excuses… He'd been working on the oversized crib that he'd accidentally made too large to fit inside the house, and planning to cut it in half and make two cribs! There was a pretty piece of burled wood in the attic that he would need to finish the project. He'd climbed the ladder and was searching for the hardwood when he'd felt tired. He'd only lain down for a nap, but the next thing he knew it was dark and he couldn't find the trap door without fear of falling down the ladder. Rather than risk certain injury, he'd decided to spend the night. It was so soothing to sleep uninterrupted by bawling and screaming. Late the next morning, he realized how comfortable he'd felt. The attic was cozy and quiet… So he'd just stayed there until his mother had come by to tell him it was time to go home.

It was all very simple, straightforward, understandable even.

But how do you explain that to your wife, who you abandoned?

He stood, frozen on the doorstep of his own house, one hand reaching toward his family, and the rest of him inclined to run back to the attic.

And he might have been there still if Rebecca hadn't opened the door and thrown a pail of dishwater and potato peels into his knees. (Chelm had no sewers; garbage was tossed into the street for the goats to eat.)

"Ahh!" Jacob yelped as the cold water soaked through his trousers.

"You!" Rebecca said, that one word both an expression of relief and a piercing accusation. She stared at him.

"I, uh…" Jacob's voice trailed off.

She wanted to scream at him. He wanted to hug her. They got to do neither because at that instant both boys began to cry.

Rebecca rushed to one, Jacob to the other. They lifted the boys into their arms, held them tight, and together sang a lullaby they had made up together:

Little baby go to sleep.
Mama and Papa are here to keep

you safe from all the things that are bad.
Don't be unhappy, don't feel sad."

It seemed to take forever, but eventually the tiny bedroom fell quiet as the boys dozed in their parents' arms.

Rebecca and Jacob stood beside each other. Tears ran down their cheeks.

"I'm sorry," he whispered. "I'm so sorry."

"I was so afraid," she said, her voice barely louder than her breath. "I thought that I lost you. And that the boys lost you. I've been frightened and sad and angry and outraged," she hissed. "And tired and alone. And finally I decided that if this was what God wished, then I would make the best of it. And then, as I planned our life without you, I found myself feeling stronger than I've ever felt in my life."

"I'm sorry."

"Sha." Rebecca scowled. "Don't be sorry anymore. Tell me where you've been."

Jacob examined his boots for a moment. Then he told her everything.

"Your Mamma sent you back here?" Rebecca said when he had finished. The scorn in her voice was so sharp he felt it bite into his chest.

"No," he said. "Yes. No. I was coming. I had already decided."

"Oh. You decided you'd had enough of a vacation, so now it was finally time to check in on your family?"

A dozen angry answers passed through Jacob's mind unsaid. Instead, he let his head drop and again whispered, "I'm sorry. I'm here now."

"Yes, I see that," Rebecca said. "The question is, do we want you?"

Jacob blinked.

"You see, we've been doing quite well without you," she continued. "The neighbors have been generous. I've even been offered a job by Reb Cantor, the merchant, when the boys are old enough to be on their own. Tell me, why should I allow you back into this house?"

In Chelm, there is a saying, "The wise man is silent when the fool is certain."

Jacob Schlemiel had no idea what this meant, but he knew that Rebecca needed an answer, and he had none. He would go back to his shop to live for a while, and then from there, who knew... Perhaps to America?

"Who am I holding?" He looked at the babe on his arm. "Is this Adam or Abraham?"

"I don't know," Rebecca said, laughing a little. "I still can't tell them apart either. Why do you want to know?"

"Because if I am to leave, I want to tell him personally. I can't kiss the boy and say, 'Farewell, Abraham,' if it's Adam. Years from now, when he grows up, he would say, 'My father left me without even saying goodbye.'"

Rebecca looked at her husband, at the sorrow and remorse in his eyes. "Well then," she said. "I suppose you'll have to stay until we figure out which one is which."

"I suppose I shall," Jacob said. He kissed the sleeping boys on their foreheads. "Thank you, little ones."

Then he looked into the eyes of his wife, their lips inches apart.

"Can you forgive me?" he asked.

"No." She shook her head. "Not yet."

Jacob Schlemiel thought for a moment that his heart would crumble. This was his punishment. He knew many men who lived without the love of their wives, but he'd never imagined that he would join their number. Perhaps some day she would look at him and know that it was love and devotion that had brought him back to their house. Until that day, he would have to make do.

"Please," he said, "let me know if you change your mind."

Rebecca felt angry. Did he really think that forgiveness came so easily? She could justifiably make him suffer for years. Who could blame her?

She shook her head and sighed. "All right. I'll forgive you."

"You will? Really?" Jacob was jolted with surprise. Then he asked, "When?"

"Now," she said, smiling just a little.

"Already? But I…"

"Shh." She leaned forward and kissed him – if only to quiet him and keep the boys asleep. "Some day, I'll ask you to do something for me to make you pay for this. No, I don't know what it is yet, but I'll think of something. Don't worry – it won't hurt. Now, set the boy down gently and let's get you out of those wet clothes…"

Jacob Schlemiel grinned with relief.

Of course, if he had known in advance the demand Rebecca was going to make to make years later, he might have kept on his pants and run off to America that instant.

Chapter Four

The Question Is Answered

When did Abraham and Adam Schlemiel begin to realize that they weren't the same person in two identical bodies? On the surface it seems like a foolish question (although in Chelm no question is considered too foolish to be asked), but from the time of their birth the twins themselves hadn't been too sure.

They were identical in every way. Their eyes, their lips, their ears, even the moles on their left elbows were in exactly the same place. They ate the same food, wore interchangeable clothes, and slept in the same crib – which Jacob had finally managed to get into the house by cutting in half and then nailing back together – because the moment their father tried to separate them they began to scream.

Not even their mother could tell them apart. When they were babies, she tried to keep Abraham on the left and Adam on the right. That might have worked, except Rebecca Schlemiel had an impossible time telling right from left. She'd set them down, turn around for a moment, and by the time she looked back, she felt certain that some impish demon must have switched the two boys.

When they were a year old, their grandmother Ruth suggested tying a piece of string around one boy's wrist. If only they'd thought of that sooner! It was decided that, as the oldest, Abraham would have the honor of wearing the bracelet. But have you ever tried to tie a string to a wriggling toddler? Five minutes after the string was secured, somehow it was gone. A new string was tied, but even in his sleep, Abraham managed to slip loose. That project was abandoned the morning that Jacob went to the crib and found both boys giggling happily with strings on all four wrists. This was but the first of the many Schlemiel twins' pranks.

They were inseparable, and still indistinguishable. As they learned to walk, they stood up together, took three steps together, and fell down together. If one bumped his head, both howled. And they loved to climb. Everyone in Chelm got in the habit of saying, "Abraham, Adam, get down from that table… that chair… that book shelf!"

Every so often, Rabbi Kibbitz would pull one or the other aside and ask, "Are you Adam or Abraham?"

"Yes," the boy would smile. "I am."

It wasn't until the approach of Passover after their fifth birthday that the boys themselves realized they had something of a problem.

You see, at the Passover Seder it is traditional for the youngest child to recite the Four Questions. Abraham and Adam's befuddled parents assumed that the boys would sing together.

But everyone in Chelm, including the boys themselves, knew that Adam Schlemiel was twelve hours younger than Abraham – and therefore only Adam was entitled to ask the Questions.

About a week before Passover, the arguments began.

"I think that I should say the Four Questions," said one boy.

"Me too," replied his brother.

"You think I should say them?" said the first. "Good!"

"No," answered the second. "I think I should say them."

"But I'm Adam!"

"I thought you were Abraham."

"You're Abraham."

"No, I'm Adam!"

It was the first time that they actually came to blows. Their mother hurried over to pull them apart.

"Abraham, Adam, stop that!" she said.

"I'm Adam!" both boys shouted simultaneously.

"You're Adam?" Rebecca asked the boy on her left. He nodded. "What about you?" she asked the other. "Are you Adam?" This boy nodded as well.

"Then where is Abraham?" Rebecca Schlemiel shouted in a panic. "I've lost my oldest child!"

Anywhere else, such a reaction would have brought healing

laughter into the room. In Chelm, however, such remarks are taken seriously. A search party was organized, and it was only after Adam and Adam had gone to bed that Jacob and Rebecca Schlemiel were relieved to count two sleeping boys instead of just one.

But the next morning, when both boys denied being Abraham, the search parties went out again.

This wasn't just malicious mischief. The truth was that neither boy was certain who he was.

On one level, they had always heard their names spoken together as "Abrahamandadam." On another level, they had sometimes answered to the individual names whimsically and indiscriminately. If Grandmother Esther offered Adam a treat, both shot forward, but if Grandfather Shmuel had a chore for Adam, neither responded. And sometimes, when neither punishment nor reward was offered, whichever boy was closest replied.

Even when they talked, it was often simultaneously, both boys speaking like a Greek chorus, or one finishing the other's sentence, as if they knew each other's thoughts completely.

It has often been asked, "When does identity begin? When does the child recognize that it is an individual and not an extension of its mother?"

For the Village Twins, individuality came on the eve of that Passover Seder.

The feast was held at Grandfather Shmuel and Grandmother Esther's house. Only four of Rebecca's six sisters and their families were coming this year, so there was a little bit of elbow room at the table. Still, Rebecca and Jacob thought that it was best if the twins were separated on opposite sides of the table, to prevent kicks, elbows, and pinches from disrupting the service.

For his part, Jacob hoped that Rebecca's newest nephew, Moishe, who was by all reports a "remarkable and intelligent boy," would be able to recite the questions and thus avoid the impending conflict. Unfortunately, even if the boy was a one-year-old linguistic genius, Moishe was fast asleep in his mother's arms.

Rebecca was worried for a different reason. If both boys really thought that they were Adam, then might they not both grow up as Adam? Then what would happen to her oldest son, Abraham? Would he simply vanish as if he had never existed?

The early blessings and songs went smoothly. Hands were washed, wine was drunk, and the tale of the Exodus from Egypt began to unfold.

Grandfather Shmuel, as the leader of the service, was seriously considering skipping the Four Questions entirely. The last thing that he wanted was a long and drawn-out argument that made dinner come even later. He came to the Four Questions in the Haggadah and said, "Let's speed this up a bit and move along to... OUCH!"

Grandmother Esther had kicked him under the table. He looked at her, she stared him down, and he said, "All right. Fine. Who's going to read the Four Questions?"

All eyes turned to the twins.

"Maybe they both can read them together," said Grandmother Ruth.

"Or take turns," added Grandmother Esther.

"No!" both boys stood up and spoke simultaneously. "Only one! The youngest reads the Four Questions."

Grandfather Shmuel rubbed his forehead and closed his eyes. Oy! He felt a headache coming on.

The room fell quiet. No one dared even to breathe. The two brothers looked at each other across the table, their faces carved in impassive stone. The candles flickered. The roast in the oven grew drier.

And then... without saying a word to each other, it was decided.

Abraham sat down, and Adam remained standing.

They looked at each other again. A feeling of sadness filled their eyes with tears.

Abraham nodded at his brother, and in a voice sweet enough for two, Adam began to chant the Hebrew, "Mah nishtannah ha-lailah ha-zeh..."

In his seat, Abraham mouthed the words, but his voice was silent.

Chapter Five

The Roma

They arrived after dark. No one saw them come. They quietly set up their camp in the round village square. There were two wagons, three horses, and a mule.

The first person to notice them was young Doodle, the village orphan, whose job it was to extinguish the gas lamp in front of the synagogue. He told Miriam, the egg lady, who told Deborah Shikker, who told her husband (the town drunk), and within an hour everyone in Chelm knew that a herd of wild elephants had trampled Rabbi Kibbitz, but were being subdued by Cossacks in the village square.

A crowd gathered.

"Where are the elephants?" asked young Avi Weiss.

"The Cossacks have gone," said Reb Cantor, the merchant. "Thank goodness."

"But what about the poor rabbi?" moaned Mrs. Chaipul.

Just then, a man's head popped out the back of one of the wagons. He had long hair, tan-colored skin, and hooped earrings in one ear. He looked at the villagers, scowled, and withdrew.

Everyone fell quiet.

Just then, Rabbi Kibbitz, still in his sleeping gown, arrived at a run. He had heard that the synagogue had been destroyed by a gigantic fire-breathing water buffalo.

Naturally, the Chelmsfolk congratulated the rabbi on his daring escape from the elephant, while he thanked them for quelling the inferno and rebuilding the synagogue so quickly.

With order restored, the two painted wagons were soon forgotten, and one by one people drifted home, to work, or to morning prayers.

Late in the afternoon, there was a timid knock on the door of Jacob Schlemiel's wood shop.

The twins pushed into each other to answer.

"Are you the carpenters?" a little girl asked. She wore a bright red dress and had shiny brass earrings. Her head was covered by a beautiful silk scarf. Beside her stood a tall man with a long drooping moustache.

"We're not carpenters yet," said the young boys, who blushed. Even though two years had passed since they had learned their identity, from time to time, they still spoke together in one voice. "We're only seven years old, but we're learning."

"Who is it?" Jacob asked.

Both boys turned to their father. "A couple of Gypsies."

The man with the moustache hissed.

"No, please wait," the girl said. She whispered to the man in an unfamiliar language. He shrugged. Then she said, "We are not Gypsies. We are the people of Romani. One of our wagons is broken, and we need some wood to fix it."

Jacob Schlemiel dusted himself off and came to the door. "There is plenty of wood in the forest."

"We need nails as well," said the girl. "And a hammer. And a saw."

"Reb Cantor's store sells those."

The girl did not answer.

"Papa," said the boys. "They need a carpenter."

"Ahh," Jacob Schlemiel said.

"No!" The man with the moustache barked, "The Kalderash need no one." He spun on his heels and departed.

The little girl looked uncomfortable. "Please. Come this evening to our camp. We have no money, but we can offer dinner at least." Then she turned around and ran after the man.

Jacob Schlemiel sighed.

"Will we go papa?" said one boy. "Can we?"

"Where are they from?" said the other. "Do you think he was her father or her uncle?"

"Abraham, Adam, shaa. Back to your chores."

Needless to say, for the rest of the day, nothing got done. The Schlemiels quit work early and went home to tell Rebecca the news.

She immediately flew into a rage. She had spent all day preparing a delicious stew and now Jacob was telling her they were going out for dinner? He couldn't have told her sooner? Look at her clothes, what would she wear?

"You look beautiful, Mama," the boys said.

Rebecca patted their heads and then snapped at Jacob, "Do they even keep kosher?"

"I didn't have time to ask," Jacob said.

"How can we eat with them if we don't know?"

"It would be rude to refuse. Why don't you bring the stew along?"

"If I bring the dinner they promised you, then how will they pay for their work?"

"I don't know!" Jacob answered, exasperated. "How often do strangers come to Chelm, knock on the door of my shop, and ask for my help? We're not so poor we can't spare a piece of wood, some nails, and few hours of our company."

Rebecca smiled. "If I'd wanted fame, I would have married an actor. If I'd wanted riches, I would have married the merchant. Instead, I married you."

Jacob's face drooped. "Are you disappointed?"

She shook her head and kissed his cheek. "Not at all."

A half-hour before sunset, the Schlemiels left their house. Jacob carried the stew pot, Rebecca carried the lantern, and the twins carried the wood and tools. When they arrived at the village square, they found that the quiet scene of two wagons, three horses, and a mule had been transformed into a colorful camp, with three small fires, bustling men and women, laundry blowing in the breeze, and a dozen or more barefoot children running after two yapping dogs and a pig.

Rebecca saw the pig and nudged Jacob.

"So?" he said. "It's alive. At least we know we're not eating that one for dinner."

They were met at the edge of the camp by the little girl, who introduced herself as Rosa. As she led them to her wagon, she apologized for her father. He was the Duke of Kalderash, she explained, a proud man.

"What of your mother?" Rebecca Schlemiel asked.

"She is with God."

"I'm sorry," Rebecca said.

"Oh, don't be," Rosa answered. "I talked with her last week and she said that she is very happy there. Heaven is a wonderful place, and she said that she'll welcome me herself when it is my time."

"Ahh," Rebecca nodded. She didn't say another word.

It was an awkward meal. Rosa's grandmother had prepared a huge feast of bread and cheese and vegetables. The stew pot sat to the side, untouched. (Rebecca had decided that it would be insulting to mention it.) While Abraham and Adam were delighted at the way the Kalderash family tore off pieces of thin bread and used it to pick up their food, Rebecca was horrified.

"Ask if they have a fork," she whispered to Jacob.

"Hush," he said. His eyes widened as the duke pulled a large curved knife from his belt, which he stabbed into a hunk of cheese before handing it, hilt-first, to Rebecca.

No one said much of anything after that.

As the sun set, they ate a sweet baked dessert in the flickering firelight and dim glow from the street lamp.

The boys wandered off to play with Rosa, and Jacob took his tools and the lantern and vanished into the back of the wagon with the duke to examine the damage.

Rebecca found herself left alone by the fire with the old woman.

"That," Rebecca said, talking loudly and slowly, "was delicious." She patted her tummy and smiled.

"I understand your language." Rosa's grandmother answered. "Give me your hand."

"Why?" Rebecca hesitated.

"I shall tell your fortune."

Rebecca Schlemiel extended her right hand. The old woman took it roughly. She peered at it in the dim firelight, examining first the palm, then the back.

"Give me the other one," she said. Her voice had the ragged rasp of a lifelong smoker.

"Maybe I shouldn't," Rebecca said. She ran her fingers over the back of the hand the old woman had touched, as if checking to be sure everything was still there.

"Are you afraid?"

If she hadn't been, she was now. What good was knowing the future? If all was to be well, then that would be revealed in time. As would evil. How could knowing the future be of any use? It would only cause worry and anxiety.

"No," Rebecca said. "I'm not afraid, I just... I don't believe in fortunes."

"The seventh daughter of a seventh daughter does not believe in fortunes?"

"How did you know that?"

"What sort of a soothsayer would I be if I could not recognize a fellow seeker of sooth?" The old woman smiled. Remarkably, she had all her teeth, though many were chipped or yellowed.

Rebecca felt her heart beating rapidly.

"I see you doubt me even now." The old woman's eyes narrowed. "Tell me, when your husband vanished for a time so many years ago, were you worried?"

"Of course I was."

"But not for long. Because you saw. You saw that all would be well."

"I didn't know where he was. It was terrifying."

"Of course it was." The woman chuckled. "Fate must jar us from time to time. How else would we learn who we are? Do you think your coming here is an accident? There are no accidents."

"My husband came to fix your wagon."

Rebecca glanced over the old woman's shoulder. The door to the colored caravan was closed. Jacob had been in there for quite some time, yet she hadn't heard the sound of his hammer or saw. The boys had been playing nearby with the old woman's granddaughter, Rosa, but Rebecca could not see them. Instead, she heard only the crackling of the fire and a man at another campfire playing a sorrowful tune on a strange stringed instrument.

All at once, the space surrounding the camp seemed to close in upon her. Was she really still in Chelm? Could this all be happening in the village square, within shouting distance of the synagogue? To escape she needed only to stand and run. It was but a few hundred yards to Reb Cantor's house, and only a short distance beyond that to her cozy home.

She did not move. Nor did the old woman.

At last, Rebecca extended her left hand. Once again the woman seized it. She squinted at it, back and front, only a glance really. Then she held it firmly and stared into Rebecca's eyes.

"You have two boys," the woman began. "They are the same. And yet they are different."

Oy, Rebecca thought, she's telling me the obvious. This is what I was afraid of? She rolled her eyes.

The old woman squeezed her hand harder.

"They look the same. They are the same. And yet they are of different countries. They have different lives. Different futures."

For a number of years, Rebecca had known that the twins, born twelve hours apart, did not share the same nationality. Abraham was Polish and Adam was Russian. It was a quirk of fate that the title to Chelm had been transferred from Poland to Russia at that exact moment. How did the old woman know?

The old woman continued, "One is a soldier, but not that one. One will be a cook, the other a carpenter. One will travel, one will stay. There is a woman. One will run. Vanish. One will live on in Chelm, the other will go."

"What do you mean?" Rebecca asked.

The woman shook her head and droned on. "The older is not one but two. The younger… one day here, the next gone."

"Now, you're scaring me," Rebecca said. "Stop it."

But the old woman would not let go. "And yet from one comes two. The years have passed. The lost son returns, but the son who has vanished has never left. They come together, meet again. One becomes two – different, and yet the same."

"You're babbling," Rebecca said. She yanked her hand away, and the old woman let it go. "You're just saying things to sound important. I'm sorry I came. I enjoyed your dinner, but as soon as my husband is done repairing your wagon, we will have to go."

"You know what the strangest thing is?" The old woman looked puzzled.

"No," Rebecca snapped. She stood up and brushed off her dress. "And I don't want to know."

"Suit yourself," said the old woman. She leaned forward and poked a stick into the fire.

Now that she was standing, Rebecca saw the twins playing tag with Rosa near Chelm's sole street lamp. They were handsome boys, seven years old. So innocent, so gorgeous. How could that witch try and scare her like that? Yes, from time to time Rebecca, like any mother, had worried and wondered about the day that her boys would leave her. But to hear of it so suddenly and with such mystery... No, she would put it out of her mind.

She paced back and forth. The sounds of Jacob's hammer from inside the wagon reassured her.

The old woman picked her teeth with a fingernail.

Rebecca looked away. Nonsense. It was all nonsense. She should just forget about it. And yet...

"What," Rebecca asked at last, "is the strange thing?"

"Are you sure you want to know?"

Rebecca snorted. The old woman laughed.

"The woman," she began softly. "The wife. She both comes between them and draws them together again."

"What nonsense!"

"Her name. Would you like to know? It is Rebecca."

"Fooey!" Rebecca spat. "That is my name."

"I know," said the old woman. She laughed louder and louder. "That is what is so strange!"

Rebecca Schlemiel spun around, wanting to strike the old woman, to silence her, but the sudden movement made her feel dizzy. She sat down for a moment and rubbed her forehead.

The next thing she knew it was morning and she was in her own bed.

"What happened?" She sat up suddenly. "Where are the Gypsies?"

"The Roma?" Jacob answered from the kitchen. "They left this morning. You were very tired last night."

"That old woman," Rebecca said, the words nearly a curse. "She told my fortune."

"The queen?" Abraham and Adam said simultaneously.

"What?"

"She was the queen," they said. "The queen of the Roma."

"What did she say?" Jacob asked.

"Nonsense," Rebecca said. "Utter nonsense."

Still, she gathered her two boys up and hugged them close until at last they wriggled away.

"Nonsense."

Chapter Six

Growing Pains

Eight-year-olds can be devious. Although the twins knew who they were, Abraham and Adam Schlemiel did their best to keep everyone else guessing. They never meant to hurt anyone, but they did enjoy the confusion. Getting into mischief could be great fun, and as they got older they got better – both at getting into trouble and at avoiding the consequences.

For example, they made a habit of never going into a room at the same time. Abraham would go in first, and then Adam, or the other way around. Then Abraham would duck out a window or another door and come in again. They could keep this up for an hour or more, until everyone else's head was spinning.

Now, in any other city, this sort of nonsense would never be tolerated. Unfortunately, the villagers of Chelm had notoriously short memories, something the brothers played upon mercilessly. And, as they got older, they kept getting better

On Friday mornings, for example, Rebecca Schlemiel would send the boys to the bakery for the Shabbas loaf of challah and a sweet roll for them to share. Abraham would enter the store and Adam would lag behind, lingering beneath a beech tree.

"Good morning," Reb Stein would say. Then he would playfully scratch his head. "Are you Abraham?"

"No," the boy would fib. "I'm Adam."

"You're not tricking me, are you?" Reb Stein would ask. "One day I will find you out! The usual?"

A nod. "The usual."

Then, the baker would reach for a challah and not one, but two sweet rolls. "Here," the baker would say, "an extra for your brother."

"Thank you." Abraham would gather up the bundle and trundle off.

A few moments later, Adam would enter the store.

"Good morning," Reb Stein would say. "You must be Abraham!"

"No," the boy would say. "I'm Adam. I need to pick up our order."

"Weren't you just in here?"

"No. Every week I come for our bread. Maybe you're thinking of my brother."

"Ahh well." Reb Stein would shrug. "One day I will find you out! The usual?"

A nod. "The usual."

Again, Reb Stein would reach for a challah and not one but two sweet rolls. "Here. An extra for your brother."

"Thank you, Reb Stein." This time, Adam would gather up the bundle and trundle off.

The boys would stuff themselves with sweet rolls and bring two challah home to their mother. Rebecca, who was embarrassed by Reb Stein's charity, always gave the second challah to a pauper or some tradesman to whom money was owed.

Thus, everyone was happy – even Reb Stein, who knew that no matter how many challah he baked, one was always mysteriously taken up to heaven as an offering.

The twins were also masters at avoiding chores.

As in most households, the everyday work no one really wanted to do was divided up among all of the members of the family.

Jacob was responsible for earning a living, for saying prayers, for heavy lifting, and once a year white washing the house and mending the roof.

Rebecca's tasks included cooking the meals, most of the shopping, most of the cleaning, most of the laundry, and sewing all the clothes.

Early on, Rebecca and Jacob had agreed that the boys needed to work, in order to help things run smoothly, and to learn responsibility.

Abraham was given the tasks of making the beds and sweeping the kitchen. Adam, as the younger boy, was given the jobs of throwing the garbage into the streets for the goats to eat and watering the garden. Both boys were responsible for cleaning their own chamber pots and fetching water from the well.

Emptying a chamber pot is a difficult thing to forget to do, but making a bed or watering the garden are the sorts of tasks that can slip anybody's mind. Whenever Rebecca was angry at the boys for neglecting their chores her brow would knit into a frown and the color in her face would grow as red as a ripe cherry. As soon as they spotted her coming in a rage, one of the boys would hide outside behind the pickle barrel, or more often duck under the bed.

"Abraham!" Rebecca would roar. "Why is this bed not made and the kitchen unswept?"

"I'm Adam," the boy on the bed would answer, regardless of the truth.

Rebecca would spin around in a rage. "Where is your brother?"

The other boy under the bed would muffle his snickers with a hand across his mouth.

Then, Rebecca would turn on the sole visible son.

"All right, Adam," she would say, trying to be patient. "There is garbage from yesterday in the kitchen and the garden is as dry as a desert."

"Why are you telling me this?" The imp sitting on the bed would look puzzled. "I'm Abraham."

Under the bed, the other one would now be holding his sides, barely suppressing his guffaws.

Rebecca's eyes would go wild. She would sputter and puff. "Fine!" she'd shout. "I'll do it all myself!" Then she would turn on her heels and vanish in a fury.

If only her anger had diminished a little sooner, her head would have been clear enough to hear the chorus of gleeful laughter behind her. But by the time she realized anything was amiss, the boys had slipped out, and she was once again left alone to tend to all the household tasks.

Now, you shouldn't think too badly of these boys. They didn't mean to be wicked or dishonest. They were youngsters, and it is as much the job of a child to escape duty and learn the boundaries of rules by breaking them, as it is the work of a parent to establish limits and lay down the law. The villagers of Chelm were kind, understanding, forgiving, and often completely ignorant that they were being made fools of. As a result, though the twins suspected that they were pulling stunts and engaging in trouble that was not quite kosher, no one ever managed to pin them down and clearly explain the difference between right and wrong.

But, you think, they surely must have learned that it is a sin to tell a lie. And when Abraham said he was Adam or Adam said he was Abraham, the boy making the claim must have known he was not telling the truth. You would think.

If this were so, then the story of the Village Twins would be far shorter and much less interesting than it really is.

Because, although they had chosen their identities on that Passover evening so many years earlier, both Abraham and Adam knew that on some level the decision had been somewhat arbitrary. Abraham was secure in his identity, and Adam was fairly certain about who he was, but really who could be sure? If you had asked Abraham to stake his claim to paradise on the fact that he was born first, he would have shaken his head no. If you had turned to Adam with the same offer, he too would have found himself unable to claim his place as second born with complete certainty.

So, with the logic and precision worthy of the greatest legal minds, the boys assumed whichever identity was most convenient for them at that particular moment.

They were happy and everyone else was confused and more than a little frustrated.

It wasn't until the arrival of the new schoolteacher that the boys found their inventiveness severely tested…

A New Teacher

Rumors had it that the new schoolteacher was nine feet tall and as thin as a fence rail. They said his hair was as red as a blacksmith's fire and his beard was striped, red and white, like a big city barber's pole. They said his smile was a snarl, his laugh a cackle, and his sneeze like opening a door into a raging thunderstorm.

They said all this never having met him.

Needless to say, the children of Chelm were terrified at the prospect that this half-human half-demon was about to become their new schoolteacher.

"Why can't we study with Rabbi Kibbitz," Abraham and Adam Schlemiel asked their father, "the way that you and Grandfather did?"

For a moment, Jacob Schlemiel smiled faintly at the memory of the doddering chief rabbi of Chelm trying in vain to control a room full of rowdy, screaming, laughing, shouting youngsters. Then it occurred to him that he was a parent now, and that kind of chaos was exactly the sort of behavior he didn't want from his children.

"Rabbi Kibbitz is too old," Jacob said. "Young Rabbi Abrahms will be a fine teacher."

"He is an ogre," said Abraham.

"A monster," added Adam.

"A lunatic madman!" they said as a chorus.

"Stop!" Their father raised his hands. "How dare you speak ill of a stranger. After all, it is because of you that Rabbi Abrahms has moved to Chelm."

Both boys looked at their boots in shame. It was true. If they had heard it once, they had heard it a hundred times. It was all their fault.

One summer afternoon, not long before, the newly ordained Rabbi Yohon Abrahms had been scouring the Yiddish newspaper's help wanted ads in search of a position, when he learned that the village of Chelm was in urgent need of a mohel's services. He immediately pawned all his possessions and spent his last kopek to catch the fastest train to Chelm. Of course, it is a rare train that comes anywhere near Chelm, so after arriving in Minsk, Rabbi Abrahms was forced to travel by goat cart through Pinsk to Smyrna, and from there walk. Or rather run. After all, in Jewish tradition, the circumcision must be performed on the eighth day following a birth, and it had already taken Rabbi Abrahms seven days just to reach Smyrna!

At last, exhausted, hungry, and broke, he arrived at the synagogue, knocked on the door, and breathlessly told Reb Levitsky, the synagogue's caretaker, that he hoped he wasn't too late to circumcise the twins. Naturally, this troubled Reb Levitsky, since at eight years old the Schlemiel twins were already more than half way to bar mitzvah age. It wasn't until Rabbi Kibbitz arrived and Rabbi Abrahms showed them the tattered clipping that they began to understand.

"Ah."

It was such a typical misunderstanding. Rabbi Kibbitz had forgotten to tell the newspaper when the advertisement was to expire, so it had been running every day for eight years.

Rabbi Abrahms looked dumbstruck. The poor man was shattered. "Then it's all a mistake? I don't belong here. All right, I'll go. I'm sorry for bothering you."

With that, Rabbi Kibbitz and Reb Levitsky broke into broad grins, clapped the young rabbi on the back, and shook his hand firmly. "Welcome to Chelm!"

Young Rabbi Abrahms looked confused, so Rabbi Kibbitz explained.

"Anyone who comes to Chelm on purpose we assume is lost," Rabbi Kibbitz said. "Only those fortunate few who arrive by accident are welcome to stay and make their homes here. After all, is it not written that 'the lost are found and the found are lost?'"

"Is it?" Rabbi Abrahms asked. "Where? I don't remember."

"It must be written somewhere," Rabbi Kibbitz answered, offhandedly. "Nearly everything is."

"Ahh!" Rabbi Yohon Abrahms's face broadened into a wide grin. All his life he had searched for a wise teacher to study with, and now purely by chance he had found him!

So, over a nice chopped liver sandwich at Mrs. Chaipul's restaurant, it was settled. Young Rabbi Abrahms would take over all the duties that Rabbi Kibbitz was getting too old for. He would teach all the children at the Yeshiva; he would lead the early morning services when there was snow on the ground; he would become the new mashgiach (making sure that all the meat served in Chelm was kosher); and since they had promised it in the advertisement, he would become the village's new mohel.

"Unfortunately, you're a little late," Reb Levitsky whispered while Rabbi Kibbitz settled the restaurant bill. "The last boy Rabbi Kibbitz performed a circumcision on is a double amputee."

Rabbi Abrahms looked horrified.

"I'm kidding!" Reb Levitsky burst out laughing. "Welcome to Chelm. We have the biggest sense of humor in all of Russia."

"I thought Chelm was in Poland?" Rabbi Abrahms said.

"Poland, Russia, Austria, Russia, Poland, China, who can keep track? We pay our taxes, and they leave us alone." Reb Levitsky knocked three times for good luck on the wooden table.

Now, all of this had occurred at the end of the growing season when the harvest was beginning, and naturally school was not in session. Rabbi Abrahms found himself busy building a house to live in and tramping around the countryside from farm to farm examining the cattle, chicken, ducks, and goats for impurities.

All of this activity was debilitating. Yohon Abrahms had been born and raised in a city. What little he knew of farming and house building could have been written on the back of his left hand in chalk and then washed away. So, instead of rising with the sun and greeting the morning with prayers, he slept. And on Saturdays, when most of the village was in the synagogue welcoming the Sabbath with prayers, he slept.

And so it was, that at the end of the summer, when it came time for school to begin again, the children of Chelm realized that none of them had ever actually seen their new schoolteacher. It seemed impossible. How could anyone living in a village as small as Chelm escape their notice? Did he even exist? Perhaps he was a demon, hiding during the day, coming out only at night, and biding his time. Yes, that was it. He was a demon, waiting for the right moment when he would devour an entire schoolchild whole!

"Father, you must understand," Abraham said. "Since it is our fault that Rabbi Abrahms is here, it is up to us to make things right."

With a serious face, Jacob Schlemiel listened to his boys' fears.

"Don't worry," he said, stroking his beard thoughtfully. "There are two of you. If he is a demon and he eats one, the other is bound to escape."

Their young eyes widened in horror. Jacob Schlemiel winked, but his sons were too afraid to understand that the wink meant he was kidding. This was not the first time that the famous Chelm sense of humor resulted in unexpected consequences, but it was one of the more dramatic.

Because, it was right then and there that Adam and Abraham Schlemiel decided that, since no one else was going to do it, they needed to take care of the demonic schoolteacher themselves – if only to save the village.

The Plot

In every duo there is a leader and a follower. One has the idea, and the other reluctantly agrees. One is more cautious, the other impulsive. So it was with the twins.

As the older brother, Abraham felt it was his duty to be responsible. When Adam made mischief, Abraham took the blame. Or so it seemed most of the time.

What, you may wonder, does this have to do with the heroic plot Adam devised to rid the schoolchildren of Chelm of their demonic teacher?

Shortly after the long conversation with their father, Adam wondered aloud what would happen if the tea kettle's spout was plugged with a potato. He convinced Abraham to steal a potato from the root cellar. They waited until their mother went to the market, and then pressed the potato onto the kettle and blew on the coals. The kettle first hummed, then vibrated, and finally shook like a goat gone mad. The two giggling boys ducked underneath the kitchen table. Then there was an awesome explosion. The potato shot out of the kettle and blew a hole in the roof.

"Oy!" Adam shouted with glee. "Did you see that?"

"See what?" Abraham said. "There's rain pouring into the kitchen."

"I know, but it went off, bang! Like a gun."

Just then, Rebecca Schlemiel returned home. She was already dripping wet and had been looking forward to sitting down for a nice hot cup of tea in front of a warm fire. She saw the pool of water forming on the kitchen floor and began screaming.

"Who did this? Who is responsible?"

Silence. There was nothing but the steady dripping from the roof on the damp wooden floor.

"You want to tell me, or do you both want to suffer?"

Glumly, Abraham stepped forward and received a long and heartfelt tongue-lashing. He was now responsible for cleaning the floor, emptying the rain buckets, and patching the roof. He would also, his mother said, move his half of their bed underneath the leak so that he would learn the value of sleeping under a roof at night. Abraham nodded, lips tightly pressed together, and agreed. Adam stood silent and shameful, a few steps behind his brother, and wondered if he shouldn't have taken the blame instead.

It is well known in mystical circles and even in the scientific community that some phenomena cannot be explained. So, although Abraham took the formal responsibility, Adam only appeared to escape the suffering. The truth was that even though they lived in two different bodies, the twins shared their discomfort equally.

And not just punishment. Both pain and pleasure were, from time to time, transferred from one of their bodies to the other. Sometimes, when Abraham tripped over a log, Adam felt the bruise grow on his knee. If Rivka Cantor pulled Adam's hair, Abraham winced and felt his head jerk sideways. Once, when Adam had stolen a blueberry strudel and eaten the whole thing himself, Abraham (who was working in their father's wood shop at the time) had found himself grinning a blueberry smile, which was unfortunately followed by a severe stomachache. This wasn't something they had ever discussed. Why should they? At the age of eight, they simply assumed that everyone shared pleasure and pain evenly.

So, although Abraham went without dinner that evening, he felt nourished every time Adam took a bite. And, while Abraham slept soundly in the puddles, Adam, whose pillow was as dry as the bottom of the Red Sea when Moses and the Israelites fled from the Egyptians, somehow felt his hair was soaking wet and his skin cold and damp.

Unable to sleep, Adam stayed awake thinking. The idea came three hours before dawn.

"Abraham."

"Glug."

"Take your head out of the puddle."

"What?"

"We can't kill him, right?"

"Huh? Kill who?"

"The schoolteacher," Adam reasoned. "He's a demon. You can't kill demons."

"That's true, but they say he's only half a demon. We could kill half."

"No," Adam shook his head. "Chickens run around after their heads have been cut off. I don't want to think about what a demon might do."

"So," Abraham said, wiping rain from his eyes, "when school begins, he'll eat us one by one and eventually Chelm will become a village with no children."

"But I know what we can do!" Adam said. "What do demons fear most of all?"

"The master of the universe," answered Abraham with certainty.

"Yes, that's true," Adam agreed. "But I was thinking more of humiliation. Think about it. In every story I've heard about demons, the only way people win is by making a fool of the demon. So, that is what we have to do."

"Is that all?" Abraham asked.

"Yes."

"Can I go back to sleep?"

"No! We have to make more plans. School starts next week. We have to drive the demon out of Chelm, or else we'll all be doomed!"

"Uh huh."

"Doomed!"

Abraham rolled over. Even his blankets were sopping. "I heard you the first time. But, in all the stories, the demons are fighting with grown-ups. We're just boys. How can we possibly outwit a demon?"

"You forget that we live in Chelm, the center of wisdom in all of Poland."

"In all of Russia," Abraham countered.

"If the demon was from Chelm, we'd be in trouble. But isn't it said that the youngest baby in Chelm is as wise as the oldest sage in Warsaw? We are going to be nine years old next spring. Surely we can outsmart one feeble demon."

"Yes!" Abraham agreed. He was beginning to feel excited by the prospect. "I think you're right. So, what shall we do?"

"What is the most humiliating thing you can think of?" Adam asked.

"Playing tag with Rachel Cohen when she wins."

"Good one," Adam said. "More humiliating."

Abraham thought for a moment. "The time I thought I had an accident in my pants in synagogue and had to stand there for two hours knowing that everyone was watching."

"Yes," Adam said. "Closer. Now, think of something that would be even worse."

"That was pretty bad," Abraham shuddered. "I can't think of anything worse."

"It's when people laugh at you. When everybody laughs at you."

"Sure," Abraham nodded.

"Naked."

"Naked?"

"No clothes. Not a stitch. Maybe a yarmulke."

"Wait a moment," Abraham said. "You're suggesting that we get the entire village of Chelm to laugh at the demonic schoolteacher naked?"

"Exactly!"

Abraham shuddered. "I don't think I want to look at Rabbi Kibbitz or Mrs. Chaipul without their clothes on."

"No! Not the villagers," Adam insisted. "The schoolteacher. Just the schoolteacher would be naked."

"Oh. That's all right." Abraham nodded. "But how are we going to do that?"

"I don't know, yet." Adam shrugged and then shivered. Although his nightshirt was dry, it still felt wet…

"Wait," both brothers said it together. "I know!"

And they laughed and plotted until dawn.

The Demon is Banished

Getting the schoolteacher naked turned out to be both easy and complicated at the same time.

On the very first day of school, Abraham stood on a chair, while Adam sat on his shoulders, and balanced a bucket filled with water on the partially opened classroom door. Then, Adam tied a short rope from the bucket's handle to a nail above the door. The other schoolchildren giggled with barely suppressed glee.

The schoolteacher would open the door and the bucket would fall and drench him, but not bash him on the skull. Humiliating a half-demon was one thing, cracking its head open was another. They wanted to embarrass the monster into running away from Chelm, not enrage it enough to destroy the village.

Their major concern was that the new teacher might be wearing his broad-brimmed hat as he opened the door. In that case, most of the water would be diverted onto the floor.

"One of us will have to wait outside," Adam said.

"But then he'll know it was us," Abraham argued.

"By then, it'll be too late. He'll vanish in a puff of smoke."

"We hope." Abraham knocked three times on the wooden door. "Careful!"

The bucket wobbled, but did not fall.

"Is everyone else in the village coming?" asked Rachel Cohen, the first girl who had ever been admitted into the formerly all-male school.

"They'll be here." Adam nodded. "Everything is timed out to the last moment."

"Hsst! He's coming!" hissed Rachel's brother, Yakov.

Abraham looked at Adam and then sighed. "You know, as long as I'm going to get blamed, I might as well do the deed." Adam nodded. They shook hands solemnly. Then, Abraham squeezed out a window and ran around to the front of the synagogue, just barely catching up to the new schoolteacher.

As he got closer, Abraham started to feel puzzled. Rabbi Abrahms looked rather normal and harmless, like a skinny young man. Ahh, he realized. It's a perfect disguise.

"Good morning, Rebbe," Abraham said.

The schoolteacher looked surprised. "Good morning, ahh…"

"Adam," Abraham lied, smiling. "Adam Schlemiel."

"Ahh," Yohon Abrahms said. "So, you're one of the boys who brought me to Chelm. I trust your bris went well."

Abraham blushed. He couldn't think of anything to say to that, so he just nodded and kept walking. But at least now he was certain the "rabbi" was actually a demon. After all, what kind of a man would ask a boy such a thing?

Abraham looked over his shoulder to see if the villagers were gathering to watch the spectacle. But the round village square was still empty. Where was everyone?

Not far away, the breakfasters in Mrs. Chaipul's restaurant were in heated discussion about a note Mrs. Chaipul had found that morning nailed to the door of her restaurant.

"A demon?" Reb Cohen, the tailor, scratched his head.

Reb Gold, the cobbler, shrugged. "That's what the note says. 'The demon will be driven from the synagogue at nine o'clock sharp.'"

"Nonsense," said Reb Cantor, the merchant. "There hasn't been a demon in Chelm for generations."

"How would you know?" Mrs. Chaipul asked. "Is there a regulation that visiting demons must receive the merchant's approval?"

When Reb Levitsky laughed, tea came out of his nose , which prompted a sneezing fit.

"No." Reb Cantor looked hurt. "But wouldn't the demon seek to corrupt the richest man first?"

"Or the poorest," said the cobbler, glumly.

"Why not the wisest?" said Reb Cohen. "After all, why should a demon visit Chelm but to destroy the wisest of the wise?"

Mrs. Chaipul looked worried. "Do you think Rabbi Kibbitz is in danger?"

The restaurant grew quiet and serious.

"Perhaps," said Reb Cantor at last, "we ought to go and find him."

Throughout the small village, dozens of notes were being found, variations on this conversation repeated, and similar conclusions drawn. Coats were thrown on, bootlaces tied, and all at once, the citizens of Chelm converged on the village square.

Just outside the synagogue, in front of the booby-trapped door that led into the school, Yohon Abrahms stopped suddenly. He barely noticed as Abraham Schlemiel bumped into his leg.

The young rabbi shivered.

Me, a schoolteacher? he thought. I have never felt so nervous in all my life.

It was a cold autumn day. He rubbed his hands together and blew into them to get warm.

If I am to become a wise and respected schoolteacher, he told himself, then I must make a strong and powerful first impression. I must not be afraid. He drew a deep breath and stepped forward.

"Rebbi!" Abraham said. "Your hat…"

"Thank you, young man." Just as he reached the door, Rabbi Yohon Abrahms removed his broad-brimmed hat and stepped inside.

So, the first part of the plan went perfectly.

The door opened, the bucket tipped, the icy water spilled, and the schoolteacher was soaked!

"The demon!" one of the excited children shouted.

Young Rabbi Yohon Abrahms, the new schoolteacher of Chelm, was stunned.

"Quick! Out of those wet clothes," said Adam Schlemiel, trying to sound just like his mother. "Hurry, hurry, before you catch your death of cold."

Without thinking, the poor young rabbi obeyed, shedding his clothes even as his teeth began to chatter.

"The demon, the demon!" the chorus of schoolchildren chanted.

Slowly the words began to penetrate the rabbi's frozen brain. A demon? In my school? Where?

Even as he poured the water from his boots and slid his wet trousers off, hopping first on one foot and then the other, he scanned the room. He saw nothing aside from a gaggle of frightened and shocked schoolchildren.

Using his most commanding schoolmaster tone, he bellowed, "Where is this demon?"

"Outside!" Abraham and Adam Schlemiel replied. "Outside!"

So, without a stitch of clothing, the brave young rabbi turned and rushed back out into the square.

There he came face to face with the entire assembled village of Chelm. There was a gasp.

"Have you seen the demon?" Rabbi Abrahms shouted.

"No!" they answered as one.

"What demon?" someone asked.

"I didn't see a demon."

"It's as good as gone!" Abraham and Adam Schlemiel said to each other, shaking hands in premature celebration.

"It's gone!" someone else said. "Is it really gone?"

"It's gone," Rabbi Abrahms said. "It must have flown away."

The villagers began to cheer. "The demon is gone! It has fled. Rabbi Abrahms the pure has chased the evil demon away!"

An instant later, amid cheers and song, the stark naked schoolteacher was lifted off his feet and paraded through the village as a hero.

All the other children ran after the crowd, leaving behind a worried Abraham, and a confused Adam.

"What happened?" Adam asked.

"I don't know," Abraham answered. "But we'd better clean up."

Just then Rabbi Kibbitz walked in the door. He looked at the bucket dangling on its rope and at the pile of damp clothes on the floor.

"I see that there was at least one demon in Chelm this morning." His ancient voice creaked. "Maybe two."

The Schlemiel brothers stood as still as statues, their faces as white as marble.

"I trust those demons have been banished," the old man continued, "and that they will give Rabbi Abrahms no more trouble?"

Adam and Abraham nodded their heads. "Yes, Rebbe."

"Good," said the rabbi. "And in honor of your new teacher, Rabbi Abrahms, and his accomplishment in facing such a terrifying ordeal naked, I believe that you both will happily volunteer to clean the classroom every day this year."

Abraham and Adam nodded their heads again.

"Good," said the rabbi. "Very good."

Had Rabbi Kibbitz winked at them before he left the school that morning? Neither brother could be sure.

Only two things were certain.

Every day after school, much to their mother's surprise, Abraham and Adam Schlemiel could be found clapping out the erasers, washing the blackboards, emptying the garbage, and scrubbing the school's floor.

And, after his defeat of the demon, Rabbi Yohon Abrahm's position as the second wisest man in Chelm was secured forever.

Chapter Seven

Separation Time

Jacob Schlemiel yawned. "It's getting late."

Late? Abraham and Adam Schlemiel exchanged looks. The sun had barely risen in the sky, and they had only been in their father's wood shop for a few hours. The ground was still moist from the dew, and their classmates in Chelm's small school would only just be getting out of bed. As always, it had still been dark when their father had wakened them with three short knuckle raps on the forehead. ("To knock the knotholes out," he always joked.) They had dressed, done their morning house chores, eaten breakfast, stumbled out of the house, and opened up the shop all before dawn. Since then, they had sawed, sanded, planed, hammered and beveled. How late could it be?

As if on cue, Mordechai Blott, the village timekeeper, bellowed the hour, "Three o'clock in the afternoon!"

"You see," their father said. "Before we know, it will be dark again."

Adam and Abraham rolled their eyes.

It is said that time is money. Although Chelm was known far and wide as the wisest village in Poland, it was also one of the poorest. Money was always a problem in Chelm, so was time. Wealthy towns like Smyrna could afford to indulge in fanciful construction projects, like a railroad depot or a central clock tower. Such expenses were unthinkable in Chelm, where brainpower was in greater supply than gold.

For centuries the villagers had relied on hourglasses. At sunrise, the head of the house would turn the glass over and the day would officially begin. If you said to someone, "I'll meet you five hours after sunrise," you'd bring a book and read a few chapters until he arrived. It was a pleasant and relaxing system, unless your meeting was outside and it was raining or snowing.

When word reached Chelm about the invention of minutes and seconds, life was transformed. All of a sudden, these new increments added measurably precious moments to every day. It was one thing to nap for an hour, but to spend sixty minutes dozing seemed so frivolous. And if you broke that into seconds – thirty-six hundred seconds – think of the waste!

The villagers became obsessed with time. Everyone wanted a clock, but timepieces were too expensive. So, Jacob Schlemiel's grandfather Adam had seized the opportunity. "Tick tock, tick tock," he'd said. "A couple of gears, a few wheels, a ratchet or two, how hard could it be?" And, with no plans whatsoever, he began construction.

His first clock was the size of a small barn. Not only did it count the seconds, it shouted them out in four languages – Hebrew, Yiddish, Russian, and Polish – simultaneously. Tourists traveled for miles to listen to the din and watch the twelve-foot-long second hand spin around and around at unbelievable speed. Day and night the clock bellowed the exact time, so that everyone in Chelm lying in their beds awake knew exactly how much sleep they were missing. No one, including the inventor, was particularly upset when the thing inexplicably burst into flames and burned to the ground.

Having learned from his mistakes, the next clock Jacob's grandfather built was a masterpiece of simplicity. It was a small device, about the size of a muskmelon, had no moving parts, and made no sound. In fact, the second hand didn't even move because it was painted onto the clock's face.

The odds of this clock keeping anyone awake or bursting into flames were minimal.

"But does it tell time?" the villagers asked.

"Pff," answered the master clockmaker. "Clocks never tell time. People tell time."

"Ahh," the villagers nodded. "Then what time is it?"

"It's now," the Schlemiel clockmaker had said wisely.

This new system functioned perfectly for more than a

generation. No one in Chelm spoke of tomorrow or yesterday or even lunchtime. There was only now. They ate now, they slept now, they worked now. It was amazing how much got done, and at the same time how little got done.

Then one day, the present Reb Cantor's father returned from Moscow with a cartload of clocks.

"They were factory seconds," he explained. "Such a deal I got." And he sold them for a small profit to every household in Chelm. Now everyone had a clock of his own, but none of them kept the same time.

Smyrna had solved this problem by building the huge clock tower in the center of town. The villagers of Chelm knew that it would only be a matter of time before this building would burst into flames and explode, so rather than waste their money on construction they devised another plan.

They pooled their resources and hired Mordechai Blott to become the village timekeeper. His job was to count the seconds, add up the minutes, and call out the hours. If Reb Blott called out two o'clock and your clock said it was seventeen minutes past two, then you knew you were running fast.

Reb Blott was zealously dedicated to his job. He bragged that he never missed a second. Every night, he made a point of remembering the exact second at which he fell asleep. Then, when he woke in the morning, he began counting at the next second.

Anywhere else, it might have been unsettling to see the sun rise at ten-thirty one day and four in the afternoon the next, but no one in Chelm had the heart to fire Reb Blott. As long as they ignored their clocks everyone kept more or less the same time, and within a few years, they all got used to the situation. After all, given enough time people can get used to just about anything.

All of this is a very roundabout way of explaining why Jacob Schlemiel was certain that it was getting late, while Adam and Abraham Schlemiel were equally certain that since it was not even midday there was plenty of time left before dark. So, as children often do when their parents say or do something that is patently absurd, they laughed to themselves, shrugged, and went back to work.

They were nearing the completion of a fine oak chest that Reb Cantor had commissioned Jacob to build as a gift for the new provincial governor. It was a beautiful piece of furniture – seven-sided and with ten legs. "It should be unique," Reb Cantor had ordered. And so it was. Jacob had even specified that it should be finely polished on the inside, while the outside remained rough and splintery. "You keep valuables inside a chest like this," he planned to tell Reb Cantor, "not on the outside."

Then, all of a sudden, Jacob smacked his head. "Adam!"

"I didn't do it!" Adam said quickly.

"Do what?" Jacob asked, his eyes narrowing.

"Nothing. Nothing."

"Good," Jacob said slowly. "Adam, I need you to go to Smyrna. Go to the coppersmith's shop and pick up the brass clasp that I ordered last month. It's a good thing I remembered it. What good is a chest for valuables if you can't lock it shut?"

Brightening at the thought of a nice walk on a pleasant spring day, Adam and Abraham set down their hammers and reached for their coats.

"Not you, Abraham. Just Adam."

Abraham looked puzzled. "But, Father, we always go together."

"You heard me," Jacob said. "Adam will go by himself. I need someone to go to Smyrna and bring back the clasp, and I need someone to stay here and help me."

"But," Abraham said, "we've never been so far apart."

Jacob smiled and nodded. "Then it is time that you were."

Adam, his heart filling with pride at the thought of being sent on such an important mission, grinned widely, crinkled his nose at his brother, and was out the door before another word could be said.

Abraham jumped as the door slammed shut. Through the window, he watched as his brother danced up the road and out of sight.

"Come on," Jacob said, putting a hand on his older son's shoulder. "Let's go back to work. It's getting late."

Abraham nodded quietly. He didn't know what he felt, and he

wasn't sure he could explain it, perhaps because it was the first time in his life he had felt frightened and alone.

Adam Alone

Two farmers stood on the outskirts of Chelm, leaning against their rye rakes in the late morning sun.

"There go the Schlemiel brothers on the Smyrna Road," said one. "Running as usual."

"What brothers?" said the other. "I only see one."

"It's a trick of the light," said the first farmer. "If you squint, you can see them both."

The second farmer squinted. "Ahh yes. In fact I see three!"

"Hmm," said the first farmer. "I wonder if their mother knows."

Adam Schlemiel, completely alone perhaps for the first time in his life, enjoyed this newfound sense of freedom. He ran, he jumped, he twirled in mid-air. Then, he caught his foot on a rock and stumbled head first in the dirt. But nobody saw. When he got up and looked around, the laughing, mocking face of his twin brother Abraham was nowhere to be seen. His mouth opened into a wide grin and he howled at the clear blue sky like a wild animal.

"Yip Yip Yip! Yooooh!!"

"What are you yelling about?" Jacob Schlemiel barked angrily at Abraham. "When I'm about to saw a board the last thing I need is for you to howl like a wild animal so I lose maybe a finger or three."

Abraham was just as surprised as his father at the strange yapping noise that had emerged from his mouth. Not only that, but the palms of both his hands smarted.

"Nothing, Papa," Abraham said. "I was just thinking of Adam."

"Well, stop thinking of him and go back to your sanding and polishing. Some day you'll inherit this business and you need to pay attention to the details."

"Yes, Papa," Abraham said, glumly.

It isn't far from Chelm to Smyrna, maybe ten miles by road. Still, it is not a journey that is taken on a whim, since the road twists and winds through the heart of the Black Forest. During the daytime, this part of the Schvartzvald wasn't so bad. Just a lot of trees and leaves and the occasional chipmunk.

But after dark, the stories said that the woods were transformed into the kind of nightmarish place where wolves howl, bears prowl, and woodcutters abandon their poor defenseless children to wicked witches in gingerbread houses.[2] Not only that, there were thieves, brigands, robbers, and cutthroats who lurked in the shadows ready to leap out at the least provocation.

In other words, it wasn't such a nice place to spend the night.

Adam Schlemiel should have been home in plenty of time. Even though he had left his father's shop at three in the afternoon (according to Reb Blott, the time keeper of Chelm), he managed to reach Smyrna shortly before lunch. He went straight to the coppersmith's shop and bought the brass clasp that his father had said would be waiting for him.

His errand accomplished, Adam then did what any normal boy will do when left to his own devices – he went to buy food with the leftover change.

The marketplace was nearby, and he had a wonderful time wandering up and down the crowded streets, nibbling first on a loaf of bread, then a chunk of cheese, an early apple, an orange all the way from Spain, a piece of halvah, a chunk of Turkish candy, a bowl of chicken soup with matzah balls, half a chicken roasted with garlic and herbs, a baked potato with fresh black pepper and salt, and some more Turkish candy followed by almost a gallon of water

---

[2]Actually, the villagers of Chelm originally had a different story. In the Chelm version, two wicked children, Haimy and Gittel, ate a house that their grandmother had built out of mandlebread, and they got stomachaches. The Brothers Grimm heard the Chelm tale, changed the names, and made the grandmother into a witch. The revised story was so scary that the villagers promptly believed it, and never made mandlebread houses again.

drunk from the town well.

With the sun still high in the sky, Adam smiled, patted his belly, and lay down on the side of a grassy hill just outside the marketplace for a nap.

"Abraham, wake up!" Jacob Schlemiel yelled, shaking his son by the shoulder. How was it possible for a nine-year-old boy to doze off in the middle of hammering? One moment he was banging away, and the next moment the hammer had fallen to the ground and the child was snoring like an elephant. "What's the matter with you? Wake up! Hey! Hey!"

"I don't feel well," Abraham mumbled, clutching his stomach.

"It can't be food poisoning," his father said, "because you didn't eat a thing for lunch. Come on, get up. Walk around a little."

But despite Jacob's prodding, the boy would not be moved. His eyes closed, his chin fell against his chest, and he was out cold once again.

Jacob put his hand on his son's forehead but felt no fever. He shook his head, picked up the hammer, and began whacking away. Eventually the noise would rouse the boy.

The sun was just going down when the sound of a woodpecker roused Adam from his slumber. The marketplace was already shut up. The streets of Smyrna were nearly empty. It was time to hurry home. With luck, he would get back to the shop just as his father was closing up for dinner.

He jumped up, patted his pocket, which held the brass clasp, and started walking. But which way should he go? Smyrna looked so different in the twilight. Even worse, all the roads looked the same. From Chelm there were only two roads, the Smyrna Road and the Great Circular Road. But Smyrna was a big city. There were at least six roads leading away from the marketplace.

That was when Adam Schlemiel realized he was lost. And it was getting dark. And cold. And he had spent all of his money on the brass clasp and food he had eaten for lunch without saving even a crust of bread for dinner.

"Don't panic," he said to himself. "Just ask Abraham what to do…"

But Abraham was in Chelm, now lying safely in bed with the stomachache he had gotten from Adam's lunch.

At first, Adam tried to stay calm. He didn't panic. He ran back and forth, up and down the streets of Smyrna, trying to find a landmark, something that would point him in the direction he needed to go to get home.

Every passerby on the street he asked, "Excuse me, can you tell me where the Smyrna Road is?"

But no one knew. It was as if the people of Smyrna had never heard of the Smyrna Road.

"Where are you from?" one kind woman had asked.

"I'm from Chelm," Adam answered.

"Oh," the woman smiled. "You want the Chelm Road."

"No, thank you," Adam said. "There's no Chelm Road in Chelm. Only the Smyrna Road and the Great Circular Road."

"Silly boy," the woman began. "From Chelm, the road is called the Smyrna Road, but from Smyrna it is called the Chelm Road."

Adam ran away from her, certain that she was a witch trying to trick him into her gingerbread house. Finally, exhausted and frightened, he threw himself down on the hillside where he had napped and began to cry. He sobbed and he sobbed until at last he felt a soft and gentle hand on his shoulder.

"Adam, are you all right?"

Adam looked up and saw the face of a young girl.

"Rosa?"

"I don't know what's the matter with the boy." Jacob Schlemiel had been watching Abraham carefully. "One moment his stomach hurts, the next it's fine. One moment he's crying like a baby, and the next he's got a smile on his face like he's met a long-lost friend."

"Why didn't you send both of them to Smyrna?" Rebecca whispered angrily.

"They're nine years old. Old enough to go their own separate ways for once. I thought I might get some work done. It was a mistake."

Rebecca Schlemiel nodded as she and her husband stared out the window into the darkness.

Adam in the Black Forest

"Tag!" Rosa said. "You're it." And then she took off at a run.

Adam Schlemiel grinned as he chased after her through the woods. Never mind that the Schvartzvald was quiet and creepy. Never mind that it was after dark and a full moon was rising in the sky. Even when thin branches whipped by his cheeks, and he heard the howl of a wolf in the distance, his smile never faltered.

He trusted Rosa. She said that she knew a shortcut, a secret way through the Black Forest that would have him home in time for dinner. And she was a Gypsy princess, so she should know such things.

Just ahead of him, Rosa laughed and dodged around a large boulder. Adam hurried to catch up. She was fast and clearly knew her way through the woods after dark. But Adam was as fit and fleet as a hunting dog in its prime. Even though he stumbled and tripped, slowed by the shadows and the underbrush, he knew he would catch her at any moment. His smile grew broader with the anticipation.

But the next instant Rosa was gone. Vanished – as if whisked from the face of the earth. Where was she? Adam continued to run, peering ahead. Had she hidden herself behind a tree or fallen over a cliff? Maybe this was a trap. Now he remembered the rumors he'd heard about Gypsies, that they were witches and did magic. Rosa hadn't seemed evil. She was just a young girl, around his age. But perhaps this wasn't really Rosa but a demon luring him deep into the woods to eat him. Had she led him somewhere to kill him? Adam slowed as he felt the panic begin to rise in his stomach.

Then something soft wrapped around his foot. Adam stumbled and fell, sprawling head first into a pile of soft leaves and moss.

He jerked his leg free and was about to shout when a thin hand clamped over his mouth.

"Shhh," Rosa whispered. Her face was close to his.

"Brrfrum," Adam said, his words muffled by her palm.

"Shhhhh," she insisted.

Something urgent in her shushing told him to stop for a moment, catch his breath, and wait. If he needed to, he could always fight her. If nothing else, he could peel her fingers away and scream.

"Shh." Rosa took her hand away and held her finger to her lips. Then she pointed to her ears. Listen.

So he listened. That's when he heard them. Footsteps. Hooves.

There was someone out there – and not far ahead. Adam squinted and saw three men leading their horses through the woods. Two of them were cursing the third loudly.

"He knows a shortcut," said one. "A quicker way to Chelm."

A second voice said, "We'll be there in no time. We'll steal everything in town and be gone before dawn.'

The first voice replied. "Of course Alex Krabot, the great criminal mastermind, has no sense of direction, so here we are lost in the woods…"

A second robber giggled.

"Shut up, Dimitri," said the third thief, who had been silent until then. "Do you hear something?"

All three men stopped. Their horses began to graze at the leaves. Adam and Rosa held their breaths. A horse whinnied.

"Alex, you think it's a werewolf?" said the second thief, clearly terrified.

"Bertie, there are no such things as werewolves," said the first one. "Now, vampires, ghosts, and demons, maybe…"

"Shut up!" hissed the third, as he slapped the others across their cheeks.

Adam winced at the sound. Then his heart began to pound. That was why Rosa had stopped him. These men were bandits, maybe murderers. They planned on sneaking into Chelm and robbing everyone of everything! If they heard him, they would surely kill him.

"Who's there?" shouted the third thief, who was clearly the leader. "Who's out there?"

Rosa made a hoot like an owl.

The robber leader's head spun, listening.

The first robber said, "Alex, it's just a bird."

"Oww," said the second. "That hurt."

The leader waited another moment, nodded, and then the three men and their horses continued along their way.

Rosa and Adam lay very still for a long time after the men had gone.

Then Adam leaped to his feet. "They're going to rob Chelm!"

"I know," Rosa said. "I'm trying to think."

"But there's nothing in Chelm to steal!"

"I know," Rosa said. "And when they find that out, they're going to be angry. And angry men do stupid things."

Chelm was a peaceful village. Three men with guns and swords could hold the entire town hostage – or worse.

"What are we going to do?" Adam asked.

"We need help," Rosa said.

"What about your family?" Adam asked. "Are they nearby?" It was funny, he thought, only a few minutes earlier he had been afraid that Rosa was leading him to her family's stew pots. Now he hoped that the Gypsies might be close enough to offer assistance.

"No." Rosa shook her head. "They are in Minsk."

"Your family is in Minsk and you're here? You're just a girl."

"In my family, when you reach a certain age you must spend some time alone. It's a long story."

Adam sat down on a rock. "Then my village is doomed."

Rosa put her hand on his shoulder. "Don't give up. Not yet."

"What can we do? It's a long way back to Smyrna. We're not so far from Chelm, but the bandits are between us and the village. Even if we could get home in time, the only weapons my people have are rakes and shovels and scissors." Adam felt despair rising in his heart. Before, when he had thought himself lost in Smyrna he had been afraid, but that was only fear for himself. Now he worried for the people of his village.

"You still have a brother?" Rosa asked. "Abraham?"

"Yes, of course."

"You are twins?"

"Yes," Adam snapped. "What about it?"

"Do you ever talk to him without talking?"

"What do you mean?" Adam began, but then he fell quiet. He knew what she meant. He couldn't believe he had forgotten! He pursed his lips and then told Rosa, "Yes, sometimes Abraham and I talk without talking. Or at least we used to. How did you know?"

"Among my people," Rosa nodded, "twins are often very close. Can you call him now?"

"I don't know," Adam said. "When we were very little, it seemed as if we were the same person. But now… This is the first time we've ever really been apart. I don't know… It's so far."

"You must try." Rosa took Adam's hand. "Close your eyes. Think of your brother. Call to him."

"All right. Quiet, please."

Abraham! he thought. *Abraham! Can you hear me?*

"It's not working. I can't hear him."

"Shh," Rosa said. "Be patient. Close your eyes. Don't hold your breath. Listen for Abraham. Picture him. Feel his breath."

Adam sighed. He shut his eyes and took a deep breath.

Abraham… Abraham…

Less than three miles from where Adam and Rosa sat, Abraham Schlemiel sat at the dinner table; his eyes were closed as he prayed for his missing brother's safe return.

Adam… Adam…

Abraham… Abraham…

Then his eyes snapped open.

"Mother, Father," Abraham said, his voice firm. "Trouble is coming."

Chapter Eight

Thieves

The robbers arrived at dawn. Alex Krabot, Bertie Zanuk, and Dimitri Dimitriovich, known from Yalta to Yaktusk as three of the deadliest bandits in Eastern Europe, had planned to appear in Chelm just after sunset the day before. Unfortunately, they had been delayed in the woods. First they were lost. Then there were the mysterious sounds. Then a shower of acorns, as if the squirrels themselves were defending their territory. So, instead of three terrifying figures on horseback riding mysteriously out of the dusk, the three men stumbled into the small village in the early morning, tugging on the reins of their exhausted nags, and cursing.

"Alex, where is everyone?" asked Bertie. "You think the spirits of the forest told them we were coming?"

The streets were deserted. The farms they passed were empty. They peered into several windows, but saw no one.

"Maybe they're in church," Alex Krabot said. "You know these Jews, always celebrating or mourning something."

"I think they call it a synagogue," said Dimitri.

Alex shot him a murderous stare, and the bandits continued to search the village for signs of life.

Meanwhile, in the synagogue's social hall, the entire village of Chelm had gathered to argue about Abraham Schlemiel's strange warning. For what seemed like the thousandth time, his father, Jacob Schlemiel, explained what had happened.

"Aren't you listening?" Jacob said, exasperated. "Just after dinner, Abraham went all stiff. He said, 'Trouble is coming.' I said, 'What kind of trouble?' He said, 'Robbers.' I said, 'So, Mr. Smart Guy, how do you know this?' He said, 'Because Adam told me.'"

"But Adam wasn't there," said Reb Gold, the cobbler.

Jacob nodded. "I pointed this out to him. The boy says he heard Adam's voice in his head."

"But you said he was acting strange all evening," Reb Gold insisted.

"Yes!" Rebecca Schlemiel snapped. "Yes, yes, yes. For a hundred times, yes!"

Jacob patted his wife's shoulder. "She's had a long day."

"A long day?" Rebecca hissed. "A long day? Yes, I've had a long day. You send one son off by himself on an errand to Smyrna and he doesn't return. And the other one is acting like a diseased lunatic. Yes, it's been a long day!"

Jacob stood still, a smile frozen on his face. Rebecca buried her head in her hands. Abraham sat next to her, still in a daze, nodding his head and talking to himself. He paused for a moment, smiled, and patted his mother's knee.

Whispers filled the social hall. No one in Chelm knew what to make of Abraham's strange warning. Was it true or had the boy lost his mind in grief over the disappearance of his twin brother? Everyone had an opinion, and they had been arguing for hours. There were even two farmers who swore that the boy who had gone to Smyrna was not Adam, but Abraham.

Then, the doors at the back of the social hall opened and three men, filthy with dust from the road, walked in.

"What's going on?" Alex Krabot barked.

"We're waiting for the robbers," said Reb Shikker, the town drunk.

"You see, Alex," Dimitri said. "They knew we were coming."

"Oh, you're them?" Reb Shikker smiled. "We've been expecting you. Hey, they're here! The robbers are here!"

The three wicked thieves stood with their legs planted firmly on the ground and their meanest grimaces fixed on their faces. Usually the announcement of their arrival to a crowd was good for a shriek, a scream or two, and at least a couple of faintings. Then someone, usually a young man, stepped forward and tried to stop them. He was usually killed quickly, as an example. After that, everyone else was much more cooperative.

Instead, much to the thieves' chagrin, the villagers began to applaud.

"Hooray! The thieves are here!"

"At last!"

"It's about time!"

"Can I go home now?"

With a flourish of pride, Reb Shikker escorted the three dazed bandits to the stage at the front of the hall. There they were introduced to the rabbi, the merchant, and the caterer.

At last, Rabbi Kibbitz held up his hands. "Sha, shaa." The crowd fell silent.

"So," Rabbi Kibbitz said, "you're here to rob us?"

Again, the villagers cheered, clapped, and stomped their feet until they were silenced by a wave from the rabbi.

By now, the bandits were completely confused.

"Yes, we are here to rob you," Alex Krabot snarled, stifling any cheers before they could begin. "Bring us all your wealth."

All of a sudden, there was a noise like a donkey with hiccoughs. "Ha HAW! Ha HAW!"

Everyone turned and stared at Reb Shikker, who was doubled over with laughter, his face as red as a boiled tomato.

"You!" Alex shouted. "What's so funny?"

The other two thieves dragged the helpless Reb Shikker onto the stage.

"Who is this man?"

"He's the town drunk," said Reb Gold.

"Oh," said Dimitri, about to punch Reb Shikker in the face.

"And our bookkeeper," Reb Gold quickly added. "He keeps all our accounts."

The bandit leader stared at Reb Gold. "You let the town drunk keep the books?"

Reb Gold shrugged. "He's got a gift."

"Enough!" Krabot shouted. "Bring all your gold here."

"Gold?" Everyone laughed now. "HA HAW!"

"Stop it!" Alex Krabot fired a gun into the ceiling and didn't even flinch as plaster and chunks of wood fell at his feet. Then he handed the gun to one of his men to reload and said, "Who is the wealthiest man in Chelm?"

"Ahh, that would be me. Reb Cantor, the merchant." He performed a low bow. "At your service."

"You, bring me your money."

"Excuse me," Reb Cantor said. "May I have a word with you?"

Alex threw his hands up. "Why not?"

They both stepped to one side of the stage.

"Let me be blunt," Reb Cantor whispered. "I don't have any money."

"What? You're the richest man in Chelm, and yet you say you're penniless? What kind of a fool do you take me for?"

"None at all," Reb Cantor said quickly. "I buy and I sell. Right now, I'm arranging one of the largest shipments of caviar to Egypt! So, all my money is in caviar."

"Bring me the caviar," Alex Krabot said through tight lips.

"Well, the caviar is in the sturgeon. The sturgeon is in the Caspian Sea. The sea is in Russia. The governor of the province, who is Russian, needs to sign the papers. He needs a bribe. I have no money, so I'm having a chest built. A beautiful thing…"

"Shut up!" Alex Krabot spat. "Bring me the chest!"

"Well, it's not quite finished."

The bandit leader spun around. "I'm going to kill someone!"

Just then, a boy of nine years stood up and said, "Kill me!"

"Sit down, Abraham!" Rebecca grabbed at his hand, but missed as he jumped onto the stage. "Are you crazy?"

"No. Take me outside and kill me," Abraham Schlemiel said. "I'll volunteer."

"Abraham, no!"

"Shh, Mama. I know what I'm doing. Look, Mr. Tough-Guy Robber, kill me."

"Abraham?" Rebecca stood up. "You come back here at once. If anybody is going to die, it should be me."

Jacob Schlemiel fidgeted uncomfortably in his chair. Truth was, he didn't want to die, but he glumly stood and volunteered. "Okay, Okay. You can kill me instead."

"This is a very strange town," Alex muttered. "Take the boy outside."

"No, not him!" Rebecca shouted.

Krabot held up his gun. "Lady, sit down or I'll kill you both. Take the boy."

"Can I do it?" Bertie asked. "I'll do it!"

"No, me," Dimitri said. "Bertie got to do the last one. Please."

Alex Krabot shook his head in disgust. "Why don't you both do it? Take the boy outside."

"Both?" Abraham's eyes widened in fear. "Don't you think that one of them should stay inside to protect you from this crowd?"

"From this crowd?" Krabot chuckled. "No, you're right. Caution is prudent. All right, fine. Dimitri Dimitriovich you go. Bertie Zanuk, don't say a word. He's right, you did the last one."

Dimitri stuck his tongue out at Bertie and dragged Abraham off the stage, through the crowd, and out the front doors.

"My boy," Rebecca moaned. She collapsed into her chair. Jacob put his arm around her, wondering if he should have done more, and if so, what, and if it would have made any difference.

Everyone fell quiet. Alex grinned. At last there would be fear.

The villagers of Chelm had watched with sinking hearts as the notorious thief dragged Abraham Schlemiel from the synagogue's social hall.

A few moments later, everyone in the synagogue heard a bloodcurdling scream.

Rebecca Schlemiel screamed and fainted. Jacob Schlemiel burst into tears.

"Now," Alex Krabot said firmly. "Bring me all your silver, all your gold. Everything you have of value."

Caught

When the villagers of Chelm watched Dimitri Dimitriovitch,

the notorious thief, drag Abraham Schlemiel from the synagogue's social hall, their hearts sank. When they heard his long and mournful howl of agony cut short, "YaaaH-OoooWWWWW-rp!" they felt despair.

Outside, however, it was a different story.

Squinting as he had emerged into the sunlight, Dimitri had been trying to decide whether to waste a bullet on the boy or just cut his throat with a knife. The bullet was less bloody, but the blade was less expensive. He had just about settled on the knife when he heard a voice behind him.

"Let me go!" the voice had said.

He spun around and saw something that made him blink.

The boy he was about to kill was standing behind him.

He turned again. No, the boy was still there in front. Dimitri was still holding him by his shirt. For a moment, he thought he was seeing double. Then, Dimitri actually heard double.

"Whatever you do," two voices echoed in both of Dimitri's ears, "don't look up!"

He was just in time to watch as hundreds of potatoes fell out of the sky smacking him right between the eyes. Then everything went black.

"I meant you should drop an empty sack of potatoes over his head," Adam Schlemiel said. "I wanted to tie him up."

"Now you tell me." Rosa Kalderash panted with exhaustion as she jumped down from the social hall's roof. "Abraham, are you all right?"

She leaned over and gave Abraham a kiss on the cheek.

For the first time since he had learned that three thieves were going to rob Chelm, Abraham Schlemiel smiled. "Yes, I'm fine. Where have you been?" Abraham asked his twin. "He almost killed me."

"I got lost in Smyrna," Adam said. "Rosa found me. We took a short cut through the woods, and we saw these thieves sneaking up on Chelm. That's when I mind-talked the warning to you."

Abraham nodded. "How did you do that?"

Adam shrugged. "I don't know. It was Rosa's idea. You remember, Rosa. Father fixed their wagon once a few years ago."

"Of course I remember her," Abraham said, blushing. "Always a pleasure."

"You were very brave," Rosa said. Abraham blushed again. "You and Adam are twins," Rosa continued. "Your bond is close. Still, we don't have much time. In a few minutes, the other thieves will begin to wonder what happened to this one."

"Yes," Adam said. "And that was too quiet. The robber was supposed to make some noise when we hit him."

Adam reached over and pinched Abraham hard, right under the armpit.

"YaaaH-OoooWWWWW-rp!!" Abraham wailed until Adam slapped his hand over his mouth.

"All right, all right," Adam whispered. "That's enough."

Abraham slapped Adam's hand away. "That hurt!" he hissed.

"Sorry," Adam grinned.

Rosa frowned. "Stop it," she said. "Abraham, how many guns do they have?"

"I don't know," Abraham said, still rubbing his armpit. "There were three robbers. They each have at least one gun, maybe more."

Adam got up and began searching the felled thief. He spotted a pistol butt sticking out of the unconscious man's pocket. "This one only has one gun." He pulled it free.

"Do you know how to shoot?" Rosa asked.

Both brothers shook their heads. "Do you?"

"No," Rosa said. "I know if you pull the trigger it goes off, but as for hitting something…"

Abraham shook his head. "Mama says that guns are dangerous, and I tend to agree with her."

"Abraham, if you won't," Adam said, "I will…"

"No. You can't," Abraham said. "There are too many people inside to take the chance."

"Well, I'm going to keep this thing just in case," Adam said, examining the heavy pistol.

"We don't have much time," Rosa said. "We need to do something."

"I know, I know." Abraham paced back and forth.

Adam sighted down the barrel of the gun and said, "Bang." Then he slipped the gun into his pocket.

"I've got it!" Abraham said at last.

"What?" Adam asked. Then he nodded. "Oh. That's a pretty good plan."

"Thank you," Abraham agreed.

"Would you mind telling me?" Rosa asked.

Abraham smiled and explained. "You are going to run back to Smyrna for help, while Adam and I..."

On the social hall's stage, Alex Krabot, the bandit leader, listened impatiently as the villagers begged and pleaded.

"We don't have any gold."

"We have nothing of value. Our silver candlesticks are made of tin."

"The kiddush cup from the Holy Land? It's brass."

"What about my mother's diamond wedding ring?"

"Sarah, I'm telling you for the last time, it's not a diamond, it's a piece of glass!"

"You know, I should invest in diamonds," Reb Cantor muttered, "they're easy to hide."

Krabot wanted to kill them all, but he knew that if he let them complain and moan and deny they had any money, eventually they would wear themselves out and reveal all their secret hiding places. If not, then as soon as Dimitri got back from killing the boy, he'd have another one taken out and killed.

But where was Dimitri? What was taking him so long? He'd told the fool to kill the boy, not bury him.

Just as he was about to send Bertie out to look, the doors to the social hall opened. In ran the boy. His hands were covered with blood, screaming, "Murder! Murder!"

Of course there was a murder, Alex Krabot found himself thinking. Only you're supposed to be the dead one.

And then the boy vanished into the crowd of people.

"Alex, what was that?" Bertie asked in a quiet whisper.

"I don't know," Krabot said. "Go and find him."

And then, again the boy appeared. This time he was at the door at the front of the room, near the stage. His hands and face were red with blood, and he was shrieking "Murder! Murder!"

"How did he get there, Alex?" Bertie asked nervously. "You said that the forest wasn't haunted."

"Idiot, we're not in the forest," Krabot said. "He ran. Boys are fast."

But just then the boy appeared in two places!

"I'm dead!" the boy on the floor yelled

"I'm dead!" the boy near the stage yelled.

Bertie's face was as white as a sheet. "A ghost. We killed a ghost!"

"You can't kill a ghost," Krabot said. But it was too late. Bertie Zanuk's eyes rolled back in his head and he collapsed in a terrified faint. Alex Krabot sighed. Good help was so hard to find these days.

"I'm dead!" the two bloody boys were yelling. "A ghost!"

A cry rippled through the crowd. "They're dead. The twins are dead."

"Twins?" Alex said. "Twins?"

"Oh, yes," said Reb Shikker. "Abraham and Adam Schlemiel are twins. It's impossible to tell them apart. They're quite the troublemakers. Still, it's a shame that they've been murdered."

Alex smacked his forehead. Twins. Somehow they had overpowered Dimitri and scared Bertie half to death by covering their hands and faces with wine and screaming like castrated pigs.

"Enough!" Alex bellowed. "Shut up! Everyone!"

He grabbed the woman nearest to him, the one who had tried to prevent Dimitri from taking the boy in the first place.

"Stop it!" he shouted. "Or I will kill your mother."

The room fell quiet. The two boys stood still.

Alex Krabot stuck his pistol in Rebecca Schlemiel's ear. "You, Merchant, get your wealth. Get everything of value in this godforsaken village. Put it in that chest you were having made for the governor and bring it here. Now! Otherwise, I'll blow her head off."

The whole village gasped.

"You," Rebecca Schlemiel said to the thief, "are not a very nice man."

"No," the thief said. "I'm not."

Then, Alex Krabot, one of the bloodthirstiest cutthroats in all of Eastern Europe, threw his head back and laughed.

The Robber's Story

It was hot in the social hall. This was taking forever. After the robber leader sent Reb Cantor and Reb Gold out to gather up the wealth of Chelm, he had the twins brought up on the stage, where he could keep an eye on them. Bertie and Dimitri were still laid out cold. Alex wondered if he'd ever manage to find good help. Still, one thief with a gun was more than a match for an entire village of fools. He huddled everyone else into one corner, far away from both doors. Some of the villagers gossiped, some prayed, some complained, others napped. A quartet of yeshiva students was playing pinochle.

"Come here, boy." Alex Krabot beckoned with his gun.

Abraham came closer.

"What's your name?"

Abraham told him.

"Abraham, you were very brave earlier," Krabot said. "Like when I was a boy. Feisty."

Abraham nodded. He glanced over at his mother, who looked scared. "Why are you doing this?" he asked at last.

Krabot laughed. Adam, who had been dozing, was startled awake and briefly thought about pulling out the gun he'd taken from the other robber. No, it was still too dangerous.

"You mean aside from the money?" Krabot scratched his beard. "Excitement maybe. Like a cowboy in America, you ride into town and everyone is watching you. They treat you with respect, and then they give you all their money. Then you go somewhere else and you drink and play cards and meet ladies. Everyone treats you like a big shot, at least until the money runs out. Then you find a new village, ride into town, and start all over again. It sure beats killing pigs for a living. Abraham, you're what, nine years old?"

Abraham nodded.

"When I was your age, I had already killed my first man. He was a Pole, a real hard case. He deserved it." Krabot's voice trailed off.

After a while, Abraham asked, "Why?"

"What's that?"

"Why did he deserve it? The Sixth Commandment is 'Thou shall not kill.' You put yourself in God's place when you killed that man. I was wondering why."

Krabot's eyes narrowed. For a moment, he thought about backhanding the boy. Instead, he coughed, spat, and said, "No one else has been stupid enough to talk to me like that since I was a child. They've all been afraid. Aren't you afraid of me?"

"Yes," Abraham nodded. "I'm sorry. I shouldn't have…"

"No, no," Krabot said. "You should know. You live in this nice village. Your parents and your brother love you. Other people don't have it so good.

"I was born in a Russian village on the border of Poland. My father worked at a slaughterhouse. Everyone in the village worked at the slaughterhouse. He killed pigs all day, and when he came home he was drunk and he beat me and he beat my mother. That would have been my life, too. It was the way things were.

"One day, he didn't come home. It was payday. And on paydays, like most days, he went to the tavern. But it was getting late. My mother was afraid that he would drink all his pay. So, she took me and we went to the tavern. I was eight years old.

"Well, my mother and I arrived and found the tavern filled with song and cheer. My father was playing cards and laughing. I don't think I'd ever seen him so happy. I didn't know why my mother was so anxious. That tavern didn't seem like such a bad place.

"But then this Polish man grabbed my mother, and started to kiss her. If my father saw it, he ignored it. I ran to him and he told me not to worry, that it would do her good. She was screaming. So, I killed the man. I grabbed my father's sharp butcher's knife and stuck it in the man's gut. It was awful. The blood went everywhere.

The tavern fell silent. My mother was in tears. 'Run boy,' my father said. 'Before the police come. Run.' And so I ran. I left my village, I left my parents, and I never saw them again. Once I went back. About ten years after that, and everything was gone. The whole village, as if it never existed.

"And that, Abraham, is why I am who I am today. What do you think?"

Abraham whispered, "Am I supposed to be sympathetic?"

Krabot laughed. "You're either a hero or a fool. I've killed men for less."

"Violence again," Abraham said. "Where has it gotten you? No home, no family. You come to my village and you threaten my mother. You've turned into the man you killed."

"Shut your mouth, boy," Krabot said, his lips tight with rage. "What do you know about violence? I'll teach you about violence." He stood up and drew a knife from his belt. "You see this knife? This was my father's knife. He used it to slit the throats of the pigs. You keep kosher, boy, don't you? This is not a kosher knife."

Abraham's eyes were wide. Adam was reaching for his gun. The social hall was as silent as a graveyard at midnight.

Just then the front doors burst open and in came Reb Cantor and Reb Gold dragging the beautiful seven-sided chest that Jacob Schlemiel had been making for the provincial governor. They tugged the chest up the center aisle and brought it to the edge of the stage.

"Just in time, boy," Alex Krabot said, putting his knife back in its sheath. "Open it."

Reb Gold looked at Reb Cantor, who nodded. Together they pulled back the lid.

It was filled to the brim with books.

"Books?" Alex Krabot roared. All the sleeping villagers awoke with a start. "Books? I don't want books. I want gold. I want silver. I want jewelry."

"We told you," Reb Cantor said. "We don't have any of that. You wanted our wealth? This is our wealth. You've got the Torah, you've got the Mishnah, that's part of the Talmud… you've got the stories of Sholem Aleichem. This is pretty good stuff!"

Reb Shikker moaned. "No! You can't give him my accounting books. I won't know where to begin!"

Alex Krabot was dumbfounded. Was the entire village insane?

"Empty it," Krabot ordered, waving his guns at the men. "Pile the books in the middle of the room, and burn them."

"Burn our books?" Rabbi Kibbitz said. "But this is our wealth. Our heritage. Our entertainment. We have little enough already!"

"Burn them!"

Moving quietly, the villagers formed a line. One by one, they gently removed the books from the oak chest and began passing them down the rows into a pile in the middle of the hall. Occasionally, someone would stop to brush away a tear or sigh at the memory of a particular volume.

At last, the chest was empty. Krabot stood at the edge of the stage, grinning. "Set that pile of books on fire," he said. "I'll burn the whole building!"

Adam leaned next to Abraham and whispered, "Ready?"

Abraham looked at the thief and nodded.

Adam drew his gun and shouted, "No!"

Krabot turned and saw the boy with the gun. "Are you going to shoot me? I don't think you will." He turned his back on the boy. "You. Rabbi. Light the match."

Adam's face grew white as a sheet. His hands were trembling. "Now, Abraham," he said. "Now!"

Abraham took one step closer to the robber and gave him a push. Alex Krabot, gun in hand, toppled forward off the stage and landed in the seven-sided oak chest with a thud. In an instant, Reb Gold, Reb Cantor, and Reb Shikker slammed the lid shut and jumped on top. There was a gunshot, and a small hole exploded out of the chest not two inches from Reb Shikker's bottom.

"Oy gevalt!" Reb Shikker shrieked. The box shook with angry pounding from the inside.

"Adam, the latch," Jacob Schlemiel shouted.

Quickly, Adam ran down from the stage, reached into his pocket, and removed the small brass latch he had purchased in

Smyrna. Jacob took the gun from his son's hand, spilled the single bullet on the floor, and used the gun's butt as a hammer to attach the latch to the chest, locking it securely.

"Done!" Jacob shouted. A cheer erupted from the villagers. Jacob and Rebecca Schlemiel hugged their boys close.

At exactly that moment, the doors to the social hall opened once again, and in strode five provincial constables, followed closely behind by an exhausted Rosa Kalderash, who had run all the way back to Smyrna to fetch help and had ridden back with the police.

"Where's the trouble?" one constable asked.

Reb Cantor stepped forward. "No trouble at all. Only two unconscious robbers, the one on the stage and the other one you passed on the way in. And this other one in this box, which by the way is a gift from me to the Governor in Minsk. Please give him my regards."

In the end, the puzzled looking constables had nothing to do but haul away the criminals while the villagers of Chelm raised their voices in a song of joy and relief.

Chapter Nine

Trouble

Avi Weiss strode into the classroom a quarter-hour late, went right up to the front, and handed Rabbi Yohon Abrahms a note. Then he sauntered to his seat, whispering to Abraham and Adam Schlemiel as he passed, "You're in trouble…"

The twins, who had been mind-talking with each other, plotting a daring egg-bombing raid on Rabbi Abrahms's house, looked up with a start.

The schoolteacher glanced at the note and said with a sigh, "Abraham, Adam, go and see the Rebbe."

They stood, glared at Avi, and left the classroom. Then they dawdled in the synagogue's cellar until Reb Levitsky, the janitor, caught their arms and dragged them into the chief rabbi's office.

"Adam, Abraham," said Rabbi Kibbitz. "Sit down. Sit down." He gestured to the chairs in front of his table.

Puzzled, the boys sat. Usually, when they were in trouble, the grown-ups made them stand at attention for hours while they were lectured and scolded.

This time, Rabbi Kibbitz was smiling.

We're in for it now, Adam's voice echoed in Abraham's mind. *What did you do?*

It wasn't me, Abraham mentally whispered back. *What did you do?*

Then both pointed at the other and shouted aloud, "He did it!"

Rabbi Kibbitz jumped with a start. "Did what?"

"He put the congealed chicken fat in Rabbi Abrahms's shoes."

"Well, he put the book paste in the shoes so that the rabbi couldn't take them off!"

Rabbi Kibbitz covered his mouth, gave the boys a stern look, and giggled behind his hand. His poor young colleague had been trapped in his boots for six weeks, and the rancid smell had been beginning to cause the village elders to reconsider his contract.

"What did you say?" Rabbi Kibbitz said. "I'm deaf in one ear. I didn't quite hear you..."

"Umm," both boys said. "Nothing. Nothing."

"All right..." the rabbi said slowly. "Well, I wanted to talk with you about the robbery."

Two heads perked up with smiles. Less than a month had passed since the Schlemiel boys had apprehended Alex Krabot and his henchmen, and no one in Chelm, let alone the heroes, had tired of retelling the story. Two boys and one girl capturing three of the most notorious thieves in Europe was something impressive.

"Rosa and I were in the forest," Adam began.

"Wait, wait," the rabbi said. "I know more or less what happened, but I do have some questions. May I?"

Adam nodded his head.

"Tell me, Adam, why didn't you and Rosa go straight back to Smyrna for help? I am told that you followed the bandits through the Schvartzvald for several hours. And your plan? Ghosts? Really?" The rabbi raised his eyebrows as though he didn't think much of the idea. "Thank goodness your friend Rosa was able to run all the way to Smyrna and return with the constables in time."

Adam's brow creased. He had never really thought about it, but the rabbi was right. If he and Rosa had just turned around and hurried back to Smyrna, they could have gotten the police and been back in Chelm almost before the robbers arrived. Adam's mouth opened and closed.

His brother rescued him. "He was lost," Abraham said. "And he was tired and scared. He's only nine years old."

Rabbi Kibbitz nodded. "Tell me, Abraham, how did you know the robbers were coming?"

Abraham's eyes widened. The twins exchanged glances. How could they explain it? The fact was they weren't sure themselves. Rosa had told them that twins often had such a bond. Still, it was something that the boys had instinctively kept quiet. Should they tell the rabbi?

What harm will it do to tell him? Abraham thought-spoke to Adam.

He might think we're demons and kill us, Adam answered.

But we're not demons.

Maybe we are.

Abraham had never considered that, and it stumped him.

During the long pause, Rabbi Kibbitz looked from one boy to the other. At last he said, "It wasn't the Gypsy girl, was it? She didn't do anything to you? Cast a spell?"

"No," they both said. It would have been easy for Adam and Abraham to blame it all on Rosa. That would have handled their problems in an instant, but despite their propensity for troublemaking the twins were relatively honest. "She didn't. It wasn't her."

"Then what?" the rabbi asked.

"I can hear his voice in my head," Abraham said at last.

The rabbi looked startled. "Whose voice? The Almighty's?"

"No," Abraham said. "Adam's voice. I heard him speaking to me when he was in the forest."

"We don't know how we do it," Adam said. "It's just like talking to each other, but without moving our lips."

"Oh," Rabbi Kibbitz said, relieved. Historically, whenever somebody thought he or she personally heard the voice of the Creator of the Universe, it meant that person and everyone else who lived nearby were in big trouble. If the two boys thought they were talking to each other, well, that was a little strange but not such a major problem. "Okay. So, one more question."

That didn't seem to bother him, Adam thought.

I don't think he believed us, Abraham answered in his brother's mind.

"Are you boys doing it now?" Rabbi Kibbitz said. "If you are, please stop. It's a little rude, like whispering."

"Sorry, Rabbi."

"All right." The rabbi waved his hand. "This question is harder to ask. I want you to think before you answer."

The boys fidgeted uncomfortably.

"Adam," Rabbi Kibbitz said at last, "how did you feel when you were holding that gun? Were you going to kill that man?"

Instantly, both boys remembered the moment at the edge of the stage when Adam had pointed his pistol at Alex Krabot and the thief had laughed. The gun was loaded and aimed. Then Abraham had pushed Krabot into the trunk and it was all over.

Adam stared at his feet. He felt sick to his stomach. "I…"

"He didn't shoot him, did he?" Abraham said.

"Shh," Rabbi Kibbitz said. "Abraham, you're a good boy, but this is important for Adam. You thought about it, didn't you? Here was this man; he had threatened your parents. He held everyone hostage. He was going to rob the village. And then burn our shul and all our books. You held the gun. It was aimed at him. Pulling the trigger would have been very easy, wouldn't it?"

Deeply ashamed, Adam nodded his head, and began to cry.

"But he didn't do it!" Abraham shouted.

Rabbi Kibbitz winced and rubbed his good ear. "No, he didn't. And in some ways that was the most heroic deed I have ever witnessed. To hold another person's life in your hands and save it is a blessing. But to hold a wicked man's life in your hands and let him live… That is most dangerous and very courageous and a little bit stupid."

"What?" Abraham said, not certain he had heard the rabbi correctly. "You mean it was okay?"

"Who knows," Rabbi Kibbitz said. "It's difficult to say this, because I applaud what you both did. But, I just received a letter from the Provincial Governor inviting me to accompany the two boys who captured Krabot and his men to Minsk, where they will stand trial. It's an order, really. It means that the governor wants you to testify. One of two things will happen. Either the bandits will be convicted, or they will be released. Either way, these men will probably want to kill you. Can you imagine the humiliation they must feel at having been defeated by two boys? Although you spared Alex Krabot's life at great risk to your own, men of violence rarely see that as a blessing."

"So, I should have killed him?" Adam asked quietly.

"Well, it would have been easier," the rabbi said. "But no. I don't believe so. Yes, if you had killed him, this would all be over and done with. But you? You would have changed. I think you made the right choice, although it does create a problem. But what is life without a few problems? We'll leave tomorrow."

The two boys were quiet.

"Don't look so glum!" The rabbi laughed. "We'll figure something out. After all, what chance does a thief stand against the accumulated wisdom of Chelm?"

Somehow, neither Adam nor Abraham felt reassured.

The Man Who Complained Himself To Death

"All the way to Minsk?" Rebecca Schlemiel said. "They're only nine years old!"

"Shh!" her husband, Jacob, said. "Rebecca, they're sleeping. Yes, all the way to Minsk. You've only said it a million times. But the Rebbe is going with them. And it's not as if you can ignore a request from the provincial governor to meet the heroes who captured the Krabot gang."

The boys, of course, were not asleep. Abraham and Adam Schlemiel lay in their bed, wide-awake.

Abraham whispered. "We're going to go to Minsk!"

"All the way to Minsk," Adam said. And both boys convulsed with muffled laughter.

Three days later, trudging through a barren field, the twins already wished they were back home. So far, their great adventure had consisted of a waterlogged schlep to Smyrna in the rain and then hours standing in the mud beside the railroad tracks in what passed for a railroad station.

The rabbi had asked when the train would come, but the villagers of Smyrna had just shrugged. "Sometimes it comes.

Sometimes it doesn't come. When it does come, sometimes it stops, sometimes it doesn't stop."

Rather than stay still, the rabbi had decided that they should start walking. So they did. Two more hours they had spent trudging through the mud alongside the railroad tracks.

The twins were quietly miserable. Ordinarily, they might have complained, but they were too tired and uncomfortable even to moan. This was just as well, because struggling along beside them, Rabbi Kibbitz was complaining enough for an entire army.

"Oy, my feet are soaked," he was saying. "You could fill the ocean from my boots. There's enough mud in my socks to plant a garden in. I think my hat has turned into a sponge, and I think that water is leaking into my brain through my ear!"

At any other time, the boys would have laughed.

"It's so dark, I can't tell if it's day or night," the rabbi said. "I'd look up at the sky, but then my eyes would be flooded by a bucket of rain. If this keeps up, maybe we can swim to Minsk. Of course, I can't swim, so I'd drown. What a way to go, to drown in the middle of a field. All we need now is lightning."

As if on cue, a thunderbolt cracked and the three travelers watched in amazement as a lightning bolt split a nearby elm tree in two.

"Oy!" Rabbi Kibbitz said. He closed his eyes in prayer for a moment. When he had finished, he removed his gigantic backpack and brought out a large cloth tent. "Let's make camp."

It took an hour, and they lost half the tent spikes, but at last the twins and the rabbi were inside the tent, cozy and dry, wearing nothing but their underwear.

"Look at me," the rabbi said. (The boys did their best not to look.) "I'm nearly Moses' age. I've got corns on my feet the size of apples. And my boots are soaked. At least the Almighty was merciful and let Moses walk through the Red Sea dry-shod." He heaved a big sigh. "You two are very quiet."

Abraham and Adam nodded.

"No complaints?" the rabbi asked.

They shook their heads.

"Why not?" the rabbi said. "It's rotten outside and not that much better inside. I wouldn't be surprised if the tent sprung a leak or was full of spiders."

Both boys squirmed.

"Our mother says we shouldn't complain," Abraham said. "She says we're very fortunate."

The rabbi looked thoughtful. "It's true, we are all very fortunate. But complaining is one of the greatest pleasures in life. Why, without complaints, my wife (may she rest in peace) and I would have had nothing to say to each other."

"Our father says that complaints are a waste of breath," Adam said.

"Nothing is a waste of breath so long as you enjoy it," Rabbi Kibbitz said. "Let me tell you the story of the man who complained himself to death."

Once upon a time, not so long ago, there was a kvetch. This man was known far and wide as the greatest complainer the world has ever known. You could give him a silver piece and he would complain it wasn't gold. You could remove a splinter from his toe and he would say that by mistake you'd pulled out a bone.

He lived in a house that was too small, on a farm that was barren. He had a skinny cow, a flea-ridden dog, and a wife who was deaf, which was fortunate for her because she couldn't hear his constant litany of woe.

From morning until night he whined, he cried, he kvetched. The sun was too early, it was too bright, it was too hot, and then it was dark already. Why bother planting a seed? It would just encourage the weeds. Every day he ate a rotten breakfast that gave him indigestion, and then he sat on his porch until lunchtime, wondering aloud what horrible misfortune would come his way.

His neighbors avoided him like the plague. Not only did the kvetch's moaning make them miserable, but so did his smell. The man refused to bathe for fear of catching pneumonia, so he stank like a moldy dead skunk smeared with Limburger cheese.

One day a giant arrived and declared himself the ruler of the land.

This giant was a cannibal who demanded to be fed. In an instant, the neighbors decided that the kvetch would be the first to go. They sent a committee to the farm to inform the kvetch of their decision.

He nodded glumly and said, "Of course. Just my luck." Then off he trundled to the giant's palace.

When he got there, the door was open, so he walked inside. Then he heard a voice, a big booming loud voice. "Fee Fie Foe Fum, I smell… GAAAH! What's that horrible smell? Ugh!"

The kvetch lifted his arm, sniffed underneath, and gagged. "It's me," he said, at last. "Something's growing under my arm."

The giant held his nose and peered down at the thin pitiful man. "Why don't you take a bath?"

The kvetch explained at great length about pneumonia, the number of people who drown in bathtubs every year, and the possibility of leeches.

"Shut up!" the giant said at last. "Stop complaining or I'll cut off your head!"

For a moment, the kvetch looked thoughtful. Then he shrugged. "Why bother?" he said. "If I were going to live forever in paradise, then maybe I could keep my tongue. As it is, I'm starving, I'm miserable, everyone hates me, and you're going to eat me anyway…"

With that, the giant drew out his great knife and with one stroke cut off the kvetch's head.

Amazingly enough, that's not the end of the story, because with his last breath, even as his head was flying across the room, the kvetch managed to groan, "Oy! My neck!"

This so infuriated the giant that he picked up the kvetch's body and swallowed it in one bite, without even chewing. A moment later, the giant's face turned blue, he coughed, gagged, sputtered, and died on the spot.

The giant was dead, and when the kvetch's neighbors found the poor man's head, they were surprised to see that he had a big fat smile on his face. Everyone realized that he had died complaining.

By now, the two boys were nearly asleep. Abraham, however, managed to open his eyes just enough to ask, "Rabbi, what's the moral of that story?"

"Moral shmoral," Rabbi Kibbitz laughed. "Does every story have to have a moral?"

<u>Training</u>

In the morning, the rain stopped, the sun came out, and chirping birds dove through the field beside the railroad tracks. Abraham and Adam Schlemiel rubbed their eyes and poked their heads out of the tent. It was a beautiful day. The grass glistened wet and twinkling, and mist rose from every puddle.

"It's so different from Chelm," Abraham said.

"What's so different?" Adam answered. "Same birds, same grass, same sun."

"It's peaceful and quiet," Abraham said. "And there is no one around who we know."

Just then, from inside the tent, Rabbi Kibbitz let loose an earth-shaking snore.

Adam raised an eyebrow, and both boys giggled.

Then they heard another sound, even louder than the rabbi's snore. The train was coming.

"Rebbe, Rebbe, the train!" the boys shouted.

Startled from fond dreams, Rabbi Kibbitz leaped to his feet, which was unfortunate because his head tore a hole in the thin top of the tent. He blinked twice, and then felt the wind blowing across his bald skull.

"You two are going to kill me," he said, snatching his kippah from the roof of the mangled tent. "Quick. We'd better get packing, unless you want to walk all the way to Minsk."

Without another word, the boys leaped into action, and by the time the train puffed into sight, they were all dressed, and the tent was folded (more or less) and stuffed into the rabbi's huge backpack.

Abraham and Adam stood by the side of the tracks, waving handkerchiefs and jumping up and down.

"Do you think it will stop?" Adam asked.

"Oh, it will stop," the learned sage answered with certainty. "The question is, 'Will it stop for us?'"

It didn't.

If the rabbi and twins had been Cossacks, the train would have stopped in an instant. If one of them had been the czar, it would have expelled all the other passengers to make room. The engineer had just enough compassion to slow the train down barely enough to give them a slim chance of running alongside and then jumping onboard.

Among the passengers, wagering was fierce. The conductor gave the boys even odds. The rabbi, however, started at ten to one, but as his breath began to falter the odds skyrocketed to fifty kopeks to a zloty. If a sly merchant from Moscow hadn't dashed up front and bribed the engineer with a percentage of his profits, the rabbi would have been left standing alone in the field, with his young charges lost in the distance.

The engineer slowed the train just a bit more, and Rabbi Kibbitz was finally pulled aboard to a chorus of cheers from the winners and boos from the losers. New wagers were immediately placed about whether he would keel over and die of a heart attack.

Fortunately for himself, the twins, and the entire village of Chelm, Rabbi Kibbitz eventually caught his breath and at last gasped, "Oy... vey..."

Everyone laughed, and more money changed hands.

The Governor's Palace... in Pinsk

By the time the train approached the city, Rabbi Kibbitz was fully recovered. The merchant, who had made a small fortune betting on the rabbi's survival, shared a goat cheese pie with the travelers from Chelm.

The train blew a long and loud whistle.

"... insk!" the conductor shouted. "Last stop! Everyone off!"

All the travelers clapped and stamped their feet with joy that the long cramped ride was about to end.

"Such a din!" Rabbi Kibbitz said, although no one could hear him. The crowd surged toward the doors. "Stay near me boys."

They were, of course, immediately separated. Adam went this way, Abraham went that way, and Rabbi Kibbitz, with his gigantic backpack, was lucky to get off the train at all.

The station was a whirl of people, animals, machinery, and smoke. Using their mind-speech, Adam and Abraham agreed to meet at the far end of the station, near the ticket seller's booth. They picked the right spot because as the station slowly emptied out, Rabbi Kibbitz tottered toward them, his face white with fear and exhaustion.

"Yes, you boys are definitely trying to kill me," he said with relief. "I am an old man, and it occurred to me, why am I doing all the schlepping? You youngsters should carry this while we search for the Governor's Palace." He dropped his backpack onto the ground with a thud.

"Of course, Rabbi," the boys said. They each took a hold of one strap and lifted. The pack didn't budge an inch. "What's in this?" Abraham asked.

"Besides the tent and a week's worth of clothes?" Rabbi Kibbitz said. "Food of course. I have some blintzes, two kugels, and fifty dehydrated matzah balls for an emergency. Then there are the books. I couldn't leave Chelm without something to read. There's the Torah, a haggadah, and twenty-six other books I've been meaning to read."

The boys looked at each other dumbfounded.

"Maybe it's time we hire a cart," the rabbi said with a sigh. "You boys wait here."

A few moments later, Adam saw Rabbi Kibbitz waving him to bring their bags outside. Just in front of the train station, Rabbi Kibbitz stood, haggling with a man. Grunting with effort, Abraham and Adam dragged the rabbi's pack outside, and hoisted it with their bags into the back of the small cart. They wondered if the man's old donkey would be able to pull such a heavy load.

"Where to?" the carriage driver asked.

"The Governor's Palace," Rabbi Kibbitz said.

The carriage driver laughed. "The Governor's Palace? The three of you?"

"I'll have you know that I am Rabbi Kibbitz of Chelm, and these boys are the Schlemiels who defeated the famous Krabot gang."

"Oh, really?" the driver smirked. "And I'm the lover of Catherine the Great."

"Shh!" Rabbi Kibbitz said. "A man oughtn't to say such things in public. Especially in front of young boys."

The driver shook his head. "Are you sure that you don't mean the Governor's Palace in Minsk?"

"Isn't that what I said?" Rabbi Kibbitz asked.

"You said you wanted to go to the Governor's Palace. That means something quite different in Pinsk than it does in Minsk. And this is Pinsk, not Minsk."

"Pinsk, Minsk, Sminsk," Rabbi Kibbitz said. "How can the Governor's Palace be anything other than the Governor's Palace? I have heard that people in the big city sometimes like to play jokes on those of us from small villages. Take care, because I am on to your tricks. Now, please, take us to the Governor's Palace."

"All right," the driver said. "But don't say I didn't warn you." With that, he cracked his whip, and the donkey grunted in momentary agony before the cart began to roll.

"Rabbi Kibbitz," Abraham said, "aren't we supposed to be in Minsk, not Pinsk?"

The rabbi smiled, and patted the boy's arm. "Minsk and Pinsk are hundreds of miles apart. We started our journey on the train to Minsk. When we got off the train, how could this be Pinsk?"

"But it might have been a different train," Adam said.

Rabbi Kibbitz didn't seem to hear. He had opened his pack, removed a book, and was reading intently.

"What are we going to do?" Adam asked his brother.

"Minsk or Pinsk, we're here now," Abraham said. "We'll go to the Governor's Palace. How different could it be?"

They'd imagined the Governor's Palace as a splendid castle, high on a hill, overlooking fertile green fields, lovely gardens, and well-tended woods filled with deer. Instead, the carriage was rumbling down a rutted road through a part of Pinsk with open sewers, broken-down hovels, and the unmistakable stench of a glue factory. At every intersection, a dozen children swarmed out into the street begging for kopeks until the cart driver chased them away with his whip. When Abraham reached into his pocket to throw one of the more pitiful little girls a copper, the cart driver hissed that it would only encourage them. Even the sun seemed to go into hiding in this neighborhood. It was hardly a regal landscape.

"The wise ruler does not set himself apart from the people he governs," Rabbi Kibbitz explained when Abraham asked. "For, if he lived apart, how would he know their problems or understand their troubles?"

"This governor must be really wise," Adam said wryly.

"Perhaps the wisest," the rabbi agreed.

The cart driver snorted and then announced with a grand sweep of his hand, "The Governor's Palace!"

The visitors from Chelm turned their heads and stared.

"This is not what I pictured." Rabbi Kibbitz said.

Abraham had to agree.

"It's a tavern," Adam said.

The building was two and a half stories tall and not quite as broken down as the rest of the neighborhood. The windows were intact, although covered with soot, and the roof looked as if it should have been replaced ten or twenty year earlier. Above the door was a sign of crossed scepters over a mug of ale.

"Are you sure you took us to the right place?" Abraham asked. "You're not trying to cheat us?"

"I tried to explain this to you," the cart driver began. "In Pinsk, this is the Governor's Palace."

"Of course! It's perfect," Rabbi Kibbitz said, jumping to his feet and hoisting his backpack, his energy quite refreshed after the long cart ride. "What better place for a wise man to rule from than a tavern? It is a gathering place, a meeting house. A center both of social and political life. I can hardly wait to meet this governor!"

"And I can't wait to see this," chuckled the cart driver. He tied his donkey to a pole and followed the trio up the three broken steps to the front door. Rabbi Kibbitz led the way, Abraham stayed close behind, and Adam kept his eyes open for robbers and thieves.

Inside the tavern was dark, almost pitch black. It wasn't even noon, and already the room was filled with smoke and the stink of stale spilled beer that was never completely washed away. Several heads turned when the rabbi, two boys, and the carriage driver entered, but most of the two dozen denizens of the Governor's Palace ignored them.

As Rabbi Kibbitz's eyes adjusted to the light, he began to look for the governor and immediately spotted him – an elderly and distinguished man with a long flowing beard sitting on a stool at one end of a long table.

With a broad smile, Rabbi Kibbitz rushed over to the governor, took his hand, and began shaking it vigorously. "Your Excellency," he said. "We came as soon as we could. It isn't easy to travel from Chelm to Minsk. Or to Pinsk for that matter, especially with two young boys."

The rabbi paused to take a breath, and the old man whose hand he was still holding tottered, wobbled, and fell to the floor with a thud.

"Oy! I killed the governor!" the rabbi gasped, his eyes growing wide. He let go of the governor's limp hand in horror.

The room filled with laughter.

Rabbi Kibbitz looked as if he was about to burst into tears. He began chanting the prayer for the dead. Abraham and Adam were terrified that, having killed the governor, the three of them would probably be executed on the spot.

Just then, a hefty woman with the shoulders of a mule and the face of a weather-beaten Madonna climbed out of a trap door in the floor. She took in the scene with a single glance, and then shouted,

"Quiet!"

The room fell silent, save for the rabbi's chanting.

The woman strode over to the fallen man and gave him a soft kick. The man moaned.

"He's not dead," she scowled. "Just drunk."

Rabbi Kibbitz opened his eyes. "The governor is drunk?" he said. "How can that be? How is it possible that a governor so wise would fuddle his mind with drink, especially before lunchtime?"

"He's not the governor," the woman said, squinting at the rabbi.

"Ahh." Rabbi Kibbitz sighed with relief. "You see the governor asked me to bring these boys to see him, so... Um, where, may I ask, is the governor?"

The woman stared at him. Then she looked at Adam and Abraham. The boys flinched under her gaze and stepped behind their rabbi's long black coat.

"Who brought these idiots here?" she bellowed suddenly.

The cart driver's hand shot into the air. "I did. They asked me to take them to the Governor's Palace. What was I supposed to do? They're from Chelm."

Again, the dark room filled with laughter until the woman silenced it with a stare.

"It's important," said Rabbi Kibbitz. He paused as the drunken man, who he'd thought was the dead governor, began crawling across the floor toward the door. When the man crawled outside, the rabbi continued, "It's important that we see the governor immediately, if not sooner."

"And who exactly are you?" the woman asked, her polite words undercut by contempt and exasperation.

"I am Rabbi Kibbitz of Chelm," said the rabbi proudly. "And these are Abraham and Adam Schlemiel, the two youngsters responsible for the defeat and capture of the notorious Krabot gang."

Another roar of laughter was cut short as the woman held up her hand.

"Is it true?" she asked. "My Alex finally got captured?"

"And Dimitri Dimitriovitch and Bertie Zanuk as well," Adam added.

"Hush, little one," Rabbi Kibbitz said. "Let us save your heroic story for the governor, whom I am certain would like to hear it in person."

"You really did it, didn't you?" the woman asked quietly. "I'd heard rumors, but I assumed that they were lies…"

"Yes, we did," Abraham said.

A startled murmur rippled through the room as all eyes turned to the boys.

Adam and Abraham felt like running, but they bravely stood and weathered the unwanted attention.

"So, you see it is important," Rabbi Kibbitz said, "that we speak to the governor as soon as possible. The boys need to give evidence at the Krabot gang's trial. Then, I would like to get back to Chelm before Shabbas. If we can catch the evening train to Smyrna, then by tomorrow afternoon…"

"Excuse me," the woman interrupted.

"Yes?" said the rabbi.

"You wanted to speak to the governor, so shut up and speak already."

The rabbi looked confused.

The woman narrowed her eyes. "My name is Babushka Krabot," she said, a wicked smile cutting across her wrinkled face. "And I am the governor."

The Trial

Abraham was terrified. Rabbi Kibbitz was confused. And Adam was looking for a way out.

In the poorest section of Pinsk, the small tavern facetiously named The Governor's Palace seemed more crowded now, as if somehow word had gotten around that the young boys who had captured the notorious Krabot gang had stopped in and asked to see the Governor. Worst of all (for them) their request seemed to have been been granted.

"But… but you're a woman," Rabbi Kibbitz sputtered. "I don't remember the governor being a woman." He reached into his pocket and withdrew the sheet of parchment that had summoned the Schlemiel boys. He reread the paper and showed it to the large old woman who owned the inn. "This isn't your name, is it?"

Babushka Krabot took the paper from the rabbi, glanced over it, and said, "No. And this isn't Minsk. This is Pinsk."

"Minsk Pinsk Shminsk!" said Rabbi Kibbitz cheerfully. "Mrs. Krabot, it's clear that we've made a mistake. We won't trouble you any more. If we can just find our driver, we'll hop back on the cart, go to the train station, and…"

"Wait," Babushka Krabot bellowed.

Rabbi Kibbitz fell silent. Adam wondered if this might be a good time to bolt for the front door. Abraham put an arm on his brother's shoulder and whispered, "Wait."

Babushka Krabot frowned, her face a road map of displeasure. "You come into the Governor's Palace and ask to see the governor. You tell an incredible story about how these two boys have captured my son, Alex, and then you want to just leave?"

"Your son?" Rabbi Kibbitz said. "Yes, we did make a mistake. A big one. Oy vey."

The crowd closed in around the three travellers from Chelm.

"What shall we do with them?" a one-eyed man hissed.

"String them up?" said a man with a wart on the tip of his nose.

"I'm hungry," said a girl wearing what looked like a wolf's head for a hat. (Or maybe, Abraham thought, it was a wolf wearing a girl's head as a necklace…)

"Shut up!" Babushka Krabot roared. "You're all giving me a headache."

"Let's put them on trial," said the one-eyed man. "Give them a taste of their own medicine."

"Well, first, we're not sick," said Rabbi Kibbitz, "so we won't need any medicine. And second, these boys were supposed to testify at the trial, not be on trial. The distinction is small but nevertheless important."

"Just kill them," said Wart-Nose. He drew out a long sharp knife.

"Then eat them!" giggled the girl.

"A trial," said Babushka Krabot, smiling. "All right, a trial. Set the room up. Enough of you good for nothings have been dragged into court to know what it looks like. Get moving!"

The next instant, two dozen men and women began hurrying about to transform the Governor's Palace from a dark and dingy barroom into a dark and dingy courtroom. All the chairs were arranged in rows. Tables were set for the prosecution and the defense. A platform was constructed from old vodka crates, and the judge's bench appeared tall and threatening.

During the chaos, Abraham, Adam, and Rabbi Kibbitz began edging their way toward the door. They might have made it, if Abraham hadn't accidentally stepped on Wart-Nose's cat, which hissed and snarled.

"Bailiff," shouted Babushka Krabot, as she hoisted her huge body into the judge's chair, "grab those prisoners and bring them to me!"

"Clumsy," Adam whispered.

"Shh," Abraham said. "I'm beginning to have a plan."

"Don't worry, boys," Rabbi Kibbitz said. "This is a court of justice. We are innocent. I have no doubt that the truth will set us free."

Abraham and Adam exchanged looks. They were now more concerned than ever.

The Rabbi was shoved into a chair. Abraham and Adam were brought before the governor.

"Mr. Prosecutor," Babushka Krabot said. "What case have you brought before me?"

"Your immenseness," One-Eye began, "these two boys claim that they are responsible for the imprisonment and imminent demise of your one and only son, Alex."

"Objection!" said Rabbi Kibbitz, rising to his feet. "Your son is not dead."

"Not yet," hissed One-Eye, "but when he is found guilty of attempted armed robbery, he will surely be sentenced to the gallows."

"Objection! Who is to say that he will be found guilty?"

"Rabbi," Abraham said, "Krabot and his gang tried to rob Chelm. Remember?"

"Oh," Rabbi Kibbitz said, nodding. "Well, he was definitely guilty of that."

"Abraham!" Adam looked aghast. "What are you doing?"

"The witnesses have admitted their own guilt," One-Eye said. "The prosecution rests. We demand the death penalty."

The spectators in the gallery cheered and stamped their feet. The wolf-girl hurried behind the bar, brought out two bottles of vodka, and began filling glasses for a toast.

"Death to the righteous!" Wart-Nose said, raising his glass and tossing down the clear liquid in a single burning gulp.

"Death to the righteous!" everyone echoed – except for the Schlemiel brothers and Rabbi Kibbitz.

"Oy," Rabbi Kibbitz said, rubbing his forehead. "Oy."

Abraham, if you have a plan, Adam said into his brother's mind, *this would be a good time…*

You're the one with all the ideas.

Not today. I'm sorry.

All right, I'll try something…

"Your giganticness," Abraham said. "May I speak in our defense?"

Babushka Krabot's eyes narrowed, but she banged her glass on the podium for silence. "Speak."

"Your son, Alex, spoke kindly of you," Abraham said. "He told me how you tried to protect him from a wicked world."

"Objection!" One-Eye stood. "The guilty party is clearly trying to influence the judge with a pack of patently false lies."

"If they're false lies," Rabbi Kibbitz said, "then they must be true!" No one listened.

"What did Alex say about me?" Babushka Krabot asked.

Abraham tried to remember exactly what Alex Krabot had said about his mother. "He said that the last time he saw you, he was trying to protect you. That he killed a man and hadn't been home since. I think he misses you."

"You think?" One-Eye said. "Pure speculation!"

"Go on," Babushka Krabot said.

"He said that you told him to run from the police," Abraham said. "You thought he would get away safely. And he did. He has been on the run, living in danger for years. And he might still be free if only he hadn't tried to rob Chelm at gunpoint and then threatened everyone, including my mother."

"You see," One-Eye smiled. "A full confession!"

"He did that?" Babushka Krabot said. "Alex did that?"

Abraham nodded sadly. "Yes. He held a gun to my mother's head and told my father and our village to give him all we had. It was only by luck that no one was hurt and, that our village was not burned to the ground like the one that you and your son once lived in."

Babushka Krabot frowned. She stared at her fingernails, which were black with grime.

"It has been fifteen years since he ran away," she said. "And never a day passes that I wish I hadn't told him to run. If he had stayed he might have been found innocent. Or served his prison term already. Instead, I hear my son is a big shot robber. Sometimes I think he is doing well for himself, but other times I wish I could bring him here to my palace, give him a good dinner, and tuck him into bed. I miss him."

"Your hugeness," the prosecutor began. "Don't be swayed by this obvious ploy. Your son is going to die because of these two. The people demand revenge!"

"Fyodor, shut up. The game is over. We've had our fun. We scared them, and that is enough."

"So, are we free to go?" Rabbi Kibbitz asked, jumping to his feet with surprising agility for a man so old.

Adam grinned at Abraham. Abraham held his hand up, and shook his head.

"But tell me," Babushka Krabot looked at One-Eye. "What will happen if these boys do not appear at the Governor's Palace in Minsk to testify at Alex's trial?"

One-Eye stood and thought for a minute. "If there are no witnesses at Alex's trial, then he will surely be found innocent. You cannot convict a man without the testimony of his accusers. The court will have to let him go.

Babushka Krabot waited for him to sit back down before she continued. She looked first at Abraham, and then at Adam. "You are sentenced," she said, "to return to your Chelm with your sacred promise never to leave that village. You will not be able to testify at my son's trial. He will be released. And then perhaps he will at last come home."

"Babushka," One-Eye said. "You can't be serious."

Then Rabbi Kibbitz asked, "You mean that they just can't leave Chelm to testify at the trial? Or are you talking about something broader than that?"

"Forever," she said. "My son may be a thief and worse, but he is still my son. Will you abide by my judgment, or should I leave you to them?"

Abraham and Adam stared out at the leering crowd in the derelict tavern. Then they slowly nodded. "We promise," they said, their voices barely a whisper.

The weary woman banged her empty vodka glass on the podium, sealing her judgment. She climbed down from the bench and without another word vanished through a door behind the bar.

The stunned crowd remained silent as Abraham and Adam Schlemiel and Rabbi Kibbitz gathered their belongings and made their way outside into the gray and rainy afternoon. They paused for a moment, greeting the fresh damp air with relief. Then they climbed into the donkey cart and set off on their way back to the train station.

"A good show," the donkey cart driver said. Then he pulled out a cigar and chewed on it.

"You see?" Rabbi Kibbitz told the boys. "All is well."

Adam frowned and stared blankly ahead. Rabbi Kibbitz patted him on the shoulder.

Abraham looked back at the tavern and wondered how many more years Babushka Krabot would have to cry before her lost son came home.

Chapter Ten

Let's Not Talk About It...

Babushka Krabot's sentence hung over Abraham and Adam's heads like a millstone. It weighed them down and made them weary. By unspoken agreement, neither they nor Rabbi Kibbitz mentioned the mistaken trip to Pinsk to anyone in Chelm.

When they first returned to yet another hero's welcome, Mrs. Chaipul asked Rabbi Kibbitz, "So, how did the trip go?"

There was a long pause, as every ear in the room strained to hear.

"Well..." Rabbi Kibbitz began. He nodded. He pursed his lips. He nodded again.

Everyone waited.

Rabbi Kibbitz took a sip of water. He nodded a third time, and then he rubbed his beard.

"What did he say?" asked Oma Levitsky, who was eighty years old, hard of hearing, and had assumed that she'd missed something.

"Shh, Mamma," said Reb Levitsky, the janitor.

"And the Governor," asked Reb Cantor, the merchant. "Did he like my gift? What did you think of him?"

"Him?" Rabbi Kibbitz frowned. He raised an eyebrow and smiled in an awkward way. "Well..."

"What?" asked Oma Levitsky. "What?"

"Shhh."

"And the trial?" Jacob Schlemiel asked his boys. "That went well, too?"

Abraham looked at Adam. Adam looked back. They both looked to the rabbi, who smiled and shrugged. "Well enough."

"What?" the old woman asked. "What?"

"Well, Mamma, well," her son replied.

"Well?" Oma Levitsky looked puzzled. "Well what?"

"Well enough!" Abraham shouted with frustration. This the old woman could hear.

"Well enough!" Oma Levitsky repeated, grinning from ear to ear.

Well enough. Such a wise man Rabbi Kibbitz was. So succinct. And it was also clear that the Schlemiel brothers, who everyone had pegged as troublemakers from birth, were finally learning and growing more mature under this mensch's influence. What more could anyone ask for?

Glasses were lifted and a cheer was raised to "Well enough!"

Everyone went home happy. Everything went back to normal – or as normal as it gets in a village such as Chelm.

But for Abraham and Adam, the world had changed very much. It had grown smaller, confining. They had given their promises, and now they were in prison instead of Krabot. It was true that their prison was as large as a village, but it was a prison nevertheless.

"What if I want to travel?" Adam grumbled one day as they hauled water from the well.

"You can't," Abraham said.

Another day, their father ordered them into the Black Forest to help him cut down trees. They hesitated. Where did Chelm end and the rest of the world begin? The forest, they decided, mind-talking back and forth, could be considered within the realm of Chelm, but not Smyrna, which was another village entirely. So, while they were free to cut trees or pick mushrooms in the forest, they weren't free to go to Smyrna. The next time Jacob asked the boys to go there for brass tacks they refused.

"I don't know what's wrong with them," Jacob said to Rebecca that evening. "They used to jump at the chance to go to a big city like Smyrna."

"They're frightened," Rebecca soothed her husband. "They're young. Give them time."

"They're nearly ten years old. It wasn't as if I was going to ask one of them to go off by himself again. Although, when I was ten years old I was sent off to be an apprentice by myself."

"Times change," Rebecca said. "Children today don't understand."

But months passed and still Abraham and Adam Schlemiel would not set foot beyond the bounds of the Schvartzvald. It was sad how much such a small promise had changed their lives. From all appearances, their lives went on as might be expected. In addition to their schooling with Rabbi Abrahms, they took on new chores around the house and began to learn Jacob's trade. They learned how to saw, plane, hammer, sand, and polish wood. They learned that if a chair's legs were too skinny it would break, but that if they were too thick the chair would be as ugly as a stone.

After a particularly prosperous winter, their father suggested a family trip to see Warsaw and visit distant relatives. A look of such sheer panic filled the boys faces that he never again mentioned such a thing.

More months passed. They had a birthday, and then another.

Now they were eleven years old and their days seemed long and exhausting. Summer mornings were filled with chores and work in the shop. Then it was time to go to school to learn to read and write and understand the ways of the world. Rabbi Abrahms couldn't open the windows because then everyone would look outside, so the classroom grew hot and stifling. Dozing was not allowed, and whenever a head began to nod, Rabbi Abrahms brought his ruler down on the offender's desk with a loud WHACK!

In the old days, the other children had looked to Abraham and Adam for comic relief and retribution, but now they were disappointed to find the boys too worn out to play the sorts of tricks they had played in the past. No longer were Rabbi Abrahms's feet glued into his shoes, nor was the seat of his chair covered with grease so that every time he sat down he slid to the floor with a thud.

These were sad times for the children of Chelm, tired times. But it was summer, and summers were always this way. Days were long, and the growing season was short. Everyone had to work their hardest to store enough food and firewood to last the long cold winter.

So, after school, it was back to more chores – cleaning the shop, sweeping the kitchen, peeling the potatoes, weeding the garden. It never ended!

One morning, in the long summer following their eleventh birthday, Adam said to Abraham, "Well enough? I've had enough. We need a break."

They were dragging a load of water back from the well, and Abraham sighed. "Adam, it's Tuesday. We'll have a break on the Sabbath."

"No." Adam shook his head. "On the Sabbath we'll spend half the day in shul and the other half studying with Rabbi Kibbitz. Today is going to be hot, the sun is already high, and I need a break now."

"Stop talking such foolishness," Abraham said. "There is work to be done."

At the door to their house they stopped to wipe their feet and made sure they didn't spill a drop of water on their mother's carefully polished floor.

Adam gave him a look. "There is always work to be done. There always will be work to do. You sound like Father. What happened to my carefree brother, who once managed to tie the schoolteacher's bootlaces to a billy goat's beard?"

Several months before the Krabot disaster, Rabbi Abrahms had taken the class to a farm to observe his work as a mashgiach, and while the rabbi had been inspecting a goat's kid Abraham had sneaked up behind the teacher... The billy goat had butted the poor rabbi in the tuchas fifteen times before the laces finally snapped. For a week afterward, the sore man had sat on a pillow.

It had been brilliant. For once Abraham had even managed to escape punishment because no one had seen him do it, and the goat had eaten both the shoelaces and the rabbi's shoes.

"All right," Abraham grinned. "What do you propose?"

Adam's smile grew broad.

Before he could answer, they heard their father's voice from behind the house. "Boys! Come on already. Give me some help with the wagon."

Even if they hadn't been able to read each other's minds, they would have known what to do. They looked at each other, nodded...

And ran away.

To the Gold Mine!

Their father's shouts quickly faded in the distance. Abraham and Adam ran all the way out of the village proper, off the road, across the farm fields, and into the edge of the Schvartzvald before they at last collapsed, laughing with exhaustion.

They lay on the ground of the dark forest for a long time, clutching their sides and giggling. Just as one boy began to settle down and breathe calmly, the other would snort or guffaw, and they'd be off again, laughing like two maniacs.

"Oww!" Abraham said at last.

"Ow-wow!" Adam agreed.

They each took a deep breath and held it. One, two, three. And slowly they let their breaths out. Adam felt his stomach jump, and Abraham nearly giggled, but at last they had managed to contain themselves.

Now they rested, enjoying the soft crinkle of the fallen elm leaves, the smell of moss and dirt, the light breeze, and the rustle of the trees. It felt good to be away, out of town. It felt even better to finally relax and be themselves once again. In the year and a half since their trip with the Rabbi, everyone had treated them like grown-ups, as if they had somehow improved, and without realizing it they had found themselves doing exactly what was expected of them. It wasn't that they had been deliberately malicious before, but they were boys. They needed to have some fun. If everything was all chores, work and study, then what would be the point?

When they got back this afternoon, they would be in big trouble. They knew that. But for now the air was cool in the forest, the birds were chirruping, and their father's wood shop was far away.

"So, shall we go swimming?" Adam said.

Abraham thought for a moment and nodded. "Maybe we can catch a fish and bring it home for dinner."

"There are no fish in the Uherka," Adam said. "You know that.

Why do you always have to try and do something nice? Why can't we just go for a swim?"

"Fine," Abraham said. "Fine. We'll swim."

Although it was a tributary of the great Bug River, most of the Uherka River was nothing more than a trickle. Its water was used to irrigate the farm lands of Chelm, Smyrna, and three other villages. Any fish that accidentally made their way into the Uherka were caught long before they reached Chelm. (Although Bulga the fisherman did brag that he had once caught a nine-foot sturgeon with his bare hands, but it was too heavy for him to carry home so he had let it go.) In fact, the river was so shallow that there was only one spot deep enough for swimming – the Gold Mine.

Once upon a time, a visitor to Chelm said, "You can't get blood from a turnip."

"You can't?" his host answered. "How do you know?" And he immediately devoted the rest of his life to extracting blood from turnips.

That, in a nutshell, was the story of the Gold Mine.

Reb Gold, the cobbler, was a very poor man. His hobby, of course, was getting rich. He always had brilliant ideas about packaging this and selling that. None of them worked. One winter, he built a large box, which he filled with cold air. "In the summer time," he told his wife, "people will pay dearly for a cool breath." Unfortunately, the box wasn't big enough, and when he opened it on the hottest day of the year, he felt only a momentary breeze. "Well," he sighed. "If only I could sell ideas, I'd be the richest man in Chelm."

Since his name was Gold, and he wanted gold, Reb Gold was always reading about gold. One day, he read about a gold strike in America. Evidently millions of people in California were wading into rivers and coming out with pots and pans filled with gold. It seemed like a long way to go just to get wet, and since the Uherka was so close, Reb Gold put two and two together and got five.

The next morning, he dragged his wife's largest soup kettle to the banks of the river. "If I fill a big pot with gold," he reasoned, "then I'll have to make fewer trips."

Unfortunately, the river was so shallow and the kettle was so big that it was impossible to fill with water.

"If I dig a hole," Reb Gold said to himself, "I can put the pot in the hole. The pot will fill with water, the water will be filled with gold, and I will be rich!"

Using his bare hands, Reb Gold got down on his knees in the mud and began to scoop. It's not easy moving mud out of a running stream, but after a few hours, he finally managed to get the pot under the surface. Water began to dribble in, and Reb Gold began to think about lunch.

"I'll go home and get a bite. By the time I get back, I'll be rich."

Unfortunately, Esther Gold had been planning on making soup that morning, so there was nothing to eat when her husband returned. In fact, she was so furious at him that he immediately turned around and headed back to the river to retrieve the kettle.

"She'll be so surprised when I return with all the gold that she'll forgive me, and we will live happily ever after. Now, if I can just remember where the pot is…"

Reb Gold looked at the river. He squinted at it. He tried to retrace his footsteps, but all to no avail. The surface of the water was smooth and flat, and there was no sign of his wife's soup kettle.

At last, he took off his shoes and began walking through the stream, certain that at any moment, he would step into the kettle. No luck. Or perhaps it was the greatest stroke of luck that had ever come his way!

If he had stepped into the kettle, then he could have dug it up and brought it home, but without any gold. Since he did not step in the kettle, that meant it had already filled to the brim with gold!

Forgetting his shoes, Reb Gold ran back to Chelm with the good news. An hour later, every man, woman and child in Chelm was at the edge of the Uherka, digging for the gold. They brought shovels and pickaxes and wheelbarrows, so the work went quickly. Great heaps of dirt were dug from the Uherka and piled up on either side of the bank. But as quickly as they dug, the water flowed into the hole. Even if the hole was filled with gold, then how would they know?

At last, Rabbi Kibbitz suggested that they build a dam and dig a hole big enough to supply the entire village with gold. No sooner was it said than it was done. A dam was built, a hole dug, and it filled with water.

"What if there's not enough gold?" said Reb Gold, "Maybe we should dig a bigger hole?"

An even larger hole was dug behind the first hole. When this hole was finished and filled, yet another hole was dug.

By now several weeks had gone by, and the piles of dirt on either side of the Uherka had grown monstrously large. Neighbors from Smyrna came to watch and laugh. "Only in Chelm," they said, shaking their heads.

That summer was nearly over and still no gold had been found. One by one the villagers went back to their farms and shops. In the end, only Reb Gold was left, and he too would have given up – except that even with all the digging, he had never quite managed to find his wife's soup kettle.

At last, Esther Gold came out to visit her husband. Come home, she begged him. There were shoes to be mended. She would buy another kettle. A broken man, Reb Gold turned away from the huge lake he had helped to dig, and went home to mend shoes and dream of his lost pot of gold.

Summer Day

Abraham and Adam Schlemiel climbed the grass covered hill on the south shore of the Uherka, near the Gold Mine, stripped off their clothes, looked down at the cold clear water, and dove into the small lake. It was cold and refreshing!

They swam and played for hours in the icy water, until their lips turned blue and their fingers and toes went numb. Abraham liked swimming down to the bottom and tugging on Adam's leg as if he were a monster from the deep. Adam liked waiting until just after his brother surfaced to splash a handful of water into his open and gasping mouth. All in all, it was just about as much fun as two brothers could possibly have together.

At last, half frozen and shivering, they climbed out and found a grassy spot high on the banks of the river to warm themselves in the sunshine.

"We should have brought towels," Abraham said.

"We should be hard at work in Father's wood shop," Adam said. "I think we can live without towels."

Abraham nodded. His eyes were closed and he felt the warm orange glow on his face. "Do you ever worry that Alex Krabot might come and kill us?"

Adam sighed. "I didn't until just now."

"It scares me some times," Abraham said. "I'm not even sure that we should be this far outside of Chelm. We did give our promise to the governor."

"Abraham, stop it. We've discussed it over and over," Adam said. "She wasn't the governor, she was his mother. And the whole point was to prevent us from testifying at her son's trial so he'd be set free. That was almost two years ago. He must be free by now. As far as I can tell, it worked and we have kept our end of the bargain. Even if we hadn't, I don't think Alex Krabot would care if we sneaked out to go for a swim. He might kill us, but I doubt he'd blame us."

"I suppose so," Abraham said glumly.

"Why can't you just relax and enjoy yourself?" Adam asked.

"I'm hungry."

Adam laughed. "Me too. I can't wait for dinner."

"We're probably going to get sent to our room without dinner tonight."

"Stop it." Adam swatted at Abraham. "Enough of that. If you could have anything you wanted for dinner, what would it be?"

"Brisket," Abraham said without hesitation, "and kasha varnishkas with plenty of gravy."

Adam nodded. "But no kale. It doesn't matter what Mama does to it, I hate kale."

"I kind of like it. Especially when she cooks it with garlic and onions and vinegar."

"Eccch!" Adam shuddered. "Eruwaaagh!"

Abraham laughed.

They lay silently for a while. The grass was cool and tickled their naked backs. Every so often, a cloud would slip in front of the sun, enveloping them in shadow until it blew away. Nearby they heard the sounds of two squirrels fighting over a nut and a tree filled with birds cawing at the sky.

At last, Abraham said, "What do you want to do?"

Adam thought for a moment. "I want to marry Rosa and live in a house as big as Reb Cantor's. Maybe bigger. I want to have plenty of money and never have to work. I want to be respected in the shul, but not be the kind of person who they talk about when he doesn't show up. I want to have a garden. And I'd like to visit Moscow. And maybe Arizona, too. What about you?"

Abraham had propped himself up on one elbow. He stared at his brother in amazement. "Actually," he said, "I was just wondering what you wanted to do now. This afternoon."

"Oh," Adam said. "I want to take a nap." Adam's eyes were closed, and even though he was hungry he felt happy and safe.

"Are you asleep?" Abraham asked.

"Yes. Definitely."

Abraham poked him.

"What?" Adam said.

"You really want to marry Rosa Kalderash?"

"Sure," Adam shrugged. "There's nobody in the village that I'd want to marry. Can you see me married to Rachel Cohen? She would talk my head off. Or Rivka Cantor? She's so mean to me."

"I think that means she likes you," Abraham said.

"That kind of liking I can do without."

"But you can't marry Rosa. She's not Jewish."

Adam sighed. "I know. Maybe she'll convert. Or I could become a Gypsy."

"I don't think you can become one of them. And if you did, then you couldn't own a house. They're travelers."

Adam opened his eyes. He realized that Abraham wasn't going to let him nap. "So, what's your perfect plan, Mr. Smart Guy?"

Abraham smiled. "That's easy. I thought I'd marry someone like Mother, take over Father's shop from him, and live happily ever after in Chelm."

"Boring," Adam said.

Abraham shrugged. "After facing the Krabot gang and traveling to Pinsk, I don't care if I never have another adventure."

"It wasn't so bad," Adam said.

Abraham snorted. "You complained the whole time."

"Well, so did you," Adam said. "During our travels it was pretty miserable. I was scared or wet. Who wouldn't be? But now we're heroes! People as far away as Pinsk know that the Schlemiel brothers are not to be trifled with. Ha!"

"They do?" Abraham said. "I think you have an over-inflated sense of our reputation."

"So? You can get old and fat in Chelm, and I'll send you a letter from Arizona."

They both laughed. At the bottom of the hill, the Uherka River gurgled along. If either of them had opened their eyes, they might have seen a family of deer nibbling at the wild flowers on the edge of the clearing.

"Do you think we'll ever live apart?" Adam asked.

Abraham didn't answer with words. Instead, he spoke directly into Adam's mind. *Don't worry, little brother. No matter where we live, I'll always be close by.*

They reached out and held hands in a comforting squeeze.

And then, since they were normal eleven-year-old boys, the handshake turned into a tug of war, which turned into a tussle, and in two minutes they were rolling together head over heels back down the hill and into the river.

Splash! The cold water startled them apart. They opened their eyes and saw that the sun was almost below the tops of the trees.

"Father and Mother are going to kill us," Abraham said as he stumbled to shore.

"Yes," Adam said. "But it was worth it. We'd better hurry, though. Where are our clothes?"

"Where are our clothes?" Abraham asked. "Aren't they right there?"

They looked at the log where they'd put their clothes.

"You're kidding, right?" Abraham said. "While I was asleep you swam across the river and hid the clothes, didn't you?"

Adam shook his head. "I was going to ask you the same thing. Do you think Alex Krabot stole our clothes?"

"No," Abraham said. "He would have killed us. Maybe one of the boys from the village did it."

"We would have heard them. And they just would have thrown mud at us and woken us up. It must be a tramp. It doesn't matter so much who took them or why. What are we going to do?"

There wasn't much to do. Clutching twigs covered with leaves, Abraham and Adam sneaked their way back to Chelm, hiding behind bushes and rocks. They stayed off the road and cut through the farm fields high with unharvested rye, but when they reached the edge of the village, the going was trickier. They ran in short bursts from the edge of one house to the next, hoping that no one would see them scurrying around naked.

At last, their house was in sight.

"We'll go in through the bedroom window," Abraham whispered to Adam, as they ducked behind a stable near their house. "I'll go first. We'll get dressed quickly and then afterward worry about what Mother and Father will do."

Adam nodded. Together they stood up, ready for the last dash home.

"Well, hello there!" said Rabbi Yohon Abrahms, the schoolteacher. Beside him stood every schoolchild in Chelm, laughing and pointing. "We were just coming out to watch the sunset. It's been such a lovely day, hasn't it? You two weren't in school today. I suppose missing class is one thing, but missing your clothing is something else entirely..."

Adam and Abraham turned as red as the sunset and ran. They didn't stop to think that their window might be shut; they just dove inside. Fortunately, the window was open. There, on the bed, neatly laid out, were their missing clothes.

"Abraham," Mother called from the kitchen. "Adam. After you're dressed, come out. It's nearly dinner time."

Adam looked at Abraham. "Do you smell kasha?" he said.

"She's torturing us," Abraham said, terrified.

A few minutes later, they sat down at the table, surprised to see that portions of brisket and kasha were laid out in front of their seats as well.

"Wasn't it nice," their mother said as she poured them each a cup of water, "that young Rabbi Abrahams found two sets of clothing and shoes that looked exactly like yours. I didn't ask where they came from, I just accepted the gift. What a sweet man."

"I missed you today," their father said softly. "But I'm glad to see that you've come back safe and sound. Next time you run off, make sure you tell somebody. Something horrible might happen to you and we'd never know."

Jacob Schlemiel winked at his wife, who patted his shoulder and shook her head. Abraham and Adam stared at their shoes and mumbled apologies.

"Eat up before it gets cold." Their mother's face was stern, but her eyes twinkled with a barely suppressed smile.

Chapter Eleven

A Girl

Rebecca Schlemiel smiled. She always smiled. She had smiled as she had watched her babies grow into boys, and she smiled as she watched her boys growing into men. Sometimes, of course, she wanted cry – when she was tired or frustrated, but even then it didn't last.

"If you ever run out of smiles," the saying in Chelm went, "visit Rebecca Schlemiel. She's got so many, she'll be happy to give away one or two."

Once, a few years earlier, Adam had told her that he felt as if everyone liked Abraham better than him. Rebecca had felt the tears of sympathy welling up inside her. What a beautiful and wonderful boy he was. And that made her smile. She held Adam close, hiding her smile so he wouldn't think she was laughing at him, and told him how much she loved him.

Rebecca, you see, had learned a secret that many people know in their brains, but only a few know in their hearts. She knew that her life was good and perfect in all ways. No, she didn't have much money. Yes, there were times that she coughed so hard it turned her cheeks almost purple. True, Abraham and especially Adam were always getting themselves in trouble of one kind or another. Still, it was a perfect world, and she would not change a thing.

Maybe one thing.

More than anything else, Rebecca Schlemiel wanted a daughter. The boys were wonderful, and her husband was fine, but there were days when she longed for the company of women. She wanted to teach someone how to bake, how to sew, how to look at a field of wild flowers and know exactly which seven to pick to make a perfect bouquet. She wanted a baby to tickle, but not one who would grow up to make even more trouble. A little girl, who would stay at home and help her fix dinner, instead of going to the shop with her father. A young woman who would tell her of problems with boys and whose hair she could help pin up on her wedding day. A daughter wasn't so much to ask for, was it?

So far, though, nothing. Jacob and Rebecca had tried. And tried. No luck. Jacob had even gone to Rabbi Kibbitz and asked his advice. He'd told Rebecca later that the old man's face had turned so red that his beard looked as if it were going to catch on fire. After the rabbi had caught his breath, he'd gone to his bookshelf and found an old book with strange letters and pictures of men and women with slanted eyes. Those pictures! Rebecca had no idea that human beings could be so inventive. But the magic book hadn't worked either, even though they'd gone through it from cover to cover twice. (Rebecca smiled fondly as she remembered the last time the boys had gone to bed early…)

Now, however, it was time to try something else.

After Jacob and the boys went to the shop, she put on her shawl and hurried across town to Mrs. Chaipul's restaurant.

It wasn't often that a woman went alone to Mrs. Chaipul's restaurant. Mostly the women of Chelm were too busy to sit around a table and drink endless cups of tea, as some of the men did. And they were frugal, also. Why buy a meal when you could make it at home, especially if you were a better cook? It wasn't that Mrs. Chaipul was a bad cook, but…

When Rebecca opened the door to the restaurant, Mrs. Chaipul looked up from behind the counter with surprise, as did her three usual customers – Reb Cantor, the merchant, Reb Cohen, the tailor, and Reb Gold, the cobbler.

Rebecca smiled at them, and they all nodded back. Then she sat at the counter, and they all looked at her nervously.

"Are you going to the market?" Mrs. Chaipul asked.

"Not today," Rebecca Schlemiel said. "I wanted to talk with you." Her voice dropped. "You see, I have a bit of a problem…"

At their table, the three men pretended to talk among themselves while their ears grew eager to hear what that problem was.

"You think you have a problem?" Mrs. Chaipul said. "I have customers who sit here all day, drink one cup of tea for hours at a time, and then wonder why their businesses make no money."

A silence fell over the restaurant. The three men shifted uncomfortably in their seats for a moment, then Reb Cantor rose and paid the bill, and with another set of nods they all left.

"Good customers," Mrs. Chaipul said. "So, what is it? You've got a cold? I noticed you coughing the other day. Some of my chicken soup with knaidels will cure that in a minute."

"No!" Rebecca raised her hands perhaps too quickly. Mrs. Chaipul's soup dumplings were famous for being as heavy as lead and tasting nearly as good. "What I meant to say is, thank you, but the cough comes and goes. What I want is a girl."

"I completely understand," Mrs. Chaipul said. She poured them both tea and sat down next to Rebecca at the counter. "I want one too."

Rebecca looked at Mrs. Chaipul in amazement. The woman was a widow, in her sixties at least, and she wanted a girl?

"Girls are so wonderful," Mrs. Chaipul continued. "They cook, they clean, they do laundry."

Rebecca laughed. "But not right away."

"Oh, no," Mrs. Chaipul agreed. "It takes a day or two to train them. They need to learn what goes in which cabinet, how many cloves of garlic to put in the soup, and so forth."

"Only two days? Boys take forever. I had no idea girls learned so quickly."

"Girls these days are very smart. That's why they're so hard to come by."

"Ahh," Rebecca nodded. That explained a lot. "Why do you suppose it takes so much longer with boys?"

"Boys are impossible," Mrs. Chaipul said. "It's a girl you want. Shoshana Cantor, she just got a girl last week. She was telling me about it. Now she has so much more free time."

"Mrs. Cantor? The merchant's wife?" Another woman in her fifties. "Isn't she a little old?"

"Exactly. But now, the girl even does the shopping for her.

Cooking, cleaning, shopping, the girl does it all. Shoshana hardly knows what to do with her days. I told her to come in here, have breakfast with her husband, and talk with the men, but she just laughed."

Rebecca smiled. "I had no idea she was even pregnant. I'll have to get a gift."

"Pregnant?" Mrs. Chaipul laughed. "No, she hired a maid."

"A maid?"

"Yes, a servant girl. To live in. They have such a big house, with empty rooms and…" Mrs. Chaipul's voice trailed off. "You thought I meant… you thought that I wanted a baby?"

Rebecca Schlemiel looked at her teacup and nodded.

"Ha!" Mrs. Chaipul cackled. "That's a good one! I wouldn't have another baby if you paid me all the gold in the Czar's money locker. Let the children have the babies. I'll visit them. Hee hee hee. Me having another baby, who could imagine such a thing?"

Embarrassed though she was, Rebecca managed a smile.

That was when Mrs. Chaipul noticed that she was laughing alone. She giggled a moment longer and then calmed herself down.

"Oh, I see," Mrs. Chaipul said at last. "You meant that you want a baby girl. Not a servant."

Rebecca nodded.

"Okay. All right." Mrs. Chaipul rubbed her chin. "Let's see what we can do…"

Ups and…

It was a bad idea from the start.

Adam was halfway up the roof, and Abraham was keeping lookout. Ordinarily, it wasn't a difficult climb. Just outside their bedroom window were a series of spikes they had hammered into the wall when they had helped their father build the addition to the house. Jacob Schlemiel had been a little angry at what he thought was the waste of a half dozen perfectly good spikes, but by the time he saw them, they were driven in too deeply to be removed without leaving six gaping holes in the new room. The boys had played innocent, and endured the loss of dessert privileges for a week. Now, whenever they wanted to get away from the family, they could scramble out the window, step onto the pickle barrel, which was stored just outside their bedroom window, reach up and grab the spikes, climb onto the roof, and be hidden in plain sight in a matter of moments.

Except this time, Adam had decided that he wanted to practice his violin on the roof. He had heard stories of the roof fiddler who had (long ago) thrilled all of Chelm with his legendary playing. "If Mama is going to make me learn the violin," he'd told Abraham, "I'm going to learn it my way." Abraham had tried to dissuade him, but once Adam got an idea into his head, there was no turning back.

Abraham poked his head out the window and hissed, "Hurry up!"

Not only was it taking Adam three times longer to scale the roof with the violin, but once he began practicing, the screeching and scrawling would certainly draw attention. Their secret spot would be a secret no longer. Adam didn't care. He was certain that once he got his feet off the ground, his playing would improve and no one would mind where he practiced.

And it might have worked. Perhaps as he sat near the chimney, one leg slung over either side of the v-shaped roof, Adam would have tucked the fiddle under his chin, raised the bow, and played the kind of beautiful soft, gentle, yet thrilling note that made the violin an instrument of beauty – instead of the usual horrifying wail his efforts produced, like a cat being twirled around through the air by its tail.

The boys would never know.

"Jacob?" Abraham heard his mother calling from inside the house. "Have you seen Adam and Abraham?"

Abraham jumped up on the windowsill and stepped onto the lid of the pickle barrel. If his parents found him alone, they'd begin asking questions. Better for both of them to be out of sight.

"No. I think they're in their room," his father answered.

"Could you go get them," Rebecca Schlemiel said. "I want to have a talk with everyone."

Abraham reached up for the first spike.

"What's going on?" Adam whispered.

"I don't know," Abraham said. "Are you up yet?"

"No."

"Come on!"

For all their seeming carelessness, both boys knew that it wasn't a good idea for the two of them to stand on the same part of the roof at the same time. Jacob was a good carpenter, but wood was wood, and they didn't want an accident.

Abraham heard his father's footsteps approaching their bedroom door. He pulled himself up to the second rung.

The door to the bedroom opened. "Abraham? Adam? They're not in here."

"Where else could they be?" Rebecca asked. "Did you look under the bed?"

Abraham didn't dare move. He heard his father's footsteps, imagined him crouching down and looking their bed. "No. Not there."

"Is the window open?" Rebecca asked.

Abraham made a face. Usually he remembered to shut the window when he went out. It was one of the key elements to their vanishing act. He cringed as his father's footsteps drew near. All Jacob had to do was stick his head out the window, and he would see his oldest son, pressing against the wall like a frightened squirrel.

The window slid down and Abraham heard his father's muffled, "The window's shut."

Abraham sighed with relief. "Aren't you up yet?"

"Almost. Will you stop bothering me? It's kind of trick…"

Adam's voice cut off. Abraham's eyes widened. In his mind, he saw his brother teetering on the edge of the roof, balancing on one leg, the violin case in one hand and the bow in his other.

"Adam?" Abraham whispered. "Adam?"

"Abraham!" their mother shouted from the front door. "Adam!"

"Yaaah!" Adam yelped from the rooftop.

Oh no, Abraham thought. He let go of his perch, dropped to the ground, and stepped back to see what was happening.

Just then he heard a loud "Crak!" and a sliding scraping noise.

And he knew. Any second, Adam was going to come flying off the roof like a boulder off a cliff. He would tumble and spin through the air, twirling like a leaf, land on his head, and snap his neck like a twig. Abraham could already imagine his mother's wails and his father's shouts.

"I'll catch you!" Abraham shouted. "I'll catch you!"

He held out his arms, hoping Adam wouldn't land on top of him and break both their necks.

Just then, the violin came careening off the roof. Abraham's hands went up, his fingers closed around it, and he pulled it into his chest, cradling the fragile instrument as if it was a baby. Thank goodness he hadn't dropped it. The violin was rented, and while a broken leg would mend, a broken violin would cost a fortune.

"Did you catch it?" Adam shouted.

"I got it!"

"Are you boys behind the house?"

Abraham heard her coming, looked both ways, but knew it was too late.

She saw the violin, smiled and said, "Adam, where is your brother?"

Abraham sighed. It was inevitable. Whenever Adam got into trouble, Abraham was blamed.

He couldn't exactly say, "I'm Abraham. Adam's up on the roof giggling madly."

Instead, he said, "He's probably playing clarinet somewhere."

"Clarinet?" Rebecca said. "Since when does he play the clarinet? We don't have a clarinet!"

Adam, who had just managed to hook his arm around the chimney, couldn't help himself. He had to laugh.

Rebecca heard the hidden laugh and grew angry. "Abraham, I'm going to count to five. One. Two. Three... You don't want to know what's going to happen if I reach five. Four...

Still, Adam couldn't help himself. His laughter grew louder, and his grip on the chimney loosened.

Abraham heard his brother's scream of terror in his mind an instant before the sound reached his ears.

Rebecca began to look up, but Abraham pointed toward the forest in the distance. "Look over there, Mama!"

Rebecca looked, and didn't see anything except trees.

She didn't see Adam fall from the roof like a loose brick. She didn't see him land on top of Abraham.

She, however, did hear the "Thud!" and Abraham's loud gasp.

And she turned around to see both her boys collapsed in a heap at her feet, one holding the violin and the other holding the bow.

"Abraham," Rebecca said. "How many times have I told you not to run like a wild man? Especially with a sharp stick in your hand."

"This isn't a stick. This is a bow," Adam said, suppressing a smirk. "And I'm Adam."

"That's not the point," Rebecca said.

Adam pushed himself to his feet. "I'm sorry, Mama."

"Come on, get up," Rebecca said, shaking her head at Abraham. "I want to talk with you both."

Abraham rose, took one look at his twisted left leg and said, "I don't think I can walk."

His face turned white, and he started to collapse.

Adam caught Abraham as he fell, and panic rose in his eyes. "Mama!"

Good News

Abraham's leg was broken. His father and Adam carried him into bed, while Mama ran for Mrs. Chaipul, who came with her carpetbag full of medical equipment and supplies. Mrs. Chaipul looked at the strange way the leg was bent, clucked to herself three times, and then (without any warning) snapped the bone back into place. Abraham howled like a dying wolf. Adam felt a blast in his mind like a thunderbolt. Rebecca Schlemiel fainted, and even Jacob looked stunned.

Mrs. Chaipul shrugged. "You think it would have felt any better if I told you what was coming?" she said as she splinted the leg, and then bound it firmly with lengths of white plaster-dipped cloth.

For the next week Mrs. Chaipul came by every day to check on her patient. And once the initial shock wore off and the plaster dried, Abraham found that he could actually walk, albeit stiffly.

"No chasing around like a wild animal for six weeks," Mrs. Chaipul warned. "Two months if you want to be sure, but you're a boy, so… six weeks. Okay?"

"Okay." Abraham looked ashamed.

The boys had lied about the accident. You can't just say to your parents, "I broke my leg trying to catch my brother from falling off the roof." That would raise all sorts of uncomfortable questions like, "Why was he on the roof in the first place?" or "What kind of idiots are you two?" Instead, they told her that he'd been playing keep-away with Adam's violin when the two of them had collided. That wasn't much better, but their mother and father felt that the broken leg was punishment enough.

And it was actually punishment for both of them – Abraham, because he felt hobbled, and Adam, because for the first time in his life he didn't have a partner in crime to run around with. Abraham spent his days and nights in bed, while Adam did both of their chores and all of the work helping their father in the shop.

Nearly four weeks sped by before Rebecca Schlemiel finally remembered the important thing that she had meant to tell her family.

She gathered everyone together in the boys' room. Abraham lay in bed, Adam sat next to him, and Jacob stood near the door.

"I have such good news!" Rebecca said. "I can't believe I forgot to tell you!"

"You mean," Adam said, "Mrs. Chaipul doesn't have to amputate Abraham's leg?"

"You mean," Abraham retorted, "Mrs. Chaipul is finally going to cut that unsightly bump from on top of Adam's shoulders?"

"What bump?" Adam asked.

"The one that starts at your neck and ends with your kippah."

"Boys," Jacob warned. "Your mother is being serious. Go on."

"It's wonderful news, actually," Rebecca said.

"You mean he's adopted?" both boys said, simultaneously pointing at each other. They grinned until their father gave them a look that could have stripped paint off a canvas.

"No," their mother said patiently. "This is something very, very special. I want you to know that we're having…"

"A pot roast for dinner on Friday night?" Adam interrupted.

"With roasted potatoes and gravy?" Abraham continued.

"And an apple strudel for dessert?" Jacob said, his mouth salivating at the thought.

Both the boys and Rebecca were staring at him. "Sorry. It sounded good."

"You think it's funny?" Rebecca said quietly. Her head was nodding now, up and down like a fishing bob that had just hooked a snapping turtle. "You think that my good news is nothing but jokes and food?"

"No, Mama," Abraham said.

"We like your food," Adam said.

"Please, Rebecca," Jacob said. "Nothing was meant by it. Go on."

"I don't know if I should tell you now." She scowled. "And if I didn't have to tell you, I wouldn't. I'd just keep quiet about it."

Then, much to her family's surprise, Rebecca Schlemiel burst into tears.

"Mama!" Abraham said.

"We didn't mean to hurt you," Adam said.

"My sweetness." Jacob tried to put his arm around Rebecca, but she shrugged it off and stepped away.

"I try to tell you something so beautiful," she sobbed, "so special, but you have to ruin it. Men. You're all boys. Like children. Why would I want any more children? Already I have too many!"

"No, no," Jacob soothed, patting her back. "It's not ruined.

Merely delayed. Please. Please. We're listening now. Go on. Sit. Adam, get a chair for your mother."

Adam hurried into the kitchen and brought back a chair. Rebecca sat and daubed at her tears with a handkerchief.

"We're going to have an addition," she said, still crying. "An addition!"

"You want me to build another room onto the house?" Jacob said. "This is good news? I've got paying work to do. Ever since Reb Cantor commissioned me to do the box for the Governor, I've been very very busy...

"Besides," he continued. "What do we need another addition for? We have our room, the boys have their room. There's the kitchen, where we also eat. How many rooms does a house need? You want maybe a library? We don't have so many books. And where would we put it? We can't build into the road. You've got your vegetable garden on the south side of the house. The outhouse is on the west, and the Lieberman's house is very close on the east... What? What?"

Abraham and Adam were giggling. Even Rebecca, who had been half an inch from losing her temper, was now shaking her head with amazed amusement.

"Don't laugh at me," Jacob said, which just made things worse. "What? Am I completely out of line here when I say that adding a room to this house is not something that this family needs at this time? What? WHAT?"

Adam and his mother were rolling on the floor while Abraham rolled around on the bed, slapping the pillows with his hands. Their laughter was so loud and so infectious that it was heard throughout Chelm. Across town in the restaurant, Rabbi Kibbitz looked up from his chicken soup and grinned at Mrs. Chaipul.

"Fine," Jacob scowled. "You want an addition. You want another room? You boys are going to help with the work. It's labor we're talking about. Hard labor. Do you boys even know what labor is?"

By this time, the twins and their mother were gasping for air. "Stop! Stop!" the boys begged.

"No," Jacob said, shaking his head firmly. "No. You can't just stop something like this. Once an idea like this is conceived it must be planned, it must be nurtured..."

At last, Jacob stopped. No one was listening to him. Or if they were, they were completely ignoring his point. He threw up his hands in exasperation. "What is so funny?"

"Papa," Abraham sputtered at last. "We're not *building* a new addition, we're *having* a new addition."

"Oh," Jacob said. "You think there's a difference? Building, having. Life doesn't come so easily..." Jacob broke off. "Having an addition? You mean having a new addition?"

Rebecca nodded, smiling at her husband.

Jacob Schlemiel grinned in amazement, ran over, picked up his wife, and twirled her around three times before setting her back down gently.

"An addition?" he asked.

"And it's a girl. I think."

"Well then," Jacob shrugged, "I suppose we will need to build a new room for the new addition."

This time, their laughter could be heard all the way to Smyrna.

The Eighth Light

Chanukah was early, and Rebecca Schlemiel's baby was late. The sky was clear, and there were only ten inches of snow on the ground, crusted over by a thin layer of ice. The conversation in Chelm was a mixture of excitement for the coming festival of lights and anxiety because the czar of Russia was threatening the king of Poland over something or another.

On the first night of Chanukah, as was their custom, the Schlemiel family gathered in the kitchen to make latkes. Everyone knew his or her job. Jacob grated the potatoes while Rebecca mixed the recipe and cooked the pancakes. The boys would eat the latkes – as many and as fast as Rebecca could make them. The smell of frying potatoes filled the warm air. As they lit the candles, Abraham (whose broken leg was completely healed except for the occasional throb) held the shammos, and Adam lit it with a match and then said the blessings.

Rebecca sighed. "We are truly blessed."

Jacob nodded. "Truer words were never spoken."

"Come on," Adam said. "I'm getting hungry."

But Abraham would not be hurried. He knew enough to savor the delicious moment before the other candles were lit.

"It's time," his mother said.

"Yes, Abraham," Jacob agreed. "It's time. Before the shammos burns down."

"No," Rebecca said softly. "I mean it's time. Now. I'm going to have the baby."

Jacob blinked. "Right now?"

"Yes!"

Jacob blinked. Adam grinned. Abraham quickly lit the first candle.

Everyone sighed.

Then the peace and quiet was broken with sheer panic. Adam began jumping up and down. Abraham had to grab the chanukiah to prevent it from falling to the floor. Jacob ran back and forth like a chicken with its head cut off. Rebecca just rolled her eyes and moaned.

"Go," she sputtered at last. "Get Mrs. Chaipul."

"I'll go!" both boys said it together. And in the next moment they were off, running barefoot and without coats through the snow-covered streets, slipping and sliding on every patch of ice before scrambling to their feet and dashing off again.

Mrs. Chaipul lived upstairs from her famous restaurant, and since all her children were grown, the midwife was in the habit of lighting the candles in a quiet and private ceremony. Only on the evening of the town's Chanukah party did she venture out in public.

Even though everyone in Chelm knew that Rebecca Schlemiel was overdue, the furious banging at her door startled the old woman. She peeked down through her curtains and grabbed her carpetbag as soon as she saw the twins. She pulled on her coat and ran downstairs.

Now, all three of them ran barefoot back to the Schlemiels' house.

Jacob met them at the door with his finger to his lips. "Shhh," he said. "She's asleep."

"Are we too late?" Adam asked. "Did we miss it?" Abraham said.

"No," Jacob whispered. To Mrs. Chaipul he said, "Rebecca said that the pains stopped and she was tired. I'm sorry for getting you out of your house on such a cold night."

Mrs. Chaipul plopped herself down in a chair next to the fire and set her feet on the hearth to warm. "False labor," she said. "It happens. You two, wrap yourselves in blankets and sit next to the fire."

Teeth chattering, the two boys hurried to obey the old wise woman. When she got warm, Mrs. Chaipul finished cooking the latkes, which fortunately had already been mixed and were just waiting to be fried. While their mother slept in peace, the four others spun dreidels and ate latkes until late in the night.

The next day the temperature dropped and a new snow began to fall, but the baby still did not come. Once again, night fell and the Schlemiels gathered around the kitchen table to light the menorah. This time the grins and laughter had a different flavor because they all expected that tonight would surely be the night. Jacob grated the potatoes and Rebecca cooked them. Adam held the shammos and Abraham set it afire with a match.

"Well?" Adam looked at his mother. "Is it time?"

"Go on, light the candles," she said, swatting at him with the wooden spatula. "Oof."

"Careful," Jacob warned.

"It's time," Rebecca whispered.

"Really?" Jacob said. "Are you sure?"

"It's TIME!"

In an instant the boys were off and running, again without their shoes and coats. Again Mrs. Chaipul nearly leaped out of her skin when they bashed on her door. And again, Rebecca was asleep before they arrived back.

"She said she was sorry for causing all this trouble again," Jacob apologized.

"Nonsense," Mrs. Chaipul said shivering. "Maybe I'll just keep my shoes and coat on tomorrow night."

The next three days were almost exact repeats of the first two, only the snow was deeper and the winds were colder. Each day Rebecca felt wonderful and fine right up until the moment before the first candle of the evening was about to be lit. Then the pains started like a sudden landslide and the boys were off and running.

By the fifth night of Chanukah, Mrs. Chaipul had decided that it would be smarter to sleep at the Schlemiels' house. She also thought it would be prudent to send for the doctor. One or two days of false labor the old midwife knew about, but this repeated threat of imminent birth frightened her. She could see that even though Rebecca Schlemiel got up every morning with a smile on her face, the mother-to-be was growing weaker.

Reb Cantor had business in Smyrna and promised to see (and pay for) the doctor as soon as he got there. But with all the snow, it would take the merchant at least a day to travel to the neighboring village, and it would take the doctor another day to arrive back in Chelm. Even worse, no sooner was the merchant on the road than the blizzard began in earnest.

In Smyrna they tell a story that – a long time ago, the villagers of Chelm had hired porters to carry them, so their footsteps wouldn't ruin the beautiful carpet of snow. Snow only that deep would have been nice. This year the winter snows were so deep, everyone was stuck at home and the farmers had to dig tunnels just to go to the outhouse.

Rabbi Kibbitz was forced to cancel the annual Chanukah party, not because he wanted to, but because he was afraid someone would freeze on the way home. And even though in every house candles were set in the windows, not a flicker could be seen in the snow-covered valley.

The Schlemiels were cranky by now. For seven days they'd eaten nothing but latkes. Abraham and Adam slept on the kitchen floor while Mrs. Chaipul rested warm and comfortable in their bed. It was impossible to sleep because whenever they did manage to doze off they'd be awakened by one of their mother's moans or groans.

On the eighth and last night of Chanukah everyone was on edge. Jacob grumbled as he grated potatoes. Rebecca scowled as she cooked the pancakes. Abraham and Adam argued over whose turn it was to hold the shammos. Mrs. Chaipul kept looking out the window into the great wall of snow and wondering whether the doctor would arrive or if he would be too late.

At last, Rebecca Schlemiel slammed down her spatula and shouted, "Enough! Both of you hold the shammos. Jacob light it. I'll say the blessings and let's get this over with!"

The room fell silent.

"But Mama," Abraham said, "that's not how we…"

"NOW!"

Jacob's hand shook as he touched the match to the shammos. Rebecca said the blessings so quickly you couldn't have sneezed twice before they were done. Because they couldn't take their eyes off their mother, Abraham and Adam nearly set Mrs. Chaipul's hair on fire.

At last all eight lights were burning brightly.

"There," Rebecca Schlemiel sighed. "I'm going to go to bed now."

After she had gone, Jacob turned to Mrs. Chaipul. "Is she all right?"

"I'll go check," the old woman said.

"Come boys," their father said. "One more game of dreidel. This time we'll play for latkes."

Abraham and Adam groaned but joined their father at the kitchen table.

A few moments later, they heard a loud cry from their parents' bedroom. Both boys and their father were standing at the door when Mrs. Chaipul opened it, her eyes filled with tears of joy.

"It's a girl!"

Abraham and Adam stared open-mouthed at the tiny baby

cradled in Mrs. Chaipul's arms, while Jacob rushed to his wife's side. "How is she? Her hand is cold."

"She's tired," Mrs. Chaipul said.

Rebecca opened her eyes and managed a weak smile. "Shemini," she whispered. "We'll name her Shemini."

Chapter Twelve

Drudgery

Abraham and Adam had assumed their lives would get easier now that they had a new sister. Another woman around the house would naturally mean fewer chores for the men. Girls were good at those sorts of things. Little Shemini could help their mother with the cooking and the cleaning and the straightening up and the laundry.

They were wrong.

First of all, they completely forgot that Shemini was only a baby, and that it would be years before she could be trusted with anything so fragile as washing a plate, or as dangerous as chopping turnips for a cholent.

Worse still, after eight days of labor, Rebecca Schlemiel was completely exhausted. Every bone in her body ached, and she was always tired. She barely had enough strength to care for herself and to nurse Shemini, let alone perform any of the more disgusting tasks like changing diapers or washing spit-upon clothes.

"Babies are revolting!" Adam complained. He wrinkled his nose as he lifted another one of Shemini's soiled linens with a long stick and dropped it into a vat of boiling water. Immediately a sickly stench filled the kitchen.

"Adam," Abraham yelled, "I said you're supposed to scrape and rinse before you drop it in the pot!"

"You do it your way, I'll do it mine," Adam said, barely suppressing a gag. Privately, he wished he'd listened to his brother.

"What's going on in there?" Rebecca's feeble voice came through her bedroom door.

"We're making soup, Mama," Adam said.

"Soup?" Rebecca said. "Let me get up to help you."

"No, Mama," Abraham said, slapping his hand over his brother's mouth. "Everything's fine. You rest."

"All right. I'll be up in a day or so. You're such a good boy, Abraham."

Abraham smiled. Adam stuck his tongue out and ended up licking Abraham's palm. "Eww!" Abraham made a furious face and wiped his hand on his trousers.

"Adam!" Rebecca Schlemiel warned. "Just because I can't see you doesn't mean I don't know you're up to something."

Adam threw his hands up in the air and snorted to himself. It's not fair! "Abraham, you're a Mama's boy."

"You could try a little harder," Abraham said. He took the stick and fished the stinky diaper out of the soup pot.

"Try harder? I go to school. I do my homework. I help in Papa's shop. I do Mama's chores…"

"Half of Mama's chores." Using a heavy towel, Abraham picked up the pot, lugged it to the door and poured the polluted water into the snow.

"Half shmaff. Plus I do all of my old chores. How could I possibly try any harder?"

"You could smile," Abraham said. He filled the pot with fresh snow and set the pot back on the stove. "You could not complain."

Adam sneered. "Saint Abraham the cheerful martyr."

"Hush. Don't say things like that." Abraham frowned as he picked up another soiled diaper and began scraping it off. "I'm just trying to do my best."

"You like it! You like cooking. You like cleaning. You probably even like changing Shemini's diapers."

"She giggles," Abraham said, smiling.

"You see. My point exactly. You're completely hopeless."

"Oh? And what should I do, sulk and mope and then mangle the job so badly that somebody else will have to come and do it over?"

"Exactly." Adam grinned. "And they'll eventually realize that they shouldn't have given you do that kind of a job in the first place."

"And I'm hopeless?" Abraham said. "You're the hopeless one." He poked Adam in the belly.

Adam poked Abraham back, and ten seconds later, they were rolling on the floor, punching and hitting each other like a pair of wild dogs.

"Take it back," Adam said, as he rolled on top of Abraham.

"Take what back?" Abraham said.

Adam paused, puzzled. "I don't even remember." He raised his fist.

"Boys, stop fighting!" Rebecca's thin voice wafted through the closed bedroom door. Her command was punctuated by a series of hacking coughs.

The twins leaped to their feet, brushed themselves off, and rushed into their parent's bedroom.

"Are you all right, Mama?" Abraham asked, hurrying to fluff up her pillows. Shemini was peacefully asleep beside her.

"Nothing happened," Adam said.

"Oh?" Rebecca coughed. "If nothing happened, then why is your nose bleeding?"

Adam felt his nose, saw the red drops on his fingers, and immediately passed out cold.

Abraham caught his brother before his head cracked on the floor, and wiped Adam's face with a clean rag.

"Mama, that's not fair," Abraham said. "You know that Adam can't stand the sight of his own blood."

"He needed a little rest." Rebecca took Abraham's hand. "You're a good boy, Abraham. You're smart. You work hard. You can do or be whatever you want. I just don't want you to get caught up in someone else's trouble. You know who I mean."

At first Abraham nodded. Then he shook his head. "No, Mama. Adam's a good boy, too."

Rebecca raised an eyebrow. "Good? Maybe. But he starts the trouble, and you take the blame. You think I don't know what's what? You're a good brother, Abraham. I just don't want to see you hurt."

Abraham shifted from one foot to the other. He had nothing to say.

"Okay. All right," Rebecca said. "I'll be quiet. I won't say another thing. I just want you to know I love you."

"I love you, too," Abraham said. He leaned down and kissed his mother's cheek. Shemini burped, and they both giggled.

On the floor, Adam stirred, opened his eyes. "What happened? Did I miss something?"

"Nothing we should mention," Rebecca said. "But I understand that you don't like your chores."

"No, Mama," Adam began, "that's not true."

"Don't lie," Rebecca said, sternly. "If you lie, your tongue might fall out. In any case, I think I have a solution. I've already talked this over with your Father, and he agrees with me."

The boys listened warily.

"Adam," she continued, "you will work exclusively with your father in the wood shop. Abraham, you will work only with me. And Adam, don't think that you're getting the easier job. Your father has a new order from Reb Cantor for more jewelry boxes. That's in addition to everything else you both have to do, going to school and so on. Until I get better, your father and I both think this is the best way."

"Yes, Mama," they both said.

When their father heard the news that they'd agreed, Jacob Schlemiel first giggled, then smirked, and finally jumped for joy. This made both Abraham and Adam very nervous. Their mother smiled, and for the first time in weeks, Rebecca actually got out of her sick bed. Then, to their dismay, their parents joined hands and danced around the house, until Rebecca, exhausted, collapsed into a deep but happy sleep.

The next morning, Abraham rose early, went to the well for water, and fixed breakfast. After saying his morning prayers, Jacob ate with Adam, while Abraham brought a dish of food into his mother's room. He came out just in time to say goodbye as his brother and father went off to work at the wood shop.

"Don't feel bad," Adam said, patting his brother on the shoulder.

"I don't feel bad," Abraham lied. "I know that Father is going to work you harder." He smiled. "Get going. I'll bring you lunch before we go to school."

Adam felt as if a huge weight had been lifted from his shoulders.

Abraham wasn't sure how he felt. He started scrubbing the dishes and cleaning up the mess his brother and father had made.

A few minutes later, he heard a soft voice from the other room. "Abraham…"

He ran in. "Yes, Mama? Is everything all right? Is there something I can get you?"

"No, nothing," Rebecca said. She took his hand. "You're a good boy, Abraham. You work hard. You're smart. You can do or be whatever you want. I just don't want you to get caught up in circumstances surrounding somebody else. You know who I mean?"

At first Abraham nodded. He had heard this speech before. Then he shook his head. "No, Mama. Adam's a good boy, too."

Rebecca raised an eyebrow. "Good? Maybe. But he starts the trouble, and you take the blame. You think I don't know what's what? You're a good brother, Abraham. I just don't want to see you hurt."

Abraham shifted from one foot to the other. He had nothing to say.

"Okay. All right," Rebecca said. "I'll be quiet. I won't say another thing. I just want you to know I love you. Your father told me that you're helping me at home. Thank you. "

"You're welcome," Abraham said. "I love you, too." He leaned down and kissed his mother's cheek. Shemini burped, and they both laughed and watched as she wiggled her tiny fingers.

Early One Morning

Weeks turned into months and soon spring was in the air. Even though Rebecca was growing stronger, she was still too weak to do more than hobble around and care for Shemini.

By now, Abraham realized it was possible that his mother might never fully recover. He was also surprised by how much he enjoyed keeping her and the baby company. He liked listening to her recipes, which were one part tradition and three parts whatever happened to be fresh at the market or old in the pantry. Even cleaning wasn't so bad as long as he stayed on top of things. Still, he missed feeling as if he was doing man's work. Every morning, while he watched Adam and their father leave the house, he felt a twinge of regret.

For his part, Adam was finding out that being the only carpenter's apprentice was no easy job. When Abraham had been in the shop there was always someone to laugh or joke with. Now, Adam was frequently left alone, and even when his father was around, he didn't have much good to say. Jacob was always criticizing Adam's craftsmanship, showing him what he'd done wrong and how to make it better. Adam tried and tried, but nothing he did seemed to be good enough.

Their parents noticed that the boys seemed troubled. Late one night Rebecca and Jacob stayed awake whispering, and the next morning, an hour before sunrise, there was a sharp rapping at the boys' bedroom door.

"Time to get up!" Jacob shouted.

"Rise and shine!" Rebecca cheerfully agreed. She poked her boys with the end of the stick she'd started to use as a cane.

Abraham and Adam groaned. "It's still night time."

"That's the best time to pick mushrooms," Rebecca said.

"And to find the dawn hardwood," Jacob added.

None of this made sense to the twins, who were barely awake. They got dressed with their eyes half-open, buttoned their overcoats, and stumbled out of the house into the chilly morning.

"G-goo!" Shemini chortled merrily. She was warmly bundled in a scarf beneath Rebecca's coat. Only her face was peeking out, enjoying the cool morning darkness.

Adam glared at his baby sister and then stubbed his toe and tripped over a rock. "Ow!"

"Goo-boom!" Shemini burbled.

"You hear that, Jacob?" Rebecca said. "She's talking already."

Everyone laughed except Adam, who limped for ten minutes until he forgot which foot was supposed to hurt.

The whole family headed north out of Chelm. They walked slowly, allowing Rebecca to set the pace. At the edge of the Schvartzvald, they separated. Jacob took Adam to the east, while Rebecca took Abraham and Shemini a little west into the forest and then south.

By now, Abraham was awake enough to ask his mother, "I didn't think mushrooms grew in winter."

Rebecca smiled. "They don't. Not generally, but I am going to take you to a secret hot spring that my mother showed me and her mother showed her. Even in the deepest of snow, the ground surrounding this spring is rich with mushrooms."

"But why do we have to go so early?"

"Because it's a secret." Rebecca's smile widened into a grin. "This is something special. We wouldn't want everyone in Chelm to know about such a treasure. Everyone knows that the Schlemiel family always has fresh mushrooms year round and they want to find out how such a thing is possible. But there are only so many mushrooms, and if everyone went to pick them soon there would be none left for us. So, we leave before dawn, we head in the wrong direction, circle around for a while to confuse any busybodies, and then as the first hints of the sunrise flicker through the trees, we pick only the best and only what we need. Always use a knife to cut the mushroom close to the ground so that you leave the root to grow another mushroom for our next visit. You understand?"

Abraham nodded, but only a fraction of what his mother said was sinking in.

"Never mind," Rebecca said. "Just remember that this is a precious secret, one that I am sharing with you and you alone."

Meanwhile, on the other side of the forest, half a dozen steps behind his father, Adam kept tripping over branches and stumbling over logs.

Papa, what is dawn hardwood?"

"Pfff," Jacob said, using the opportunity to catch his breath. "There's no such thing. I made it up."

"What?" Adam blinked. "I don't understand."

"Your mother was so gung-ho about getting you boys up and

out of the house early that I had to think of something."

"Then where are we going? And why are we in such a hurry?"

"Shh," Jacob said. "You'll see. Come along. We don't have much time."

Adam sighed, picked himself up, and reluctantly trudged along.

"Come! Come!" Jacob urged.

"I know where we are," Adam panted as he climbed. "This is East Hill."

"Two shekels for the boy with a sense of direction," Jacob said. He pulled Adam along. "Over there. Hurry."

"Why over there? Why not just right here?"

"Adam, do you trust me?" Jacob asked.

"No."

"Well, it's an honest answer at least. How about I tell you the same thing my father told me when he first brought me here." Jacob paused for a moment. Then he shouted, "If you don't move your lazy tuchas as fast as you can, I'm going to think of some horrible punishment and make you suffer for three days! Maybe four."

Adam sighed and hustled after his father. They came to a rough clearing where three fallen trees had been arranged in a triangle.

Jacob sat on one log, and Adam flopped down beside him.

"A triangle on top of a hill in the middle of a forest," Adam said. "Big deal."

"Shh," Jacob said. He reached into his coat and pulled out a small tin flask. "Have some of this and keep your mouth shut."

Adam opened the flask, took a good long draft, and gagged.

"Aaaaagh!" he said, spitting the burning liquid onto the ground. "What is that?"

"Potato vodka. Don't waste it!" Jacob said, grabbing the flask before any more could spill. "If you get cold, drink some. Otherwise, shut up. Listen."

"You're cheerful this morning," Adam mumbled.

Jacob poked him in the stomach with his elbow. "Shaa."

"All right, all right!"

"For the last time," Jacob hissed. "Be quiet!"

All right, all right, Adam said to himself. Maybe if I close my eyes I'll get a little rest… Just as he was beginning to doze off, Adam felt his father's elbow nudging him. His eyes shot open. "Wha!" he began, furious at being awakened, but his father quickly clamped his hand over Adam's mouth.

"Shhh."

Adam frowned, thought about biting his father's hand, and then decided to play it safe. A moment later, Jacob peeled his hand away and pointed.

There in the east, just creeping over the horizon, was the edge of the brightest reddest fireball Adam had ever seen. Although the sky had been getting brighter for some time, Adam found himself gaping in awe as bright flickers of red and orange flew across the snow-covered forest. The sky above was black and then blue and then orange and even purple. The few clouds shone like white silver. And then in a few minutes, or an instant, the red was gone and the world lived in all colors. Green and white and brown and blue…

"That was…" Adam began.

"Shh," Jacob whispered. "Wait. Listen."

So, Adam waited. Five, ten, maybe fifteen minutes passed. He began to fidget. Jacob passed him the flask.

Adam was about to take a sip when he heard a sharp twang. It was the sound of the snow melting. Of the trees breathing, of the ice breaking. It lasted for just a moment, rolling like thunder, in and then away.

And then the birds sang and the wind blew and the day was begun.

"Drink up," Jacob said, slapping his son on the back. "Now you know what they mean when they talk about the crack of dawn."

Adam smiled, took a long pull from the flask, coughed and sipped a little more.

Chapter Thirteen

Double Bar Mitzvah

When Mrs. Chaipul learned that Rabbi Yohon Abrahms, the schoolteacher, had begun tutoring Abraham and Adam Schlemiel for their bar mitzvahs, she shivered with delight.

A bar mitzvah was coming! And not just one, but a double!

In Chelm, bar mitzvahs are a big deal. It's a small village, so they aren't that frequent, and when one comes around, it's an excuse for a big party. On the first Saturday after a boy's thirteenth birthday he is called to read from the Torah, and then… food and dancing. Everyone in the village contributes. The music doesn't stop until the musicians can no longer play.

Mrs. Chaipul was already imagining the double – no, quadruple – layer cake she would bake, with butter cream frosting!

For their part, Abraham and Adam felt as if they were in the middle of a rising storm, as though a hurricane was building. All around them people were buzzing and whistling cheerfully.

One day, while Adam was hurrying to his bar mitzvah lesson, Rivka Cantor caught up and fell into step next to him.

"My mother is making me a beautiful dress for your bar mitzvah celebration," she said, chattering away.

He kept walking, trying to ignore her, but she jumped in front of him. "It's made of white silk, and it's absolutely lovely. If you'd like to come over and see the fabric, which came all the way from China, just say the word." Then she winked.

Adam just smiled, but he shuddered inside. Rivka Cantor, the merchant's youngest daughter, wasn't ugly. In fact, by most standards she was quite pretty, but there was something about her winking smile that made Adam think of a leering one-eyed lizard. He nodded, thanked her politely, and hurried on to his lesson.

As usual, Abraham had arrived at Rabbi Abrahms's house first. Also as usual, the rabbi scowled as Adam came in. So, Adam dropped into the uncomfortable chair next to the fire and sulked while the rabbi and Abraham went over Abraham's Torah portion in minute and exhausting detail.

It isn't fair, Adam thought. I was on time. I would have been. It's Abraham who comes early. Mother lets him out of the house while Father keeps me until the last minute. And then I couldn't just ignore Rivka Cantor, even if I had wanted to.

Adam stared into the fire and listened absently as the rabbi patiently showed Abraham just how to chant each and every phrase…

"It's time for you boys to go home."

Adam felt someone nudging his shoulder. He must have dozed off. He shook his head and blinked his eyes open. Rabbi Abrahms stood beside him, frowning as always.

"Go. Go! I have to see to my dinner," Rabbi Abrahms said.

"But my lesson…" Adam said.

"There isn't time today." Rabbi Abrahms shrugged. "Next week be early and we'll start with you."

Adam opened his mouth to argue and then closed it. What was the point? His father couldn't let him out early, wouldn't let him out early. At this rate he would never get a lesson. He pulled on his coat and joined Abraham, who was waiting outside the rabbi's door.

"I'm sorry," Abraham said.

"Oh, be quiet," Adam snapped. "I needed the nap anyway."

Abraham grinned. "So, what did Rivka Cantor have to say?"

Adam gave his brother a furious look. "Were you listening to my mind?"

"No," Abraham smiled. "I just happened to be looking out the rabbi's window. I saw her winking at you."

Adam got a solid punch into Abraham's shoulder before the two of them ended up tussling on the ground in the mud and the snow.

"Look at all this mud on our clothes," Abraham said while they sat catching their breaths. "Mama's going to kill us."

"Nonsense," Adam said. "She'll just blame me."

"Well, you did start it."

Adam looked at his brother. "Do you want to go another round? Now, get up and let's face our punishment – or should I say my punishment."

After dinner, Abraham was told to wash and dry their clothes while Adam was set to scrubbing and polishing the floor in Shemini's room until it was shiny enough to see his reflection.

So the weeks passed, the double bar mitzvah grew closer, and at last the big day came.

Just after breakfast, Rebecca Schlemiel inspected her boys for the last time. They looked so handsome in their new clothes – perfectly matched shirts, trousers, coats, socks, and shoes. Their mother smoothed their hair, kissed their cheeks, and smiled sadly. It took every ounce of her willpower not to burst into hysterical tears.

"You boys look good," Jacob Schlemiel said.

"You can't call us boys after today," Adam said.

"I know." Jacob nodded. He smiled, remembering the first time he had held Adam in his arms. Or was it Abraham?

Shemini, who was sitting up in her crib, said, "Bloooger!" and everyone laughed.

The Schlemiel family walked to the synagogue together. With one last kiss, Rebecca took Shemini upstairs to the women's balcony, while Jacob and his boys walked in the front door.

The sanctuary was packed. Everyone was there. They watched as the three Schlemiels made their way to the front and took the seats of honor between the rabbis.

For Abraham, it seemed like an eternity before Rabbi Kibbitz turned and called him to come and stand before the entire village to read from the Torah. He rose from his chair and took his place before the great scrolls of law.

For Adam it seemed like just a moment had passed. Had he dozed off again? He glanced up at the balcony and imagined he could see his mother looking down at him, so he moved his fingers in a little wave.

Then Abraham began to sing. His voice was loud and sweet, filling the synagogue with his chant.

Adam, with nothing better to do, found himself mouthing

along. He had heard Abraham's Torah portion so many times that he knew it by heart. He moved his lips in perfect time to Abraham's chant and even remembered to hesitate and make the little eyebrow shudder that Abraham always made when he came to a particularly difficult passage.

The congregation observed this strange performance with a stunned silence. While one boy sang, was the other mimicking him? On the bimah, Jacob couldn't see what was happening. In the balcony, Rebecca Schlemiel watched in horror with her hand clasped over her mouth.

Then Abraham was done, and there was a pause. Abraham shook hands all around and sat down next to his father, who put his hand on his son's knee and gave it a squeeze.

Then Rabbi Kibbitz turned to Adam with a kind smile.

Adam stood, walked confidently to the Torah, took a deep breath, looked down at the scroll, opened his mouth, and froze.

The words on the parchment looked like squiggles. Completely meaningless. He stared. With a book at least there were pages and page numbers. Where was he supposed to begin?

Rabbi Kibbitz, who had led generations of boys through countless bar mitzvahs, took the pointer and aimed its finger directly at the word where Adam was to begin.

Still, nothing came. Even after he heard Rabbi Kibbitz begin whispering the opening passage, his mind remained a blank. Adam knew Hebrew, he knew Yiddish, and German, some Russian, some Polish, but his brain was empty of words. If someone had told him that the fate of the world hung on his recitation, he would have had to admit that the world was doomed. His eyes darted back and forth, but nothing came.

At last, Adam Schlemiel did the only thing he could think of. He took a deep breath and began chanting Abraham's Torah portion. He sang it word for word and note for note. He even remembered to hesitate and make the little eyebrow shudder.

And when he was done, there was silence in the shul. Dead silence. Then a prayer book rustled. Whispers began.

Adam turned to slink back to his seat, but Rabbi Kibbitz

stopped him.

"You were supposed to read from the Torah," Rabbi Kibbitz said loudly. He paused, squinting at Adam. "And you read from the Torah! Mazel Tov!" Then he shook Adam's hand vigorously.

"Mazel tov!" the entire village of Chelm shouted.

Abraham jumped up from his chair, gave his brother a big hug, and the party began.

Chapter Fourteen

Bad News

"Boys, wake up. I've got some bad news."

Adam and Abraham blinked their eyes slowly open. It was the morning after their bar mitzvahs, and their father was standing over their bed, somberly looking down at them.

"Is Mama all right?" Abraham asked.

"Oh, yes," Jacob said. "She's fine. This isn't about anybody sick or dying. In some ways it's worse."

Worse than sick or dying? The boys sat up. What could be worse than sick or dying? Torture, imprisonment? Mrs. Chaipul's potato latkes?

"What is it, Father?" Adam asked.

Jacob Schlemiel shook his head. "Not here. We need to go somewhere else. Get dressed. I'll pack some breakfast."

The boys looked out the window. It was still dark outside. Their heads hurt.

Their bar mitzvah was only yesterday. The party had lasted late into the night, or was it early into the morning? Who knew? They had danced and ate and drank and then danced some more.

Adam grinned at Abraham as they pulled on their pants.

It had been some fun. They had stayed on even after Rebecca had taken Shemini back home, even after their father had said that he was leaving. After that, the party had gotten even wilder, as the younger men in the village told stories that made them blush even now. In fact, now that they took a moment to think about it, neither of them could remember exactly how they got home…

Abraham grinned back at Adam. Yesterday they were boys, and today they were men.

Of course, they had expected to sleep late this morning – at least until dawn.

"What do you think he's going to tell us?" Abraham asked Adam.

"If I knew I wouldn't be getting out of bed," Adam said. "He probably wants us to cut down some tree and drag it half way to Moscow."

Abraham looked puzzled. "Why would he do that?"

"I don't know. I'm barely awake."

Together they went into the kitchen, where Jacob Schlemiel was wrapping half a loaf of brown bread and a big chunk of cheese in a towel. "Get me a knife, would you?"

"Are we cutting down a tree?" Abraham asked, as he found a kitchen knife and wrapped it in another towel.

"A tree?" Jacob's face took on exactly the same puzzled expression as Abraham's had. "Why would we be cutting down a tree?"

"It was Adam's idea."

"Adam? Why do you say such a thing?"

Adam frowned. If their father hadn't been watching, Adam would have punched his brother. "I don't know. It was the stupidest thing I could imagine doing before dawn. I don't know why I said it. Forget it!"

Jacob shook his head. "It's happening already."

"What?" Adam said.

"Let's go." Jacob and his sons went out the door, careful not to let it slam behind them.

In her bedroom, Rebecca Schlemiel heard the door creak open and then shut. She hoped the boys would take the news well. Then she coughed, covering her mouth so she wouldn't disturb Shemini.

The Curse of the Schlemiel

By the light of the half moon, Jacob Schlemiel led his boys through Chelm's darkened streets. They passed by the round market square, where the single street light burned, and headed north through the farmlands.

It was early springtime, with some days above freezing and others just below, so the ground was treacherous with mud and ice. For a long time they didn't talk. Every so often, Jacob cursed as his foot slid into a deep puddle or a pool of slush. The boys were lighter and more careful, but by the time they reached the edge of the Schvartzvald, their boots were soaked and their trousers were muddy up to the knees.

"Welcome to manhood," Adam muttered.

"It's like being in the Russian army," Abraham agreed. "Do you have any idea where we are going?"

Adam nodded. "Actually, I do."

"Really?"

"But I'm not going to tell you."

"You don't know," Abraham said. "You don't really know."

"Oh, yes I do," Adam said with a teasing lilt.

"Stop bickering!" their father ordered.

"Yes, Papa," Abraham said.

"I do, I do, I do," Adam hummed.

"Do not, do not," Abraham hummed back.

"I can hear you boys," Jacob said, without turning around.

"We're not boys any more," Adam said. "We're men."

"All right, then act like men and be still."

Adam pursed his lips. If being a man was all about not teasing your brother – especially when you actually did know where you were going – he wasn't sure he liked it so much.

"We're going to East Hill," Adam said as they began climbing up the gentle slope that led to one of the two hills north of Chelm.

"I can see that," Abraham said. "It doesn't take a genius to figure that out when you're climbing the hill."

Adam frowned. "At the top of the hill is a triangle of logs. We're going to sit there and drink vodka until the sun rises."

"Oh, really?" Abraham said.

"Don't believe me then."

The three men climbed in silence until they reached the clearing at the top of East Hill. There, as Adam had predicted, were the three logs in the shape of the triangle. Panting, Jacob sat down on the east-facing log. He reached under his coat and removed a flask. After taking a drink, he offered it to Adam.

"Told you," Adam said, sticking out his tongue at Abraham.

Jacob scowled. "This isn't funny. You're not boys any more."

"Papa," Adam began, but a look at Jacob's face told him that he'd better not go on. He took a drink from the flask and then made a face. "What is this?"

"Strong tea," Jacob said, smiling just a little. "You were maybe expecting vodka? This is sober business, Adam, not fun and games."

Adam passed the flask to Abraham, who covertly stuck the tip of his tongue out and then covered the move by taking a long drink of tea.

When Abraham was done, Jacob took the flask, drank, and screwed on the top.

He sighed and peered at their faces. They were still so young. They didn't look any different from yesterday, and yet…

"Boys," he said at last. Then he corrected himself. "Young men," he paused, "it is time for you to learn the true meaning of being a Schlemiel."

"It's the family name," Abraham said. "Right?"

Jacob nodded, and then he shook his head. "It's much worse than that. Much, much worse…" Jacob Schlemiel took a deep breath and then sighed. "So, you wonder, what is the true meaning of the name Schlemiel?"

His children yawned deeply.

"What, you're bored already?" he said. "I haven't even started, and already I'm putting you to sleep? You don't want I should tell you about the great Schlemiels throughout history? About Libby Schlemiel and the Egyptians? Judah Schlemiel and the lion? About Samson Schlemiel and the bald barber? No?"

"Papa," the twins protested. "We had a late night. It's barely daylight."

Jacob raised his hands. "I know. I know. History is boring. Bad news. You're young. You think that there is nothing to learn from the mistakes of the past. Still, what I have to say to you is important. Vital, you might say, to your future. And you need to know it now because it is the bar mitzvah that activates the Curse of the Schlemiel. But if you don't want to hear it, go ahead. Take a nap."

"Papa? A curse? What is it? Please. Please tell us."

And so, Jacob Schlemiel began…

No one knows the origin of the Curse of the Schlemiel. Some say that it is as old as the world itself, that ancient biblical figures such as Cain and Esau were among the original Schlemiels.

Others claim that the first Schlemiel was a fellow named Libby, a friend of Moses, who, as the Israelites fled dry-shod across the Red Sea, decided that his feet had gotten a little too dirty. Just as the Almighty unleashed the flood on the Egyptians, Libby Schlemiel paused to clean off his toes. Naturally this poor Schlemiel was caught in the deluge and washed downstream. The Hebrews wandered in the desert for forty years, eating manna from heaven while following a pillar of fire by day and a pillar of smoke by night. Libby Schlemiel, however, went the other way. For forty years he ate nothing but bugs and weeds and was pursued by pillars of fire and smoke. He wasn't the brightest of fellows. At last, decrepit and dying, he was stumbled upon by a group of Hebrew scouts and brought before Moses.

"You look good," Libby told his friend Moses. "What have you been up to?"

Moses told Libby about his journey to Sinai, about the Golden Calf, about the giving of the Law…

"And what have you been doing all these years?" Moses asked his friend.

Libby smiled and patted Moses on the knee. "I've been looking for you. And I'm glad I found you."

Moses stared in amazement at his long-lost friend and shouted, "You couldn't turn around and figure it out? There's a pillar of smoke and a pillar of fire pointing straight to our camp. Would it have killed you to follow directions?"

But it was too late. Libby Schlemiel had happily closed his eyes and breathed his last.

"That's not true," Adam said.

Abraham laughed nervously. "Papa, I never heard that story before."

Jacob Schlemiel shrugged. "It's family history. Legend if you will. I don't know if it's true, but it is a perfect example of the curse."

"You're making us nervous," Abraham said.

Jacob nodded. "I know. You ought to be. As children, you were protected, but now that you are men…" Jacob shook his head sadly. "It's going to start. Better you should know, not that it will do you much good, but at least perhaps you won't take it all so personally."

Jacob took a long drink of tea from his flask and stared out at the red dawn rising in the east.

Adam jumped to his feet, tripped over a branch, and fell to the ground with a thud.

"You see?" Jacob said. "It's right on schedule."

Adam got up and brushed himself off. "Nonsense," he said. "Ridiculous. I fall all the time. Now you're saying that I fall down because we're cursed? That there's some mystical magical hoo-ha that causes bad things to happen to our family?"

"Not to our family," Jacob said. "Just to the people in it. The men mostly."

"That's silly!" Adam shouted. "That's the most foolish thing I've ever heard."

"Shh," Abraham said, taking his brother's hand. "Calm down."

Adam shook himself free. "I can't believe you're listening to this as if it's real."

"I've heard the whispers," Abraham said softly. Jacob nodded.

"What whispers?" Adam asked.

"People talk," Abraham said. "They think that the children aren't listening or can't understand, so they say things."

"What kind of things?"

"That I'm lucky for a Schlemiel," Abraham said. "That they were amazed that a couple of Schlemiels could capture the Krabot gang."

"Yes," Jacob said. "That one surprised me, too."

"I don't understand," Adam said, pacing back and forth inside the triangle of logs. "There is nothing wrong with me. There's nothing wrong with you. And aside from this legendary nonsense there is nothing wrong with our father. Why shouldn't we capture the Krabot gang? Why shouldn't we be lucky?"

Abraham stayed silent.

"What can I say?" Jacob asked. "It's a curse!"

"Curse shmurse," Adam snorted. "It's a silly story to scare children. I'm not a child anymore."

"No, you're not," Jacob said. "You're an adult now, old enough to start your own family and old enough to know the story of your family. Now, are you awake enough to listen? Will you sit down?"

Adam stared at his father. His nostrils flared, and he slowly sat back down.

"All right," Adam said. "So, talk."

Jacob Schlemiel took a sip of tea, licked his lips, and began. "You think I'm an old fool trying to scare his children with nonsense?"

Adam and Abraham both cautiously nodded their heads.

"Feh," Jacob said. "The curse is not just a silly fable. The Schlemiels are not like other families. Maybe it's just bad luck, but I don't think so. It seems inescapable… You doubt me?"

"Yes," Adam said. "I do. Frankly, I expected some sort of fatherly talk, but not this."

"And you?" Jacob looked at Abraham. "You think your father ought to be dispensing words of wisdom?"

Abraham winced and then nodded.

"All right," Jacob shrugged. "Fine. One more story, and then I'll give you my wisdom. You think you can sit still long enough?"

A Schlemiel Grows in Brooklyn

"My father's older brother, Shmuel, decided that his future lay in America. It was said in those days that the streets of America were paved with gold. Uncle Shmuel left Chelm when he was sixteen and it only took him seven years to arrive in New York. At last his ship came in and he saw the miraculous Statue of Liberty holding her torch high....

The immigration official asked for his name and then laughed. Shmuel Schlemiel? He couldn't even pronounce it. So he wrote something else down on the paper, "Samuel Samuels." Of course he didn't bother to tell my Uncle Shmuel, who couldn't read English. Instead, he just slapped him on the back and sent him on a ferry boat.

As he got off the ferry, Uncle Shmuel bent over because he thought he saw a gold coin. The fellow behind him gave Shmuel a kick in the tuchas and the poor man went flying.

"Welcome to Brooklyn!" everybody laughed.

The streets in America were not paved with gold. I learned all this because my father read us the letters Uncle Shmuel wrote. The streets were made of stone and mud. There were so many houses that the sewers would overflow regularly, and in the summertime the whole city smelled like a stable, or worse.

Brooklyn, as it turned out, was across a wide river from another city called Manhattan. The day after Uncle Shmuel arrived he saw an opportunity, and he seized it.

He was walking along the banks of the river when he realized that a bridge connecting Brooklyn to Manhattan would make its owner a fortune. Even better, such a bridge was already under construction. It was a beautiful bridge, made of stone and hung from cables. Uncle Shmuel hurried toward it, admiring the ingenuity.

He asked who the owner was. No one understood a word he said. At last, he found a kind man who spoke Polish. This man told him that the bridge was in fact for sale. Best of all, the price was good because it had been on the market for so long. Coincidentally, Uncle Shmuel had just enough in his pockets to buy the bridge. He gave the kind man every copper and gold coin that he had.

The man slapped him on the back. "How does it feel to be the first man to buy the Brooklyn Bridge?

"Not bad," Uncle Shmuel answered.

The stranger said he'd be right back with the deed. By the time night fell, Uncle Shmuel had begun to wonder if the kind man had gotten lost.

Fortunately, Uncle Shmuel had taken a room nearby and paid a month's rent in advance. For three weeks, he walked to the bridge every morning and waited patiently. At last, he went to the police and explained his predicament. He told them he was afraid that the kind man had been robbed because of the enormous sum of money and might be lying somewhere dead or dying. Uncle Shmuel couldn't imagine what the translator and police sergeant found so funny. Finally, they told him he had better find some way of getting more money to pay for food and shelter before winter came, and he was thrown into the streets as a pauper.

Everyone from Chelm knows about poverty, so that didn't frighten Uncle Shmuel. Still, he thought the advice was sound. He went to his bridge and signed on as a laborer. Every day he went to work, and he worked hard. Weeks and months passed. His landlady began to worry because the poor man was wasting away from a lack of nutrition and he hadn't even paid his rent.

"Don't you have a job?" she asked.

"Of course," he said proudly. "I am self-employed as a worker on my own bridge."

"If you work on the bridge," the landlady asked, "where is your pay?"

"I don't know," Uncle Shmuel said. "Every week, I wait but they never call my name."

The landlady took pity on Uncle Shmuel and went with him on the next pay day. When the foreman called out, "Samuel Samuels!" the landlady looked at my uncle. He smiled at her, but he made no move to claim his pay.

"That's your name!" she said.

"Nonsense," my uncle said. "I'm Shmuel Schlemiel."

"You're an idiot," she told my uncle. Dragging him along by his ear, she pulled him to the front of the line and demanded not only that week's pay, but also all of his back pay. Even after she and the foreman had split half of what he'd earned, Uncle Shmuel found himself once again a very wealthy man. He thanked his landlady, quit his job, and

strolled with confidence across the nearly completed bridge. When at last he reached Manhattan, who did he find but the kind stranger!

"Where have you been?" my uncle asked, embracing the stranger. "I thought you were dead."

Well, the stranger explained, there was a problem. The money my uncle had given him had only been enough to purchase the Brooklyn side of the bridge, not the Manhattan side.

Once again, Uncle Shmuel happily gave the kind man every dollar in his pocket. And once again the man promised to return shortly with the deed.

Uncle Shmuel didn't bother to wait this time. He went back to Brooklyn and the next day begged for his job back. They gave it to him at half his old salary, and he lived happily. He worked hard and eventually met and married my Aunt Sarah, who demanded that he stop making payments on the bridge. Better to be a partial owner and save some money, Aunt Sarah said, than to own the whole thing and be bankrupt.

So, every week, when the foreman called out, "Samuel Samuels," Uncle Shmuel collected his pay and said, "Call me Schlemiel!"

And every week, they all did.

"Words of wisdom you want from me?" Jacob Schlemiel asked his sons. "Here is what I have – listen carefully for your name."

Abraham and Adam waited for more.

"That's it," Jacob said with a shrug. "I'm not a very wise man. Let's go home before we miss lunch."

Chapter Fifteen

The Prank

Abraham and Adam didn't have much of a chance to talk about their father's strange warning after they got back from the woods. By the time they reached the village, they were already two hours late to school, and then there were chores at home for Abraham and work in the shop for Adam. Plus, they were still suffering from their late night bar mitzvah celebrations. By the end of that very long day they were exhausted.

Lying in bed, Adam whispered, "Abraham? Abraham? Are you awake?"

"Hfm? I'm asleep."

"Do you believe what Father told us? Do you think that we're doomed to be failures?"

"Mmmm. No."

"I don't either. We need to do something about it."

"That's nice," Abraham mumbled.

"A prank," Adam said. "A nice solid prank. Something glorious that people will talk about for years. If we come up with something good, you'll go along, right?"

"Mmm hmm."

Abraham was fast asleep, but Adam stayed awake late that night thinking, and by dawn he had what he thought was a pretty good plan.

He explained it to Abraham as they walked to school the next day. A light snow was falling, and Abraham listened to his brother's idea with growing disbelief.

"You want the King of Poland to come to Chelm?" Abraham said. "Why?"

"Or the Czar of Russia," Adam said. "I don't care which. But it won't be the real king or czar."

"You want a fake king…"

"Or czar."

"… or czar to come to Chelm? And then what? I don't understand."

Adam hopped in front of his brother and stopped. "Just picture this. It's a cold winter morning. Or maybe early spring time. There are birds in the trees, the flowers are just beginning to bud, and throughout all of Chelm there is only one topic of conversation. The Czar is coming. When is he coming? Nobody knows. Is it this week? Is it next week? Did we miss him somehow? What are we going to serve him for lunch?

"Everyone will buy new clothes and wear them all the time. There will be a vote to clean up the streets and paint the houses.

"At last, word comes that the Czar will arrive on Friday afternoon, just before sunset. This causes great consternation because of the conflict with the Sabbath. But the Czar is the czar. If the people of Chelm don't show him proper respect then who knows what will happen?"

Abraham shook his head. "And this is supposed to be funny?"

"It's a prank," Adam said. "It's not funny, it's profound. It's like looking at a chicken and discovering that it's really a horse."

"Chickens are never horses," Abraham said, stepping around Adam and resuming his walk.

"No, but imagine if you looked at a chicken for a day or so and suddenly realized that it wasn't a chicken at all, but a horse. How would that feel? Now, imagine being the young men who managed to convince everyone that the horse was really a chicken. That is something that would be talked about for years to come!"

"I think," Abraham stared at his brother, "that the Curse of the Schlemiels has already started messing with you."

"No, listen! This is funny!" Adam hustled after Abraham. "So, we don't do it on the Sabbath. Fine. Another day. Any day. It doesn't matter, because the Czar is never going to come."

"But if the Czar never comes," Abraham said, "how can we convince everybody he's a chicken?"

"Idiot!" Adam said. "The Czar's not the chicken, he's the horse. They just think he's the chicken. But he doesn't exist. Not in Chelm anyway."

Abraham blinked. "That is so much clearer now. Thank you for explaining it to me."

They had arrived at the back door to the synagogue. Abraham smiled, opened the door, and went inside. Adam threw his hands up in the air, stomped his feet in the snow three times, and followed his brother. "Wait, Abraham. It makes perfect sense…"

"Late again, Adam," Rabbi Yohon Abrahms said. "I would have thought that your bar mitzvah would have taught you the value of being on time."

The whole class laughed. Adam found his face turning red.

"How is it possible," he sputtered, "that I am late but Abraham is on time?"

The rabbi looked at his pocket watch and shrugged. "A fact is a fact. Before the hour you are on time, and after the hour you are late. It's only the matter of a few seconds, but it is a crucial distinction. It's like circumcision – there isn't much to cut off, but that little bit makes all the difference in the world."

Again the class laughed, and Adam turned even brighter red.

"Take a seat. This is as good a place as any to start our lesson. Who of the younger students remembers where in the Torah the Almighty pledges the covenant through the bris?"

At supper time, as they walked home through three inches of new snow, Adam began again. "We can do this, you know. To create an idea in the mind, all it takes are a few well-placed words. A little bit of evidence here and there."

"But I think you're going to have to decide," Abraham giggled, "whether the Czar is going to be a chicken or a horse."

"Forget about the horse and the chicken!" Adam said hotly. "It's like a magician showing you a coin and then making it vanish."

"Oh, so now you're going to kidnap the Czar of Russia?"

"NO!" Adam shouted. "I'm not going to kidnap anyone. He's never going to be here, but everyone is going to think he is."

So involved in his explanation was Adam that he didn't notice

Abraham bending down, picking up a large handful of snow, and patting it gently into a firm ball.

"Look over there." Abraham pointed. "It's the King of Poland!"

"Where?" Adam's head swiveled.

This is too easy, Abraham thought to himself, as he fired the snowball into the back of Adam's head.

"You!!" Adam roared.

The race was on, and by the time the boys reached their house their coats were soaking wet and their fingers were blue from cold.

When Rebecca Schlemiel opened the door to find her two sons, half-frozen with their teeth chattering, she shook her head, chuckled, and said, "I bet you're glad that I made chicken soup."

"I'm just glad it's not horse soup," Abraham said. Their mother looked puzzled and Adam scowled as the two boys hurried inside to get warm.

Grrrr

Weeks passed, and then months. Nothing changed. Nothing happened.

It wasn't that life in the village was boring. Far from it. One day the baker's oven would catch on fire, the next month a farmer would find a goat on his roof, eating the thatch. All right, so it was boring. Every day was pretty much like the rest.

And for Adam Schlemiel, life in Chelm seemed twice as boring.

Every day was pretty much like the next. Every morning Adam and Abraham woke at dawn and said their prayers. Then there were the morning chores. Abraham's primary job was still helping around the house. Adam, who did his work in Jacob Schlemiel's wood shop, needed to shovel a path to the shop, light the fire, and tidy up the previous day's mess. Then it was time for school, then lunch, then back for their afternoon chores, then late afternoon prayers, dinner, and bed.

Adam couldn't stand it. Everything was always the same. Only the Sabbath was different. On the Sabbath, instead of work, there were prayers and walks and readings and long discussions about all the important issues of the past thousand years. Adam wasn't sure which he dreaded more, going to work in the morning or staying up late listening to his father, Reb Cantor, and Rabbi Kibbitz argue about which came first: the chicken or the egg, the matzah ball or the matzah ball soup.

It was an exhausting and mundane life. And what was there to look forward to next week, next month, next year? More of the same.

No wonder Adam plotted and planned. Small surprise that an impish glint entered his eyes every time he imagined his prank. The only thing that kept him sane was his prank. It wasn't an idle fantasy. He knew the prank could happen because he had a model. History was on his side.

You see, in Chelm, the villagers still spoke in somber tones of the day two-hundred years ago that the Governor of Warsaw had visited Smyrna. Not only visited, but nearly died in the marketplace! A cabbage had rolled down the street. The Governor's horse had shied and the Governor had plunged to the ground. "Whose cabbage is this?" cried the mud-soaked Governor. A meek voice admitted ownership. "And where are you from?" roared the great man. Chelm, of course. And that was how the infamous cabbage tax had fallen on the poor and innocent village.

In Adam's mind, a visit to Chelm by the Czar of Russia would be spoken of until the end of time!

Unfortunately, the prank was still in the dream stages. Nothing was happening yet. The whole process was taking longer than he'd expected. He just couldn't figure out the details. Adam was both overworked and easily distracted. Between the business of his father's shop, his studies in school, meals, and prayers at shul there was barely a moment to think, let alone formulate a coherent plan.

Winter snow became spring mud. The mud solidified and the flowers bloomed. The Schlemiel twins' fourteenth birthday came and went. Crops grew, the harvest was gathered, and again snow fell.

Every so often, Abraham would tease his brother. "So, when are the king and the czar coming to visit?"

Adam would frown or snarl or growl. The truth was, he didn't know how he was going to make it happen.

"What?" Abraham would say, "I thought that the rulers of Russia and Poland kept you fully appraised of all their travel plans."

"Grrrr," Adam would answer.

Then Abraham would laugh.

Adam scowled. Didn't Abraham understand? A prank like this wasn't as simple as putting a bucket over a door. It was maddening. And yet, where did one begin to start on a project of such overwhelming magnitude?

Meanwhile, in the Schlemiel household, all was not well. In fact, things seemed to be getting worse.

Although little Shemini was now two years old, Rebecca Schlemiel had not fully recovered from the girl's strenuous eight-day birthing. Their mother still had a smile as lovely as an upside down rainbow, but her glow wasn't quite as strong, and her coughs grew louder and more frequent.

"That's too much salt in the soup!" she would shout from her bedroom. Abraham would jump in the air, put down the salt cellar and wonder how his mother could see through walls.

"But…" he'd sputter.

"Just put some more water into the broth," she'd say.

Jacob was also worried about his wife. If it had only been himself and the boys it would have been easier, but with the little girl running around like an eager mouse always underfoot, he became more and more concerned. He would spend long hours by his beloved wife's side, holding her hand, and whispering the gossip of Chelm.

His father's absences kept Adam even busier in the shop, taking orders and paying bills.

One day, Adam was trying to make sense of a nearly unreadable blueprint. When his father finally came in, he asked, "Is this supposed to be a bed or a bureau?"

Jacob Schlemiel turned the paper around. The design was a

rocking horse for Shemini. A rocking horse?

That was the last straw! Adam tore off his apron and slammed out of the shop.

"The boy is crazy," Jacob said, shaking his head sadly.

Abraham saw his brother stampeding through the round village square and called, "So, Adam, the King of Poland is coming when?"

"SOON!" Adam yelled back. "And maybe the Czar himself is coming too!"

Everyone in the square heard Adam Schlemiel's shout.

The questions began almost immediately.

"The Czar?"

"Coming?"

"Here?"

"To Chelm?"

"Soon? Really? How soon?"

The rumor began spreading like the belly of a fat man at a wedding feast.

But by then Adam was gone, stomping across a rye field into the forest, where he half-seriously considered drowning himself in the Uherka River. Fortunately, the flow was low, and the river bottom was mostly frozen dirt. Adam stared into the muck and wondered what it would feel like to breathe in mud. He could become mud. Baah. He kept walking.

Back in the square, Abraham was surprised to hear all the villagers buzzing excitedly about the Czar's upcoming visit. He was about to explain that no, there was no such thing as the Czar coming to Chelm, when he realized that maybe Adam's plan might work.

"Did you hear?" Reb Shikker caught up with Abraham at the well. "The Czar of Russia is coming to Chelm next spring!"

"No! Really?" Abraham said, hoping that the grin he was trying to hide would look like surprise.

"Yes," Reb Shikker said. "And he's bringing an elephant with him!"

"An elephant!" Abraham laughed. "You're not serious?"

Reb Shikker raised his hand. "On my mother's grave – may she live a long life."

"That's strange," Abraham said.

"What's strange?"

"You know what I heard?" Abraham looked both ways and then spoke in a low whisper. "I heard that it's not the Czar, but the King of Poland."

"Now that's foolish," Reb Shikker said. "What would the King of Poland be doing in Chelm with the Czar's elephant?"

"He borrowed it so that he could visit Chelm," Abraham said quite seriously.

"Oh!" Reb Shikker's eyes widened. "Now, that makes perfect sense. I have to tell my wife. She's a big fan of the King of Poland." And off he hurried so quickly that he forgot to pretend he was drunk.

Abraham laughed so hard he nearly dropped the water bucket back into the well. He could hardly wait to tell Adam.

He was about to run across the square, but he changed his mind.

Mama needed that water right away, and Adam wasn't in the shop anyway.

Abraham lifted the yoke with its twin buckets, and grinned as he walked home. He wondered if he might be able to play Adam's prank on Adam…

Guess Who's Coming to the Village

Rumors in any small village, and especially in Chelm, are like the fruit of a ripe cherry tree. One takes a taste, and it's so sweet and delectable that you have to tell someone else, and soon everyone is savoring the flavorful fruit.

Reb Shikker told his wife he'd heard that the King of Poland was coming, but she was hard of hearing and thought he said the King of Prussia. Worse still, she had a bad memory, so when she mentioned the gossip to Mrs. Chaipul, she said that her husband had told her that the King of Persia planned to fly into town on a magic carpet, or some such nonsense.

"Ridiculous," Mrs. Chaipul said. "First of all, if carpets could fly, do you think anyone would buy a horse? Second, I heard from a very reliable source that it's actually the Emperor of China who will be visiting us in disguise!"

"Disguise?" Mrs. Shikker shouted back. "How will we know he's the Emperor?"

"He'll be wearing a fur hat," Mrs. Chaipul said, tapping her nose knowingly.

"But it's winter. Every cart driver from Berlin to Siberia wears a fur hat," Mrs. Shikker reasoned.

"That," Mrs. Chaipul said, "is why it's such a good disguise."

Within a day, everyone in Chelm knew that someone was coming. By Thursday, it was generally agreed that the important visitor would arrive some time in the late spring, just after the last snow had melted, but before Passover.

"What if it snows on Passover?" one child was heard to ask her father.

"Hush," the father answered. "The President of America always knows the weather. Why I've read that he is so wise he changes his policies depending on which way the wind blows."

The youngster was suitably impressed.

Less than a month later, word reached Smyrna, and there the question was, "Why would anybody of importance visit Chelm?"

"You want to know why?" asked Esther Gold, the cobbler's wife, who was in Smyrna to buy shoe leather. "Exactly because no one of importance has ever visited Chelm before."

The shopkeepers glanced at each other and nodded. "And the funny thing is," they said, "that makes perfect sense to someone from Chelm."

Although outsiders continued to laugh, in Chelm preparations began and plans were made. After all, it was wintertime, when the snow was shoulder high and a careless sneeze froze before it hit the ground. What else was there to do?

Rabbi Kibbitz began writing a speech. Reb Stein, the baker,

pored through recipe books for the perfect bread. Mrs. Chaipul wondered if the social hall would be big enough to hold all of the Emperor's horses and half the Emperor's men.

Reb Cantor, the merchant, nearly went mad wondering which of two dozen kings, princes, czars, or presidents he would be discussing trade agreements with. And what if they all came? Then perhaps Chelm would become a center of commerce, a hub, with caravans passing through on their way to Cairo or from Sicily. And who would become the most important businessman in the world? Why the ever-modest Reb Cantor himself! It was all so exciting that he was bedridden for a week, and after that he began a furious study of Hindustani languages, going on a hunch that the mysterious guest would be a Rajah from the Indian subcontinent.

Even in the Schlemiel household the question was raised late at night after the children were asleep.

"You should build something special." Rebecca nudged her husband. "Something wonderful."

"What can I make," Jacob asked his wife, "that any king will not have a million better?"

"A clock perhaps." Rebecca smiled.

"Again with the clocks!" Jacob Schlemiel buried his head under his pillow until he fell asleep, dreaming of a pocket watch the size of a horse carriage. He woke himself up, jotted down the plans, and returned to sleep with a contented smile. In the morning, however, he was disappointed to discover that he had written the following: "Corned beef and onions. Bury it far from the ocean. Tell Rebecca my left nostril is orange. Borscht." He then spent the remainder of the morning peering into a mirror trying to tell whether his nostril really was orange or if it was just the light.

With all this hubbub and commotion, it seems almost inconceivable that Adam Schlemiel would have no idea of the trouble he had started. Yet, he remained ignorant.

Of course, Abraham didn't tell his brother what their shouted conversation in the marketplace had begun. And no one else in Chelm had any reason to talk with the carpenter's youngest son about the impending arrival.

All around Adam, the villagers were excited. People were talking, whispering, sometimes shouting with anticipation. In all the centuries that Chelm had existed, nestled in its small valley, nothing so momentous or significant had ever happened in Chelm. Nor was it likely to happen again. This was probably going to be the single most important event in the history of Chelm. It would be in the newspapers. Books would be written. And, finally, perhaps those know-it-alls in Smyrna would wipe the grins off their faces.

Oblivious, Adam Schlemiel went about his business. He worked hard in his father's shop, studied as diligently as he could at school, and tried to figure out some way to bring the Czar of Russia or the King of Poland to Chelm. He kept a thick bundle of papers on which he jotted each new idea.

And, every evening, after Adam fell asleep, Abraham leafed through his brother's plans and giggled softly to himself.

Macarooned

Young Rivka Cantor had had her eye on Adam Schlemiel for years. Even though she was fourteen and Adam was just shy of fifteen, Rivka didn't think it was too early to begin planting the seeds for matrimony in the poor boy's head. But she had to be subtle about it. Her father was the richest man in Chelm, and if he had his way, he'd marry her off to some importer from Warsaw as part of a trade deal. Still, her father did have a soft spot for the Schlemiel boys, whom he thought were both handsome and heroic. Perhaps if Adam presented the case himself (or even better conspired with a yenta to make the match in secret) then her father could hardly object.

Unfortunately, so far Rivka's plans were all for naught. Every time she spoke with Adam, his face turned bright red, he stuttered, and ran off as soon as he could come up with a polite excuse. Her best friend, Rachel Cohen, assured Rivka that those were signs of true love. All Rivka needed to do was be persistent, keep calm, and above all keep herself in Adam's mind. Don't throw yourself after him, Rachel warned. Just feed him food and laugh at his jokes.

A perfect opportunity presented itself when Adam came to her father's house to collect a long overdue bill. Rivka snatched a platter of cookies from the kitchen and, as if by chance, passed through the sitting room.

"Adam Schlemiel!" she said. "What a wonderful surprise. Would you like a macaroon?"

"Yes, thank you," Adam said. He took two.

Rivka giggled. "What brings you to our fine home?"

"Business." Adam blushed. "It's about the chest your father commissioned us to make for the regional governor two years ago."

"Why don't you have a seat and tell me about it?"

"Well," Adam began, "you would think that the merchant would have the decency to pay a hard-working craftsman on time."

"As I understand it," Rivka said, smiling, "the chest was never inspected by my father. When it was inspected, it was only after a gaping hole had been blown in the lid by the robber Krabot. And my father told me he never formally took receipt of the chest. It was confiscated by the regional police inspector, was it not? We never even heard if it was received by the governor."

Adam's mouth dropped open and a few crumbs fell on the Persian carpet.

"Not that I ever pay attention to my father's business," Rivka added quickly.

"But we did the work! Is it our fault that it became a piece of state's evidence?"

"And is it our fault," Rivka asked, "that the Schlemiel boys never showed up at the trial to claim the evidence? Should we pay for your mistakes? Have another cookie sweetie… I mean, sweet cookie."

Adam didn't know what to say, so he took another macaroon even though he hadn't quite finished chewing the first two.

"But," he said in a muffled voice. "We tried to…"

"Enough," Rivka said, waving her hand. "My father will be here soon enough. Let us talk about something more interesting than money. Tell me, Adam, what do you think about the Sultan of Tunisia's visit to Chelm?"

Adam coughed and a piece of macaroon became lodged in his throat. "Thbm sbutan ob Fubgrezia?"

"Are you all right?" Rivka asked. "Can I offer you some tea?"

"Pbfleas."

Rivka poured, and Adam sipped. A moment later he regained his voice.

"What makes you think that the Sultan of Tunisia is coming to Chelm?"

"Well, it's either the Sultan of Tunisia or the Czar of Russia," Rivka smiled. "He's supposed to be coming tomorrow."

"Tomorrow?" Adam was dumbfounded. "Tomorrow?"

Rivka, who had no idea why Adam suddenly seemed so upset, answered innocently. "Yes, but we don't know what time," she said. "Kings, czars, sultans, and emperors always set their own schedules."

Adam's eyes opened wide in fury. His nostrils flared. His lips curled into a snarl. "How dare you make fun of me!"

"I don't understand."

"My brother put you up to this," Adam said. "First you won't pay us, then you have the gall to torment me?"

"No, no," Rivka said quickly. "I just thought that the arrival in Chelm of the Czar or the Sultan, or maybe it's the King of Poland…"

"Oh, really? Why not the King of Romania?" Adam shouted and stood up. The tea spilled on the rug, but he didn't care. "It's a good idea! But it's my idea, not Abraham's. Is it my fault that I don't have a moment of free time to myself?"

"Adam, please," Rivka said. "Your heart." It was something her mother often said to her father when he got over-excited.

"My heart? My heart is fine, but my head is throbbing. Tell your father I would like to speak with him, if his daughter can be less insulting."

And then he stormed off without even a thanks or goodbye. The door slammed and he was gone.

Rivka Cantor sat in her chair, tears rolling down her cheeks. How is it, she wondered, that I made his head throb instead of his heart? It had all been going so well, and then suddenly... What had she said?

"Rivka?" came her father's voice. "Is someone there?"

"No, Father," Rivka said, managing to choke back her sobs. "No one at all."

Much Ado

Adam Schlemiel banged in through the front door of the house shouting, "Abraham!"

Abraham, who was stirring a pot of stew, turned around just in time to see his brother's fist coming straight for his face. The punch struck Abraham in the forehead. He stumbled back, tripped, and fell to the floor, barely missing the hot stove.

"How dare you!" Adam shouted, standing over his brother's crumpled form. "Isn't it enough for you to make fun of me without telling every girl in Chelm?"

"What are you talking about?" Abraham said. He could feel the knot rising on his skull.

"My plan!" Adam's hands were still clenched into fists. "My prank. You've ruined it. And you've ruined my life."

"What's all the fuss?" came Rebecca Schlemiel's feeble voice from her bedroom.

"Nothing, Mama!" Adam said. Then he hissed at Abraham, "A foolish girl told me that the King of Poland was coming to Chelm next week."

"Nonsense," said Rebecca, her voice faint from the effort. "It's not the King of Poland. It's the King of Prussia. He's due to arrive tomorrow morning."

"AAAAAGH!" Adam shrieked. He pulled at his hair. "Is everyone in on this?" Then he ran from the house.

"In on what?" Rebecca said. "Adam, is everything all right? Abraham?"

"Fine, Mama," Abraham said, picking himself up. He giggled softly to himself and then winced as he felt a twinge above his nose. "Adam's just a little excited about tomorrow."

The next morning, Adam awoke, stiff and shivering, having spent the night in the unheated attic of his father's workshop.

Something was wrong. There was a noise outside, a sort of shouting roar. It rose and fell like a pigeon in the wind. Then it stopped. Then it started again. He couldn't figure it out, but it was coming from the round village square.

It sounded like a cheering crowd. But that was absurd. The only time crowds ever cheered in Chelm were on Holy Days, at weddings, births and bar mitzvahs, or at the arrival of some good news or some important visitor...

In the attic's workshop, Adam sat up suddenly, bashed his head against a low crossbeam, and fell back with a wounded yelp. He rubbed his forehead, saw no blood, crawled furiously through the trap door, and stormed down the ladder.

Abraham! Adam called out in his mind as he ran outside. He didn't know how it was possible, but Abraham had stolen his plan!

It was a beautiful morning in the village of Chelm, that rare perfect day between winter and spring. The snows had melted, the roads had turned to mud, but a week of cold air had frozen everything solid, and icicles glistened from the trees. The sky was bright blue, and a few early birds sang.

The villagers filled the round square with their bright, cold, smiling faces. Banners fluttered from poles. Every house in Chelm had been freshly painted. How had he not noticed it before? How could he have missed it? So much activity, so much excitement, and he, Adam Schlemiel, had been too busy wondering how to put his prank into effect to notice that it had taken off on its own, or that Abraham had been sneaking around behind his back to make a fool of him.

Adam looked for his brother, but couldn't find him in the sea of people. There couldn't be this many people in all of Chelm. No, he recognized visitors from Smyrna, and some strangers, too. They were all expecting somebody, but it was clear that Abraham hadn't told them who. Some were whispering that the Czar of Russia would be arriving any moment. Others argued that it was certainly the King of Poland. Or the Emperor of Ethiopia.

Adam grinned. Boy, were they in for a surprise when the day dragged on and nobody showed up.

Then he frowned. With so much uncertainty, there would be anger and fist fights, and that wasn't what he'd had in mind. No, the people needed to be unified, so that when it finally dawned, their disappointment would turn into dismay.

Adam smiled. Abraham hadn't thought that far ahead, had he? Maybe there was still time to take back some control. Give them all a single point of focus. Yes, that was it. But creating a consensus in Chelm was like training a mule to play the piano. Misdirection was the key. Yes! Abraham had given him that much to work with. Now, who was the best person to begin with?

Adam spotted Reb Shikker, the town drunk, talking with Reb Gold, the cobbler. "What's going on?" he asked innocently. "What's happening?"

"I'm so excited," Reb Shikker said. "As a longtime vodka drinker, I've always wanted to meet the Czar of Russia."

"Not the Czar of Russia," Reb Gold said. "The Czar of Prussia."

Reb Shikker frowned. "Isn't there a King in Prussia?"

"The King of Romania," Adam answered back with authority.

"Oh," said Reb Shikker, clearly puzzled. "But what kind of drink do they make in Romania?"

"In Romania," Reb Gold said, "they make rum!"

A smile blossomed on Reb Shikker's face. "Ahh! Rum is even better than vodka!"

Next Adam targeted Mrs. Chaipul, possibly Chelm's foremost gossip.

"I suppose," he said, "the banquet is ready?"

"Of course, Adam," the old woman said, "I understand that the

Emperor of China loves dumplings, so I made kreplach."

"That's good," Adam said, "because Reb Shikker says that the King of Romania loves dumplings."

Mrs. Chaipul's face grew serious. "Reb Shikker says it's the King of Romania?"

Adam nodded. "He should know. That's where rum comes from."

"I know," Mrs. Chaipul agreed. "Are you sure the King of Romania likes dumplings? I've made quite a lot of them, and I would hate to see them go to waste."

"Absolutely," Adam said. "Now, if you will excuse me, I must talk with Reb Stein."

So it went. Bulga the Fisherman had told the baker that it was the Prime Minister of Canada, but when Adam told him that Mrs. Chaipul said the King of Romania was coming for her dumplings he agreed that she must be correct.

It was all too easy. Adam moved quickly through the crowd. Each new conversation, pointed to the one immediately before, until at last everyone in the square was trying to remember the national anthem of Romania.

"There you are." Abraham's voice came from behind. "Mother was worried when you didn't come home last night. I told her you were safe in Father's attic. She said she wasn't surprised, because that's where all the Schlemiel men hide, when they're ashamed."

Adam turned and stared at his twin brother. For a moment, his ears reddened with anger, but then it passed. "I'm sorry I hit you."

"Thank you," Abraham said. "I'm flattered that you whacked yourself as punishment."

Adam touched the lump on his head. "Low ceiling."

"So, this prank is turning pretty good, isn't it?" Abraham said.

Adam nodded. "How did you manage it?"

"Purely by accident," Abraham said. "Do you remember, about a year ago, when you shouted at me in the square?"

"A year ago?" Adam thought and nodded.

Abraham shrugged. "Some things take time. What puzzles me is that everyone came today expecting to see someone different, but now they're all talking about the King of Romania."

Adam laughed. "That part was me. I wanted the prank to be more focused."

Abraham wrinkled his lips in respect. "Well done. But why?"

Adam shrugged. "So when no one shows up it won't start a fight about whose fault it is."

"Hmm." Abraham nodded in respect. "That's good thinking. But how did you do that?"

Adam touched his nose. "I'm a Schlemiel. Shall we find a place to watch? I can't wait to see what happens. I was thinking about the roof of the synagogue."

"You read my mind," Abraham said.

"Yes, indeed." Adam grinned. "Sometimes I do."

<u>Oops, Wrong King</u>

"I don't like being made a fool out of," Reb Cantor said, pacing back and forth. "I've spent months learning both Hindustani to speak with the Raja of Punjab and Farsi to impress the Sultan of Persia, and now everyone agrees that our visitor will be the King of Romania?"

"Father, calm yourself," Rivka Cantor said soothingly. "I'm sure it was an honest mistake."

Reb Cantor's face grew red. "Fortunes are lost by honest mistakes!"

Everywhere in the village square reactions were similar. The sun was going down. They'd been shivering with cold for hours and the King of Romania was nowhere to be seen. Mrs. Chaipul was afraid her dumplings were drying out. Jacob Schlemiel wondered if the special clock that he had designed for the Queen of England still would work in Romania. Infants dozed. Children and dogs ran through the square. All of the visitors from Smyrna laughed and smirked at yet another example of the foolishness of Chelm.

At last, one traveler, who had come all the way from Minsk, shouted, "Enough already. Forget about the King. It's another piece of idiocy from Chelm. The King's not coming! Let's eat!"

A cheer went up. On the roof of the synagogue, Abraham and Adam Schlemiel grinned at each other.

Only Rabbi Kibbitz managed to maintain his equilibrium. "Friends, friends," he said calmly. "So, the king is late. How many of you have ever tried to get your family up and out of the house on time for the early morning services? Imagine if you have an entire retinue. Horses, soldiers. These things take time. So, we'll be a little bit hungry. We'll give them another ten minutes. Fifteen. Okay? The food will taste all the better."

"I certainly hope so," Mrs. Chaipul muttered.

"I, for one, could really use a drink," agreed Reb Shikker

The rest of the crowd grumbled but conceded.

"All right," Abraham said. "So, that's about it. We should head down to the social hall to be first in line."

"Wait a second," Adam raised his palm. "This is my prank. I want to see how it turns out."

"This is our prank," Abraham corrected. "And I'm hungry." He stood up and was about to slide down the drainpipe when he was stopped by a shout.

"I see it! I see it! I see the caravan!"

Abraham nearly fell off the roof. Adam grabbed his brother by the coat and pulled him back from the edge.

"Who said that?" Abraham asked. "Where did that come from?"

"The elm tree," Adam pointed. "Doodle has been up there all day."

"Doodle the orphan? He's crazy."

"Maybe," Adam said, "but look over there."

Like all of the other boys on the roofs, and the ones in the trees, and everybody down in the square, they squinted into the distance.

At first it seemed like nothing. But then the nothing moved. Barely visible in the growing darkness, it bounced. It wasn't people walking. There were horses. And wagons with flags and banners. And they were all coming closer.

"No. It's impossible. It's a prank," Adam said. "I made it all up."

"I know," Abraham agreed. "I helped. But someone is coming. Come on, let's get down there and see who!"

One right after the other, the two boys slid down the drainpipe and ran to the square.

"The King of Romania!" Doodle shouted. "He's really here!"

"And just in time," Rabbi Kibbitz sighed with relief. He was hungry. Fasting all day on Yom Kippur was one thing, but at least then you were inside and distracted by prayer...

"Fooey," Reb Cantor hissed. But then he put on his best smile, and stepped forward with the Rabbi to greet the visitors.

The crowd slowly parted as the horse-drawn wagons reached the edge of the square. One wagon, two, three, four... Only four wagons? What kind of a king only traveled with four wagons?

Everyone was quiet. It was nearly dark now, and the shadows fell long and deep across the square. The wagons were painted, their drivers dark and somber. The horses weren't exactly royal stock. They looked as if they traveled thousands of miles for years at a time. There were no soldiers, no jugglers, no long procession of slaves bearing gifts for the villagers of Chelm.

At last, the tiny entourage stopped in the middle of the square. A door in the back of one of the wagons opened, and everyone inhaled, waiting for the red carpet. Instead, a rickety wooden block of steps was unceremoniously dropped.

Out stepped a large swarthy man wearing not a crown, but a purple scarf on his head.

"Welcome to Chelm, oh King of Romania," Rabbi Kibbitz said. Then he peered up at the tall man. "You look very familiar."

"It's just the Gypsies," spat a disappointed visitor from Smyrna.

"Hush, don't be rude," Rebecca Schlemiel said, nudging the man in the ribs with her elbow.

"Don't be rude," little Shemini Schlemiel echoed.

"I am Egon Kalderash," said the man in the purple scarf to Rabbi Kibbitz. He looked out at the crowd. "I have visited Chelm many times. Never have I been welcomed so."

"Well," Rabbi Kibbitz said, "this time we were expecting you."

"We were expecting," corrected Reb Cantor, "the King of Romania. You're not the king of Romania, are you?"

"I, Egon Kalderash, am a leader of my people. Although the Roma are scattered like dust around the world, we are still a nation. For my whole life I have been called a Duke, but at our last gathering, I was recognized as the true King of the Romany."

For once in his life, Reb Cantor had nothing to say. He opened his mouth and then closed it again.

"Mazel tov!" Rabbi Kibbitz shouted loudly. "A King, Egon? Who knew? You should have told us years ago. Nevertheless, Kings and commons are always welcome in Chelm. Although as far as I know, you're the first king we've ever had. Now, I know that you've had a long journey, and we are all absolutely famished, so I think it would be prudent to go inside and have some of the wonderful nosh."

"Romany, Romania, Rumania," said Mrs. Chaipul, "I just hope you like dumplings. Let's eat!"

A stampede of elephants wouldn't have emptied the village square faster.

Only two young men remained, standing still and dumbfounded.

"It was supposed to be a prank," Adam mumbled. "A practical joke."

"I suppose," Abraham said, "the joke is on us. Remember when you said that you wanted us to use this prank to dispel Father's curse? I don't think it worked."

"But," Adam said. "But…"

Without another word, Abraham took his brother by the elbow and led him out of the cold dark square into the warm and sweet-smelling hall, where there was still enough food to fill their plates high with soft kreplach, sweet noodle pudding, and savory brisket with kasha varnishkas.

At first Reb Shikker was disappointed there was no rum, but a visitor from Minsk had vodka and the Gypsies brought wine, so he made do.

Chapter Sixteen

A Visitor

Most shops have a little bell over the door that politely jingles whenever a customer enters. Jacob Schlemiel would have no such thing. "This is a carpenter's shop," he scoffed. "I'm not going out and buying a brass bell."

So, Jacob had designed what he called "The World's First Ratchet-and-Hammer Wood Block Chime." When the front door opened, the hammer went up with a "click." When the door closed, it came down with a "cl-ahk." Or at least that's how it was supposed to work. Sometimes it "clicked" open, but "clucked" closed, sometimes it "clomped," and sometimes the entire door got stuck. Jacob kept tinkering, but nothing seemed to help. If anything, it just got worse.

On this particular morning, Adam Schlemiel was working in the back of the shop while his father was out running errands – which Adam knew really meant he was at Mrs. Chaipul's having a second cup of tea and schmoozing with the other lazy shopkeepers.

Reb Cantor had finally paid for the governor's chest. Now, Adam was making a prototype of a seven-sided jewelry box that the merchant said was going to be all the rage in England next year. How Reb Cantor knew these things was anyone's guess, but he promised that once the Schlemiels manufactured an original, he'd place an order for as many as they could build at a fair price. The fact that Reb Cantor had finally paid for the governor's chest had been enough for Jacob Schlemiel. As long as the merchant paid cash, what he did with the boxes afterward was his problem.

"Fooey!" Adam cursed. His thin finishing nail had just split another piece of mahogany. This was his third attempt at nailing the sides on the bottom, and he was getting very frustrated. Reb

Cantor's design called for exactly thirteen nails along each side of the box. What did a merchant know about carpentry? Nothing! Twelve nails Adam could manage, but the thirteenth… Still, money was money and Reb Cantor had supplied the mahogany, so Adam picked up another piece of wood and started over.

He had just finished nailing three sides and twelve nails when he heard the front door "clink" open. He smiled. At least Father would see that he'd accomplished something.

He raised his hammer high to tap in the final nail when the door went "Clank-crump-twang…" and then "CRASH!"

The noise startled Adam, whose hand jerked. The hammer smashed down, shattering the nearly perfect box.

"Oy gevalt!" With the hammer still clutched in his hand, Adam ran full tilt into the front showroom. "What do you mean," he screamed, "making such a racket like…"

He saw the young girl just a moment too late to stop. Bam! He slammed into her. She went sprawling. He tumbled over her. The hammer went flying up into the air.

"Duck!" he said, pushing the girl's head down against the sawdust-covered floor and snatching the hammer in mid-spin, just before it could smack her on the back of the neck.

"Okay," Adam said, sitting down in the dust. "All right. It's okay."

The girl sat up with a look of absolute fury. In some language Adam had never before, a string of what must be curses spat from her mouth so fast that he felt stung. He held his hands up to shield himself, realized he still had the hammer, and quickly put it down.

"Relax," he said. "Relax. I'm okay. You're okay. Are you all right?"

"Yes, I'm all right," the girl said. Even those words sounded like curses. "How can you work in a wood shop with a door that falls off the hinges? First it nearly killed me, then you nearly killed me."

Adam looked. She was right. The shop's front door was lying flat on the floor not five inches from where the girl must have been standing. He took a deep breath, stood, and extended his hand to help her up. "I'm sorry."

"Yes," the girl said, "you are sorry." She ignored his hand and stood on her own. "You are Adam Schlemiel."

"No," Adam smiled. "I'm Abraham. Adam's my twin brother." It was an old trick, but at least Abraham would take the blame for this incident.

"You are Adam," the girl insisted.

"No, actually, I'm Abraham. We look a lot alike, so most people can't tell us apart. Are you looking for Adam?"

The girl shook her head. "I know Adam Schlemiel. Although I have not seen him in many years, I believe that I would know him in an instant. I came to see him, but you say he isn't here."

Adam shrugged. The girl looked familiar, but she wasn't from Chelm. She wore a dark fur coat and a bright red scarf over her hair.

"All right," the girl shrugged back. "Can you give to him a message?"

"Sure."

"Tell him I am sorry that I missed him, and..." She beckoned with her finger for Adam to come closer.

He leaned forward.

Then she kissed him on the cheek. It was a gentle touch, like a feather brushing warmly against his skin.

Adam felt his face flush red. He looked into her eyes. Then he remembered.

"Rosa? Rosa Kalderash! Of course! I didn't see you at the celebration the other day. Where have you been?"

Rosa smiled. When the caravan arrived in Chelm, she explained, she'd been too sick to go to the party, but now that she was feeling better she had wanted to say hello to Adam.

"Umm, why Adam? Why not Abraham?"

Again she smiled, and Adam thought about springtime and summer. "Don't take it personally," she said, as she turned to the door, "but I like the other brother better."

"Wait." Adam put his hand on her shoulder. "I'm Adam. Really."

"Really?"

"Yes. Really."

Then Rosa spun around and slapped Adam on the cheek she'd just kissed.

"Ow!"

"I will always know when you are lying, Adam Schlemiel," Rosa said. "But you will never know when I am lying. Maybe it really is Abraham I like better. Now, are you coming for a walk or not?"

Adam rubbed his cheek and winced. "I have work."

"Work will wait. When you come back, you will be able to bang thirteen nails in a row without accident."

"How did you know?"

"I am a Gypsy. Come."

It was impossible to argue. Adam set his apron on the counter and, stepping over the front door, followed Rosa into the sunshine.

An Innocent Walk

When Jacob Schlemiel, buzzing from six cups of tea, returned to his workshop to find the front door broken down and his son missing, he tried not to panic.

Keep calm, he thought. There is a rational explanation.

Unfortunately, the first rational explanation he thought of was that the murderous thief, Alex Krabot, had finally returned to Chelm to take vengeance. So he immediately panicked.

"Kidnapping! Robbery!" Jacob shouted. "Destruction of property!"

Within moments, a dozen villagers had gathered outside the wood shop.

"What's the matter? Jacob, calm down. What in the name of Jericho happened to your door?"

"Adam's gone," Jacob wailed. "He was working on a box. Look, one of them is smashed. I don't know what happened."

"Are you sure it was Adam?" Reb Shikker asked.

Jacob spun around. "What do you mean by that?"

Reb Shikker shrugged. "They both look the same to me."

Jacob's eyes widened, and without another word he brushed

through the crowd and raced to his house. If anything had happened to Adam, Abraham would know.

"Father," Abraham said as Jacob came panting through the front door, "is everything all right?"

"You're Abraham?" Jacob asked, leaning against the kitchen table to catch his breath.

"Yes."

"What's the matter?" Rebecca's voice came from her bedroom.

"Nothing," Jacob gasped. He stepped closer to Abraham and whispered, "Adam's missing. Do you know where he is?"

"He's missing?" Abraham said. "I didn't know he was missing."

"Shh," Jacob ordered, but it was too late. Rebecca was standing in the doorway, frowning.

"What do you mean Adam's missing?" she said. "You didn't send him off to Smyrna by himself again, did you?"

"No. I just left him in the workshop while I got a cup of tea."

"You left him alone?"

"Don't start that with me again. We don't have time."

By now, the crowd from the shop had grown and assembled outside the Schlemiel home.

Reb Cantor knocked on the door. "Jacob? Is everything all right?"

"I don't know," Jacob shouted back. "Go away!"

"But Jacob, perhaps we can help."

"Will everybody please be quiet!" the poor man yelled.

"Shh!" Rebecca hissed. "Shemini is taking a nap!"

A silence instantly fell. Jacob took the opportunity to explain what he had seen at the shop. "I don't know what to do," he whispered. "Abraham, can you help? That mind-speaking thing you do with Adam. Can you find him?"

Abraham hesitated. He knew his father had guessed that from time to time he and his twin brother were able to communicate without words, sometimes across vast distances. But as they had grown older, they'd begun to lose the knack. It had become uncomfortable and awkward for them to eavesdrop on each other, so they hadn't been doing it so often. He wasn't even sure that he still could, but what else could he do?

"I'll try," Abraham said. "First of all, Mama, you need your rest. Sit down at least."

Rebecca threw up her hands, then sat in a chair. She shot Jacob a look that said, "You're the one who left my son alone – again – and he'd better be all right, or else."

Jacob's eyes widened in exasperation, and he gave her a look of "What?! The boy is almost sixteen years old and you want me to keep him under lock and key, give me a break!"

Then they were quiet.

Outside the Schlemiel house, the people in the crowd, which was now about half the population of Chelm, were whispering among themselves.

Abraham closed his eyes, and reached out with his mind...

Adam... Adam...

He thought he felt something. So he tried again.

Adam... Adam...

What? came the answer, faintly.

Adam!

Who is this? Abraham?

Abraham smiled. *Who else would it be?*

"What?" Rebecca whispered.

"He's okay," Abraham answered.

"So, where is he?" Jacob demanded.

"Shhh..." Abraham said. He closed his eyes again.

Adam?

What?

Are you there?

Where else would I be? Go away!

Where are you?

I said go away!

BAM! Abraham felt as if he'd been smacked behind the eyes. "Ow!" he said.

"What? What happened?" Rebecca and Jacob said as one. "Is he all right?"

"He's fine," Abraham said. "He said he didn't want to talk just now."

"What do you mean he doesn't want to talk?" Rebecca said. "You tell him that I want to talk with him."

Adam.

I thought I told you to leave me alone. I'm busy.

Wait! Mama wants to talk with you.

What? Mama? Now? Why?

Abraham sighed. *Papa says that the front door to the shop has been demolished and you are missing. They're worried. Can you blame them?*

Oh. Well, tell them I'm all right.

I already did that. They want to know where you are.

There was a pause. Abraham ignored his parents and listened for Adam. At last an answer came.

Okay, but you can't tell.

What do you mean I can't tell?

Promise me.

They're going to kill me. But all right. I promise.

Another pause. Then…

I'm with Rosa.

Rosa?

Rosa Kalderash, the Gypsy princess. I'm with her.

What do you mean you're with her?

Think about it you nudnik!

Then, as understanding dawned, Abraham's face turned red from blushing.

"What's the matter?" Rebecca demanded.

"Nothing, it's tiring," Abraham said.

You see why you can't tell them?

Yes. So, what do I tell them?

I don't care. Just leave me alone.

Not a chance! Abraham thought at his brother. *This is your mess.*

Abraham thought he heard a laugh inside his head.

Rosa says to tell them that I'm learning how to drive thirteen nails in a row.

"Rosa…" Abraham began, then he stopped. "Rows of nails. He says he's learning how to bang thirteen nails in a row. Does this make any sense?"

"Yes," Jacob nodded. "The prototype box. But why can't he do that at the shop? And what happened to the door?"

Abraham listened and then reported. "The door fell down when the ratchet-and-hammer wood block chime broke. It startled Adam, and he smashed the model. After that he had to go for a walk."

"A walk?" Rebecca Schlemiel frowned. "A walk? Tell him next time he should write a note."

Abraham closed his eyes and tried to pass on his mother's message, but all he could get from Adam was giggling and then a contented silence.

Abraham pursed his lips, opened his eyes, and said, "Adam says he's sorry, and he'll be back soon."

Relieved, Rebecca Schlemiel went back to bed. Jacob opened his door, stepped outside, and announced that everything was all right.

One by one, the villagers dispersed, most of them mumbling something to the effect of "Trouble. Those Schlemiel boys are nothing but trouble."

Chapter Seventeen

A Very Schlemiel Wedding

"Tell us about your wedding, Mamma," little Shemini Schlemiel squeaked.

Abraham and Adam rolled their eyes and said, simultaneously, "Not again!"

"Your brothers are right," Rebecca Schlemiel said. "I wouldn't want to bore our guest." She nodded at Rosa Kalderash, the Gypsy girl who was visiting for dinner.

"Not at all," Rosa said, her right foot kicking Adam under the table. "I would love to hear the story."

"Ow!" Adam said. "I mean, me too."

Rebecca Schlemiel's face brightened, and her smile danced. "Well…"

I was supposed to marry Reb Cantor. Isaac his name was, and still is. We had been betrothed almost from birth. My father was a goldsmith, but I was the youngest of his seven daughters, so there wasn't much left over for my dowry. It was my father's dream that my husband become his apprentice and take over the business.

So, after his bar mitzvah, the papers were signed, and Isaac moved in to the small room over the shop. The plan was that he would live there, eat with our family, and work with Father. After five years, if all went well, we would be married.

Unfortunately, Isaac Cantor was born with five thumbs on each hand. He couldn't pick up a hammer without dropping it on his toe. My father would give him a thin strand of gold wire to make into earring hooks. Simple enough, all you need to do is to cut a small piece and bend it into a U. Two hours later, Reb Cantor would give back a handful of little golden pretzels and knots. And wedding bands?

Forget it. You have never seen such an assortment of knobby, bumbled, misshapen rings.

It was getting to the point where Father joked, half seriously, about burning down the jewelry shop rather than turning it over to Reb Cantor.

As to the question of marriage? Four years had passed and Isaac seemed to know even less about making jewelry than on the day he'd begun. How could he possibly earn enough to keep a family? My father was at his wit's end.

"What about you?" Shemini interrupted. "Did you love Reb Cantor the way you love Papa?"

Rebecca patted her young daughter on the head. "Never. But, remember, when I was a girl, your father didn't live in Chelm. He had gone to Frampol to become a carpenter's apprentice. Reb Cantor, however, I saw every day…"

I liked Isaac Cantor. Even though he was a klutz, I liked him a lot. He had kind brown eyes, and he worked hard. Every day when I brought lunch, Isaac would joke with me.

He would smile. "I can't wait until we're married."

I'd laugh back. "I can wait."

After lunch, Isaac would go back to his work bench and demolish fine jewelry, while Father held his head in his hands and prayed for a miracle. It wasn't going to work. We all knew it wasn't going to work. But we couldn't say that. We were going to be married. What else could we do?

One day there was an emergency. Mrs. Chaipul had gotten her favorite gold necklace caught in the meat grinder. Even though it was choking her, she refused to cut it. Father was summoned and, reluctantly, he left Isaac in charge of the shop.

It was a delicate operation, but fortunately both the patient and the gold necklace survived. Mrs. Chaipul happily fed Father chocolate and cinnamon babka until he could eat no more.

When he finally returned to the shop, Father was surprised to find the door shut and the "Closed" sign hanging in the window.

Frowning, Father unlocked the door and stepped inside.

Everything was gone. Every bracelet, every ring, every piece of fine jewelry that my father had made – years of stock – had vanished from their cases. Staggering under the weight of the blow, Father ran to the back and opened the safe. Only then did he relax slightly. The large bar of gold that he used to make the jewelry, and the small box of precious stones were still there.

Isaac Cantor, however, was nowhere to be seen.

Such a scandal, you wouldn't believe! The cobbler reported that he had seen the young apprentice riding north out of town in a wagon with a foreigner, and that was that.

I was broken-hearted. True, I hadn't been in love, but my life was over. Father was impoverished, and my fiancé had stolen nearly everything. Who would want to marry me now?

Months went by. Slowly Father rebuilt his business. He even began looking for my new husband, but every time he mentioned someone to me, I shook my head sadly and said, "I'll wait."

Years passed. My mother warned me that, if I didn't get married soon, no one would have me. To be sure I felt the same way, but still I said, "I'll wait."

And then a letter from Italy came addressed to Father.

"Prepare the wedding feast," it read. "Arriving in Chelm on Thursday with riches beyond belief. Best regards, Isaac Cantor."

"Best regards?" Father shouted. "A wedding? After all these years he expects a wedding?"

He threw the paper into the fireplace, but before it could burn, I snatched it out.

"Father," I begged. "You all say you want me to marry. Please."

"A thief you should marry?" Father frowned. "A man who would leave for years without a single word?"

Glumly, I nodded. I was still young, but getting old fast. I didn't know what else to do.

So the preparations began, but without joy. The social hall was decorated, food prepared, and the wedding cake was baked seven layers high.

On the great day, almost as soon as the cake was delivered, the rain began. It poured, it pelted, it bucketed, it drenched.

"Perfect," Father said, looking out the window of our house. *"Just perfect."*

And then I, not for the first time that week, burst into tears.

My father took me into his arms and patted me. *"Daughter, Daughter, it will be perfect,"* he repeated over and over.

The rain hid my tears as we arrived at the synagogue at the appointed hour.

"So, where is he?" Father asked.

No one answered. The entire village of Chelm had gathered for the ceremony, but Isaac Cantor was nowhere to be seen.

Father fumed and ranted.

"The rain," I said. *"The rain has delayed him."*

And just then the door at the back of the synagogue opened. Everyone turned and stared.

There stood a man covered in mud and soaked from the brim of his hat to the soles of his boots.

His beard was full. He had lost weight. It had been five years since we had seen Isaac Cantor, but to my eyes at least he had grown even more handsome.

"YOU!" my Father shouted. *"Where have you been?"*

"I got lost," came the quiet response.

"Well, you're just in time," Rabbi Kibbitz said, calmly hurrying down the aisle with a towel. *"Come in. Come in."*

He seemed nervous. He seemed frightened. Who wouldn't be? Not only was this his wedding day, everyone in Chelm thought the man was a thief.

"This is the man you want?" my father whispered to me.

"Yes," I hissed. *"Now be quiet."*

The shul was as silent as a tomb as the wedding began. The groom stood stiff and still. He answered by rote, barely moving his eyes as I walked around him seven times.

When it came time to give me the ring he froze for a moment and then reached into his shirt, bringing out a chain on which hung a thin gold band.

"Is that all that's left?" my father mumbled.

"It was my grandmother's," he said, slipping the ring onto my

finger. Even though he looked scared, his smile was kind to me.

He raised his foot. The glass was shattered. And in that moment all was forgiven as the synagogue resounded with a loud, "Mazel tov!"

I looked at my husband, tears in my eyes, and saw that there were tears in his eyes – blue eyes.

Just then, the doors at the back of the synagogue banged open, and a strong voice shouted, "I'm here! I'm here!"

Oy, what a mess.

All the Schlemiels laughed. Rosa Kalderash looked shocked. "What happened?" Rosa asked.

"I married the wrong man." Rebecca's smile was as bright as a star.

On the day Reb Cantor vanished, a stranger had come into my father's shop and had marveled at the craftsmanship. The stranger said he would buy everything, but that he had no money with him. Reb Cantor told us that he believed the man, but wouldn't trust him with the jewelry. So he wrote my father a note, which we never found, and traveled with the man all the way to Paris. There the man paid him, and Isaac Cantor discovered that his true calling was not as a jeweler, but as a merchant. Taking the long way back to Chelm, he bought and sold and traded his way to a small fortune. Unfortunately for him, he was twenty minutes too late for his own wedding.

Oy, there was screaming and shouting. Once again, I was in tears.

"You said you'd wait!" Isaac yelled at me.

"I waited," I shrieked back. "I waited!"

Not having a clue about what was going on, my new husband tried to protect me.

"Who are you?" he asked Isaac. "What do you want?"

"I'm Isaac Cantor, the merchant. I'm the groom. Who are you?"

In an instant there was silence again. All eyes went to the stranger.

"My name is Jacob Schlemiel," he answered quietly. "I'm a carpenter. And I'm the husband."

At that moment, my heart melted. I looked into my husband's eyes and saw his kindness. I knew that I was his, and he was mine. And that made me so happy. So so happy.

In the Schlemiel house, the only sound was the crackling of the hearth fire. Jacob Schlemiel reached across the table and squeezed his wife's hand.

"Mazel tov!" little Shemini shouted.

And everyone laughed.

Chapter Eighteen

The King and the Carpenter

Egon Kalderash, the king of the Roma, peered into the dim wood shop. The door still lay on the floor as if it had been knocked down by the police.

"Schlemiel?" The question was softer than it might have been.

A head poked from the back room. "Ahh, your Majesty, come in," Jacob Schlemiel said. "Don't mind the mess. I've been meaning to clean it up, but the weather's been nice, and I enjoy the fresh air."

Kalderash strode in.

"Now, your Royalness," Jacob Schlemiel said. "What can I do for you? One of your wagons needs repairs? I'll get my tool box."

Kalderash put a heavy hand on Jacob's shoulder. "The wagons are fine."

"Oh. You need a table? A throne? What?"

"Your son has been seeing my daughter."

"Yes," Jacob agreed. "Both my sons have been seeing your daughter."

A dark line formed across Egon Kalderash's brow. "Both of your sons?"

A nod. "Yes. In fact, I've been seeing your daughter, too."

The Gypsy king's eyes widened in instant rage. "You have been seeing my daughter?" he roared.

"Yes! Calm down! My wife saw her too. She came over for dinner last night. You didn't know? We thought she told you."

Kalderash coughed as he struggled to regain his demeanor.

"She's a nice girl," Jacob said. "A very nice girl. Polite. Well behaved. Wonderful table manners. Do you want a cup of water?"

"Enough about table manners." Kalderash took a deep breath and then sat down on the floor. "We have to talk."

"Egon, I have chairs."

"Sit," Kalderash said.

Jacob scanned the floor as if trying to gauge whether the layer of sawdust would stick to his black coat because if he came home filthy Rebecca would want him to wash it, and then it would take forever to dry… At last he shrugged, grabbed an apron from behind the counter, and sat down on it.

"Well, this is uncomfortable," Jacob said with a smile.

"Your son," Kalderash said quietly, "has been seeing my daughter."

"I thought we went through this already."

"No," Kalderash said. Even seated he looked gigantic. "He has been *seeing* her. Not just at dinner. In private. Not in public. In the woods."

"Well, that's where they met, wasn't it? I mean years ago…"

"Listen," Kalderash said. "Let me be blunt. I don't want them to be married."

"Married? The boy is barely a man. What would he be doing getting marri…" Jacob paused. Now his eyes widened. "You mean they've been *seeing* each other?!"

A nod from Kalderash.

"Oy."

"Yes, oy," Kalderash agreed. "So, what do we do?"

The two men sat on the floor in silence. Several minutes passed.

"Can I ask a question?" Jacob said.

"Go ahead."

"So, why shouldn't they get married?"

"You're a Schlemiel," Kalderash said, as if that were answer enough.

It wasn't enough for Jacob. "A couple of years ago you were just another Gypsy. Now you're the King, you think that makes you better than me?"

Kalderash leaned back and roared with laughter. Jacob looked nervous.

At last, Kalderash managed to regain his control. "It's nothing to do with royalty. Neither you nor I are what we might call high-class fellows."

"If you hadn't said that so nicely," Jacob said, "I might have taken that as an insult."

"No offense meant. It's nothing to do with my position of leadership. It's tribal. Think about the religious differences. It is a gap as cold and wide as the steppes of Siberia, and as lonely as the deserts of the Sahara."

"And as salty as a kosher pickle," Jacob added.

"Plus you're a Schlemiel."

"So?"

"So, your entire family is cursed. The last thing that I want for my little Rosa is for her to become a victim of that curse."

"I..." Jacob opened his mouth. Then he closed it.

"You see my point?" Kalderash said.

Jacob nodded. "It's not such a bad curse. I've lived with it my whole life, and I'm not miserable."

"No," Kalderash shook his head solemnly. "But we want for our children what is best for them. Living here, Rosa would be miserable. She would never be accepted by your people."

"Now, that's not true..."

"Even if she was, Rosa is a traveler. She would become restless. And if your son came with us, my people would never accept him. He would be miserable on the road. And then there's the curse."

"Yes, yes. There's always the curse. Do you happen to know any Gypsy magic to get rid of the curse?"

"No," Kalderash shook his head. "I am sorry, but I don't."

"Too bad," Jacob said. "Ask around, will you?

"I wouldn't hold out much hope."

"Perhaps your mother?"

"She died. That is why I am the king."

"Oh, I'm sorry."

Kalderash touched his fingers to his forehead. "It was her time."

They were quiet a moment, then the Gypsy King said, "So, is it settled?"

"What if they're in love?" Jacob asked.

"Love?" Kalderash rubbed his mustache thoughtfully. "That would be a shame. But young love is sudden and passionate. It's like a torch in a wind storm. It burns bright and hot… And then flickers out in a matter of minutes. When I think back to my young days, and my first loves, I regret none of them. I am only thankful I did not marry a single one of those young ladies. You see my point?"

"No," Jacob said. "I married my first love, and I don't regret it for a minute."

"Ahh." The Gypsy's single word held layers of meaning that were left unsaid. "Then what?"

"I think," Jacob said, "we should blame each other. You tell your daughter it's my fault. I tell my son it's your fault. At least then they don't hate us."

A smile appeared beneath the bushy mustache. "You're sneaky. I like that."

"It makes me sad," Jacob said.

"They're children," Kalderash said. "Next week they will find something else to make us crazy about. At least this time we can do something for them. Something to help them."

"But what if we're wrong?"

"It would be worse if we were right and did nothing."

The low afternoon sun peered in through the open front door and began to vanish in the distance. Still they sat.

At last, Jacob Schlemiel spoke. "Can we get up now?"

"I'm stuck," Egon Kalderash said.

Laughing heartily, the two men creakily helped each other to their feet. Silently, they picked up the door and working together hung it back on its hinges. They shook hands, and after Kalderash left, Jacob Schlemiel stared at the closed door for a very long time.

The next morning, both Jacob and Adam were quiet as they walked the short distance between the Schlemiel house and the carpenter's shop. Jacob unlocked the front door while Adam took the shutters off the windows. Inside, Jacob lit a small fire and peered at the day's list he'd written in chalk on the wall.

1) Prototype for Reb Cantor
2) Bread box for Mrs. Chaipul
3) Talk with Adam about problem

Jacob frowned. He glanced over at his son and for a moment thought about erasing the third item, but Adam was too quick.

"What problem?" Adam said. "I told you yesterday that I should have the prototype ready this afternoon. Reb Cantor didn't change the requirements again, did he?"

The merchant had been notoriously fickle about getting the design exactly right for the jewelry boxes he planned to mass produce and export to England.

"No," Jacob said. "It's not that. It's about Rosa."

Adam looked up. "What's the matter with Rosa?"

"Nothing," Jacob said. "She's a nice girl."

"If you don't like her, just come out and say so."

"I do like her."

"It's her family, isn't it? You have something against her family?"

"Adam," Jacob said. "Relax. And yes, it is her family."

"I knew it!" The young man spun around in a full circle. "I knew that you would be too small. It's just so obvious that…"

"Her father forbade it."

"Her father? Her father? I don't believe it." Adam pointed his finger at his father. "I think it's your fault."

"Adam." Jacob put his hand on his heart. "I have nothing but your best interest…"

"You hate her, and I love her. It's that simple!" He turned and ran from the shop. The door slammed behind him, and Jacob watched it wobble, wondering if it would fall from its hinges again. The door stayed on, but his son was gone. Again.

Jacob sighed. Rebecca would kill him.

<u>Breathless</u>

Adam Schlemiel ran through Chelm, as only a boy in love can — like a hawk in frantic pursuit of a dove. Down the street he raced. He ignored the stares from neighbors and friends as he zigged and zagged and made his way to the village square where the Romany caravan had been camping for the better part of a month.

He turned the corner around the side of the synagogue and saw...

The round square was empty. The Gypsy wagons were gone.

Adam searched frantically, as if four horse-drawn wagons could somehow be hidden behind the square's eight elm trees. Nothing. Just matted down grass and the ruts from four sets of wagon wheels heading north toward Smyrna.

In an instant his mind was made up. Adam ran after them.

Only two roads lead from Chelm, the Smyrna Road and the Great Circular Road. When he was a boy, it had taken Adam the better part of a morning to travel from Chelm to Smyrna. At top speed, he thought he might be there in an hour and a half.

He had to see her. He had to. It couldn't just end like that. No.

Adam felt his resolve harden. He took a deep breath and ran even faster.

Without warning, Abraham dropped the soup ladle on the floor.

"Abraham, what's wrong?" Rebecca Schlemiel's eyes widened.

"Eccccch," Abraham answered. His face turned red.

They had been preparing a cholent, a three-day stew that would feed the family over the Sabbath, getting better and better so that by Sunday, when only the pot drippings were left, the family would almost fight to dip the last of their challah into the wonderful gravy.

Abraham's breathing had become short and sudden. He fell to his knees.

"Abraham!" Rebecca shouted. "Shemini, run and get Mrs. Chaipul."

The little girl heard the seriousness in her mother's voice and without hesitation, without even asking a question, she snatched her coat from a hook and ran from the house.

"Abraham, you're scaring me," Rebecca whispered as she knelt down beside her boy. She rolled him onto his back and forced his mouth open, but he wasn't choking on anything she could see.

His breathing was ragged. His hands were clenched into fists. His arms were feebly pumping back and forth. His feet were twitching as if he were having a fit.

And it didn't subside. If anything, it only got worse. You would think that in such a state he would grow weaker and weaker and slow down with exhaustion. Rebecca wasn't sure which scared her more, that the fit might suddenly stop or that it might just keep going.

By the time Shemini returned with Mrs. Chaipul and her carpetbag, Rebecca had managed to get a towel under her boy's head, thrown a soup bone into the pot, and was adding a dozen cloves of garlic, plus twelve turns of pepper. The garlic and pepper were the secret. You needed to have exactly the same number of cloves as turns of the pepper mill.

"You're cooking?" Mrs. Chaipul asked as she unpacked her bag. "It smells good."

"You want I should stand here like a lump?" Rebecca snapped. "I would hold him and comfort him, but he won't sit still. So, at least we won't have to worry about supper."

"That wasn't what I meant," Mrs. Chaipul said. She removed a tube from her bag and listened through it to Abraham's chest. "When Shemini came into the restaurant, I thought it was you who was in trouble."

"I only wish," Rebecca said. "So, what's wrong?"

The old woman, who was the closest thing Chelm had to a doctor, tapped, prodded, and poked. At last, she shrugged. "I wish I knew."

The fit went on for more than an hour. Jacob was summoned home, but there was little he could do to comfort his son, wife, or daughter. He didn't dare mention the fact that Adam had also run off.

The three grownups started a game of canasta while Shemini played jacks dangerously close to the thrashing boy.

And then all of a sudden, Abraham stopped moving. His eyes snapped wide open. He took one deep breath, and then screamed at the top of his lungs, "ROSA!"

Then, his eyes shut, all the tension left his body, and a moment later he was asleep, snoring loudly.

Abraham's shout had startled everyone. Cards flew across the room. Jacob leaped to his feet, stepped on one of Shemini's jacks, and began cursing.

"Rosa?" Mrs. Chaipul said. "What's a rosa?"

"Rosa," Rebecca whispered, "was Adam's girlfriend."

"Adam?" Mrs. Chaipul said. "I thought you said this was Abraham."

"Abraham and Adam share everything," little Shemini said helpfully.

"Hush," her mother ordered, as Mrs. Chaipul's eyes widened. "It's nothing like that. Nothing at all."

"Whatever you say." Mrs. Chaipul bent over her patient. "He seems to be resting well now. Make sure you give him some water and some chicken soup when he wakes up. Let me know."

After the old woman left, Rebecca Schlemiel turned to her husband. "You told him, didn't you?"

Jacob nodded glumly. "Not him, but Adam."

"Papa," Shemini said, "Can you give me back my jack?"

Broken

Three days later, Abraham's eyes finally fluttered open. He blinked twice, saw his brother staring down at him, and smiled.

"What's the news?" Abraham croaked. His mouth was dry, and Adam held a cup of water to his lips. "So?"

"Well," Adam began, "It looks like there's going to be a war. Russia is building up its army, but it's not really clear who's attacking who."

A crease appeared on Abraham's brow. "Rosa?"

"I don't think she has to worry. They're not conscripting girls."

"Adam," Abraham insisted. "Tell me."

Adam sighed and looked out the window. It was raining. "They're gone. She's gone."

Abraham closed his eyes. If he had been any stronger, he would have cried. "I knew it. I knew the moment you left."

"And yet you gave me your strength to run even faster."

Abraham made a small shrug. "It was worth a try."

"I didn't know you cared about me that much," Adam said. He stared intently at his brother. "Or was it Rosa?"

"I…" Abraham began.

The door to the bedroom banged open. "Talking?" Rebecca Schlemiel said. "I'm hearing talking. You're awake! Jacob, he's awake! Oh, he's not here. Adam, run to the shop and tell your father. Shemini, Abraham's awake. Go get him a bowl of soup. Never mind. I'll get it myself. I'm so happy that you're awake. I was worried."

Their mother bent down, gave Abraham a soft wet kiss on the forehead, and then whisked out of the room.

Abraham's eyes glanced around. "I can't remember the last time I saw Mama so excited."

"Your illness is doing wonders for her health," Adam said, standing. "It's been years since she had so much energy."

"Maybe I should get sick more often."

"No," Adam said. "Don't." He bent down, wiped Abraham's forehead, and then kissed his brother in the same spot, but without any spit. "Get better."

Rebecca bustled in with a tray piled high with a soup bowl, a spoon, and a chunk of challah the size of a large hen. "What, you're still here?"

"I'm going already," Adam said.

"So go already. Skit skat."

As soon as her brother was gone, little Shemini bounded into the bedroom and immediately jumped on top of Abraham.

"Shemini," her mother warned, "you'll kill him!"

"No, it's all right," Abraham grabbed his sister and hugged her deeply. "I need all the simchas I can get."

"Fine," Rebecca said. "But if you spill soup in that bed, you still have to sleep there."

Abraham smiled. Everything was back to normal.

Not Really Normal

On the surface, all seemed well. Now that Abraham was awake and eating solid foods, he quickly regained his health and was back up on his feet in no time. Jacob and Adam finally finished the prototype jewelry box for Reb Cantor, who promised that after he returned from his next trip to London, he'd take as many as they could build. Now that she didn't have to tiptoe around the house, four year-old Shemini was making up for it by banging pots and singing ten hours a day, until her mother finally threatened to send her out in the rain if she didn't put a sock in it. Best of all, Rebecca Schlemiel, who had been mostly bedridden herself since Shemini's birth, was up and about and as filled with smiles and joy as she had been for years.

Meals at the Schlemiels' house were raucous and exuberant. Bowls were filled, passed, emptied, and refilled. Everything was discussed all at once, from the nature of heaven and the universe to Mrs. Chaipul's opinions on the coming spring planting.

Only one subject was not discussed, but that was the most important.

Rosa Kalderash, the Gypsy princess. She was gone from Chelm, but not far from the minds of any of the Schlemiels (with the possible exception of Shemini). At work in their father's wood shop, Adam fell quiet, straightening bent nails for hours at a time without a single complaint. Jacob Schlemiel watched his son and hoped the boy's heart would mend.

Nobody even thought to talk about it with Abraham. It was as if they all agreed that his collapse was a fluke, a sudden illness that came and (fortunately) went.

For Abraham, though, the world was a suddenly darker and more somber place.

Abraham had fallen in love with Rosa. It wasn't something he meant or intended to happen. Rosa had been in love with Adam. There was no mistaking that. He didn't want to get in between. Still, Abraham had managed to find ways to spend time with her while his brother was working. At first, he'd pretended to be just her friend, as if all was innocent. But then there was that one day when...

He didn't dare think about it. He had no idea how anything so brief could hurt so much. He never would have let himself get so close to her if he'd known the pain it would cause. It was as if the inside of his heart has been removed. Perhaps if he had been kept busy, he could have buried himself in his work like Adam. But with Mama feeling better, there was less and less for Abraham to do around the house. She insisted that he rest or go into the forest to look for mushrooms.

And so he was alone, more alone than he had been in his entire life.

Sometimes, when he was deep in the Schvartzvald and far from Chelm, he lifted his head to the sky and shouted her name, screaming "Rosa!" until his throat was scorched and his cheeks were wet from crying.

Far away, back in the village of Chelm, Adam's hammer would grow still and then tremble in his hand until at last a single tear welled up and fell into the sawdust.

Then the hammer would rise and fall with renewed vigor, pounding bent nails straight in one solid blow.

Chapter Nineteen

The Wisest Rabbi

"Did you hear the one about how the villagers of Chelm tried to lock the moon in a rain barrel? They saw the reflection of the full moon and decided to hammer a lid onto the barrel and let the moon out later in the month!" The fishmonger's head tilted back with laughter.

The marketplace in Smyrna was busy. It was open six days a week, and was ten times larger than the small weekly market in Chelm. Still, some things never changed. Whenever they got a moment, the villagers of Smyrna enjoyed making jokes at their neighbor's expense.

Now the pickle man roared with glee, "How about the time it had just snowed, and they thought the snow was so lovely that they didn't want to leave footprints, so they hired a band of Russians to carry them on their backs!"

Abraham Schlemiel's face turned as red as a boiled beet. Every week, after filling him with dire warnings about returning straight home, his mother sent him alone to Smyrna to do some shopping. For years, Abraham, who was already on edge from breaking his promise to Babushka Krabot, had heard these men making jokes about his home. Enough was enough!

"Chelm is nothing like that!" His sixteen-year-old voice squeaked with anger.

The merchants of Smyrna turned toward him.

"And who are you, schlemiel?" the fishmonger asked.

"Yes," Abraham said.

"Yes? Now that's a name from Chelm!" The pickle man giggled. "I can just see his mother calling, 'Yes! Yes!"

Now the spice vendor and the tea salesman added their guffaws.

"No," Abraham said. "No."

"Ahh," the pickle man said. "That's his last name. Gentlemen, I would like you to meet Mr. Yes No from Chelm!"

The laughter was deafening.

"My name," Abraham shouted, "is Abraham Schlemiel!"

Suddenly, there was a moment of silence, and then the fishmonger said, "Even better, a real Schlemiel from Chelm!"

"He's doomed," giggled the pickle man.

Abraham thought about turning on his heels and storming off. His shopping was done, but he wasn't about to let these men get the better of him.

He waited for the laughter to subside, and then he said, "In Chelm, we have the wisest rabbi in the world!"

"You're serious?" the tea salesman said. "You think Rabbi Kibbitz is wise?"

Abraham nodded, as serious as a cow waiting to be fed.

The tea salesman splurted, "Braahh hahaha!"

More laughter and more waiting.

When at last the merchants of Smyrna could laugh no more, Abraham began…

When Rabbi Kibbitz prayed, he davened. Now, davening is not rare. Most men daven when they pray, bowing at the waist forward and backward, or from the knees, rocking back and forth.

Rabbi Kibbitz, however, davened from left to right, from side to side like a stalk of wheat blowing in the breeze.

So wise was Rabbi Kibbitz that when the other villagers of Chelm tried to copy his davening, he put a stop to it right away.

"You can't daven from side to side," he told everyone. "Your shoulders will bump into each other. I can only get away with it because I've got more room up here at the front."

"Ahh," said the people of Chelm. And from that day on, they davened backward and forward while their rabbi rocked from left to right, stamping his feet in a quiet rhythm.

Now, one day a troublemaker thought it would be funny if he played a trick on the rabbi.

For years, for decades, Rabbi Kibbitz had stood in the same place at the front of the shul as he davened, and over time ruts just the size of the rabbi's feet had been worn into the synagogue's wooden floor. Ordinarily, Reb Levitsky, the synagogue's janitor, would have repaired such a defect, but the people of Chelm were proud of their rabbi. In fact, when Rabbi Kibbitz was sick and Rabbi Yohon Abrahms, the mashgiach and head of the yeshiva took his place, he always stumbled in surprise at how deep and wide the ruts had become.

"Nobody," bragged the villagers, "can ever fill the shoes of our rabbi."

Well, one day this troublemaker decided to fill the ruts with wood glue.

Wood glue, if you're not familiar, is a thick and sticky substance designed to match the color of the wood it is applied to. This particular batch of wood glue was very quick drying.

The glue was applied on a Friday, just after the morning prayers. That would give it a chance to set and become invisible, but not harden completely.

The synagogue filled for the evening service. Sabbath greetings were shouted, backs were slapped, and at last Rabbi Kibbitz made his slow way to the place of honor.

As usual, he stepped right into his ruts. A momentary look of puzzlement crossed his brow as his feet sank slowly into the floor. By then, however, the sun was going down and the synagogue had grown dim. It was impossible to see that there was anything amiss, so he shrugged and began the service, davening as was his habit from left to right.

One thing I forgot to mention… The more you churn wood glue, the stickier it becomes. This glue, which was almost set, took hold of the Rabbi's boots and began to pull.

Side to side the Rabbi rocked as he quickly chanted the prayers, but then he slowed. He hesitated. Where were the soft thumps of his feet as they lifted right-left, right-left? In fact, he noticed now that he could barely lift his feet.

"Am I dying?" Rabbi Kibbitz wondered, not realizing that he spoke aloud.

Naturally, this upset the congregation.

Mrs. Chaipul, the midwife, hurried down from the women's balcony. She listened to the Rabbi's heart. It sounded fine. Still, Mrs. Chaipul suggested that the Rabbi take a seat.

But this was impossible. The glue had solidified, and by all appearances, the rabbi's feet had vanished into the floor.

Worse still, because this was a Friday night and the beginning of the Sabbath, no tools could be brought into the sanctuary to free him.

"It is a sign from the almighty!" Rabbi Kibbitz declared. "I shall pray all through the Sabbath, and by the end of Havdalah, the blessed one will set me free."

All night the rabbi prayed. Mrs. Chaipul came and brought him sandwiches, but he refused to eat because the crumbs would muffle his voice. In the morning, he was still there, barely awake. He couldn't move his feet, but his body still swayed, right to left, left to right, lurching with exhaustion like a drunkard on Purim. Through lunch, his rocking continued. All afternoon he prayed, until his voice became hoarse.

At last, the sun went down. The Havdalah candle was lit, held high, and then extinguished in the wine with a sputter.

Finally the rabbi was freed!

"A miracle," the pickle man said, somberly.

"Wait a second," said the fishmonger. "You mean to say that he actually managed to daven his way out of the glue?"

"Well, no," Abraham admitted. "After sunset, the carpenter ran back to his shop and brought back drills, hammers, a saw, and a pry bar."

Then the pickle man said, "How come your rabbi didn't just take off his shoes?"

"Yes, what's so wise about standing there like that?" asked the tea merchant.

"I'm glad you asked," Abraham said at last. "After he sat down, the rabbi said that whoever had poured the glue should be forgiven, because that person had taught him the true meaning of the word Eternity."

With that, Abraham smiled, picked up his purchases, and began the long walk home.

The merchants waited until he was out of sight, and then laughter once again filled the marketplace in Smyrna.

"A Schlemiel from Chelm," the pickle man said, clutching his sides. "Oy!"

Chapter Twenty

Well, Well...

Adam hated going to the well for water. First of all, it was supposed to be Abraham's job, but Abraham was off somewhere, still – after more than a year – moping about Rosa Kalderash, the Gypsy princess. Second of all, going to the well was women's work. There was always a line, and the women and girls in line would chatter like a flock of hens. Adam was supposed to be the carpenter's apprentice, not some scullery maid. Third of all, it meant that his family was poor. The wealthier families all had wells of their own. Some of them, like Reb Cantor, even had a well pump inside the house! All in all, Adam thought, going to the well was about as much fun as having a tooth pulled by tying it to a string, the string to a door, and slamming the door shut – only slower.

Enough with this pouting about Rosa, Adam had told Abraham. Yes, Rosa was a nice girl. For a time, Adam himself had thought he was in love with her, but she was gone. Long gone and far away. Abraham should forget about her.

Adam shlepped the two buckets all the way to the village square and then sighed as he saw the length of the line. There must be at least fifteen women standing around waiting their turns. How long did it take to lower a bucket, turn the crank, dump the bucket of water into your pail, and then head home? Hours, it seemed. And because it was a pleasant and sunny day, nobody was in much of a rush.

Father would be furious at him for coming into work late, but wouldn't say a thing because Mother had given Adam the task. Not to mention the likelihood that one of his friends or schoolmates might see him in the line and take the opportunity to taunt him about it. When you're a seventeen year-old boy, you don't want to be called "waterboy". Maybe Abraham didn't mind, but for Adam, who saw himself as a carpenter's apprentice, it was humiliating.

It wouldn't even be so bad if he just could sit down on one of the buckets, but if he flipped it over, then he'd get dirt in the water and his mother would be livid.

Adam sighed deeply and took his place in the line.

"How can you be sad on such a beautiful day?" came a voice.

It was a sweet voice, and when Adam turned around he was stunned to look into the face of the most beautiful girl he had ever seen.

She had long brown hair tucked into a beautiful red and white silk scarf. Her skin was fair and smooth. Her nose was long and slender. And her eyes were brown and deep, as rich and as full of life as a garden in full bloom.

Naturally, he couldn't say a word.

"Abraham," the girl said. "I haven't seen you in so long. I've been away, you see. Traveling. My father thought it would broaden my horizons to see some of the world, so I've been out of Chelm for almost a year now. How have you been?"

"Ff... fine," Adam sputtered. She looked familiar, but for the life of him he couldn't place her. "I've been very fine."

"Well," the girl said, "you look very handsome."

Adam was mortified. His heart was pounding like a hammer, his knees felt weak, and he could barely stand.

"You were always a good-looking fellow," she went on, "but time has treated you well."

"Thank you," he mumbled. He wanted to say, "You're the most beautiful girl I've ever seen." But he couldn't. He could barely look at her face. Instead, he looked at her shape, which was slim and tall and lovely, and found himself even more dumbstruck.

"Always polite," she said. "Not like your brother, Adam. Did you know I once had a crush on Adam? I don't even know if he knew. He was downright mean to me the last time I saw him."

"Well," Adam said at last, "he was a fool. How anyone could be unkind to someone as lovely and sweet as you is beyond my comprehension."

Now it was her turn to pause. She scanned him up and down and nodded, obviously pleased.

"So, Abraham," she said at last, "why do you sigh on such a beautiful day? The sun is high, the air is cool, spring is upon us, the mud is gone, and the world is filled with wonders."

"I, ah…" Adam paused. He couldn't tell her a thing that was wrong because all of a sudden nothing at all was wrong. So he said, "All the clouds on my darkened horizon were blown away the moment you spoke to me."

"A poet too!" she said. "How wonderful."

And so they talked about this and that and nothing at all. All around, the gaggle of women watched with smiles and nods and winks. The line moved slowly, slower than ever, but Adam didn't notice and wouldn't have minded if he did.

When they arrived at the head of the line, he drew her water first and then his own. He offered to carry her water back to her house (if only to find out where she lived). She laughed and asked him how could he possibly manage to carry four buckets at once. Two trips, he suggested. She shook her head no and said she would make her way home by herself. It wouldn't do for people to talk.

He nodded glumly and then asked if he might help her at the well again, and she said, "Of course, at least until my father's pump is fixed."

So he smiled and said, "Shalom."

And she smiled back, a smile as bright as a rainbow, a smile that he promised himself would live in his mind forever. And he watched her lift the two buckets and make her way slowly and elegantly across the square.

Adam sighed again, but this time the sigh was one of happiness.

"She's turned into something," said Mrs. Shikker, nudging Adam in the ribs.

Adam blushed. Then he had a thought. "Who is she?"

"You don't remember?" Mrs. Shikker smirked. "That's Rivka Cantor, Reb Cantor's daughter."

Oh no, Adam thought. He picked up his buckets and made his way slowly home. Oy.

A Half-Bucket of Tears

Every morning for the next two weeks, Adam Schlemiel grabbed the water buckets and hurried to the village well. ("Without being asked," his mother whispered to his father. "Without even being reminded. Something's wrong with the boy.") There he waited patiently for Rivka Cantor, and when she arrived his face brightened and his whole day turned to light.

They talked about everything and about nothing, about animals and springtime, about the world that Rivka had seen in her travels, and about life in Chelm, which (although often boring and slow) now seemed so cheerful and filled with promise.

And every day when Rivka left she smiled and said, "Until tomorrow, Abraham."

Her smile made him melt, but her parting words – 'Until tomorrow, Abraham' – made him grimace.

So every day, he trudged home both exalted and diminished.

Then, one day, Rivka Cantor didn't come to the well. Adam waited and dawdled. One after another, he helped the women of Chelm fill their buckets from the well, all the while listening to their praise. "Abraham, you're such a good boy." His mind was elsewhere, his eyes darting around the village square, looking for her quick and lovely shape…

At last, with noon fast approaching, Adam made his way home, his heart crushed.

"Where have you been?" his mother asked. "It's bad enough I've got one good for nothing son who does nothing but run off into the woods when there's a sign of a chore to be done. Now I've got two? Your father was looking for you. He's got work to be done. He says that it's Abraham's job to get the water, not yours, so enough with the nonsense. And where's the water? Three hours you've been at the well, and you forgot to bring back water? What is going on here?"

Adam peered into the empty buckets and immediately burst into tears.

"Okay, okay. It's not such a big deal," his mother said. "So, you forgot the water… If Abraham ever gets back, I'll send him to the well…"

Adam's sobs grew even louder.

"Madmen," his mother muttered. "I gave birth to a matched set of lunatics. One falls in love with a Gypsy. The other tries to fill the water bucket with tears."

Then, as any mother would do, she opened her arms and hugged her boy tight, patting his back and smoothing his hair. "Sha… Shaa."

Eventually, Adam's crying subsided and he dried his eyes.

"So?" his mother said. "Tell me."

"It's a girl."

"A girl?" Her voice brightened.

Adam nodded and then it all came out in a rush. "I'm in love. I love her. She's beautiful. She's smart. And she's rich."

"Mazel tov! Is she kind?"

"As kind as a kitten."

"Does she have a sweet disposition?"

"Like honey."

"She's not married or betrothed, is she?"

Adam shook his head. "No. No. I don't think so. No."

"That's good. So, what's the problem? Doesn't she like you?"

"Yes." Adam began to sniff. "No. Maybe. I don't know. Sometimes yes. Sometimes no."

"So far, everything you're telling me seems normal, if a bit confusing. We'll call the matchmaker and ask her to set up a meeting with the parents. A six-month waiting period should be long enough to make sure that everything could work. What do you say?"

Adam hesitated. He sputtered. He stuttered. "She… She thinks… She thinks that I'm Abraham."

Rebecca Schlemiel blinked. "You're not Abraham?"

"No, I'm not Abraham! I'm Adam."

She looked at her son carefully. "You're sure you're Adam?"

Adam nodded.

"Because with you two," his mother continued, "even though I'm your mother and after all these years I should know,

I sometimes get confused. It's not surprising she thinks you're Abraham some of the time. At the well! Ah. That makes it clear. Everybody in Chelm knows that Abraham goes to the well while Adam works in his father's shop. So, it's an honest mistake. Just tell her the truth."

"But she doesn't like Adam. She hates Adam."

"But you said she likes you."

"She likes me when she thinks I'm Abraham."

"So, you tricked her." His mother frowned. "Did you do this on purpose?"

"No. I didn't know," Adam explained. "I hadn't seen her before. Not in a long time. I didn't even recognize her. Believe me, by the time I found out who she was, and who she thought I was, it was too late."

"So, who is she?"

"Rivka Cantor."

Rebecca Schlemiel's eyes widened. "Reb Cantor's daughter?"

A nod from her son.

"You remember that I was once engaged to Reb Cantor?"

Another nod.

"But that's not the problem, is it?"

Adam shook his head. "No."

"Good," said his mother. "You have enough troubles of your own without adding another generation's problems. So, listen, Adam. Tell her. Tell her the truth."

"I can't."

"What's the worst that could happen?"

"The worst? She could slap me across the face and say she hates me and never wants to see me again."

"You think she'd do that?"

He nodded. "I think she might."

"So," his mother said thoughtfully. "You think she loves you too. But not you. Not exactly. She only loves you when she thinks you're Abraham? Oy."

"That's about the size of it," Adam said.

"Hmm," his mother said. "It sounds hopeless. But then again, love usually is. Hopeless, but wonderful."

Rebecca Schlemiel put her hands on her hips and frowned. "You're going to sit there and tell me that there is a beautiful girl who is rich and kind and sweet. You love her, but... never mind. You're just going to pretend it's another one of your practical jokes? Something that doesn't matter? So, what happens when Abraham finally bumps into this girl and she accidentally tells him how much she loves him?"

That last thought was too much. Adam started crying again.

"More tears? Don't look at me for sympathy. Aim your tears for the bucket. You've been meeting this girl every day for weeks, but you couldn't be bothered to mention that, by the way, my name isn't Abraham, it's Adam? And now you think I'm going to help you?"

Rebecca Schlemiel looked at her son, whose shoulders were heaving with every sob.

"All right. All right," she said. "I'll help you. We'll figure out something. So stop already, your nose is running on my nice clean blouse."

Chapter Twenty-One

Signs in the Forest

Abraham looked up from the rock he was sitting on, and smiled. It was strange. Deep in the Schvartzvald, the black forest, he could still sense his brother's emotions. Sometimes, he could even hear into Adam's mind, but that ability had grown dimmer as they'd grown older. But that wasn't the strange thing. Today, Abraham could tell that Adam was miserable. And for some reason that particular thought made Abraham feel happy.

The next moment, he questioned it. "Why should I rejoice at my brother's unhappiness?"

But then another wave of pleasure lifted him up onto his feet, and Abraham found himself standing on the rock high above the forest's floor, laughing aloud for what seemed like the first time in months.

'This is incredible!' Abraham thought as he laughed. 'Sad, but incredible. Sad in the sense that I am benefiting so gloriously at Adam's expense. Incredible because I feel hopeful. I want to dance. I want to sing!'

And so, Abraham sang.

"Rosa! Rosa... Rosaaaaah!"

As cheerful as Abraham had suddenly become, such cheerfulness hadn't transformed him into a witty lyricist. Nor had it made his voice trill like the song of an angel. When he hit the highest note, a flock of birds lifted out of a nearby elm tree and sped away west, never to be seen in Eastern Europe again.

He took the sudden flight of the birds as a sign.

"To the west." Abraham danced. "To Rosa... To the west..."

It's one thing to stand on a boulder and sing a silly song in the middle of a forest. It's another to perform a jig on a rock. All at once, and without warning, Abraham's feet slid out from under him. He fell and landed with a thud, his head cracking against a nearby log.

When Abraham finally regained consciousness, it was dark. The sky was filled from horizon to horizon with stars.

He blinked twice, winced, and then sat up suddenly. Where was he?

A wave of dizziness nearly knocked him back into blackness.

He set a hand down on the damp ground and steadied himself. With his other hand, he reached behind his head, and felt a sticky patch of scalp with a few crusts of blood. He'd obviously cut himself, but he didn't seem to be bleeding at the moment. One small blessing to be thankful for.

Now came a more important question. Which way was home?

He squinted in every direction, but after nightfall one tree looks pretty much the same as the next. Abraham looked up at the stars. He knew one was the North Star, but which one? There were so many. Truly they were like grains of sand on a beach.

Ever since he'd lost her, for almost a year, Abraham Schlemiel had been seriously considering leaving Chelm and taking to the road in search of Rosa Kalderash. That was the reason he'd been spending so much time in the Schvartzvald, not simply to get away from his family, but to learn the ways of the woods. He'd practiced walking along narrow trails like a Gypsy. He'd taught himself which tree roots and berries were edible and which should be avoided. He'd become a master mushroomer, and made many a lunch from fat morels roasted with onion grass over a slow fire.

And he'd dreamed he was out of Chelm, out in the world. On the road, making his way, living by his wits and skills, in search of his true love.

But every night he'd gone home. There, he'd eaten his supper in silence, listened to his family bicker and laugh, and climbed into bed beside his brother with barely a word.

Perhaps this really was a sign. It was past dark and he was alone still. The birds had flown to the west. He had heard that when the Gypsies had left Smyrna they had been seen heading toward the west. Maybe it was time.

But could he really go, just like that? Without a word of goodbye?

It would break his mother's heart, and she was so weak. Of course, if he ever got enough courage to tell her to her face that he was going, that would probably break her heart too. In his mind, he could hear her saying, "All right, Abraham, you want to leave me here to get sick and die? Fine. Do what you want."

So much thinking caused Abraham's head to spin. Sometimes he hated his family's curse. Perhaps it was best to give in to it and know that no matter which choice he made everyone would be miserable, so why not make a bad choice for a good reason?

"Idiot!"

The loud word startled Abraham. For a moment, he thought the shout was Adam yelling from inside his skull.

"I can't believe you lost the road," said a voice in Russian.

"What road?" said a second voice. "You said you wanted a drink of water, and I said that I heard water. It's not my fault the river is all mud."

"You were supposed to remember how to get back to the road."

"You called that a road?" said the second voice. "Two ruts in the mud? That's like a farmer's cow path."

"Moscow prejudice," said the first voice. "Sergeant, if you're not careful, I'll report you."

"And I'll tell them that my captain, Boris Plotz, got us lost in the woods."

"You're the one who led us astray."

"But you're the leader."

There followed a volley of cursing so intense that if words were cannonballs the entire forest would have been flattened.

Abraham sat still, his face red as he imagined some of the things these men had just called each other.

At last, the shouting stopped, and he heard their footsteps drawing closer.

"So, where's this water?"

"Who can hear water with all the yelling?"

"Sergeant," Captain Plotz warned. "You are coming dangerously close to insubordination!"

Just then, the Sergeant's boot kicked Abraham soundly in the thigh.

"Yow!" Abraham yelled. He jumped to his feet and was about to run, but the world began to spin and he had to steady himself on the boulder.

This was all for the better because a moment later he heard two sharp clicks of rifle bolts being drawn back and two men ordering in a single voice, "Halt!"

Two Soldiers

"Stop!" barked the Captain. "Turn around slowly."

"Come here, boy," ordered the Sergeant.

"Stop!" shouted the Captain. "Turn around slowly."

"Come here," insisted the Sergeant.

Abraham did what any boy from Chelm would do, he began spinning around slowly as he walked toward the soldiers, which wasn't easy because he was still dizzy from his fall.

The two men, with their rifles raised, squinted in astonishment as Abraham slowly swirled toward them like a drunken ballerina.

Then they smiled.

"Stop!" they both barked.

Abraham stopped. The men exchanged glances.

"Stand on one foot," ordered the Captain.

"Touch your left hand to your nose," added the Sergeant.

"Keep turning," said the Captain. "Start again."

"And hop, too!"

Poor Abraham did his best, hopping on one foot and spinning around while touching his nose. Round and around. He actually managed to keep it up for a while. Of course, by then the soldiers had changed the rules. Soon he was patting his head, rubbing his belly, and bouncing from one foot to the next while saying,

"Boingo-boingo smlutt-nik flokka-flokka-flue!"

Eventually, Abraham's foot found a tree root and he fell to the ground with a thud. The Russians also fell to the ground, laughing.

"Sergeant, get off me!" laughed the Captain.

Abraham tried to use this as an opportunity to crawl away.

"Don't move," the Sergeant said, getting to his feet.

Abraham stopped. He whimpered, "Are you going to kill me?"

"I think you are trying to kill us," said the Captain as the Sergeant helped him to his feet. "Kill us with laughter."

"No, no," Abraham said seriously.

The soldiers guffawed.

"Poor kid," said the Sergeant. "He has no idea."

"No, you're right," the Captain agreed. "None whatsoever. What's your name and where are you from?"

"I'm Abraham Schlemiel. I'm from Chelm."

"Schlemiel, that name sounds familiar…" The Captain stared at Abraham. "Are you one of the two boys who captured Alex Krabot?"

Abraham blushed and nodded. "Yes. That was me and my twin brother."

Then the Sergeant smacked himself on the forehead. "We're near Chelm!"

"So?" said the Captain. "Chelm is on the list?"

"Yes, but the river dries up near Chelm. There's no water here."

"Then why we are wandering blindly through the woods, Sergeant?"

The two men argued for a few minutes while Abraham sat on the ground, brushing dirt and dried leaves from his coat.

At last the Captain spoke to him. "You must have a well in Chelm, right?"

Abraham nodded. "Yes."

"Let's go then. Get up. No more nonsense."

Abraham rose to his feet. "Ummm…"

"What?" the Captain snapped.

"I don't know which way to go."

"You're lost?" the Captain said. "You live here and you pretend you're lost? What kind of fools do you take us for?"

"Sir," said the Sergeant, "he is from Chelm."

"So?'

"So, the people of Chelm are idiots. Once, the story goes, the villagers of Chelm were trying to move a mountain just by pushing on it. The day got hot, so they took off their coats and a thief stole them. A little later, they turned around and saw their coats were gone. 'Wonderful!' the villagers of Chelm said. 'We pushed the mountain so far that we can't see our coats anymore.'"

The Captain was puzzled. "Is that supposed to be funny?"

The Sergeant shrugged, "It is when you've drunk half a bottle of vodka."

"It worked," Abraham said, suddenly defensive. "Do you see any mountains around here?"

The two men stared at the boy, and then laughed.

"Come on," said the Sergeant, poking Abraham with the barrel of his rifle. "Let's find our way back to the road. You'd better remember your way from there."

An hour and two bramble bushes later, the trio were making their way south along the road from Smyrna to Chelm. The two men had slung their rifles across their shoulders and were trudging along wearily, while Abraham tried to think of the best way to escape.

"So," he said at last, "what brings you gentlemen to Chelm?"

"Gentlemen?" snorted the Sergeant.

"Speak for yourself, Vassily," Captain Plotz said. He turned to Abraham. "We are recruiting. The Czar needs more soldiers. How old are you?"

Abraham cursed his luck. "Seventeen."

"Perfect! Just the right age. If you're lucky, and you sign up willingly, they might even give you a gun."

"I recommend enlisting willingly," the Sergeant said. "When someone is shooting at you, it's better to have a gun than not."

"But," Abraham asked, "what's the point of being a soldier without a gun?"

"Target practice," said the Sergeant with a shrug. "Cannon fodder."

"Oh." Abraham wasn't sure if the man was serious. "Is that what it's like being a soldier?"

"Nonsense," the Captain said. "You serve the Czar and Mother Russia nobly and with honor!"

"In reality," the Sergeant whispered, "the food, when there is food, stinks. Literally. And your uniform probably won't fit. Even if you do get a gun, chances are it will break or be completely rusted. The bullets, if you have any, only fire once out of three times. My cousin is a colonel, which is the only reason that my rifle works and I have ammunition that will probably fire. You? Your boots will be filled with mud, your hair will get lice, and you should never ever get in the way of a cannon ball."

"You know, I think I'd rather pass," Abraham said.

"You don't want to serve the Czar and Mother Russia nobly and with honor?" said the Captain in mock horror. "Then we'll have to impress you."

"I don't know what you could say to impress me," Abraham said. "It sounds horrible."

"No, you idiot," the Captain laughed. "When we impress you, we sign you up whether you want to or not. That's how Vassily here got in the army."

"I should have run away when I had the chance," the Sergeant muttered.

But then Abraham remembered something. "I'm Polish!" he said suddenly.

"Of course you are," the Captain said.

"Do you have papers?" the Sergeant asked.

Abraham nodded. He reached into his pocket. The men stopped and looked. Even by starlight, it was clear that Abraham's papers identified him as a citizen of Poland.

"You know," said the Sergeant, "these papers could be forged. Or they might be accidentally destroyed." He held the papers in both hands and looked ready to rip them in two.

"Don't torture the boy," the Captain said. "We'll visit the records office in Chelm and find out who's eligible and who isn't. No point in starting a war with Poland over a boy from Chelm."

"But who would know?" the Sergeant asked.

"Give them back."

The Sergeant held the packet high and made Abraham jump three or four times before letting the boy grab the papers.

"Is that Chelm up ahead?" the Captain asked. "Let's go. I'm thirsty, I'm hungry, and I want to sleep in a Jewish bed tonight."

Abraham barely heard the man. He was too busy thinking about his brother, and wondering whether he might be able to warn Adam...

No, You're in Trouble

In the faint light of dawn, Abraham silently slipped in through his bedroom window and nudged his brother Adam, who lay asleep in their bed.

"Wha?"

"Shh," Abraham whispered. "You are in such big trouble."

Adam's eyes blinked open, and he nodded. "I know. And it's all your fault."

"I know," Abraham agreed. "But I didn't do it on purpose."

"I know. If I wasn't such a coward..."

"Adam, this has nothing to do with cowardice. It's self-preservation. It's about surviving long enough to build a future. You can't do that if you're dead."

"Yes." Adam rolled over onto his belly. "I wish I were dead." His voice was muffled by his pillow. Then he sat up suddenly, nearly knocking Abraham from the bed. "Wait a moment, dead? What do you mean dead?"

"Shot. You know. Dead. Bang."

Adam's face drooped. "Her father knows already?"

"Whose father?"

"Who else is going to kill me? Reb Cantor, Rivka Cantor's father. First of all, he hasn't liked me for years. Second of all, he doesn't like you much either."

"Me?" Abraham said. "Why wouldn't he like me?"

"Because you're my brother. And third of all, he's probably the only man in Chelm who has a gun."

"Not any more," Abraham said. "There are two Russian soldiers in Chelm. I just managed to sneak away from them."

"More taxes?" Adam said.

"Worse." Abraham shook his head. "They're conscripting boys into the Russian army."

"So?"

"So, you're seventeen years old, and you're Russian. Your name is on their list."[3]

Adam's eyes widened and he stifled a sob. "It's the curse. Nothing will ever turn out right."

"Sha sha sha," Abraham said. He patted his brother gently on the head. "We'll figure something out. What is this about a girl? Rivka Cantor? I thought you hated her."

"I don't. I used to. I don't anymore. I love her," Adam bawled. "But she doesn't love me. She loves you."

"Me? How can she love me? She doesn't even know me. Besides, I thought Rivka Cantor was traveling in America."

"She's back now, and she's beautiful and kind and wise…" Adam's voice trailed off into tears.

"Well, if she's so wise, how could she be in love with me?"

"She… Thinks… I'm… You…"

"Adam, you didn't?"

"I did." Adam nodded. "I met Rivka at the well. I was doing your chores. I didn't know who she was, and I didn't realize who she thought I was until it was too late. Now she says definitively that

---

[3] Perhaps you remember the earlier historical footnote? Perhaps not. It was by a strange coincidence that on the day the twins were born, the province that Chelm was located in had been traded by the King of Poland to the Czar of Russia for fifteen pounds of caviar and two boxes of Cuban cigars. This kind of somewhat random territorial change wasn't unusual. During Rabbi Kibbitz's long life, Chelm had been the property of Russia, Poland, Austria, France, and even Finland (for twenty minutes). Thus, as the firstborn, Abraham was Polish, while Adam, who was born twelve hours later, was considered a son of Mother Russia.

she'd never marry anybody named Adam."

Abraham's eyes widened. "You've had conversations about marriage already?"

"We were joking, but yes."

"Mazel Tov."

Adam jumped from the bed. "You're wishing me luck? I finally find a girl I can't live without and the next day the Russian army comes into town to put me out of my misery? That's luck?"

He took a swing at Abraham, but he tripped over his night shirt and ended up sprawled on the floor.

"Are you all right?" Abraham asked, giggling.

"Fine."

"Then shh. You want to wake Mama and Papa?"

"I'm not the one who didn't come home last night."

Abraham nodded. "You didn't have guns pointed at you all night."

"Really? You're serious?"

Abraham nodded. "Yes, but… Look, why don't we just tell her?"

"She'll think that I was trying to make a fool out of her. She's in love with you, why don't you just take her?"

"No!" Abraham said. "I'm in love with someone else."

"Still with Rosa, the Gypsy princess?" Now Adam rolled his eyes. "Abraham, she barely gave you the time of day when she was in Chelm, and that was so long ago."

Abraham blushed. "Adam, does your heart want to burst with the thought of Rivka?"

"Yes. So?"

"Do you feel like jumping with joy and crying at the same time? As if someone had cut off your arm, like a piece of you is missing? Do you feel as if your life will be over unless you can be with this girl?"

Adam nodded.

"Then you know how I feel about Rosa," Abraham said. "Don't tell me otherwise."

"Abraham," Adam said, slowly considering each word. "I spent a lot of time with Rosa. And I hate to say this, but she was more in love with me than she was with you."

"No," Abraham shook his head. "Don't say such things."

"Yes," Adam nodded. "She was."

"But, did you know that she and I..."

"Abraham, sha. I know that you love her, or loved her, or think that you love her still, but the fact is that Rosa's gone. Right now, there is a girl in Chelm, a Jewish girl, who is in love with you."

"But, Adam, she's not really in love with me. And you're the one who's in love with her."

"Oy, what does it matter?" Adam sighed. He stood and began getting dressed. "It's plainly obvious that I'm not going to get what I want. Why should everyone in the family suffer? You marry her, and I'll join the Russian army and get killed in Siberia."

"Is that where you're going now?" Abraham asked.

"Yes."

"Maybe you should take off your night shirt before you put on your jacket."

Adam looked down and frowned. "You don't think it looks distinguished?"

Abraham grinned back. "No. Now sit down and listen. There's got to be something else we can do. The Schlemiel twins have outwitted demons, criminals, and rabbis. All we have to deal with now are two Russian soldiers and a girl."

Adam sat down on the bed and said, "I'd rather face a Russian firing squad than hear Rivka Cantor say that she hates me."

"You're an idiot, but I can understand that. Now, let's think."

Chapter Twenty-Two

Over a Barrel

Shortly before dawn, a loud noise was heard rumbling through the village of Chelm. Puzzled farmers peered into the cool cloudless sky and wondered if a storm was coming. Then, as suddenly as it began, the noise stopped, and was replaced by a whispered bickering in the village square that was only heard by two young men.

"I don't see how this is going to work," hissed Adam Schlemiel. Catching his breath, he stared up at the gigantic pickle barrel they had rolled from behind Mrs. Chaipul's restaurant. The barrel was huge – four feet wide and six and a half feet high. "What would we have possibly done if the barrel wasn't empty?"

"Do you love this girl?" asked Abraham.

"You know I do!"

"Then get in the barrel."

"Get in? Why do I have to get in? Why not you?"

"Quickly!" Abraham urged. "Someone's coming!"

Cursing loudly, Adam Schlemiel jumped up and grabbed the top of the barrel. As he pulled, Abraham pushed and an instant later Adam tumbled in head first. "Ow!"

"Shh!"

"There are still some pickles in the bottom!" Adam muttered, but by then Abraham had slammed the lid back on top. "It smells in here!"

"That's quite some barrel, Abraham Schlemiel," said Mrs. Chaipul, who visited the well first thing every morning to get water for her restaurant's customers. "Is that my barrel?"

"I'm just borrowing it." Abraham began filling Mrs. Chaipul's water buckets.

"It's for a special project," he said, turning the crank to bring the water up.

"Ahh," Mrs. Chaipul nodded. "Just make sure that your brother can breathe in there. Thank you very much." And away she went.

Abraham pried open the lid. "Are you all right?"

"Yes," Adam gasped. "Aren't there easier ways for you to kill me?"

"Mrs. Chaipul must have seen us. I won't put the lid on so tightly. Be quiet. Someone else is coming."

The morning passed quickly for Abraham, who busied himself hauling buckets of water for the villagers. For Adam, squatting in six inches of pickle juice, it seemed like an eternity until he heard a familiar voice. He immediately stood up so that he could listen better.

"Hello, Abraham."

"Hello, uh…"

Adam banged the side of the barrel.

"Rivka!" Abraham said. He smiled. Adam was right, during her travels away from Chelm, Rivka Cantor had blossomed. She was stunningly beautiful.

"You don't know me any more?" the young woman said.

Abraham felt himself blushing. "I feel as if I haven't seen you in ages."

"It's only been a few days," Rivka said. "My father finally got our well's pump fixed. Fortunately, last night I accidentally broke it. What is a pickle barrel doing next to the well?"

"Get to it," Adam whispered.

"Well, it's an idea I had," Abraham said. He found himself stumbling, tongue-tied. "What if we filled up the pickle barrel with water and then filled our buckets from the pickle barrel?"

Rivka smiled. "Then we'd have pickle-flavored water."

Get in here! Adam said, using mind-speech to talk directly to Abraham.

It had been a while since Abraham had heard Adam's voice so clearly in his mind. The sudden interruption startled Abraham.

Get in here!

"No!" Abraham said. "I mean, oh, it's clean."

Now! Adam began banging on the side of the barrel.

Rivka looked puzzled. "It sounds as if there's a raccoon in there."

"No, that's just water settling. Uh, let me look." Abraham pulled himself up to the barrel's rim and whispered, "What?"

Adam grabbed Abraham's collar and pulled. Abraham tumbled down, head first on top of Adam.

"Ooof!"

"Abraham!" came Rivka's concerned voice. "Are you all right?"

Adam whispered, "Bend over," to Abraham.

"What?"

"Just do it."

"Abraham? Are you all right?"

Adam stepped onto Abraham's back and stood up. His head poked over the top of the barrel. "Fine. Fine."

"Your hair is wet. And you look taller."

"Oh, I slipped," Adam said. "There's a stool in here."

Abraham muttered, "Watch your boot."

"Why is there a stool inside a pickle barrel?" Rivka asked.

"To stand on," Adam answered. "In case you fall in."

Again Abraham muttered, "Watch your boot."

"What?" Rivka said.

"It's an echo," Adam said. "I said, you look beautiful."

Now it was Rivka's turn to blush. "Thank you. You're acting very peculiar today."

"What do you mean?

"I don't know," she said. "A moment ago you were so distant, and now you seem... Comfortable? Like yourself."

I am not comfortable! Abraham said into Adam's mind. *Ask her!*

"All right!" Adam blurted. "Rivka, would you marry my brother?"

"What?" Rivka said.

Idiot!

"Now you're a matchmaker?" she began.

"No." Adam quickly interrupted. "I mean, if I wasn't Abraham, would you still like me? Or if my name was Adam..."

"You are acting very strange," Rivka said.

Abraham could listen no longer. He shifted out from under

Adam, who fell into the barrel with a thud. A moment later, Abraham stood up on top of his still-squirming brother.

"The stool is slippery," he explained. "I'm sorry. Look, let me be honest. How do you feel about me? Right now?"

"A moment ago," Rivka said nervously, "I was feeling quite settled. But now I'm not sure. You seem, I don't know. Wasn't your hair wet?"

"Would you like a pickle?" Abraham said suddenly. He jumped off Adam, ducked into the barrel, and dipped his hair into the water.

"I…" Rivka said. She stared up at the rim of the barrel, confused.

"What are you doing?" Adam hissed.

"Shh," Abraham said. *Use mind-speak.*

– Okay, so? What are you doing?

+ She's beautiful, Abraham said.

– I know. Couldn't you marry her?

+ Yes, but no. I love Rosa. Rivka loves you. Not me.

– I know that, but she thinks she loves you, Adam said. *And I'm going into the Russian army…*

+ No, Abraham said. *Give her this pickle. Ask her to marry you.*

– Are you crazy?

"Abraham?" Rivka's voice echoed into the barrel. "I have to get my water now."

"Wait, please!" Abraham shouted. "I'm coming."

She's in love with you, Abraham said, *but she likes my name. So, I'll give it to you. You can have it. Who's to say that you're not Abraham anyway? You've heard the stories about how Mama and Papa mixed us up when we were little. You be Abraham and I'll be Adam.*

But what about the Russian army?

Here. Abraham handed Adam a damp bundle.

– What's this?

+ My papers. They prove that you're Polish. You take them.

– But what about you?

Abraham shrugged. *The Russian army I'll run away from. You stay here and marry Rivka. As you said, there's no point in both of us being unhappy.*

Adam stared at his brother in the dim light at the bottom of the pickle barrel.

"You would do this for me?" he whispered aloud.

Abraham nodded. "Of course."

The brothers hugged. Abraham twined his fingers together. Adam stepped into the stirrup. Abraham lifted and Adam was boosted up and out of the barrel.

"Whaaa!" Adam said, flying through the air. He landed, almost gracefully, just behind Rivka Cantor, who turned around and looked extremely startled.

"I thought you were getting me a pickle," she said.

Just then, a pickle soared out of the barrel toward the back of Rivka's lovely head. Adam reached past her ear and caught it, like a conjuring magician.

"A sour pickle for my sweet one," he said smoothly.

Rivka blushed.

"Rivka, will you marry me?" Adam asked.

"Abraham." Rivka blinked. "You're proposing to me with a pickle?"

Adam shrugged. "I'm not a rich man like your father. I'm not as eloquent as my brother. All I know is that I want to spend every day of the rest of my life with you."

She stared into his eyes, and then nodded. "Of course I will."

"Who hoo!" came a shout from the depths of the pickle barrel.

Rivka jumped. "What was that?"

"I threw my voice," Adam said nonchalantly. "Let's fill your buckets, and tell… I mean ask your father."

Two minutes later, the young lovers were gone.

Inside the barrel, Abraham was grinning. He couldn't help himself. So what if he was alone at the bottom of a smelly old barrel. He munched on a pickle and smiled with happiness for his brother.

Chapter Twenty-Three

Home

By the time he finally got to the front door to his house, Abraham Schlemiel was asleep on his feet. Not only had he been up for almost two days straight, but getting out of the gigantic pickle barrel had nearly killed him.

After eating a dozen pickles, he had gotten thirsty and began shouting for someone to get him some water. The women of Chelm who were at the well took him literally and began dumping bucket after bucket of water into the barrel. Then, when Abraham yelled for them to stop they decided that the barrel must be haunted and ran off, screaming. He had finally gotten out by slamming back and forth into the walls, diluted pickle water sloshing from side to side, until the barrel tilted, fell, and then rolled two hundred yards across the round village square, where it smashed into the side of the synagogue. Abraham felt sick, and it was all he could do not to vomit a mess of half-digested pickles on the steps of the shul.

Now that he was home all he wanted to do was lie down and go to sleep.

"Adam!" his mother said, as he came inside, her voice a cheerful hammer tapping against his brain. "Did you hear the good news? Abraham is getting married. Oh my god! Adam, you look awful. You smell like pickles. Abraham smelled like pickles. Why does everyone smell like pickles? Are you all right? Can I get you something? You want some chicken soup or a little brisket? I have some mashed potatoes. There's a kugel in the oven. It should be ready any minute now. Or maybe some chopped liver?"

Abraham nodded and burped greenish pickle breath that sent his mother stumbling back.

"Feh," Rebecca Schlemiel said. "Sit down. I can only imagine that this news must be shocking to you. I know that you were fond of Rivka Cantor, but... Adam, I'm sorry."

"No, it's not that." Abraham looked at his mother. She thought he was Adam. Their plan was working. "It's good. I'm all right. My brother can have Rivka. I'm just tired." He folded his arms, closed his eyes, and lay his head on the table.

His mother nodded. "There were soldiers here today looking for you. I told them you were probably at your father's shop. But then when I heard the news, I wasn't sure what had happened."

Abraham wearily lifted his head. "The soldiers were here already?"

Rebecca nodded. "They said they were drafting young men into the Russian army." Her voice was quiet and serious. "What are we going to do?"

Abraham rubbed his face. What was there to do? He knew. His mother knew. They just didn't want to say. For months he'd imagined what it would be like to be out on his own, wandering the world in search of Rosa Kalderash. Now that he had to leave Chelm, he found he didn't want to. All he wanted was to lie in his own bed, sleep without dreams, and wake up in time for dinner. Then he'd sit, crowded around the table, elbow to elbow with his brother, new sister-in-law, sister, mother, father, and whatever friends or relatives happened to be in the neighborhood for the brisket and soup and mashed potatoes and kugel. Then he and Adam would go for a walk and slap each other on the back. Joke about the future, about girls. About Adam's marriage...

Abraham roused himself from his dozing dream. "I need to pack," he croaked. "The soldiers will be back. I can't stay."

"Can't you hide?" His mother's voice was nearly begging. "The attic in your father's shop. It's a good hiding place. I'll bring you food."

"No." Abraham shook his head. "I know these men. I've met them. They seem like idiots, but they're not stupid. They'll expect me to hide. They'll wait, and they'll look, and they'll search. And if they find me it'll be worse than if I volunteered to begin with."

Rebecca Schlemiel nodded sadly, coughed, and suddenly felt

very, very old. Her heart was nearly breaking, but she dared not cry. She'd have the two of them in tears, paralyzed, and the Russians would find him there, salty and soaked, and drag him away.

So she sighed and began rummaging for a rucksack.

"You take a bath, and I'll pack for you," she said as she began bustling from room to room. "Properly, you should leave your parents' house with a wagon filled with clothing and furniture and everything you need to start a house of your own. Instead... A couple pairs of underwear, a few pairs of socks? Several shirts. A sewing kit. Your boots and coat of course. What else? Hats and gloves. An oilskin raincoat that belonged to your great uncle Noah. He always said that it would get him through a flood. A knife, a fork, and this."

Abraham lifted his head off the table again and saw his mother standing before him holding a ten-inch cast iron frying pan.

"This was my mother's," she said, "and her mother's before her." She wedged the pan into the rucksack. "Adam, I know you can't cook, but you'll need something to eat. Here's some garlic and some dried meat. A water skin. Some currant jam. There's just not enough room for everything. You'll have to be able to walk quickly and quietly without getting tired."

Abraham felt the tears rolling down his cheeks.

"Look," said his mother, sniffling, "if you're going to sit there like a lump, the least you can do is go and wash your hair. You stink of pickles. Use my Paris soap, all right?"

Abraham nodded and gave his mother a hug.

They held each other for a long time. Then he took a bucket of water from next to the stove and went outside to the bathtub.

Rebecca Schlemiel stood still, hugging her arms across her chest.

"Don't forget to wash behind your ears!" she shouted, with only a little catch in her voice.

Goodbye, Adam

After Abraham had dried himself and dressed in clean clothes, he felt much better. He still could use a good long nap, but didn't have the time. The longer he waited, the more likely it was that the soldiers would come back to the house. At last, he gave his mother a hug and swung the rucksack onto his back.

"Here." His mother handed him a cloth napkin with its corners tied into a sack. "It's a brisket sandwich. You can eat it while you walk."

Abraham nodded. He was afraid to say anything, afraid he would start crying.

"You have to say goodbye to your father," she said.

"I know."

They hugged again and kissed, and through her tears Rebecca Schlemiel whispered, "Come back soon."

Abraham couldn't speak. He gave his mother one last squeeze and slipped out the door.

As she watched her son through the crack in the door, Rebecca remembered the words the Gypsy queen had spoken so long ago, "One day here, the next gone... The lost son returns, but the son who has vanished has never left. They come together. One becomes two – different, and yet the same."

Rebecca Schlemiel found herself shivering. She shook her head and began to sob.

By now it was late afternoon, and the streets of Chelm were nearly empty. Everyone was either busy at work, at school, or making dinner. Abraham quickly looked around for the Russian soldiers, but fortunately they were nowhere in sight.

He glanced up at the sun and guessed he still had three hours until sunset. If he stopped to visit his father, how long would that take?

Abraham wasn't sure how his father felt about him. He knew that Jacob Schlemiel loved all his children, but for years, Abraham

had worked in his mother's kitchen instead of at the wood shop.
Even though he had never said anything, Abraham thought
his father was disappointed. He'd always complained that Adam
was lazy and useless, a bumbler in the shop. Once, Abraham had
overheard his parents talking. His father had suggested that they
trade twins for a while, and have Abraham work in the shop while
Adam would help around the house. His mother had said that
wouldn't be fair to either boy, so the arrangement had been left as it
was.

What would happen now that he was leaving? Abraham
wondered.

"Abraham," said a giggling voice, "where are you going?"

Abraham looked down and saw his sister Shemini smiling up at
him.

How could he have forgotten Sheminie? She was so beautiful.
And bright. A bundle of joy and mischief.

"I'm Adam," Abraham said. "And I have to go away for a while.
But I'm going to miss you."

"Abraham," Shemini said, poking him in the belly.

"No," he laughed. "And I am Adam. And I have to hurry."

Shemini looked up at her brother's face and saw how sad and
serious he looked. It didn't bother her that he was wearing a thirty-
pound backpack. She jumped up into her brother's arms and held
him tight.

"I love you, Abraham," she whispered in his ear.

"I love you too, Shemini," he whispered back, kissing her cheek
and breathing the smell of her soft hair.

Then Shemini jumped down, waved, said, "Bye, Adam," and
was gone.

Suddenly unbalanced, Abraham stumbled backward and nearly
fell. Fortunately, he caught himself. It wouldn't do to land in a mud
puddle and get soaked before his journey had even begun.

Before he knew it, his feet had taken him to the door of his
father's shop. He knocked, pushed the door open, and peeked in.

"Father?"

There was no answer. He felt relieved. He couldn't go searching all over Chelm just to say goodbye. That would be the surest way to bump into the Russians. So, he decided to write a note, but he couldn't find any paper or a pen or a pencil. At last, he saw a piece of charcoal and found a flat board that looked like the lid to a box.

It's not easy to write with charcoal. You can't make small letters, and the blackened wood begins to smudge if you're not careful. Besides, as much as there was to tell, Abraham didn't know where to begin or what to say.

"Father," he wrote. "I have to go. I love you. Ab…"

Fooey. Without thinking, he'd begun to sign his own name instead of Adam's. He looked for a cloth to wipe the board, but there was only the napkin his mother had wrapped the sandwich with. So, he ate the sandwich, which was absolutely delicious, and then tried to erase the word with the napkin. It wasn't working. The charcoal blurred, so he spat on it, and now it became a muddy swirl. He blotted the board with the napkin and tried to write "Adam" on top. Now the signature was completely illegible. All that you could read was the first letter of his name, which he'd written in Hebrew – Aleph.

That would have to do. Abraham sighed. He'd wasted enough time already. He folded the napkin so the blackened part was on the inside and stuffed it into his pocket. He hoisted the pack onto his back, gave the shop one last look, and…

That's when his father came in the front door.

Jacob Schlemiel took in the scene in an instant. He'd heard the good news about Abraham's engagement and then he'd gone to Reb Cantor's to celebrate with a little vodka. By the time he'd returned home to hear the horrible news about Adam and the Russian soldiers, it was nearly dark. Rebecca was furious at his tipsy state and horrified that he hadn't seen Adam to say goodbye. So, stumbling out of the house, he'd hurried to the shop, knowing that it was impossible for Adam to still be in Chelm, but hoping nevertheless…

"So," Jacob said, "you're going to leave me with crumbs everywhere?" As soon as the words were out of his mouth, he regretted them, but it was too late.

Abraham frowned, took a deep breath, and blew with all his might against the work table. Sawdust and sandwich crumbs flew everywhere.

Both men closed their eyes tightly and coughed.

Abraham edged toward the door, but his father was in the way.

"Son," Jacob sputtered, steadying himself on Abraham's shoulder. "Adam, I'm sorry. I didn't mean that. You and I haven't always gotten along or agreed. Sometimes I've felt that all we've done for all these years is butt heads like a couple of stupid goats."

Abraham nodded and listened, but didn't hear most of what his father said. His father wasn't really talking to him, but to Adam, and this thought made Abraham feel sadder than ever. But what could he do? He couldn't say anything. Still, he wished that Adam was there, listening to the old man's confession of mistakes made and love misplaced. Then Abraham realized something else. If Jacob had said all these things to Adam, Adam probably would have been furious. Perhaps this way was better.

"Papa," Abraham interrupted at last. "I have to leave."

Jacob stopped in mid-sentence and then nodded. "Did you pack any tools?"

"Mama packed the bag. There wasn't any room."

"Women," Jacob shook his head. "Wait a moment." He hurried into the back room and returned an instant later with a tool belt.

"This belonged to your great-grandfather," he said. "I want you to take it."

"But…" Abraham began. He knew how to use a knife, but not the saw and hammer and awl that Jacob was even then strapping around his waist.

"There," Jacob said. "I should have given these to you years ago. You deserve them."

"No," Abraham insisted, unbuckling the belt and pushing the gift away. "My brother will need them."

Jacob Schlemiel smiled at his son. "You're a good boy," he said. "I wish I'd told you sooner. Well, better late than never. I give you my blessing. Good luck."

"Thank you," Abraham said, the words coming out choked.

"Go," Jacob said, opening the door. "It's getting dark. Try to make it to Smyrna before it gets too late."

Abraham nodded. He wanted to say more, but Jacob gave his son a fatherly slap on the back, which, given the fact that Abraham was already carrying a huge pack, sent him reeling into the street.

"Oy, watch out for the mud puddle!" Jacob cried.

Catching his balance, Abraham smiled, waved, and was gone.

In the doorway to his shop, Jacob Schlemiel remembered when Adam was a baby, all the trouble he'd been as a boy, and what a good man he was becoming. He watched the empty street until the shadows grew long, and then headed home to a house that would seem much smaller now.

Chapter Twenty-Four

Adam Alone (More or Less)

In Chelm, a year can pass as quickly as the turning of a page.

For Adam Schlemiel, however, his seventeenth year was the longest of his life so far, and certainly the most confusing. His love for Rivka Cantor grew day by day, but so did his fear. Fear of her father, fear of marriage – fear of not getting married, and most of all, the fear of discovery. It was bad enough that Abraham was gone, leaving Adam with no one to talk to.

Now, Adam was pretending to be Abraham, and he was terrified of being found out.

From morning until night, every time someone called him "Abraham" he tensed. His eyes widened in panic, and he held his breath. He looked left and then right, as if sure that there must be some kind of a mistake. Then, after a moment, he found himself able to breathe and relax and continue the pretense.

He knew that some day he would be found out and called a liar and a cheat. Rivka would desert him, her father would want to kill him, his father would banish him, and his mother would hang her head in shame.

Even worse, in the meantime, everyone in Chelm seemed to be going out of their way to tell him what they really and truly thought of Adam and how much better a person Abraham was.

If one of the brothers had to leave, they all said, at least it was Adam. They were so glad that Abraham had stayed behind.

Now, Adam didn't think he was acting differently than before, but the way his family and neighbors were treating him made him unsure. Only Shemini treated him well, telling him how much she missed Adam, and that Adam was always her favorite.

Still, as he woke every morning, Adam had to remind himself

that his name was now Abraham. Then he washed and got dressed. Previously, he had considered this ordinary and unremarkable behavior. But now his mother would say, "Abraham, you look so handsome this morning." Then his father would say, "You're looking healthy today, Abraham." After a while, even Shemini seemed to have forgotten him. "Abraham, your smile is so much nicer than Adam's ever was."

By the time he finished breakfast, Adam's eyes had already glazed over.

Then he and his father went to the shop.

Before the switch, going to the shop too had been an unremarkable event. Adam would give his mother and his sister a quick peck on their cheeks and then stroll briskly to the wood shop. Now, though, everyone made a big production about how proud they were and how he should have a good time.

And inside the shop it was even worse.

"You know, Abraham," Jacob Schlemiel would say, "it took your brother months to learn how to hammer a nail in straight. You pick up that hammer and ten seconds later you're swinging it like a professional."

That was their father's highest compliment – a professional.

"And you know," Jacob would continue, "the polishing job you did on that last jewelry box? Was better than anything Adam ever managed."

Adam couldn't say a word.

He took lunches now with his father-in-law-to-be.

Reb Cantor would meet him at the door. "Abraham! Welcome!"

The meals were splendid. Every lunch was like a Sabbath feast. There was always meat, both chicken and beef. And wine. Reb Cantor prided himself on having the largest wine cellar in Chelm. Never mind that he had the only wine cellar in Chelm. He would escort Adam into the basement and say, "Abraham, you see those bottles over there? They are from France! A man who owned a vineyard told me that before you open them, you have to shake them up. That's what makes them fizzy. You should see the corks fly! The last time I opened a bottle, the cork shot out the window into the sky and killed a vulture. Now that's a good wine."

Reb Cantor ate for hours – every meal. "I like to take a half-hour break between breakfast and lunch," he laughed. "And between lunch and dinner I reserve forty-two minutes."

When Adam (as Abraham) wondered aloud how Reb Cantor got any business done, the fat merchant said, "Business is easy. Most of the negotiations take place during the meal. When my associates see how much I can eat and how much I can drink, they are in awe. They know that my appetite is huge and I will eat them alive. Well, perhaps not alive, but certainly I would eat them roasted."

And then Reb Cantor would laugh and tell stories about all the trips he had taken around the world. Every so often Rivka would peek into the room, and she and Adam would blush.

By the time Adam stumbled back to his work at the carpenter's shop, it would be late afternoon and he would be sleepy and fuddled from too much food and drink.

His father would make excuses, tolerating behavior and laziness that Adam never could have managed under his own name. "It's not easy becoming a carpenter. Your brother had years. You're learning on the run. Not only that, you're forming a partnership. This is good. Reb Cantor is powerful and rich. You nap while I finish up this table…"

Then it would be time to take Rivka Cantor for a walk.

In Chelm there weren't so many opportunities for a young man and a young woman to court each other. Most marriages were arranged almost from birth. Other weddings were usually performed quickly to avoid the embarrassment of an early bris or naming ceremony. To prevent such a misfortune, the courtship of Abraham and Rivka had to be supervised in full view of at least one, if not a dozen villagers.

So they walked. Mostly circling the village square. Sometimes they would walk clockwise: south, then west, then north, and then east. Other days, so they wouldn't get dizzy, they walked the other way around. It didn't really matter as long as they were together – and under careful observation. The most humiliating part of the entire situation was that everybody else in Chelm agreed that Abraham and Rivka were a perfect match, unlike Adam and Rivka, they all said, who couldn't manage a civil conversation, let alone a sustained relationship.

Despite all this, for Adam, these walks were the best part of the day. He found he didn't need to talk, that just being with Rivka was enough. He didn't dare hold her hand. He barely managed to glance at her because when he so much as glimpsed her smooth and perfect face he would blush and stop dead in his tracks. It seemed impossible that he, Adam Schlemiel, could be engaged to someone as wonderful in every way as Rivka Cantor.

Then Rivka would reach over, squeeze his hand, and say in a soft voice, "I can't wait for our wedding night!"

He would feel his heart race. Any other young man would have been in heaven.

The problem was that even though Adam was walking with Rivka, Rivka was walking with Abraham.

Rivka would giggle, and then, pretending to wipe an eyelash away, her fingers would brush his cheek and she would whisper, "I love you, Abraham."

Adam, his face frozen in a smile, would nod. If he had known it was going to be this difficult, this upsetting, he'd have volunteered for the Russian army himself.

Russian Around

The Russian soldiers never left Chelm. As strange as it seems, they settled in. They comandeered a farmhouse from Reb Cantor, who owned several properties and usually rented them out, and after a time it was as if they had always lived there.

At first there was quite a lot of tension. They were rude, bossy, and lazy in the manner of soldiers too far from home and without clear enough orders.

Their job, as the Captain Boris Plotz explained at any opportunity, was to round up new recruits for the Russian army and send them back to Moscow. Specifically, they were to go to every village they encountered, check the census, and send every eligible man between the ages of seventeen and twenty-three. That was the point that the Captain focused on – since he had yet to find any eligible men in Chelm between the ages of seventeen and twenty-three, he couldn't very well move on. Besides, it would be such a coup if he could enlist the famous Adam Schlemiel. After all, how many men, let alone nine-year-old boys could claim to have defeated a band of thieves?

Unfortunately, Adam Schlemiel seemed to have gone into hiding. His twin brother, Abraham was a Pole and technically ineligible to serve, so…

There was nothing to be done but to keep searching for him. Hence the initial rude bossiness, as the Captain ordered his Sergeant to methodically search every house, barn, shed, shop and outhouse in Chelm.

Sergeant Shnuck was very thorough. An inspection of a single hay stack could take as much as a week, especially as the weather grew warmer.

And did they find Adam Schlemiel? Well, no, of course not. According to two farmers, he had last been seen just after Purim heading towards Smyrna struggling beneath the weight of a backpack the size of a goat.

Such misinformation would not deter Boris Plotz. He smiled knowingly, as he moved his chess pieces across the table from Rabbi Kibbitz. Never had he encountered a man so old who knew so little of chess. Neither had he ever found an entire town that was so clearly lying about the whereabouts of one boy. Adam Schlemiel was somewhere in Chelm. He knew it in his bones.

Whenever his Sergeant returned half-drunk from a search expedition, the Captain just picked another building at random and sent him back out. He carefully watched Rabbi Kibbitz's face for signs of concern or surprise as he made these announcements, but so far the Rabbi's beard was as inscrutable as his chess playing.

For his part, Sergeant Vasilly Shnuck simply saluted, turned around, and stumbled back out into the village's streets. These

Chelmener were surprising people. Rather than treating him as a leach or a bug or a mad dog to be avoided, they were very nice. Reb Shikker in particular liked to take Sergeant Shnuck out to Mrs. Chaipul's restaurant, prop a bottle of vodka in front of him and say, "Go ahead, take a drink for you, and then one for me." Strange man.

Searching the houses was easy too. They were all small and empty of everything but a few pieces of furniture, some pots and pans, clothes, dishes, and far too many people. They also smelled delicious. Every house he visited seemed to have a stew on the stove that was just begging to be tasted. At the first few homes he searched, the Sergeant had simply taken a bowl and helped himself. Since then, however, he had grown a little more respectful, although he wasn't quite sure why. After all, he was a Sergeant in the army of Russia and these were little more than poor Jewish peasants. Still, his forbearance seemed to bear fruit, because at whatever house he entered, he was offered a meal, as long as he wiped his feet and was careful not to break anything. As a matter of protocol, he politely refused. It was one thing to take a taste as was his right, and quite another to take a helping as a bribe. So, he searched as carefully as was necessary. He opened the single closet, looked under the half-dozen beds, opened the cabinets, and peered under the table cloth. At just that moment, the house wife would usually have placed a bowl of stew with a chunk of bread down. "It's too far to go back to your quarters," she would say. "You've done your work, don't you deserve a break?"

The Sergeant shrugged and sat down. As the Captain might say, what else could he do? So, he ate well, very well. After lunch, he often napped (after taking off his boots) on one of the beds.

Even the Schlemiel family was gracious, although very sad. Mrs. Schlemiel, the Sergeant learned, had been ill before Adam fled Chelm, but now her condition had grown worse. Yet instead of being resentful, she was always kind to him. And her kasha and brisket were simply the most delicious pieces of overcooked meat he had ever eaten. If she hadn't been so sick, he might have simply camped out in their house and waited for the son to return. As it

was, his conscience would only allow him to search their house
once or twice a week, usually on Fridays. They even started setting a
place for him at the table.

And the soldier's living quarters? Well, their quarters were
nothing short of amazing. Russian barracks were never known as
four star hotels. They were shabby, cheap, dirty, dark, and always
infested with bugs, rats and worse. During their journey, the
Captain and Sergeant had grown accustomed to living in tiny
(leaky) tents. In Chelm, that all changed.

The day after they had arrived, Reb Cantor the merchant had
come to the Captain with a proposition.

"I have a small farm to the south of Chelm that is currently
abandoned," the Merchant said, pouring the Captain a glass of
wine. "The family that lived there emigrated to America, and the
land has been fallow for over a decade. I would be happy to let you
use it as long as you are in Chelm."

It was a decrepit building, but it became snug and warm after a
wall and a few new shingles were replaced. Reb Cantor was pleased
to sell them the wood and nails on credit. Of course, the Captain
had no intention of repaying the merchant, but after a time Plotz
realized that a house this size was more than he'd ever be able to
afford on his captain's salary. Besides, he had the Sergeant. So, he'd
ordered the Sergeant to clear and plow the fields.

Sergeant Shnuck had mixed feelings about this arrangement.
On the one hand, he had grown up in a Moscow slum and had
dreamed his entire life of owning a farm. On the other hand,
puttering around Chelm and pretending to look for Adam
Schlemiel was such easy work. On the other hand, he and the
Captain had been gone so long that they would probably be
considered deserters. On the other hand, he was a sergeant,
following his captain's orders; it was the Captain who would have
to answer to the wrath of the Colonel, who also happened to be
Shnuck's cousin Vladimir. On yet another hand, nothing lasts
forever.

So, in secret, he visited Reb Cantor and explained his problem.
He only had five years left in the army before he could retire.

Would Reb Cantor be willing to sell him the land?

"Of course!" the merchant smiled. "If you do all the work and take care of such land, I would be a fool not to sell it to you, Sergeant Shmuck."

"No no no," said the Sergeant. "My name is Shnuck."

"Of course it is," the merchant grinned. "In five years, we'll talk."

Chapter Twenty-Five

The Marriage

The Russians were invited to the wedding of Rivka Cantor to Abraham Schlemiel. How could they not be? Everyone in Chelm was invited, and many from Smyrna, too.

For a man and a woman, a wedding is the moment when their two fates are twined together. They walk under the chuppah separately, and leave as one. For the village of Chelm, however, a spring wedding was an excellent excuse for a big party. Winter snows were gone, enough grass had grown so your boots didn't sink half a foot into the mud, and it was time for a dance!

Why shouldn't everyone take pleasure in such a festivity?

Besides, if they hadn't been invited, the Russian soldiers probably would have shown up uninvited at the front door to the synagogue with their guns and scared the guests as they waited for the return of Adam Schlemiel.

After all, if Abraham Schlemiel was getting married, wouldn't his twin brother sneak back to attend the celebration?

There were rumors, of course, that it was not fear of the Russians that had chased the younger twin from Chelm, but jealousy.

Adam Schlemiel, it was said, had been madly, secretly and passionately in love with Rivka Cantor, even though it was also a well-known fact that Rivka despised Adam for reasons of her own.

Sadly, the rumors were more than half true. Adam did love Rivka, and Rivka said that she hated Adam as much as she loved Abraham.

All these thoughts ran through the real Adam Schlemiel's mind as he stepped into his brand new formal trousers. He was not a fool. He knew what people thought and said about him and his brother. That they'd fought, that they were enemies divided by love. Nonsense. If any of them knew the sacrifice that Abraham had made…

Yet there was some truth, too. Adam was living a lie. He was marrying under false pretenses.

In popular fiction and theater, when a hero takes on a new identity, he always disguises himself. He puts on a false beard, a mustache, or shaves his head. Perhaps he feigns a limp or wears a mask. Even an eye patch is sufficient in the world of make believe for him to be taken as someone else.

Only a villain or confidence man would steal someone's name and brazen into town without changing so much as a hat.

And yet for a year, Adam Schlemiel had walked in his brother's name, slept in his brother's bed, eaten his brother's meals, accepted his brother's praise and compliments, and courted his brother's bride.

It shouldn't have mattered so much, if at all. Before Abraham had fled Chelm, the bed had belonged to both of the boys. Their mother had always served their dinners from the same pot. It didn't even matter that the real Abraham had cared not a fiddle for Rivka Cantor.

Adam was obsessed with only one question: what would Abraham do? He kept asking himself that, but he got no answer.

For the past several weeks, Adam had actually tried to mind-talk with his brother. When they were growing up, the twins had been able to complete each other's sentences, think each other's thoughts, and occasionally converse at length without uttering a sound. It was a wonderful thing, to always be able to confide, or complain, or to call for help. The farthest their mind-talk had ever reached was from Chelm to Smyrna. Abraham must have traveled farther away than that. In a corner of his mind that he couldn't feel, couldn't touch, could only barely understand, Adam knew only that Abraham was still alive.

Adam missed his brother, and he wanted Abraham to come home and share his wedding. Yes, it would be dangerous but the Russians were idiots and the famous Schlemiel twins could outsmart them with half a brain, let alone the two with which they were blessed.

More than Abraham's company, though, he wanted his counsel. How long could this go on? It had been a year so far. At first it was by turns amusing, disconcerting, unsettling, entertaining, discomforting, enlivening…

And then, from time to time Adam actually found himself forgetting. Days and even weeks went by when "Adam" didn't really exist. He gave it no thought. He was who he was. Whatever name people called him was his. The work that he did was his. The brief moments when Rivka Cantor brushed her hand against his cheek as they walked through Chelm were his.

She's not his bride, but my bride, he told himself. She never was his. She loves me, but not me. Or does she love me? Does she love him? She's never spent time with him, only me. She must love me. Doesn't she? It was all so confusing, and it made him feel terrible.

On the day of his wedding, Adam was shaking in his brother's best boots – and he hadn't even put them on yet. Should he tell her? He couldn't. If he told her then the Russians would come for him and put him in the army. But it was so difficult to keep lying.

This didn't feel like his wedding day. It felt like it was Abraham's. And the funny thing was that the real Abraham wasn't even here to enjoy it.

The trousers, along with the shirt, socks, boots, jacket, and even the felt hat were a pre-wedding gift from Reb Cantor. "To my new son, Abraham," the note in the box had said.

The letters on the beautiful cake that Mrs. Chaipul had baked spelled "Mazel Tov Rivka and Abraham." Even the cake was really his brother's, not his.

He sighed. Somehow, in spite of all his thoughts and worries, he had managed to slip into his wedding costume, comb his hair, and put on a smile as his father led him into the synagogue, packed to the rafters with grinning, cheering, and laughing family, friends, and neighbors.

Like everyone else, he lost his breath, his heart caught in his throat, and he felt himself warm with love and amazement as Rivka Cantor walked slowly down the aisle toward him.

She was the most beautiful woman he had ever seen, and now, brilliant in white silk, she looked even more splendid.

Joy filled the room with a river of tears!

For Adam, however, there was no one else but Rivka. They were alone. The moment stretched into an eternity. Through her veil, he could see her smile glowing just for him. And then he felt a nudge.

"So, Abraham?" Rabbi Kibbitz coughed.

Adam wasn't sure what the question was. He looked from one smile to another, from Rivka's to the rabbi's.

"Well, Abraham?"

Adam!

Adam turned around suddenly and searched through the synagogue. He thought he'd heard a voice. Was Abraham out there? Face after face grinned at him. Some nodded, some winked, some rolled their eyes, but Abraham's face was not among them.

And then, Adam saw that the two Russian soldiers standing at the back of the room were also looking for Abraham. They knew he would come back. They too were hoping to find a face identical to the one under the canopy.

"Abraham?" Rabbi Kibbitz said. "Is everything all right?"

Adam turned back. The smile on Rivka Cantor's face was flickering with doubt.

He would not allow that.

"Everything is wonderful," he said. "I was looking for my brother."

Rivka hesitated a moment, and then she nodded. The Rabbi nodded.

Then everyone waited.

"Abraham," the Rabbi said at last. "Step on the glass already."

A pang of doubt and fear and anger flashed through Adam Schlemiel's heart as he lifted his leg and smashed his new boot down on the napkin-wrapped wine glass.

CRASH, it shattered.

"Mazel tov!" the village of Chelm roared.

Then Rivka Schlemiel's lips met his and all thoughts were erased with a warm splash of joy.

The Importance of Being Mud

"Abraham."

"Mmmm." Adam Schlemiel hummed in his sleep.

"Abraham," said the musical voice very near his ear. It was a woman and she sounded lovely.

"Mmm?" He smiled.

"Abraham," the voice shouted, "get up!"

"What? Is there a fire?" Adam sat bolt upright, blinking furiously.

Rivka Schlemiel looked at her husband and laughed and laughed.

Adam felt his face widening into a grin. He picked up the pillow and threw it at her. She caught it and hurled it right back. It hit him smack in the face, and he used that as an excuse to lie down again, close his eyes, and pretend to snore. "Zzzzzz."

"ABRAHAM!"

"Mmm?" he grunted, frowning.

Rivka jumped right on top of him and began tickling him furiously. Adam was taken completely by surprise and now found himself laughing uncontrollably.

"Stop, stop!" he begged. "Someone will hear us."

"Who is going to hear us in our very own house?"

"Ahhh!" Adam said, trying to push her hands away.

Much to his amazement, it was true. Not only had Reb Cantor given Adam his daughter, he had also given them both a brand new house just on the edge of Chelm, equidistant (and equally far away) from both of the in-laws' homes. The irony of the gift was that Adam himself had helped his father with the construction and carpentry but hadn't realized that this was going to be his own home. If he had, he probably would have used better materials and been a little more careful with some of the hinges and joints...

"Stop!" he gasped. "As your husband, I command you."

"Oh," Rivka grinned. "Now you're my husband, are you?"

"Yes, absolutely." Adam tried to keep a straight face. "I am the ruler of this house, and my word is law."

"Law is it?"

"Yes." Adam nodded. "And the first law of this house is no tickling."

"And what happens," Rivka asked coyly, "if someone breaks the law?" She poked him just above the ribs. "Hmmm?" Another poke. "Hmm?"

"Stop. Stop! I'll call the soldiers."

"Call the soldiers indeed," Rivka said as her tickles grew even worse. "You can barely breathe."

"Aaack!" Adam sputtered. Here he was married less than a day, and already his authority was being undermined. Enough was enough. He reached out and began tickling Rivka. "This will be your punishment!"

"I'm not ticklish," she said.

"Nonsense." Adam tried harder, and then differently and then more and then less. No matter where he poked, prodded, or flicked, his efforts at tickling his wife didn't even provoke a smile. How could someone not be ticklish?

"You see?" Rivka said, poking him. "Now, Abraham, who is the ruler of this house?"

"HA!" Adam laughed. He grabbed Rivka and gave her a huge hug and then a soft and gentle kiss. That particular sequence of affection had its desired effect and pushed all thoughts of tickling from Rivka's mind.

A little while later they both sat at the kitchen table, sipping tea.

"You know, Abraham, your breakfast was warm when I came in to wake you up."

"It is delicious cold," Adam said. Privately, he thought that the greasy fried eggs and rock solid black bread toast would make better food for a goat, but he was lucky enough not to mention this. At least the tea was still lukewarm, and with a dollop of honey tasted like sweetened water from a swamp.

Rivka kissed his cheek. "Abraham, Abraham, Abraham," she said. "And to think that we're married."

Adam sighed.

"What is it?" Rivka asked.

"Do you love me?" he said.

"Such a question to ask me at this particular moment," said Rivka. "How can you even think otherwise?"

"Yet you didn't answer," Adam said. "Do you love me?"

"Yes," Rivka said. Her voice was patient. "I could elaborate by saying that I love you to the core of your being, from horizon to horizon, from the creation of the world to the end of eternity, but that would just be hyperbole."

"Hyper-what?"

"Exaggeration. I love you." She set her hand on his. "I love you as much as a woman can love a man."

Adam smiled. "Then I have a favor."

"Anything, so long as it is legal, moral, and won't hurt."

"Don't call me Abraham any more."

Rivka looked puzzled. "How can one distinguish between a rose and a weed except by its name?"

"Call me 'Husband.'"

Rivka snorted. "As if we are seventy years old already? Should I perhaps call you Reb Schlemiel? Or 'Your Excellency,' since you are so attached to ruling this small kingdom of ours?"

Although Rivka was being sarcastic, for Adam any name would be better than hearing her sweet lips call him Abraham day in and day out for the rest of their lives.

"Abraham," he said, "is such an old fashioned name."

"I could call you Abe," Rivka offered. "That's got a youthful sound."

"No," Adam shook his head. "It's…"

"I'd call you Ham," Rivka said, "but in English 'ham' is another word for pig, which, even though you are acting like one, is hardly kosher."

"Rivka…"

"I could call you Braham, or Abra, Abrahm, or perhaps Maharba, which is Abraham spelled backwards."

"Rivka…"

"What about Hambra? Or perhaps I should just call you Mud."

"Mud? Why Mud?"

"Because that's what your name will be in my book if we continue this conversation."

Adam sighed. "All right. Mud it is. Call me 'Mud.'"

"You're kidding." Rivka looked at her husband. "You're not kidding. You'd rather be called Mud than Abraham?"

Adam nodded.

Rivka's face looked like a confused owl's. "Why?"

He wanted to say, "Because I'm not Abraham. I'm Adam." But how could he? The truth was, he couldn't. It was insane. So, Mud he would be.

"You don't have an answer?" she said. "It seems to be a simple question. For example, 'Rivka, please don't serve me horseradish because it makes me break out in hives.' This makes perfect sense. 'Rivka, don't call me Abraham because…' Because no reason. It leaves me completely stumped."

"Rivka," Adam said, "you have a brilliant mind. You understand things. You can put words together in ways that leave a simple carpenter like me speechless."

Rivka was flattered. She paused for a moment and then asked, "So, you want me to do it? Just like that?"

Adam nodded.

"All right, Ab…" She began to say the name but then pursed her lips. "This is your house, your castle, your domain more or less. Mud it is."

Adam smiled. He set his hand on top of hers. "When you call me Mud it fills my heart with joy."

Rivka shook her head. "You are a very strange husband, Mud Schlemiel."

Chapter Twenty-Six

Where the Wind Blows...

Rosa's lips brushed Abraham's cheek like a light breeze. A kiss landed on his forehead like a wet leaf. Her finger poked into his back like a sharp stick. Another wet kiss lingered on the tip of his nose...

Abraham Schlemiel's nose twitched. He frowned and opened his eyes. Wet leaves were stuck to his nose and brow. He rolled off the sharp stick and sat up in the pile of elm leaves he had collected to sleep on. Then he lay back to fall asleep again but had no luck.

It was still dark. He could see the sky above through the leaves of the elm tree he had rested under. It was black and clear, star-lit and brilliant. More stars than he had ever imagined when he had lived in Chelm. Sometimes he spoke to them, as if they were old friends, but tonight his mind was elsewhere.

Rosa. He had been dreaming of her again, and in his dream she was so close. He knew that the Roma, the Gypsies as they were often called, believed strongly in the power of dreams. Did that really mean that Rosa was nearby? Perhaps her caravan was just a mile or two from his poor camping spot. Which direction though? In the woods in the darkness he wouldn't be able to see smoke from their cooking fires. Never mind. As a cursed Schlemiel, he could almost be certain to head in the wrong direction anyway. Still, she was there, and he had nothing better or more important to do than to look.

The world was so big. He had never imagined it to be so. As a boy, he had known only Chelm and Smyrna, the Schvartzvald and that small strip of rail and land that led to and from Pinsk. Now he had wandered for hundreds upon hundreds of miles over how many years?

He thought back in his mind and tried to add it all up. It

wasn't easy keeping track of the days when you lived outside of the villages, towns and cities. Perhaps that is why Rosa's people traveled together, to keep their own time. The only way he remembered the Sabbath was a trick he had developed. Every week he looked for a stick with seven branches, and every day he broke off a branch. When the week was over, he found a new stick.

The first year of his search for Rosa had been a disaster. He had nearly starved to death a dozen times. After leaving Smyrna he had gone the wrong way and ended up in Siberia.

One night, dug into the side of a snow bank, shivering, he thought he was going to die.

Then, inside his mind he saw a picture of Adam standing under the chupah with Rivka Cantor. That whole long evening he had fed off the warmth of their wedding, drinking their wine and eating from the wedding feast. And when Adam had danced with Rivka, Abraham had danced along. He knew he was dying, and that this was a dream of delirium, but when Adam had embraced their mother and father and little Shemini, Abraham felt as if an inferno had been rekindled in his heart. The next morning, he awoke, his cheeks covered with frozen tears, and dug his way into the sunlight to find a westbound train chugging slowly past. He hopped a ride.

After that, he had visited France, Belgium, Amsterdam, Germany... The cities and towns and villages were all a blur.

Sometimes he stopped for a while and found work as a cook or a laborer. Sometimes he begged. Sometimes he told stories that made people laugh. It didn't seem to matter what story he told; if it was about Chelm, everyone thought it was a joke, and they gave him a few coins for the entertainment.

Everywhere he went, he saw families, husbands and wives, children, aunts, uncles... The world was composed of clumps of people living together sometimes happy and sometimes sad. Whenever he was invited to a Shabbas dinner, whenever he saw a young woman smile at a young man, Abraham felt his heart yearn for Rosa.

Mostly he liked to live in the forest, alone, far from reminders that his home village was a joke and that the woman he loved was far away, just another speck underneath the blanket of stars.

Abraham sighed. He was an idiot from Chelm, and he knew it.

In Vienna, he had lived for a year with a kind family, preparing all their meals and doing odd jobs around the house. The father, he knew, thought that Abraham would eventually marry his daughter. And Abraham, after having no home for so long had almost come to think so himself. When the daughter came to him in tears, and told him that she was in love with a boy who worked at the tavern, Abraham had smiled and rumpled her hair. Then he had hung his apron on a hook, and walked away without looking back.

That would have been such an unhappy life, both of them in love with someone else. Maybe they would have gotten along eventually, but...

Abraham sniffed the air. Smoke. He smelled smoke. He sat up again. Sleep was impossible anyway. He sniffed. Where was the smoke coming from?

Reaching down, he picked a handful of dried leaves from the ground, crumbled them up, and threw them into the air. The powdered leaves blew into his face. He coughed and sputtered, rubbed his eyes, and sneezed leaf dust from his nose into his dirty handkerchief. At least now he knew which way the wind was blowing. He smiled. Perhaps Rosa's camp really was nearby.

He picked up his pack and headed off, into the dark, searching for the light of his life.

As he walked closer, the smell of smoke grew stronger and thicker. This was too much smoke for a single camp fire. If the forest was ablaze would he be better off on higher ground? He was already climbing a hill when realized the glow was growing brighter over the other side. Sunrise was still hours away. At least from the top of the hill he would be able to see what was happening and perhaps plan an escape route.

He reached the crest, and was just catching his breath, when he looked down the other side of the hill and saw...

A village in flames. Soldiers on horses!

"Get down!" a voice hissed.

Abraham felt a hand grab his ankle and pull him to the ground.

Bonfire

Abraham grimaced as his face hit the dirt, his hands barely getting up in time to prevent a serious fall.

Then, all at once, he sat bolt upright as the image of the village being burned by soldiers reached his mind. It had only been a moment, but he'd seen the villagers watching, their mouths open, their homes afire.

Abraham was about to shout with outrage when another large hand pressed over his mouth.

"Shhh!" a deep whisper in his ear urged. "If they hear us, they will come up the hill and kill us."

"Brfff," Abraham said.

"Yes," the low voice continued, "I know you didn't do anything, but the fact remains. We are alive because they are unaware we exist. May I now take away my hand?"

Abraham nodded. He was beginning to have trouble breathing. The hand slowly peeled away.

"Who are you?" Abraham hissed.

"Shhh." Now that his initial surprise was past, Abraham's eyes began to focus, and he saw a fat index finger go to an equally fat pair of lips. "The wind is blowing toward us, so we should be all right as long as you keep your voice down. My name is Vlad."

"Vlad? Is that short for Vladimir?" Abraham was unused to calling complete strangers by nicknames.

"Not any more. Now I am just Vlad. And you, my lucky friend, are called what?"

"Abraham. Abe."

"Abe!" Vlad laughed quietly. In the dim light, Abraham could see that Vlad was a big man, dressed in a long black jacket with heavy boots. He had a large head with a full bushy beard that was streaked with grey.

"Is that funny?" Abraham asked.

"No. Not particularly. I was just reflecting how incongruous it was to be having such a polite little chit-chat under these circumstances." Vlad nodded down the hill.

Abraham looked and now he saw the scene below more clearly.

He had been wrong. The village was not on fire as he had first imagined. Instead, a huge bonfire was burning in the middle of the village square. At least a dozen riders on horseback, each of them holding guns, were galloping back and forth as smoke swirled around them. Some of them carried torches, which they waved with glee.

Here and there, Abraham saw groups of people huddled together. Families watching in sobbing tears as they waited for their homes and businesses to be burned to the ground.

"Cossacks," Vlad said, simply. "Out for a night of fun. It's not easy being an underpaid soldier in the Russian army."

"How can you joke about something like this?" Abraham snapped, his voice barely kept in check.

"What else can one do?" Vlad shrugged. "I would cry, but it appears that this small horde is being somewhat merciful."

"Merciful? They're going to burn down that village."

"At least they're not killing anyone. Or worse."

Abraham found himself nodding in reluctant agreement. In the years since he had left Chelm, he had learned that the world was not always pleasant. He had felt sadness of his own, and met sorrow in others. As a boy, he had learned the tragedies of histories, but they had always seemed distant and unreal. But this was the first time that he had encountered such a horror face to face.

"Isn't there anything we can do?" he wondered.

"Well, we could charge down the hill and be shot like squirrels. If, somehow, we reached the bottom still alive, we would be surrounded and then trampled. Perhaps we could avoid those horses, in which case we could pick up handfuls of sand and throw them into the flames. I'm afraid not."

Abraham felt his stomach turn, but he knew that Vlad was correct. He wanted to crawl away, to run away. Anything to be far from the smoke and the sobs that he faintly heard blowing up the hill. But he couldn't move. Something kept him there. And he watched and he witnessed, cursing his helplessness in the face of such evil.

Except for a trick of geography, this village might very well be his home village of Chelm. Whether they were Polish or Russian or Jewish, from this distance the families waiting for their lives to be put to the torch could be his family, his friends, his neighbors. How could a man do such a thing to another man? Didn't Cossacks have families of their own? Mothers and sisters and aunts and grandfathers? What kind of idiocy was this?

Abraham closed his eyes as a billow of dark smoke floated past, and felt his body heaving with stifled sobs.

A large hand rested on his back, and patted gently.

"War is never a pleasant thing, my small friend," Vlad said softly.

"What war? Do you see these people fighting back?"

"War is not something agreed upon by all parties. It is waged by one and inflicted on the many. It is a plague as fierce as any the God of the Hebrews inflicted on the Egyptians. It cares not for children or innocents. And, once released, it is most difficult to stop, because in the midst of its destruction it strips away hope and humanity and leaves in its place the seeds of revenge. Leaders may portray war as glory, honorable, necessary, or expedient, but rarely do they lead with their bodies. Instead their words, their orders spur others on. And the enemy, whoever the enemy is, is caught up in this same fury but facing the other way. Heaven help any creature caught in between."

"How can we stop it?" Abraham asked at last. "How can we make it stop?"

"I don't know," Vlad said. "I don't know."

At that moment, Abraham felt his heart fill with rage. If he had a gun, he would begin firing and kill all of the Cossacks. But what then? What of the Cossacks families who came looking for him? The ones who would search out his village and destroy that?

He wanted to hold up a mirror and shout, "Look! Their faces are not different. They are the same as yours!"

He could make speeches. He could write pamphlets. He could throw his body in front of a horse!

But at this moment, none of that would matter. It would not change the world one tiny bit.

Abraham closed his eyes, and buried his face in his hands. He felt Vlad's hand resting on his shoulders, patting, and slowly he began to fall asleep, hoping against all hopes that when he woke in the bright light of morning this would all be a dream.

Then, just as he felt himself about to drift off, Abraham's eyes snapped open.

"I have an idea!" he whispered, as he leapt to his feet.

Out of the Frying Pan

Abraham started dancing around on top of the small hill. "I have an idea!" he was singing it now. "I have an ideeeeea!"

"Are you crazy?" Vlad hissed, his hand scrabbling for Abraham's leg. "Get down!"

"Crazy? No. I have to do something," Abraham said. "But crazy? Yes! Yes? Maybe that's a good idea, too." He dropped his pack on the ground, and began stripping off his coat. "Vlad, you might want to get out of here."

"What, and miss all the fun?" Vlad said. "Don't worry. As soon as they shoot you, I'll be long gone."

"Fair enough," Abraham answered. "Could you do me a favor? It's rather large."

Vlad shrugged. "Possibly. I never commit to anything until I know. But whatever it is, you'd better hurry. I think they see you."

Abraham looked down the hill, and saw that two of the horsemen were arguing and pointing in his direction.

"Please, if I get killed, go to Chelm and tell my mother what happened."

"All right. If I'm near Chelm, I will. What is your mother's name?"

"Rebecca Schlemiel. I'd better hurry. They're about to come this way, and I'd rather they didn't catch you as well. Good-bye."

"Good-bye," Vlad said. "And good luck."

"Thank you." Abraham took a deep breath, rolled his shoulders once, and then began running down the hill, waving his coat and flapping his arms like they were wings and he was trying to take off.

"Waaaaaga!" he yelled. "Waaga waga waga!"

The two horsemen reined their steeds to a halt as he tore down the hill like an insane gigantic raven.

"Reeeee! Raaaaaa! Waaaaga!" Abraham gabbled. "Oooga Oooga Ooga!"

He tripped, rolled three yards, and regained his feet at a dead run. "Oy! Oooooga!"

The Cossacks' eyes widened. Their horses shied and reared.

A moment later, Abraham was past them, and running through the outskirts of the village, heading toward the square. Three more riders saw him, and they gave chase. He paid them no mind.

"Glooob! Gloob! Li Li Li Li Li!"

The villagers parted as this strange apparition raced through their streets, like a lunatic demon escaped from the forest.

So far, Abraham's plan was proceeding exactly as he'd anticipated. He'd diverted the soldiers. All their attention was on him. Twelve horsemen, some with rifles, some with long sabers were converging on him at full speed. Any minute, they would catch him, and then...

All of a sudden, Abraham's brain started racing as fast as his legs. Maybe this wasn't the most well thought out plan he'd ever had. In fact, as he cleared the last house and entered the village square where the bonfire was burning as high as a house, he had a rather unsettling thought – now what? It was too late to turn around and hide. He'd never make it back up the hill alive. Perhaps Vlad had been right, and he was about to throw his life away for no good reason. But wouldn't that be better than watching a whole village burn down in flames and doing nothing?

Now Abraham was nearly surrounded. The horsemen were behind him, but closing fast from all directions. The only clear path led straight into the bonfire.

Guns and swords behind, a crackling inferno in front.

This was looking to be a stupendously stupid idea...

No! The point was to save the village. If it took dying, then so be it. But it was going to take something more…

"Li Li Li Li!" Abraham shouted, stopping in his tracks. He spun around, his arms outstretched, his coat flapping, his beard blowing wildly in the smoke from the fire. The horsemen reined their beasts to a startled stop.

"Li Li Li! Leave my village alone!" he shouted in Russian. Then he turned again, and ran straight into the bonfire, and an instant later was gone with a loud echoing scream of, "OYYYYYYYYYY!"

The horsemen remained frozen in place. A horse screamed and reared on its hind legs. Then another, a third. A strange and horrible smell wafted from the pyre, and the flames grew even higher.

"Where did he go?" one soldier shouted, trying to reign in his steed.

"He vanished," answered another.

"The Devil!"

"The Devil's village!"

Gradually, the men brought their horses under control. One soldier aimed his rifle into the flames and fired. The sound of the gunshot was drowned in the roar of the bonfire.

The Cossack Major called his men to him. They were nervous. He needed to calm them. "Whoever it was, he is dead now," he said. "Let's burn the rest of the village and be done."

"It's the devil's village," said one man. "He said to leave it alone."

"I don't mind killing peasants, Jews, and Gypsies," said another. "But the Devil…" He made the sign of the cross.

"It was just a man," the Major said, not completely sure himself. "His bones are smoldering even now."

"But what if it was the Devil? What if there are no bones?"

As a unit, the men shuddered and crossed themselves. Even the Major was becoming frightened. "We'll let the fire burn down," he said. "We'll rake the coals and find the bones. Then we'll burn the village."

The soldiers stared nervously at the villagers, who were staring back, just as surprised.

The fire had been large, but fed mainly on furniture and straw, it began to die down quickly from the lack of new fuel. Soon it was little more than ashes and embers. The Cossack Major fixed a bayonet to the end of his rifle, and began prodding it. In his head, he knew the Devil was nonsense, but in his heart he wasn't so sure. He felt as if he was poking a sleeping bear, or worse. At any moment, he expected to see a flare and a hiss, followed by a pointed head with a gigantic pair of red eyes and huge razor sharp fangs...

But there was nothing. No Devil, and no bones either. His orders were clear. Find the band of Gypsies that had been roaming the countryside. Kill the Gypsies, and kill anyone who had helped them. This village, he believed, fell into the latter category. If it was the Devil's village, then they certainly had been helping the Gypsies. On the other hand, he could easily tell his superiors that the village had proved itself to be innocent, and none would be the wiser. Certainly none of his men would whisper a word of this to anyone for fear of bringing the evil eye.

There was only one more possibility, and the Major wondered why he hadn't thought of it sooner.

"Did anyone see a man run out of the fire?" he asked.

One by one, his troops shook their heads.

"What about you?" he shouted at the villagers. "Did you see a man run out of the fire?"

"The Devil," said one old villager, "does not run from flames. He brings others into them."

The other villagers stood still and silent. Suddenly, to the Cossack Major, they seemed unafraid. That would not do.

He lifted and aimed his rifle at the old man, and pulled the trigger, but the hammer fell on a defective round of ammuntion with a dull click. The old man stood, still and smiling.

"It's a sign," the old man laughed. "Run for your lives, while you still have your souls!"

That was enough. As if they had one mind, without waiting for their major's order, the band of soldiers turned their horses away from the fire, and rode East toward the rising sun.

One by one, the villagers crossed themselves as they silently approached the nearly spent bonfire. Was it really the Devil or a demon, or just a foolish hero who had sacrificed himself for their sake?

It was a question that, even years later when they told their grandchildren the story, no one had ever answered.

Chapter Twenty-Seven

...Into the Fire

Adam felt the flames in front of his face hot as a furnace. He wrapped his coat around his head and leaped into the bonfire. An instant later, he felt his coat catch on fire. An instant after that....

"OYYYYYYYY!"

"Abraham, wake up!"

"AAAAAAAAAAH!"

"Abraham!"

Adam's eyes flew open. He focused on the dim outline of Rivka's face. She looked concerned.

"Don't call me Abraham," he snapped. "Abraham was on fire!"

"Excuse me, but you're screaming, and I should try to remember you want to be called Mud? You were having a nightmare."

"It wasn't a nightmare, it was a vision."

"A vision?" Now Rivka really looked worried. "You're having visions? What about? Was I in it? Were we in it? Are we in danger?"

Adam ran his fingers through his hair, half expecting it to be singed off. He felt his face, but there were no blisters. He sat up and rubbed his forehead. He didn't want to tell Rivka, but he knew that she wouldn't let him go back to sleep until he explained what he'd seen. He asked for a drink of water, and she hurried into the kitchen where she poured him a cup from the earthenware jug. By the time she returned, he'd composed an edited version of the dream.

He took a sip of water, and began. "You know that my brother and I are close?"

Rivka nodded. She lit a lamp beside the bed.

"Sometimes we share each other's thoughts. When we were younger, we could finish each other's sentences. When we were alone, we didn't need to speak. A number of times, we have mind-talked over great distances."

"Is Adam in trouble?" Rivka asked.

"Well…" Adam coughed. "My brother was in a forest. It was dark. Tonight, I think. And he was watching a village burn. There was a fire in the middle of the square, and in order to save the villagers, he threw himself into the flames."

Rivka's voice was quiet. "That's horrible. What happened to him?"

Adam shook his head. "I don't know. That's when you woke me up."

"I'm sorry. How was I to know? If you go back to sleep, do you think you'll be able to find out what happened?"

Again, Adam shook his head. "I doubt it." He sighed.

Rivka lifted the cup from his hands and drank. "When you woke up, you said that Abraham was on fire."

"Did I?" He'd hoped she'd forgotten, but his wife was much too smart for that.

She nodded. "What you said makes me afraid. You think it was a vision of your brother, but you called him by your name. That makes me wonder whether it wasn't perhaps a premonition. Did you recognize the village? Did you see the faces of the people? Was it Chelm?"

"No." Adam scowled. "I knew you wouldn't understand. I was inside his mind. I got confused when I woke up. That's all."

"Mud, relax."

"Why should I relax when you misinterpret everything that I tell you? All I want is to have a simple life, and raise a family. Is that such a difficult thing to understand?"

Rivka didn't answer. She didn't know how it had gotten so confused so fast. She was hurt. Yes, they had been trying to have children since they were first married, and so far nothing. Was that her fault? It could just as easily be his fault. It wasn't from a lack of trying. But recently, everything seemed to remind him of it. She wanted children, too. But not at the expense of losing her husband.

She stood, and nodded.

"Rivka," he said. His hand reached for her, but she stepped back, turned, and went into the kitchen.

"Oh, my strudel," Adam said softly. "My dumpling. How can I tell you the truth? You'd hate me."

Just then, Rivka stormed back into the room.

"I hate you already," she hissed. "You want to tell me the truth? Just start at the beginning. How difficult could it be? A dream is a dream. What are you hiding in your dream? Were you trying to save some other woman? Did you dream that you pushed me into the fire first? I don't understand how difficult this could be to talk about!"

"Rivka!" Adam laughed. "No. No, nothing like that."

"Don't laugh at me, Mud. When I married you, you had nothing. We still have nothing. My family wants to give me everything, but I said, no, my husband is too proud. They shake their heads like I'm an idiot. But do I let them get to me? No. I stand by you and support your decisions. I don't mind living like this, and trying to make a family on our own. But I can't stand the fact that we're not together any more. We live in the same house, but it's as if we don't really see each other. I ask you a question, a simple question, and you become like a madman. What can I do about this? Hmm? What?"

Adam was stunned. He looked up at her and saw the anger in her eyes. She stood with one hand on her hip, her lower lip curled into her mouth. She was, he knew, only an inch from tears.

"I love you," he said. "Can't that be enough?"

"It could be enough." She nodded. "Yes. If you allowed it to be. If you trusted it. If you were able to tell me the truth, whatever that truth is."

"You wouldn't understand," Adam said.

"No, you're right. Of course I wouldn't understand. How could I understand? I'm just a stupid woman. I'm just your wife. I'm not your long lost twin brother. I don't have the ability to read your thoughts. I am restricted to conversation, usually shouts and arguments these days. Words are the way that I learn things, but if they're never spoken, you're right. I don't understand."

She looked at him, and she could see the love in his eyes, and the confusion. What was it going to take to get through to him? She'd tried reason, she'd tried tears, she'd tried shouts, she'd tried love…

"Enough is enough." Rivka threw her hands up. "When you want to talk with me, I'll be at my mother's."

"Rivka, don't go. If you leave, the whole town will know that we're having an argument."

"As if I care? I should stay here with you so that we can argue in private? I'd rather live in a house where I'm loved without so much agitation and anger. You want me to stay? Tell me. Tell me now."

Adam opened his mouth. He closed his eyes, trying to think. He felt the heat of the bonfire searing Abraham's eyebrows, and he winced.

When he opened his eyes, she was gone.

"But I'm not angry with you," he told the empty house. "I'm angry with myself."

Too Quiet

With Rivka gone to her parents' house, Adam was at a loss. He went to work every day, and his father didn't say a word. In the evenings, he went to his parents' house for dinner, and his mother didn't say a word. He went home to his empty house, and there was no one to talk with. On Friday evening, he went to shul and sat with his family, while she sat with her family. Nobody said a word. In fact, everyone in Chelm was so busy not saying a word about the estranged couple that just about all conversation stopped.

One morning, when Rabbi Kibbitz took his usual table in Mrs. Chaipul's restaurant, she began asking, "Did you hear about…" but he interrupted her.

"Shhh," the learned man said. "Our gossiping about won't help them."

"You're right," the old woman said, demurely. "Well, then, what about…"

"I told you, I don't want to talk about it."

Mrs. Chaipul had only been trying to ask the rabbi if he wanted his usual breakfast of tea and toast. She shrugged and gave him a plate of matzah brei and a cup of coffee.

This puzzled the rabbi, but he ate it anyway.

By the end of the second week, Chelm had become as quiet as a village of deaf people. They couldn't talk about it, and they couldn't talk about anything else, so nobody was talking.

At last, a delegation of men gathered in the Rabbi's office and fidgeted quietly for an hour and a half before the wise rabbi said, "All right, all right. We'll send Doodle."

"Doodle?" said Reb Stein, the baker. "Why Doodle?"

Doodle was the village orphan. Abandoned when he was a child, he had been adopted by the entire village. His whole life, he had been shuttled back and forth from house to house, spending a week with this family, a Sabbath meal with another, while doing odd jobs for a third. He was a sweet young man, a little younger than the Schlemiel twins, but not known for being particularly bright or tactful. In fact, Doodle had the uncanny ability to say exactly the wrong thing at the worst possible time.

"Don't worry. Doodle's an innocent," Rabbi Kibbitz said. "He's friendly with both the Schlemiels and the Cantors. He can say whatever he likes, and no one will hold it against him. If he messes it up, we're no worse off than we are now."

So it was agreed.

The next morning there was a Clop-Kack-Whiing! as the latest of Reb Schlemiel's door alarms announced Doodle's arrival.

Adam looked up from the chest of drawers he was sanding. "Hello. May I help you?"

Doodle, still startled by the door's alarm, said, "What? No. Not me. Help you."

" All… right," Adam answered slowly. "Fine."

He waited. Doodle remained silent. Adam nodded politely, and asked, "Do you mind if I finish this up?"

"No. Not at all," Doodle said. "Go right ahead. Make that wonderful chest of drawers. Do a good job. It looks like a nice piece of furniture. But you're driving us all crazy! You know that you love her. She knows that she loves you. We all know that you love each other. And even so, you're married. Work it out already."

Despite the fact that, as far as Adam was concerned, all this came out of nowhere, he knew exactly what Doodle was saying. But was it all true? He missed his wife more than he had ever thought imaginable. At nights he stared at the ceiling, or sniffed at her bare pillow. Did she feel the same way? Was she as alone in her parents' house?

"She wants me to tell her the truth," Adam said.

"So, tell her the truth."

"If I tell her the truth, she'll ask me for a divorce. I don't want a divorce."

"I understand." Doodle nodded. "So, don't tell her the truth."

"If I don't tell her then our life together is based on a lie. That doesn't work. Besides, she already knows that I'm not being honest."

Doodle's head started to spin, so he sat down on the floor.

"Are you all right?" Adam stood and peered over the counter.

Doodle's eyes were crossed, and he was wondering if his brain was leaking. "Give me a few minutes, and I'll let you know."

Adam dipped a cup into the water bucket, and brought it to his friend. "Do you understand why this has been so difficult? I don't even know where to start."

Doodle drained the cup of water, and then squinted. "I don't understand it at all. As far as I can tell, you have a secret that you can't tell your wife, so you obviously can't tell me."

Adam nodded.

"And," Doodle continued, "Rivka knows this, so she's moved out. But how is telling her the truth any different from what's happening now?"

"Because right now, I have hope," Adam said softly. "Once she knows…"

"Oy," Doodle said. "That's some problem all right. Well, it can't go on like this. Not only are you two suffering, but everyone in Chelm is suffering with you. You have to tell her."

"No," Adam said, "I don't. I can't. And I won't."

"Wait, wait, wait a second, I have an idea." Doodle smiled. "First, you invite her to your mother's house for a Sabbath dinner."

"What if she won't come?"

Doodle rolled his eyes. "I'll make sure she's there. Then, after dinner but before the strudel you explain to her…"

As Doodle outlined his plan, Adam's sadness began to melt away, and he started to smile. It was the first time in weeks, perhaps months, that he had felt this happy. He tried to thank Doodle, but the young man said he should wait a while.

"After all," Doodle said, "She hasn't moved back home with you. Not yet."

I'm Telling You…

The Sabbath dinner wasn't a total disaster. Not at the beginning, anyway.

That Friday evening, Adam was distracted and nervous, but hopeful. When Rivka arrived, right on time with a bouquet of beautiful flowers for his mother, he smiled at her as sweetly as he could. She didn't scowl so much as glare back impassively, and then hurry into the kitchen to help with dinner.

His father had shrugged, and when Doodle showed up a few minutes later and asked how was it going so far, Adam had to admit that he hadn't a clue.

"Don't worry," Doodle said. "I'll take care of everything. All you have to do is stick to our plan."

Adam nodded, but now he really felt scared.

Once, Doodle had been sent by Reb Cantor to a silent auction. He was to buy a chest of caviar at the best possible price. As soon as the auction had begun, Doodle had raised his hand and said, "I've got ten gold pieces in my pocket, and I can't pay a penny more!" Everyone was overjoyed, except for Reb Cantor, who learned that every other box of caviar had sold for less than half that. "But," Doodle said in his own defense, "I got it for the best possible price!"

Still, the meal went better than expected. His mother's chicken was tender and moist. Her noodle kugel was sweet and delicious. The kasha and potatoes were well salted and filling, the challah was still warm, and the wine Doodle had brought was surprisingly delicious. (He whispered to Adam that Reb Cantor had given him the bottle from his personal cellar. "Anything to get Rivka back out of my house!")

But the conversation lagged. Jacob and Rebecca Schlemiel had been married forever, and had little new to say to each other. Shemini went on and on about a boy she had seen a week ago at the marketplace in Smyrna, which made everyone feel very uncomfortable.

At last, Doodle laughed and said, "I just remembered a story."

Rebecca Schlemiel smiled politely, and said, "I would love to hear it."

"So," Doodle began, "this rabbi walks into a tavern and orders a glass of milk with a duck sticking out of his elbow. The bartender said, 'What is this, some kind of a joke?'"

Doodle paused and smiled, waiting for a laugh.

"Milk doesn't have elbows," Shemini said.

"No," Doodle agreed. "The duck was growing out of the Rabbi's elbow. The rabbi said, 'No, I'd like some milk, please.' Then the bartender pointed at the duck that was growing out of the Rabbi's elbow and asked, 'How did that happen?'

"The duck quacked, 'Oh, I don't know. One morning, I woke up and he was just there.'"

Doodle grinned.

"A duck that studied Torah?" Jacob Schlemiel pursed his lips. "That's something impressive."

"The duck couldn't go to Moscow to get an operation?" said Rivka.

"You know," said Rebecca Schlemiel, "I don't think that making light of deformities is funny."

"Deformities?" Doodle said. "It's a joke."

"Doodle, it takes nine months to make a baby." Shemini shook her head. "And then at least another fifteen or twenty years for a baby to become ordained, and you expect us to believe that the bird just grew a whole rabbi overnight? And was this another naked rabbi? If not, where did the duck get the clothes? And how could the duck swim without the Rabbi drowning?"

Doodle threw his hands up in the air, "It's just a joke!"

All this time, Adam had been staring intently at Rivka, while she stared back. He tried sending her thoughts, as he would to Abraham.

I love you, he thought. I never wanted to hurt you.

At the same time, she was sending her thoughts to him.

You are so handsome, she thought. Why can't you just tell me the truth? I'll understand.

But men and women are not mind readers. Instead, they have a bad habit of misinterpreting anything and everything in the worst possible way.

She hates me, he thought.

He doesn't want me, she thought.

We're doomed, they both thought.

All around them the conversation swirled. It rose and fell, lived and died. Many words were spoken and almost nothing was said. Everyone knew that the purpose of the evening was to reconcile the estranged couple.

At last, Rebecca brought out the coffee. "I'll be back in a moment with the strudel."

"Let me help," Rivka said.

"No, sit, please. Shemini, come with me."

"Mama," Shemini said, "you don't need help with the strudel."

"Shemini," her mother warned.

"Oh." The girl rose and followed her mother into the kitchen.

"Reb Schlemiel," Doodle said, "I wonder if you could show me something interesting outside."

"What are you talking about?" Jacob asked.

"You know," Doodle said, winking, "that interesting thing you wanted to show me."

"Ahh! Yes. Come."

And so, at last, Adam and Rivka were left alone.

In silence.

Adam smiled. Rivka stared at her coffee cup.

"So," Adam said. "How have you been?"

"Not bad," she said. "You?"

"Lonely. I miss you, Rivka."

"I miss you too, Abraham."

Adam winced.

"What?" she said. "See? You can't stand me. Why don't you admit it? I can't even talk to you and you start to twitch!"

"No, it's not that! Not at all."

"Then what?"

"Can't I tell you later?" Adam said.

"When?" Rivka said. "You're going to tell me some horrendous, stupendous, monstrous secret that has already all but torn our marriage apart, and you want me to wait? How long? Next week, next month, next year, next decade? I can't live like that. It's like I'm a rabbi attached to a duck, living under water, holding my breath and wondering when I can surface and breathe again. Maybe I can hold my breath for a minute or two, but eventually I'll either suffocate or drown. And then what do I do about the duck?!"

Adam nodded. It had been Doodle's idea to say he would explain everything, but not just yet. So much for the brilliant plan. Clearly Rivka wasn't willing to wait. Now Adam would just have to tell her everything, the whole truth, and hope for the best.

"After I tell you," he said, "I may have to join the Russian army."

"If you don't tell me," she said, "you'll definitely have to join the French Foreign Legion."

"All right. Do you remember the day we met at the well?"

"Yes. It was like I saw you for the first time."

"For me as well," he said. "It was as if I saw you for the first time. But then you told me that you would never fall in love with Adam."

Rivka blinked. "This is about your brother? What is it about you twins? Abraham, I love you and not Adam. It's as simple as that."

"It's not so simple," Adam said, "you see..."

Just then, Doodle and Jacob burst into the room. "Abraham! There are some people to see you!"

"Not now," Adam snapped.

"It's Rosa Kalderash," Jacob said.

"The gypsy princess," Doodle added.

"And her son," Jacob whispered.

"Her son?" Adam said.

"Yes," Doodle said. "He looks just like you."

Rivka burst into tears, and fled into the kitchen.

Adam rose to follow her, but Jacob caught his arm.

"Listen, I know what's important to you," Jacob said. "You can take all the time you want trying to soothe Rivka, but until you find out what's going on out there, nothing you say is going to make the slightest bit of difference."

Rosa's Story

"Rosa?" Adam Schlemiel peered out the doorway of his parents' house. "Is that really you?"

"Over here," came a soft voice from the shadows. "Shh. I don't want anyone to see."

Adam found himself tiptoeing out of the house. "Why not?" he whispered. "Are you in trouble?"

"Ow!" shouted the voice of a young boy.

"Aaah!" Adam yelped.

"Shhh!" Rosa urged.

"He stepped on my foot!"

"I'm sorry. I didn't know someone else was standing there. If you weren't hiding, I wouldn't step on your foot."

"Will you both be quiet? I don't want my father to find out we're here."

Adam's eyes were adjusting to the darkness, and now he dimly saw the little boy nod. "Papi mustn't know," the boy said. "That's very important. Otherwise he would simply put a stop to all this foolishness."

That brought a smile to Adam's lips. The boy sounded just like Egon Kalderash; there was no doubt that this was the Gypsy King's grandson.

"Well then, you've come to the right place," Adam said. "Between Chelm and the Schlemiels, we're sitting on a gold mine of foolishness. Rosa, can you tell me what's going on? I'm having a bit of a problem at home…"

"Abraham, it's about your son," she said.

Her words didn't quite register, because just then, Rosa Kalderash stepped forward, and a glimmer of light fell across her face. The sight of her took Adam's breath away. Rosa wasn't a girl anymore. Ten years had passed since he had seen her last, and her features had filled out. She looked strong and wise. Her eyes were still a deep brown, but her smooth skin had grown wrinkled with worries and cares.

"My what?" Adam sputtered.

"Your son needs…" she began, but her voice trailed off. "But you're not Abraham."

"What?" Adam said. Now it was his turn to be afraid that someone might overhear. "What do you mean? Of course I'm Abraham." He held a finger to his lips.

She ignored it. "Kiss me. If you kiss me, I'll be able to tell for certain. I know the lips of every man who I have kissed."

A horrible wail came from just inside the house.

"No! I'm married!" Adam said it loud enough for even the neighbors to hear.

But it was too late. A moment later, Rivka burst out of the house, pausing only long enough glance from Rosa to the boy, and then glare at Adam with a tearful mixture of loathing and dismay, before she ran away in the direction of her father's house.

"Rivka!" Adam said. "Wait!"

He started to go after her, then stopped. What was there to say? His father was right. He needed to find out the truth first. He turned. "Well, now that you've ruined my marriage, what is all this foolishness?"

"Can we go for a walk, please?" she asked quietly.

"No. I want to handle this now. Right here."

Rosa stared at him. She whispered something in Romany to the boy, who nodded, and went inside the house.

Adam heard his parents and sister greeting the boy with surprise and delight.

"All right," Adam said. "So, talk."

"You are not Abraham," Rosa said, quietly this time. "I apologize. I am confused. I thought you had forgotten your promises. I heard that you had gotten married… I could hardly believe it. But then at the same time, I have had dreams that made no sense until now."

"Well, that's two of us, because none of this makes any sense to me. Rosa, I am sorry if I hurt you. I know that you loved me deeply, but you and I were together for such a short time, and it was so long ago. I don't remember making any promises…."

"Shut up," she said. "I hate to offend your pride, but I was always in love with Abraham."

"I am Abraham," Adam hissed.

"All right, fine," she said. "We'll pretend. Then I was always in love with your brother."

"With Abraham?" Adam said. He couldn't believe it. He knew that Abraham had been in love with Rosa, but he'd always assumed that it was affection misplaced.

Rosa threw up her hands. "When you make up your mind who is who, please let the rest of us know." Then she grabbed his face, and pressed her lips against him.

Adam struggled furiously for a moment, but then Rosa let go of him like he was a hot potato.

"No," she said. "Abraham is not your child."

"Abraham?" Adam sputtered, catching his breath.

"Yes. It is a tradition among my people to name the first boy after his father."

"Oy," Adam said. He leaned against the side of the house. "My head hurts."

"Your head? Do you know how angry I've been with you? Or with Abraham. Whichever! Abraham promised to wait for me, and then I learn that he married… I thought he married… My heart was broken, but I made do and raised our son. Then, one morning I looked at Abraham, my son and I saw the face of his father starting to emerge, and I wanted to kill the boy. That's when I knew I had to bring him to back to Chelm. It would be a fitting revenge, don't you think, to return the boy to his father after so many years. Why should I care if it caused a little trouble between Abraham and his so-called wife? Wasn't that retribution enough for all the pain I have felt?"

Adam nodded. It was beginning to make a little more sense. "It must have been difficult. But Rosa, Abraham left Chelm years ago to look for you. "

"And yet," Rosa continued, ignoring him, "throughout all these years I have had my dreams. During the day I was certain that my love had betrayed me, but at night he searched for me still. I dreamed of Abraham wandering through forests, calling my name. I have felt his presence in my soul. It was as if the Devil was torturing me." She made a sign against the evil eye. "Then my dreams end as he runs into a bonfire and is consumed by the flames."

"You see why I have to bring him to you? I thought the Devil was at work, and I will not bring any harm to my boy."

Suddenly, she was crying deep sobs that she muffled with her fists. Adam put his hand on her shoulder and patted lightly.

"Rosa," he said at last. "A few nights ago, I had the same dream about Abraham and the bonfire."

She looked up. "The bonfire? You dreamed that, too?"

"Yes," Adam nodded. "But however it seemed, I know that Abraham did not die."

"How can you be sure?" Rosa asked. "It was a real bonfire. We had been in that village only a few days before. When that dream came to me, I raced back there. An old man told me it was as if a demon had run into the flames and vanished. More torture from the evil one. I decided then that Abraham belonged with his father. So, we came right here."

"But I know he's alive," Adam said, smiling with relief. "And now you know the truth. He never married. I did."

"Yes." Rosa wiped her cheeks with her sleeve. "You're a good man, Adam. Or Abraham, if you like." Then she reached down and picked up a rucksack, which she thrust into Adam's hands. "Take good care of my son."

"What?"

Rosa's eyes twinkled with fire. She picked up another rucksack. "If Abraham is alive, I have to move quickly to find him. I can't be slowed by the boy. He needs to be with his father's people even if his father isn't. It will be good. Especially for you."

"What?" Adam said it again. "What?"

"You wanted children, now you have one."

And then she was gone. Running softly and swiftly, he couldn't even tell in which direction. Towards Abraham, he supposed.

"But, Rosa…"

What? Who?

"Now what am I supposed to do?" Adam stood outside, alone in the moonless Sabbath evening, and sighed. Above him, a billion stars twinkled and smiled. "Maybe I should just leave Chelm. My shoes are new, my coat is warm, and at least I've eaten dinner. I could be in Smyrna by morning, and in Moscow or Prague within a week. Why settle for Prague? I could go to Boston. Or Texas! And live with the Indians and the Cowboys. I could learn how to ride a horse and punch a cow. Although why in the world you would want to hit a poor defenseless creature is beyond me."

No. He shook his head, chasing away the errant thoughts. He would stay in Chelm. Leave the adventures to Abraham. It was time to tell the truth…

Another sigh. This one was as bitter as horseradish, and as stuffed full of despair as a gefilte fish.

Adam opened the door and heard laughter. Shemini, Doodle, his parents, the boy, and one other voice…

Rivka? Somehow while he had been outside, lost in his own thoughts, Rivka had returned to the house. Now instead of just one or two problems he had a million.

Maybe he could shut the door quietly, and board the next steamer to Japan if that's where it was going!

But it was too late.

"Abraham come back inside!" ordered his father's voice, "Your son is wonderful!"

Enough, Adam thought. Time to tell all and stop this nonsense.

"Papa," he began, "he is not my son."

The boy nodded. "My mother said that you would say that."

"Don't be silly," his mother, the boy's grandmother said. "He looks just like you."

"Abraham, why didn't you tell me?" Rivka asked. "I would have understood. You were young and foolish, and she must have been very exotic. No wonder you've been so secretive. But I'm your wife. I would understand. The past is the past. But this boy, he's not the past, he's the future. We've been waiting so long for a child, and here he is. You should have told me."

Adam was dumbfounded. "I didn't know," he said. "Besides, it's true. He's not mine. He's my brother's boy."

Again the boy nodded. "She said you'd say that as well."

Shemini grinned. "I never knew I had a cousin."

"I don't care. We'll adopt him," Rivka said. "It's clear that he has no place with the Gypsies."

"We can't adopt him, he's not my boy. His mother told me so!"

The room fell silent.

The boy stared at him, and Adam felt as if he was looking into a mirror and seeing his younger self.

"Look, I know this is difficult," Adam said. "You don't know how difficult this is for me. You seem like a wonderful boy, and I wish you were my son, but I'm not Abraham. I'm not your father. I am Adam. I'm your father's twin. Years ago, when the Russian army came into town, they wanted to draft me into the army. But I fell in love with Rivka. My brother... He took my name and fled from Chelm in my place. I took his name and stayed. That is the secret that I have been hiding. All of it. I knew nothing of this boy. I lied to everyone, so that I wouldn't have to go into the army.

"I lied to you, Rivka, so that you would marry me."

Rivka stood and moved close to her husband. "Abraham, how can you say such things?"

"It's the truth. You told me over and over that you loved Abraham and hated Adam. But you didn't, you loved me. Except you told me yourself in the pickle barrel that you would never marry Adam. So I became Abraham. And you married me. I think."

"Stop it," his mother shouted. "Stop it right now. I'll hear none of this. You've gone mad."

"Son, I understand your embarrassment," his father said, "but even a Schlemiel has to stand up and accept his responsibilities."

"Mama, Papa," Adam said, wincing. "Please believe me. Rivka, please understand. I didn't mean to hurt you. Do you think I like being called 'Mud?' No, but to hear the woman I love call me by my brother's name... That was driving me insane."

"I don't believe it," Rivka said. "I just don't believe it." She threw her hands in the air. "I knew you had problems, but I never thought you were such a coward. How can you deny that this is your son? Look at him."

Adam turned to young Abraham. "You look so like him. Me, when I was younger. If I could be your father, I would. But I won't lie any more. Maybe I could have pretended, and raised you as my own. But some day you would find out, and then you would hate me. Just as my wife hates me now. Believe me, son, this is better."

The boy's lips didn't quiver. His eyes did not fill with tears. The disappointment hadn't yet struck home. He looked at Adam, his eyes asking without hope, and the sad shake of the older man's head told him that it was true.

"I knew," Shemini said quietly. "I always knew."

Everyone but young Abraham turned to look at her.

"As he was leaving Chelm," Shemini said, "I saw Abraham, and even though he told me he was Adam, I didn't believe him. It was so long ago, I thought it was a dream, but... It wasn't, was it?"

"No," Adam said to his sister. "I'm also sorry that I lied to you."

"I'm not the one who's upset," Shemini said softly.

Rivka's face twisted into a frown. "Mud? This is why you wanted me to call you Mud?"

Adam nodded.

"Now my head is going to split," she said. She took his hand and stared at his wedding band. "You gave up your identity, your name, to marry me?"

Again he nodded. Tears filled his eyes. It had been a short marriage, but mostly happy. He stared at the floor.

"Husband." Rivka lifted his chin and looked into his face. "Adam?" She paused, winced, then continued. "Adam, I have always loved you. More now than you will ever know. You think I wanted to marry Abraham? No, I was always in love with Adam, but Adam was so cruel to me when we were younger... and Abraham asked."

"What?" Adam said.

Then Rivka's hand balled into a fist and she drove it hard into his right forearm.

"Yow!" he yelped.

"If you ever lie to me again, you will hurt even more," she said. "I love you. Even when I found out that you had a son, I loved you. I was angry, and I thought, 'This is just the sort of thing that Adam would have done.'"

"But you married Abraham," Adam said.

"No," Rivka said. "I married Adam. I just thought he was Abraham. Of course we still can't tell anyone about this. What would my father think? And the Russians must never ever find out."

Adam found himself nodding, not quite sure what Rivka was getting at.

"I can see this is a difficult time," the boy said, politely standing. "You have all been very kind. Now I'll go back with my mother."

"Oy," Adam said. "Sit down, son. We're not finished..."

Clear as Mud

"Wait wait wait," Jacob Schlemiel interrupted. "I'm so confused. Abraham, I don't understand how Rosa could have your son, but you say he's not your son."

"Papa, I'm Adam."

"It makes perfect sense," Shemini said. "Adam was only pretending to be Abraham."

The little boy looked up at his grandfather. "I'm Abraham's son."

"All right," Jacob said. "But I thought I just heard Adam say you were his son."

"Jacob," Rebecca said. "It was a figure of speech."

Jacob's eyebrows rose. "You mean you called the boy 'son' even though he wasn't your son?"

Adam nodded.

"No wonder I'm confused!" the new grandfather said. He squinted down at young Abraham. "When your father and your uncle were boys, they did this to me all the time. Who could tell one from the other? I'll give you some advice… Never have twins."

Rebecca patted her husband's shoulder. "I don't think that's something he can control."

"Now, son," Adam continued, "we need to figure out…"

"Stop calling me your son!" young Abraham said. "I'm not your son. I'm your nephew."

"But…" Adam said.

"Wait, wait wait," Jacob said. "Do you know what this all means?"

Everyone waited.

"Don't look at me." Jacob shrugged. "I certainly don't."

After a few moments pause, they all started talking at once.

"I've wanted a grandchild for so long," Rebecca said.

"I've always wanted a cousin," Shemini said.

"It was a slip of the tongue," said Adam.

"We can't let him leave," Rivka said to her husband. She was still getting used to the idea that Abraham was Adam and not Abraham.

Or was it the other way around?

"I want to see my father," young Abraham said loudly.

Everyone grew quiet.

"I want to see my father. My real father. My mother showed me a drawing she had made. You look like him, but I knew…"

The young boy burst into tears. Adam stepped forward to comfort him, but the boy shook him away. He stood in the center of the room, sobbing, until at last his grandmother put her arms around him, and hugged him tight.

"Sha, little one, sha," Rebecca whispered. "This is so hard. It should not be so."

"What are we going to do?" Adam asked.

"We adopt him," Rivka said. "What else can we do? What else would you do?"

Adam nodded. Even though Abraham was not his boy, he certainly felt responsible.

"But," said Jacob at last, "how do we explain him to Chelm?"

For that there was no immediate answer.

Shemini filled the kettle and put it on the stove to boil. Rebecca patted the boy's hair, amazed at how much he reminded her of her own boys. Rivka held her husband by the arm, as if by letting him go he might turn into another person. Jacob watched them all, still slightly confused, but with pride.

At last, tea was poured, the boy was calmed, and a plan was made.

This didn't happen right away, of course. Nothing in Chelm, let alone in the Schlemiel household, ever happened in a straightforward and easy fashion. There was arguing and crying and shouting and hand wringing, but at last some semblance of sense was made.

Jacob found a sheet of butcher paper and piece of charcoal, and tried to make a chart to explain everything – if only for his own peace of mind

While Jacob scribbled, Adam knelt down beside the boy, and began whispering. Rivka joined them, and after a few minutes, the three of them stood.

"I understand!" Jacob waved the paper. Then he stared at his new grandson. "Abraham, you grew up without your father, only to meet your father and find out he's not really your father! Such a brave boy."

"And he's staying with us," Adam said. "We are his family, and he is ours. When his father or mother returns, we'll go from there."

Young Abraham nodded. "I've never lived in a house before."

Rivka squeezed the boy's hand. She still wanted children of her own, but until then this would do.

"So that's that," Rebecca said, squinting at the chart. Jacob's handwriting was terrible.

"It still doesn't solve the problem," Shemini said.

"Which problem?" Rivka said. "The boy is staying with us."

"But, if the Russians ever find out you're Adam," Shemini said, "they'll take you into the army. Then my cousin Abraham will have neither a father nor an uncle."

Both Rivka and Adam's eyes grew wide.

"Oh feh," Rebecca said. "That's simple. All we have to do is keep up the pretense. Nobody else needs to know. Adam, you're Abraham. You're married to Rivka. And Adam's still gone. That doesn't have to change. Now, my grandson here is a little more difficult. We wouldn't want everyone to gossip more than they already will. Young Abraham here is Abraham's son, so we'll call him Young Adam. Abraham and Rivka will adopt him until his father, who we'll also call Adam, returns."

Shemini clapped her hands in delight.

Adam smiled. "Just call me Mud."

Rivka looked at her husband. "No matter who you are, I still love you."

Jacob, who had been making additions to his chart finally gave up, crumpled the paper into a ball, and threw it into the stove.

"Little one," Rebecca said, "I know this is difficult. Do you understand?"

"Backwards and forwards," young Abraham said. "Madam, I'm Adam."

Chapter Twenty-Eight

Splash

"Abraham, are you awake?" Elijah the pickle man man said.

Abraham Schlemiel blinked twice. For a moment, his thoughts had drifted, and he'd imagined himself back in Chelm, warm around the fire in his parents' kitchen, laughing and joking with his wife and family... A fantasy to be sure.

He sighed and looked at the pickle man. "I don't know."

Surviving the bonfire had been a miracle. As soon as he'd leaped into the flames, his coat had ignited. He'd stumbled in the heat of the inferno and screamed as the ground beneath his feet suddenly gave way, and he'd fallen, still screaming into the pit of hell...

Another moment later, he'd landed with a splash and a hiss. The flames on his coat extinguished and his head sank beneath the water of the underworld.

So, he'd wondered, this is death? It's very cold and wet. Not particularly comfortable, but not as miserable as it could be. Of course, since my nose is full of water it's not so easy to breathe, but if I'm dead why bother? Maybe I'll just hold my breath a little longer. After all, I've got an eternity ahead of me. This isn't so easy, though. And it's starting to feel painful. Would it hurt to swim up?

It only took two strokes and a kick for his head to rise above the surface, where he gasped gratefully. He seemed to be drifting downstream. High above, he saw flickering flames getting farther and farther away.

Well, he thought, I managed to plunge straight through hell and ended up in its sewer. Soon the current pulled him around a bend, and he was surrounded by darkness.

He bobbed and floated, not really thinking, dozing a little, until his head bumped into a wall.

Ow! So, of course you feel pain in Hell. It could be worse. He sighed and floated some more.

Finally, bored with eternity, Abraham began to paddle about.

Soon, he discovered an incoming stream branch with shallower water, then stone walls, and a narrow passageway with only a thin dribble along its floor.

Abraham stood up. If this water is running down into the river of Hell, then perhaps this tunnel will lead me up into Heaven. He put one hand on each wall, and slid his feet along the slippery floor. Heaven or not, it wouldn't do to trip, fall, and break a leg.

He felt something cold and wet wiggle past his foot, but it was gone by the time it occurred to him that the fish might make a meal. Then he shuddered. Maybe it was a fish, and maybe it was a demon-worm. Or worse. Who could tell in this darkness? He was hungry, but the idea of eating something raw and wriggling made him feel a little queasy.

Then, without any warning at all, his nose slammed into another wall. The passage had come to an end.

"Oy! Just my luck. Hell has a sense of humor."

Filled with despair, Abraham plopped down on the damp dirt floor. Maybe there really was no way out.

In the meantime, he took a sip of water from the trickle running past his ankles. At least there was plenty of that… It tasted bitter, though. A little salty, like… Corned beef?

Ah-ha! In heaven the water might taste like corned beef! There had to be a way up. The water was coming from somewhere.

He felt around and discovered that the tunnel was shorter here. He couldn't stand, but he could crawl.

By now, Abraham was becoming delirious with hunger. All he could think about was a corned beef sandwich on fresh baked rye bread, with mustard, and a pickle.

When a warmish drool of salty water dripped on his head, he looked up, and was surprised to see dim light through a wooden grate. The tunnel continued on ahead, but above him the smell of corned beef was overwhelming.

Using all of his remaining strength, Abraham gave a great push, and a heave, and the grate slowly inched out of the way.

He reached up, pulled himself out of the sewage drain, and found himself in a food warehouse surrounded by barrels filled to the brim with corned beef and pickles!

Heaven! Abraham giggled as he pried open a barrel, and picked up a five pound piece of meat. I've found my way into heaven!

He took a bite, and chewed. A bit undercooked, but delicious.

So, he thought, if this is heaven, where's the rye bread? Where is the mustard? I've made it so far, I might as well search out the rest. He took a moment to stuff one pocket with pickles, and put an extra chunk of corned beef into another pocket. Then he found his way to the warehouse door.

Naturally it was locked. So he started banging.

"What's going on?" came a voice from outside.

"Elijah!" Abraham shouted, "I need some rye bread!"

An old man opened the door, and pointed a pistol at Abraham. "How do you know my name?"

"Who else could you be?" Abraham grinned. "I need a rye bread with caraway seeds, and some mustard. And a knife also. I'd rather not eat with my fingers."

"Tell me why I shouldn't shoot you for a thief right now?"

"I'm already dead," Abraham said. "I leaped into a bonfire to save a village. I fell through the pit of hell, into its sewers. Then I swam and crawled my way into heaven. Besides, I won't eat much."

Never had the old man heard such a strange tale. Keeping his gun pointed carefully at the ragged young man, he led Abraham into a kitchen. There he gave Abraham the bread, knife, and mustard, and watched the young man eat with gleeful abandon.

When Abraham was full, the old man questioned him more carefully, and after Abraham told his story, the old man broke the bad news as gently as possible.

"This isn't Heaven," he said. "This is Bialystok. My name is Elijah the Pickle Man. The sewer drain under my warehouse must feed into an underground stream. I suppose it must connect with the old well in the village of Wasilków, which is a few miles from here. A troop of Cossacks came into town yesterday, looking for a band of gypsies. They said they had just been in Wasilków and that an insane demon had driven them from the village. I think you fit the bill. And you have mustard on your chin."

"I'm just glad," Abraham said, "that there is mustard in heaven."

Oops, Wrong Barn

"I think I'd better go visit my mother." Abraham Schlemiel nodded thoughtfully. As payment for his hospitality, Abraham had spent the afternoon helping Elijah the Pickle Man make a vat of sauerkraut. All the cooking reminded him of home.

"Won't that be dangerous?" Elijah asked. "Not only is the Russian army still looking for cannon-fodder, but that band of Cossacks you fooled is still bivouacked outside of Bialystok. If they catch you, they'll either kill you or make you enlist. Either way, you might be better off staying here with me. I could use a helper who knows his way around the kitchen and doesn't mind smelling like pickles."

Abraham smiled. "It's a kind offer. A week ago, I'd have accepted it without question, but after what I've been through… I need to see my family." He ran his hand through his singed hair. "Tomorrow, I'll go. Meanwhile, old man, what shall we eat for dinner?"

At that, Elijah brightened. "There is a sandwich I've invented. I call it Reuben. Would you like to try it?"

"All right," Abraham shrugged. "Why would you call a sandwich Reuben?"

"Well, I've always wanted a son named Reuben, but I never married. So, if I can't have a son then at least I can have a sandwich…"

The next morning, Abraham filled his coat pockets with corned beef and pickles, and left early. The Cossacks, he hoped, would still be sleeping off their latest drunk. When he saw their camp on the outskirts of Bialystok, he gave it a wide berth, cutting through a potato field. On the other side of the farmhouse, he returned to the road, and began making his way toward Chelm.

It was a lovely spring day. The sky was blue, the air was clear, and birds in the trees were singing their bright songs of love and hope. Abraham found himself smiling and humming softly to himself. In a few days he would be home, and perhaps at last he could rest comfortably in his own bed. It would be good to sleep soundly and wake to the smell of his mother's cooking. How big would Shemini be? And where would Adam and Rivka be living?

The thought of Adam made Abraham stumble over a rock.

Returning to Chelm might endanger not only Adam's life, but his marriage as well. It was something to be considered.

At the very least, Abraham could sneak into Chelm at night, kiss his mother on the forehead, and vanish again.

If only he was more like Reb Cantor. Every time the merchant left Chelm, he returned with more riches. Every time Abraham left Chelm, he returned with nothing. Less than nothing. Hands and pockets that smelled like pickles.

A string of grey clouds was looming on the horizon. The chittering birds now seemed agitated and upset. Abraham sniffed the air, and knew a storm was coming in fast.

How was it possible for such a beautiful day to vanish so quickly? The rain would be cold and heavy, and the road would turn to mud. He scanned the horizon and saw an old apple barn on a hill two or three miles ahead. It would be a good place to eat lunch in any case.

He picked up his pace and tried to hum, but no tune would stick.

His mind turned to Rosa, and he wondered how much of a fool had he been to spend so many years of his life wandering through woods and city streets in search of a girl who had probably long-since grown old and married.

Not a fool, Abraham told himself, a Schlemiel. Only a true Schlemiel would waste his time so. Reb Cantor roamed the world in search of profit. Reb Kimmelman had twice left Chelm to visit the Holy Land. Adam, at least, was building his family. Only a true

Schlemiel would hunt for a gypsy princess, and hope that she still loved him...

With a sudden crack of thunder, a bolt of lightning split the sky, striking a nearby apple tree, which burst into flame.

"Yipe!" Abraham jumped fifty feet in the air. Well, maybe not fifty feet, but it felt that far. Icy dollops of rain began splattering on the dirt road.

Now was the time for less thinking and more running.

He lurched forward, and began stumbling blindly through the thick storm. In seconds his coat was wet and heavy. In a minute the road was nothing more than a puddle of mud sucking at his boots.

He cut across the apple orchard, dodging every other branch, and stumbling at every tree root. Was he safer from electrocution in the road, a lone figure on the run, or among the trees? Who could tell? He had heard that the safest place to wait out a lightning storm was in a ditch, but the idea of spending another hour or ten soaking in muck was out of the question.

Anyway, he spotted the apple barn, not five hundred yards away.

Now the thunder surrounded him like cannon in the midst of battle. Lightning lit the dark afternoon sky like rocket fire. At least inside the barn might be dry. Perhaps some old hay for a bed...

Abraham left the orchard and ran across the open ground, then up the hill, as if his life depended on it. A door was open. He made for it, ignoring the dark shapes he saw moving inside. Probably an old blanket on a nail...

And then he was through the door and inside the barn, steam rising from his coat.

Wham! He slammed head first into a pole, stumbled backwards, and landed with a thud on his tuchas.

"Ha ha ha ha!" a voice roared. "What a sight!"

"He is funny, like monkey," giggled a second.

Abraham blinked. Water was streaming down his forehead, and his eyes were not quite focusing. "Is there someone there?"

"Ha!" said first voice. "Someone indeed. He wants to know if there's someone here. Who are you and what did you bring us?"

Abraham now heard two other voices, laughing along. Three

against one. It was better to be honest.

"Well, I have some corned beef I'd be happy to share," Abraham said. "And my name is Ab-GLUCK!"

Abraham suddenly cut his name short.

There, glowering down at him was Alex Krabot, his face even more scarred by time and hard living. Standing behind the notorious bandit leered his flunky, Bertie Zanuk and another thief that Abraham didn't recognize.

"Abe Gluck? An unusual name," Krabot said. "Give me the corned beef, and perhaps we'll let you live."

Abraham nodded silently, reached into his pocket, and put his largest piece of corned beef right into the filthy hands of the murderous villain.

Company of Thieves

"Except for the pocket lint," said the third thief as he chewed, "this is some good corned beef. It's too bad you didn't bring any sauerkraut."

The man's voice sounded familiar, so Abraham shrugged. Even though he, Krabot, and Zanuk were eating his lunch, he wasn't hungry. "No room in my pockets."

"Besides," said Bertie Zanuk, giggling, "all the juice would have leaked out."

"Idiot," Alex Krabot said, slapping Bertie on the side of his head. "That's what Vlad was talking about. He was making a joke."

Vlad? Abraham wondered if he'd heard correctly. He suddenly looked up at the third bandit, and found himself staring into the fat bearded face of Vlad, the man who had tried to save him from the Cossacks at the bonfired village of Wasilków.

"I was making a joke too," Bertie Zanuk whined. "How come you didn't hit him?"

Abraham wasn't listening. He'd been so shocked to see Alex

Krabot, he hadn't paid attention to the third man right away.

Vlad was one of Krabot's robbers. Of course. It explained how he knew so much about Cossacks. But he'd seemed like such a nice man. Another example about how little a cursed Schlemiel from Chelm would ever know about human nature.

Vlad saw Abraham watching him, and lifted a chunk of beef as a toast, and smiled.

The barn was silent except for the sounds of rain on the roof, and the loud gnawing by the hungry thieves.

Abraham would have sneaked away in the night, except he heard the creaking sound the heavy doors made as Bertie and Vlad yanked them shut. He would have jumped from a window, but the only window was in the hayloft, and he knew from experience that jumping from a high roof could easily mean a broken leg.

So, he'd spent a restless night sleeping in the hay, hoping that Alex Krabot wouldn't suddenly remember his face and slit his throat. Abraham would never forget the knife Krabot carried. It was long and curved, and sharp enough to cut through bone.

In the morning, the doors creaked open, and the bright light of dawn made Abraham's eyes hurt.

"You got anything else in your pockets, little man?" Krabot asked.

"A few pickles," Abraham said, handing them over one at a time.

"Not a bad breakfast," Vlad said. "You say you know a warehouse filled with corned beef and pickles?"

Abraham nodded, thinking what a poor guest he would be if he betrayed Elijah the Pickle Man to these brigands.

"Am I a grocer?" Krabot said, his eyes widening. "I am Alex Krabot. I am known far and wide. The mention of my name makes grown women weep and gives children nightmares. And you want me to rob a pickle barrel?"

Krabot raised his fist to strike Vlad, but the older man's hand shot out and grabbed the robber's wrist.

"You need to develop your sense of humor," Vlad said, quietly.

Krabot's fingers went white with tension. Abraham could see

the cords standing out on the bandit leader's neck. His other hand was creeping around behind his back for the long knife when Vlad suddenly released his grip.

Krabot jerked backwards, as if he'd been burned. "Tell me, Vlad. Why shouldn't I kill you right now?"

Bertie Zanuk was fumbling at his belt for a gun.

"You might not succeed." Vlad calmly took a large bite from his pickle.

"Besides," Abraham said brightly, "it would be messy and loud. And who needs that this early in the morning?"

Krabot's eyes darted from Vlad to Abraham, and back. "A sense of humor? All right."

And then he laughed.

Abraham remembered that laugh too. It was horrible, bone chilling, devoid of joy. It froze him, and he could barely breathe.

Bertie finally found his gun, and was busily trying to load a bullet. "Did I miss something?"

Whack! Bertie tumbled backwards as Krabot hit him.

"What'd I do this time?"

"You forgot who's the leader," Krabot said. "Does everybody know who is the leader here?"

"Of course, Alex," Bertie said, rubbing his cheek. "You're the leader. You've always been the leader. Isn't that right?"

Abraham nodded immediately. Vlad a moment later.

Krabot smiled. "Good."

"So, leader," Vlad asked, "where are you leading us?"

"Not back to Bialystok. The Cossacks are there. You say they came from the east looking for Gypsies?"

Vlad nodded.

"Then we'll go east. It's unlikely that they will give up their search, and more unlikely that they'll revisit covered territory."

"But Alex, they've been burning the villages to the east," Bertie said. "There won't be anything left to rob."

Krabot turned, and Bertie Zanuk shied back like a skittish horse. "That's a good point, Bertie. We'll go southeast. See where this road takes us. It's got to lead somewhere. I haven't been in this part of the world for years. And there is one place, about a week or so from here, that I need to revisit. Come along. We won't get rich standing in this barn."

Aside from their shoulder bags, the robbers had nothing to gather, and a minute later they were tromping away.

To Abraham, the road no longer seemed peaceful and pleasant. All the pleasure he had felt at the thought of returning home had vanished the moment he'd recognized Krabot. Now he was even more concerned, because he had a bad feeling that the thief had an agenda, that there was a destination in his mind, and that his intention was revenge.

What kind of a son will I be bringing this man back to Chelm? Last time, it was only by luck that we defeated him. Luck, plus… Abraham had an idea.

Adam! Abraham said, trying to send his mind, send his thoughts out to his brother. *Adam, can you hear me? Are you there? I'm coming! Trouble is coming!*

But there was only silence. It had been a year or more since they had been able to talk into each other's minds. Was it too much to ask for it to work just this once?

Yes, of course it was. Abraham sighed. The Curse of the Schlemiels.

He kicked at a rock in the road, which wasn't a rock but a tree root, so he stumbled and would have fallen face first in the damp dirt if Vlad's strong hand hadn't grabbed his elbow at the last moment.

Bertie Zanuk giggled uncontrollably.

"Thank you," Abraham said, quietly.

"Careful what you kick," Vlad said, smiling. "You never know what's buried beneath the surface."

Chapter Twenty-Nine

Wakeful Nights

Rebecca's cough was getting worse, again.

Jacob Schlemiel lay in bed, pretending to be asleep, and felt his wife's body shudder as she tried to suppress the wracking coughs that were shaking her body. It only made it worse, like trying to stifle a hiccup; eventually the sound forced its way to the surface with a loud and continuous hacking.

At first, when Shmenie was still a baby, he'd woken up with her every night, fixed his wife cups of tea with honey, and held the baby. But after six months, when Shmenie began to sleep through the night, it was clear Rebecca felt that keeping him up at night was far worse than having to stay awake by herself.

"Jacob, go back to bed," she'd said. "I'll be fine. You need your sleep. I can rest all day."

"But Rebecca, I want to help you. I want to be here for you."

"You want to help? Go back to sleep. I promise, if I'm going to die I'll wake you up."

"Don't say such things." Jacob made a sign against the evil eye.

"All right." She smiled and patted his hand. "But I know where you are. There's no point in both of us getting sick."

At last, he'd go back to bed, where he'd lay awake, often staring at the black ceiling until dawn.

She was right, though. His staying awake did neither of them good. But he couldn't help it. Whenever she had a spasm of coughing, he woke instantly, and winced.

Rebecca had been sick for years, so much that he'd nearly forgotten what she had been like before. Once he and she and the boys had gone for long walks, mushrooming together in the Schvartzvald, and gathering wood for the winter. But ever since the ordeal of Shemini's birth, Rebecca had been frail and weak.

Her smile still radiated warmth. Her spirit was still strong, but her bones seemed lighter and her body grew thin. Spring turned into summer. The New Year came and the leaves fell from the trees. Next, there was snow on the ground, and now, the coughing was growing still worse, and whenever she shuddered, he grew afraid.

He went to Mrs. Chaipul, who gave him a mixture of roots and leaves to brew into tea. That helped a little, but not enough. He returned to Mrs. Chaipul's restaurant and complained.

"Jacob, she went through eight days of labor," Mrs. Chaipul said. "The human body is not meant to take such abuse. You were lucky that both she and Shemini survived."

"But why now?" Jacob asked. "Isn't there anything we can do?"

"Take her to a doctor in Warsaw. Old Doctor Krupnik in Smyrna will want to bleed her. Whatever you do, don't let him. You want to know why there aren't any old women in Smyrna? Doctor Krupnik's bleeding cure. If Rebecca goes to Warsaw, and you find a doctor who you can afford, the man will examine her, fully dressed, of course, and give her a medicine that will cost ten times too much. It will taste awful and make her hair fall out. The unfortunate truth is that in the long run nothing is going to help."

"No," Jacob whispered, shaking his head. "I don't believe it."

Mrs. Chaipul looked sad. She hated saying these things, but sometimes lying was worse than telling the truth. "We all have to die some day."

"What about Rabbi Kibbitz? He seems to be living forever!"

Mrs. Chaipul laughed. "My husband is a special case."

Rabbi Kibbitz and Mrs. Chaipul had married a few years earlier, and she had kept her name, to avoid confusion she said.

"Sometimes I think that the only reason my Rabbi husband is still alive is because he's too absorbed in his studies to know he was supposed to be dead fifty years ago. The man says that he has too much to learn to die yet. But some day he will pass. Why do you think he invited Rabbi Abrahms to stay in Chelm? This village isn't so large it needs two rabbis, but one day…" Now it was her turn to make the sign against the evil eye.

"I won't let it happen!" Jacob declared. "I'll take her to Smyrna and Warsaw and Moscow if needs be!"

"You can do all that," Mrs. Chaipul said. "You can take her to London or even to America. But then she'll probably die on the road, or on a ship. Or in any case, she'll be far from home, far from Chelm. You can't take your whole family with you. How would you afford to live and pay for her treatments? Perhaps it's better to stay and ease her pain here."

Jacob threw his hands in the air. "She won't let me! I try. She tells me to sleep. I can't sleep while she's suffering."

"Ahh." Mrs. Chaipul nodded. "I have just the thing." She went into the back room of her restaurant and returned a moment later with another small box of sticks and herbs. "Every night you brew this tea, and just before bed you drink it with her. Tell her I said that the company will do her good.

Jacob nodded, and reached into his pocket, but Mrs. Chaipul shook her head. "This one is a gift." Again he nodded, mumbled thanks, and shuffled sleepily out the door.

Mrs. Chaipul rested her arms on her lunch counter and sighed. The new potion wouldn't help Rebecca a jot, but it would knock Jacob unconscious. His wife was right, the poor man needed more sleep. Especially if he was going to be able to deal with the unexpected.

She searched around for a pen, found a piece of paper, and began writing.

Summoned

The next day, Mrs. Chaipul gave the letter to Shemini, and told her to take it directly to her mother. No one else should see it, especially her father. When Shemini opened her mouth, Mrs. Chaipul told her "Don't ask."

Naturally, as soon as she was out of Mrs. Chaipul's sight,

Shemini held the envelope up to the sun and squinted at it. It was no good. If only she had her brothers' talent for mischief.

As quickly as she could, she hurried to her mother's bed and handed over the envelope.

Rebecca Schlemiel opened and read it immediately.

"What does it say?" Shemini asked, eagerly.

"Mrs. Chaipul wants me to go to the mikveh tonight." Rebecca sniffed her blouse. "Shemini, do I need a bath?"

Shemini shook her head. "You smell fine."

"Good, I'm relieved. But why else should I go? It's not my time. I wonder if there is some festival I don't know about…"

"Perhaps she wants to talk to you in private."

"What's so private she can't come here and talk?"

"I don't know," Shemini said, "but she was very firm about me not telling father."

"Ach," her mother tsked.

"Are you going to go?"

"We'll see," Rebecca said. "Just the thought of getting into that cold water makes me feel tired."

By evening, however, Rebecca Schlemiel's curiosity had grown overwhelming. After dinner, which Jacob now brought to her in bed, she lifted herself with a great sigh and began getting dressed.

Jacob heard the sound of the closet door opening, and rushed in.

"Rebecca, is everything all right?" he asked. "Where are you going?"

"It's fine. Relax." His wife smiled weakly. "I'm going to the mikveh."

"Is it that time of the month already? Do you need some help?"

Rebecca glared at him. "I'll be fine. Shemini will take me."

The girl, who had been listening from the kitchen table, smiled, and immediately began lacing her boots.

After calming Jacob's protests for another ten minutes, the two Schlemiel women made their way through Chelm to the mikveh.

In Chelm, the ritual bathhouse was not attached to the synagogue. Instead, it was a little way south of the village, where a small brook fed the indoor pool with continuously running water.

Rebecca Schlemiel was glad that she'd asked her daughter to

walk with her. They had to stop several times to rest, and arrived at last about an hour after sunset.

The mikveh's lights were lit, and the door opened before Shemini could even knock.

Mrs. Meier, the mikveh attendant, smiled and invited Rebecca inside. When Shemini moved to follow, Mrs. Meier shook her head. "Not tonight little one," she said. "We'll make sure your mother gets home safely."

Now Rebecca was more curious than ever. She kissed her daughter on the cheek, and sent Shemini on her way. Then she went into the changing room, and began to get undressed.

"Don't take off your clothes." Mrs. Chaipul poked her head into the changing room. She held a candle in one hand. "We could be here for a while, and the last thing we want is for you to catch your death of cold."

We? Who's we? Rebecca wondered as she rebuttoned her blouse. Still it was a relief knowing that at least she wasn't going to freeze her tush in the mikveh's bath.

Mrs. Chaipul led Rebecca into the bath area, and then through a small door in the far wall. There was a narrow passage with a low ceiling that dead-ended in another, even smaller door.

"I never noticed these doors before," Rebecca said, chatting nervously.

"That's because this is a secret passage," Mrs. Chaipul said. She rapped on the tiny door three times, and then twice.

"Channah, what's going on?"

"Shh. We have to wait."

"What are we waiting for?"

"I could tell you now, but you wouldn't believe me. In five minutes, you'll believe me."

"All right," Rebecca shrugged.

They stood, their shoulders bent so their heads wouldn't bump on the ceiling.

At last Rebecca said, "How much longer do we have to wait?"

"Oy!" Mrs. Chaipul smacked herself on the forehead in frustration. "Ow! I thought I explained this. We have to wait in silence for five minutes."

"But why?"

"Because they won't let us in until we've been quiet for five minutes."

"Who is they?"

"I told you. You won't believe me, but in five minutes you'll see."

"Oh. Fine."

Silence.

Then. "Why do we have to be quiet for so long?"

Mrs. Chaipul glared at Rebecca. "Do you want to stand here forever?"

"No."

"Did you know that they are listening, and there is an hourglass they are watching? Every time you say something, they have to turn the hourglass over and start again."

"But," Rebecca said, "if you turn a five-minute hourglass over mid-way through then you'd only get another two and a half minutes."

By now, Mrs. Chaipul's eyes were burning. "So maybe they wait two and a half-minutes and then flip it. Now we'll have to wait seven and a half minutes."

Rebecca shook her head. "I don't know if I can be quiet that long."

"Pretend you're asleep."

"What if I talk in my sleep?"

"Don't!"

Again, silence.

And then. "But why do we have to be quiet?"

Mrs. Chaipul nearly bit through her lip. "Empty your mind of thoughts. Clear all the words from your brain. Leave everything that you know and everything you don't know behind, and SHUT UP!"

"Oh," Rebecca said, "if you put it that way..."

Six and a half minutes later, the door opened.

The Council

"You know," said Mrs. Cantor, as she moved aside, "that's a new record for standing in the hall."

Mrs. Chaipul glared at the merchant's wife.

"Leave her alone," said Mrs. Levitsky. "Come in, Rebecca. You're tired, you're hungry, and you're curious."

Rebecca nodded as she ducked her head and stepped through the doorway. She let Mrs. Levitsky take her by the elbow and lead her to a chair.

The room was actually in a cave, a surprisingly cozy cave, with carpets on the floor, low tables, comfortable chairs, two sofas, and even some draperies hanging from the rough stone walls. Light from at least two dozen candles shined brightly off the whitewashed ceiling.

Almost all the other chairs and both couches were filled with women. In addition to Mrs. Chaipul, Mrs. Meier, and Mrs. Levitsky, there was Mrs. Gold, Mrs. Stein, Mrs. Cantor... in fact, nearly every woman in Chelm over the age of forty.

"Would you like a rugelah?" said a cracked voice, and Rebecca turned to see Mrs. Levitsky's ancient mother-in-law, offering her a tray.

"Tea?" asked Mrs. Gold, nodding her head toward a silver samovar with a small fire burning under it.

"Just bring her some," Mrs. Meier said. "Never mind, I'll get it."

"Is she deaf?" Oma Levitsky asked. She spoke louder. "Would you like a rugelah?"

Rebecca pointed to her mouth, and moved her lips and fingers at the same time.

"No, I think she wants to know if she can talk yet," said Mrs. Levitsky. "Yes dear, you can talk."

"What is all this?" Rebecca said. "Yes, thank you." She took the cup of tea and then a pastry. "Mrs. Levitsky, Mrs. Chaipul, where am I? What's going on?"

Oma Levitsky smiled, and pinched Rebecca's cheek. Then she passed her the platter, and slowly lowered herself into her seat.

"First of all," said the younger Mrs. Levitsky, "let us dispense with the formalities. You must call me Chaya. Here we are not called by our husbands' names."

"I never am," said Mrs. Chaipul.

Shoshana Cantor rolled her eyes. "Channah, you are always the exception. Look, let's just call the meeting to order and then maybe she'll understand."

"Shoshana," Chaya said, "when it's your turn to be the leader, you run the meeting your way."

"Fine, fine."

"But perhaps you're right. Sisters?"

The women reached out their hands and made a circle. Oma Levitsky's bony fingers closed around Rebecca's left hand while Sarah Cohen squeezed her right.

All the other women closed their eyes, so Rebecca closed hers.

"Upstairs we are individuals," Chaya intoned.

"Down here we are one," the rest answered.

"By the light of day we are separate."

"In darkness we come together."

"Except when we argue," muttered Shoshana Cantor.

"Shoshana, shh."

"She does this every time," Sarah whispered to Rebecca.

"Ladies!" Chaya insisted. "I'm almost finished." She spoke quickly. "Our strength is our voice, our intelligence, our wisdom. I call this Council to order."

Rebecca heard a loud snore, and opened one eye to see that Oma Levitsky had fallen asleep.

"At last the mumbo jumbo is done," said Shoshana Cantor. "I'll be right back." The merchant's wife jumped up, and hurried through the door that led back to the mikveh.

"Weak bladder," Sarah explained, letting go of Rebecca's hand. Rebecca in turn gently set Oma Levitsky's hand on her lap.

"So," Chaya said, "You want to know what this is. You want to know why you are here. That is natural."

"Chaya, stop beating around the bush," said Esther Gold. "This is why we don't elect you leader more often."

Mrs. Chaipul – Channah, Rebecca corrected herself – giggled.

Chaya pursed her lips and frowned. "Fine. I'll get to the point." She turned to Rebecca. "Rebecca, this is the Council of Wise Women."

Rebecca drew in a breath. She had heard rumors of the Council of Wise Women, but until now, those stories had always been myths. It was said that the Council had begun back in the days of the matriarchs, that Sarah, the wife of Abraham, and Rebecca, the wife of Isaac, had formed the Council to reconcile Jacob's two wives, Rachel and Leah. Sarah, the story went, was so filled with regret at the way Abraham's mistress, Hagar, had been sent away, that she was determined to help her grandson's wives live together in peace.

"I didn't know that the Council was in Chelm," Rebecca whispered at last.

"It's a secret," Miriam the egg lady said, holding her fingers up to her lips. "You can't tell anybody."

"I won't," Rebecca said.

"The Council of Wise Women in Chelm?" Channah Chaipul snorted. "Who would believe her?"

"Did I miss anything?" Shoshana Cantor said as she returned to her seat, stopping just long enough to pick up two more rugelah.

"Can I go on?" Chaya asked, "Or should we all just chit chat and drink tea?"

The Council members nodded and told her to proceed.

The Council, Chaya explained, had been in existence for longer than anyone could remember. Membership was open to any women who had passed a certain age and maturity. In the old days, they had met in secret, in the forest, but when the mikveh was built a hundred years earlier, the diversion of the river had left this cave open and dry, a perfect place for their monthly meetings.

"So, what does the Council do?" Rebecca asked.

"Mostly we chit chat and drink tea," Sarah Cohen whispered.

"We influence the history of the world!" Chaya continued,

ignoring the rudeness "But subtly. We wouldn't want the men to think that we're up to something. They're so happy operating under the illusion that they're in charge. Let them think it. Our influence is quiet, but firm. And, the world, we'd like to think, is a better place because of us."

"And it beats darning socks," someone else said.

The laughter woke Oma Levitsky up, and she began clapping until she dozed off again.

Much to Chaya's frustration, everyone took that as a signal to refill their tea cups, and another quarter-hour passed before she could continue.

"Rebecca, we'd like you to join us."

"I'd be honored." Rebecca blushed. She had never thought of herself as particularly intelligent, let alone wise.

"But," Chaya held up a finger, "there's a problem. You're going to die."

Rebecca gasped.

Shoshana Cantor rolled her eyes. "So much for subtle."

Chaya quickly repented. "That's not what I meant. I mean, your illness. You've been sick for years. Ever since Shemini was born. It's an excuse. It is a crutch. You've gotten lazy. You've gotten used to being an invalid. And it's getting worse. The sad part is that if you were going to die from her birth you should have done it back then. But you didn't! You lived. All right, you needed some time to recover. Fine. We can all understand. But your boys are men. One is gone and the other is married. Shemini's almost old enough to be betrothed herself. Enough is enough."

Rebecca felt as if she'd been slapped. It had come at her so quickly. "I don't understand. What do you want me to do? You think I haven't tried to get better? I've taken every potion you gave me!"

"It's not that," Channah Chaipul interjected. "It's not your body. It's your mind. It's how you spend your days. Rebecca, I know this sounds cruel, but I have been a healer for far too long to leave this unsaid. You are as healthy as you'll ever be."

Rebecca Schlemiel found herself panting.

All around her, the elder women of Chelm nodded and sipped their tea, as if discussing her death was something they did every day.

"I can't give you any more prescriptions," Channah said. "But I do have a piece of advice. And this comes from the whole Council. It is time for you to stop living as if you're sick. Get on with your life. Start something new. Build something. Get out in the world. Dig in the garden. Go to the market. Live. Or choose to die and be done with it."

Saying those last words to Rebecca made her sad, but Channah held her tears back, knowing that showing strength was important.

"You don't need to decide right now," Oma Levitsky said, her thin fingers patting Rebecca's hand.

"But I have," Rebecca said. "And you're right. I don't want to die. I want to see my daughter married. I want to play with my grandchildren, and even great grandchildren. God willing. But I've been afraid for so long." For a moment her head drooped, and the tears rolled down her cheeks. Then she looked up. "Please. I don't want to die. Not yet. I need your help. I don't know how to live."

The room was quiet, a chill blew through the cave and the candles flickered.

Then Chaya cleared her throat. "Of course we'll help. After all, what's the point of being in a Council of Wise Women if we can't help each other?"

And at just that moment, Rebecca felt the weight of fear lift from her chest as a window of hope opened into her heart. The tears didn't stop, but her cheeks lifted into a smile, her famous smile, that was a joy for all to behold.

"Have another cookie," said Oma Levitsky. "They'll taste better now."

Chapter Thirty

Deep Discussion

"Another lovely day," said Bertie Zanuk. He and Abraham always walked behind Krabot and Vlad, but not too far back. "It always impresses me how blue the sky is after it rains."

Abraham looked up at the sky, and nodded. Two days ago, he would have agreed completely.

"They say that the sky is blue because of the ocean," Bertie continued. "But I've never seen the ocean. Have you?"

"Once," Abraham said.

"Was it blue?"

Abraham shook his head. He'd been in St. Petersburg for a week, and had thought about shipping out for England or America. He'd been down to the docks, but the sea had looked so cold and miserable. America was so far from home that he'd turned around and decided to stay. "It was grey."

"See!" Bertie pointed his finger in the air. "I knew it was a lie. You know what I think? I think it's blue because all the other good colors were taken. Grass is green. Dirt is brown. The sun is yellow. Night is black, and blood is red. What other color could the sky possibly be? Purple, I suppose. That might be nice, too. A purple sky..." His voice trailed off.

No wonder, Abraham thought, that Alex Krabot loses his patience. Krabot was up ahead, walking quickly beside Vlad. Abraham sighed.

Bertie turned to look at him. "Are you all right? We can rest if you want. Alex told me to stay close by you. I must admit, it's a relief not to have to keep up with him. I've seen him walk twenty miles in a day, drink through the night, and walk twenty miles the next day as well. And, if you think about it, that means I had to do the same!"

"Why do you do it?" Abraham asked.

"Well, when you've got to be somewhere, and you don't have a horse, walking's the only way."

"I mean, why do you stay with him?"

"Oh." Bertie hesitated for a moment. Then he said, "Oh, Alex isn't so bad."

"Yes, he is."

"Well, that's true, I suppose. He is fairly bad. As far as bad goes, but it doesn't explain his good side, does it?"

"He has a good side?"

"Of course. Don't we all? Alex sends money to his mother. And he never kills anyone who doesn't deserve it."

"I see." Abraham felt suddenly queasy.

"No, no, it's true. I've never seen him kill someone just for fun, and you can bet that he's had plenty of opportunities. With Alex, there's always a motive, a clear reason. That's important. You don't want to be around some of those other crazies. Give them a knife, and they're just as likely to slit your throat as somebody else's."

I don't know who is more dangerous, Abraham thought, Krabot because he's vicious or this man because he's an idiot.

"The pay's good, too" Bertie said. "When I get paid I'm rich. I mean fabulously stinking rich!" He giggled a little.

"So why are you wearing old clothes and sleeping in barns?"

"Well, we spent it all. And if we didn't spend it all, then we wouldn't have to work any more. So it's a good thing. It keeps us busy. The food's good, too. When we have food. And I get to see the world."

"Bertie, if you couldn't be a robber, what would you be?"

"That's easy," Bertie grinned. "The Czar."

"The Czar?"

"Oh, yes. Absolutely. I'd make a great Czar. I know how to smile, and I can stand very stiffly when they take my photograph. I look good in a uniform. We've stolen a few, and they look very smart."

Bertie began ticking items off on his fingers. "I know how to eat with a fork. I've watched Alex for years, so I know how to bark orders. I can ride a horse. And I don't mind sitting around and listening to other people make plans. You know, it's important for a good Czar to know how to delegate authority. And I can grow a big mustache!"

At the last, Bertie seemed very pleased, and he resumed his humming.

A few more miles down the road, he asked Abraham, "What would you be?"

"A chef." The answer came quicker than Abraham had expected. It surprised him.

"What's that?"

"It's a French word for a cook."

Bertie nodded. "You mean like an Army cook?"

"No. I'd like to own a restaurant."

"I ate in a restaurant once," Bertie said. "It was in Moscow. Best food I ever ate. Expensive, too. I don't remember how much it was, because when the check came, Alex shouted, 'That's robbery!' and we left without paying. I say, if you're going to steal money, why not steal food, too?"

Abraham tried to smile. If only his life was so simple.

"You know, Abe," Bertie said. "You're lucky. Any time you get enough money, you can quit this business and open up a restaurant. Me, I'm going to have a harder time becoming the Czar. First of all, I'm German. Secondly, it's not a job they advertise for in the newspapers. I figure, if I'm ever going to become Czar, I'm going to have to find a new kingdom. And that's not easy to do these days."

Was Bertie serious? Abraham glanced at the man beside him. It was impossible to tell.

"I know a king," Abraham said, thinking of Rosa's father. "He didn't have to kill anyone. Now that I think of it, he doesn't have a kingdom either."

"Really?" Bertie was obviously impressed. "Did he inherit it? That's how a lot of kings get their start. But nobody in my family was ever a king."

"I think he was voted king."

"Voted! A democratic monarchy? Fascinating. It could work, I suppose. Of course you need a constituency for that, and the trouble with being on the road like this with just Alex and me is that it's difficult to build a majority. Especially when Alex is the leader."

Now it was Abraham's turn to be impressed. He hadn't heard that many big words in one sentence since Rabbi Kibbitz had been delirious with a fever. And Bertie's almost made sense. In fact, it gave him an idea.

"You know," Abraham said, "now that Vlad and I have joined your little group, you might win a majority."

That stopped Bertie dead in his tracks. "You mean you'd elect me Czar?"

"Absolutely," Abraham nodded. "And I think that Vlad might as well."

"That's something," Bertie said, resuming walking. "Two votes. Three, if mine counts."

"Of course it counts."

"Oh. That's something," Bertie repeated. "Abe, let me ask you. Czar Zanuk the First has a good sound, don't you think?"

"Wonderful," Abraham agreed.

The smile on Bertie's face grew broader, and once again he began to hum.

Chapter Thirty-One

The New Employee

Clunk-Clank. The door to the carpenter's shop opened.

Jacob Schlemiel looked up from his workbench and was surprised to see his wife standing in the doorway. He'd waited up for her the night before, when she'd gone to the mikveh, but had finally dozed off at the kitchen table. In the morning, he'd panicked, until he found her fast asleep in their bed.

"Rebecca," he said, rising, "are you feeling all right?"

"Yes, yes." She nodded. "Fine." She squinted. "Is it always so messy in here?"

Jacob looked around. Only an inch of sawdust on the floor, a few piles of short-ends, and some nails scattered here and there. "Yes," he admitted. "Actually, this is pretty clean."

Rebecca frowned.

"Mama?" Adam said, coming in from the back room, wiping his hands on his apron. "Can I get you a chair to sit down?" His adopted son, Abraham, hovered behind him.

She waved them away. "No. No.... Well, yes. Maybe that would be a good idea."

Relieved, Adam hurried forward with a chair, set it down, and wiped it clean with his apron. Rebecca lowered herself and sighed.

"Are you all right?" Jacob repeated.

Young Abraham came forward and handed her a cup of water.

"Thank you." She sipped and smiled at the boy, who sat on the floor next to his grandmother. "Yes. I'm fine."

"Is everything all right at home?"

"Of course," Rebecca said. "Why wouldn't it be?"

"Well," Jacob said, "I can't think of the last time you visited the workshop. I was just a little worried."

"Jacob, you can stop being worried about me. I'm going to die, but not soon."

"Mama, don't talk that way." Adam, Jacob, and the boy all knocked on pieces of wood.

Rebecca looked at her son, grandson, and husband. "You're being ridiculous, but not absurdly so. I have been sick, this much is true. And I'm told that I will be sick until I die, but at the same time, I've decided that's probably not going to happen for a long time. So, it's time for a change."

The two men and the boy waited. They didn't know what to say.

For her part, Rebecca enjoyed their dismay. She'd been up until well after midnight consulting with the Council of Wise Women, and together they'd come up with a pretty good plan. The problem was that this morning all the other women were safely home while she was the one about to break the news to her family...

Her eyes darted from her husband to her son, and back again. They were both so worried. She smiled. She was tempted to hesitate or stutter, anything to drag out the moment and keep them wondering. But as the Council had said, it would be better to get it over quickly. The more time she wasted, the more she delayed, the more likely she'd be to back out. She needed to move forward now while her health was relatively good and her resolve was relatively strong.

At last, Rebecca said, "I'm going to join your business."

Adam and Jacob stared at each other, and then back to her.

"Excuse me?" Jacob said.

"You're what?" Adam asked.

"I'm going to join the business," Rebecca said. "I'm not going to stay home any more. I'm going to come to work with you."

If Jacob had seemed worried before, now his face was contorted into a look of barely controlled panic.

"Mama, perhaps you should see Mrs. Chaipul," Adam said quietly. "Perhaps she has a balm or a salve..."

"Enough medicine." Rebecca spoke softly but firmly. "I already saw Mrs. Chaipul. Medicine won't fix me. I need something more. I need something else. Mrs. Chaipul runs her own business. Shoshana... Mrs. Cantor has her art, her painting. Mrs. Meier maintains the mikveh. Mrs. Levitsky and most of the others have their grandchildren. Me, what do I have? I have an illness. And not a very horrible one, either. I can walk, I can breathe. I have all my fingers and toes. My boys are grown up. My daughter is nearly old enough for marriage. My grandson doesn't need me either. I have to develop something stimulating, something that gets me out of bed. Otherwise, why bother getting up in the first place?"

Jacob's face was white. He teetered dangerously, his fingers barely touching the counter. Adam hurried forward with another chair.

"What?" Rebecca said. "What's the matter with my idea?"

Jacob opened his mouth, but no words came out.

"Nothing," Adam said quickly. "Nothing at all. I'm just... we're just. It's not expected. Yesterday you were in bed, barely able to get up, and today you're here. And you do look so much better, so much happier and healthier."

"I feel better," Rebecca said. "I can breathe again. Do you know that for years now, it seems as if the only time I got out of bed was for meals and when I had to go to shul? It's almost a miracle. Jacob, close your mouth. You'll swallow a fly. You're beginning to drool."

Obediently, Jacob Schlemiel closed his mouth.

"What's the matter?" she asked. "Aren't you happy for me?"

He nodded.

"So say something!"

He mumbled, "Mazel Tov."

Adam sensed his father's unease, and again came to the rescue. "Mama, I don't understand. What can you do here? How will you help? You don't know anything about carpentry. It's hard work, and takes many many years to develop the expertise. You may feel better, but I don't know if you're strong enough..."

"Relax, relax," Rebecca said. "I'm not going to pound nails or cut things. That's for you. But the business? The money, the advertising."

"We don't advertise," Jacob said. His voice began quietly, but rose slightly in volume. "Why should we? This is the only carpenter's shop in Chelm."

"I know," Rebecca said. "I know. It's rather sudden. I don't have clear plans, yet. I'm very open to suggestions. We'll all have to work together. That's all."

"There's no room!" Jacob said. He stood up. "Where would we put you?"

"What do you mean there's no room?" Rebecca looked around. "There's a cellar, there's an attic, there's a back room, and there's a storage shed. How can there possibly not be enough room?"

Jacob's mouth opened as if he was about to say something bitter and angry. Then it closed, and without another word, he untied his apron, dropped it on the counter, and strode out of the shop.

"Jacob, wait," Rebecca said. But he was gone.

She watched him storm off, and remembered what the Council had said. "There will be a period of adjustment," Mrs. Meier had advised. "You'll be tempted to let things be. In the short run that is the simplest solution. But you need to be strong and look to the future."

"He's angry," Rebecca said.

"He'll be fine," Adam said.

"What about you?"

Adam smiled. "I'm glad that you're feeling better. Are you sure you wouldn't rather take care of your grandchild?"

Young Abraham smiled and waved his fingers. He was such a quiet child, certainly nothing like his father and uncle had been.

"Ahh well." Rebecca sighed. She reached over and ruffled her grandson's hair. "I will always take care of him. But, meanwhile, I'd like you to explain why there isn't any room in this huge shop...."

A Good Deal of Boxes

Young Abraham finally spoke up. "It's because of all the boxes. The attic, store room, and the basement are full, top to bottom."

"What boxes?" Rebecca asked.

"The seven-sided jewelry boxes we've been making for Reb Cantor," Adam said. "He sells them in England."

Adam reached under the counter and brought up a box. It was a lovely piece of work. Smooth polished oak, with brass hinges and a brass clasp.

"I see." Rebecca Schlemiel nodded. She opened it. "This is very nice. How come your father didn't bring me one?"

"You don't have any jewelry," Adam said, shrugging. "That's just a guess."

"I suppose." Rebecca held it up to the light, turned it over in her hand. "Still, I could use it for pins. Or almost anything. May I have this one?"

"Of course," Adam said. "Keep it."

Young Abraham nodded. "I keep my dead crickets in one."

Adam patted the boy's head.

"How many of these have you made?" Rebecca asked.

Adam reached under the counter and brought out a block of wood covered with hash-marks. He counted for a moment, pursed his lips, and said, "Five thousand, four hundred twenty-two, and a half."

"Five thousand, four hundred and twenty-two?" Rebecca was stunned.

"And a half," said Adam.

"Actually, it's three-quarters," young Abraham said. "I'm almost done with this one."

Adam smiled. "His fingers are small and nimble. He's very good at nailing on the hinges and clasps."

"That's almost fifty-five hundred boxes," Rebecca said. "And of course Reb Cantor has paid for all these?"

"Oh no," Adam said. "Not yet. He gave us some money for supplies, and when we ran out we got more. He'll pay on delivery."

Rebecca looked thoughtful. "Exactly how long have you been making these boxes?"

"For years," Adam said. "As long as I can remember. I think we started around the time that Abraham left Chelm. I can practically build one of these in my sleep. In fact, sometimes I think I have."

He grinned.

Rebecca sighed. She poked her head into the back room and saw that the walls were lined with shelves full, top to bottom, with boxes. She pulled open the door that led down into the basement, and saw that it was also full, top to bottom. Then she climbed up the ladder to the attic… Full, top to bottom, with boxes.

"That's a lot of boxes," she said.

"Well, it's not so bad," Adam said. "We make them in between all our other work. It keeps us busy when things are quiet."

"I have a question. Did anyone tell Reb Cantor that the boxes were ready?"

Adam rubbed the thin beard on his chin and looked thoughtful.

"No, I don't think so," he said at last. Then his face brightened. "Do you think we ought to?"

Rebecca smiled. "I think I'll take care of it. Why don't you boys make a few more boxes, but I think you should stop when you reach fifty-five hundred."

"I'd be happy to stop today," Adam said. "I'm a little sick of making boxes."

"No," Rebecca insisted. "Fifty-five hundred is a good round number. I think I'll go and visit Reb Cantor now. It's nearly lunchtime. He should be at Mrs. Chaipul's restaurant…"

"Can I come?" young Abraham said.

"No, sweetie. You stay here and keep your uncle company."

A few minutes later, the door to Mrs. Chaipul's restaurant opened with the jingle of a little bell. Reb Cantor was sitting by himself at the counter.

"Hello, Rebecca," Mrs. Chaipul said. "He's in the back booth." She pointed with her thumb.

"No he's not," Rebecca said. "He's sitting at the counter."

"Your husband?"

"No, Reb Cantor."

"You're not married to Reb Cantor," Mrs. Chaipul said. "Your husband is in the back booth."

"Oh," Rebecca nodded. "I'll talk to him in a minute. May I have a seat?"

Reb Cantor smiled broadly. "Be my guest. What can I do for you, my dear?"

Rebecca sat on an empty stool. Mrs. Chaipul glanced over at Jacob Schlemiel, who was doing his best to pretend he hadn't heard his wife enter the restaurant.

"I think I can do something for you," Rebecca said.

"Ahh," said Reb Cantor. "A business proposition? Yes? Then you must have something to eat. I never conduct business on an empty stomach."

"Perhaps just tea," Rebecca said. Mrs. Chaipul brought a cup from the samovar. "Thank you."

"So?" said Reb Cantor. "Are you sure you want to discuss this in such a public place?"

"It's fine." Rebecca shrugged. "Do you remember the jewelry boxes you ordered from my husband?"

"Of course. I sold two hundred in England. Why? Do you have more?"

Rebecca nodded, sipping her tea. "A few more."

"Are they the same quality?"

"Better," Rebecca said. "They're beautiful." She put a box on the counter. Mrs. Chaipul came over and admired it. Jacob Schlemiel stared out the window.

"How much are these?" Mrs. Chaipul said. "Are they for sale? I would like one. I'll give you 10 rubles."

Reb Cantor coughed. "That much?"

"Done," Rebecca said. She pushed the box to Mrs. Chaipul and winked. "Why don't you start a tab for me?"

Mrs. Chaipul took the box and winked back.

"I couldn't possibly pay 10 rubles per box," said Reb Cantor.

"Oh, I understand the business," Rebecca said. "One price for retail, another for wholesale. But that's locally. If you're planning on exporting them to England, I imagine you'd get a better price than you would in Chelm."

"Of course I would, that's why I…" Reb Cantor cut himself off. "You're very good. What were you thinking?"

"I like ten rubles."

"Out of the question. I think perhaps five."

"That's much too little," Rebecca said.

Jacob Schlemiel's head spun around so fast it was a wonder it didn't fall off like an apple twisted from its stem. "Rebecca!" he hissed loudly, "what are you..."

"Jacob," Rebecca said, "don't you think that nine rubles would be a good price? That's a ten percent discount."

"But Rebecca..." Jacob began. He was about to go on when he saw a look of determination in his wife's eyes that stopped him cold.

"Do you two want to discuss this?" Reb Cantor said.

Jacob glanced at his wife, who shook her head just an inch. "Um, no," he said at last. "Rebecca is my new business partner. She'll handle this."

"Really?" Reb Cantor raised an eyebrow. "All right. Six."

"Eight," Rebecca shot back.

"Seven," Reb Cantor said. "And that's firm."

"Seven and a half," Rebecca said. "Plus materials at cost. And that's firm."

Reb Cantor squinted. "I'll cover the material costs, and take them all at seven and a quarter each, plus materials, and not a bit more."

"Rounded up to the nearest ruble?"

"Why not?" Reb Cantor said with a shrug.

"Done!" Rebecca said.

Both she and Reb Cantor spat in their palms and shook.

Mrs. Chaipul was grinning from ear to ear. "I'm so proud of you, Rebecca."

Jacob Schlemiel's eyes were wide in amazement.

"Well, my dear," said Reb Cantor. "It's a painful pleasure doing business with you. Last time your husband only charged me three rubles per box."

"Really?" Rebecca said. Jacob shrugged sadly. "Well, then I'm glad you're still happy at this price. I'm sure you'll be able to sell them all at a nice profit."

"Oh yes," said Reb Cantor. "The English, French, and even Americans love hand-crafted boxes. By the way, how many are there?"

Rebecca smiled. "Five thousand, four hundred twenty two and three-quarters. But by the time you're ready to take delivery we should have fifty-five hundred."

"Gaak!" Reb Cantor said, choking on his tea.

"Come along Jacob," Rebecca said, pleasantly. "We have to talk."

Jacob nodded, slapped the sputtering Reb Cantor on the back, and followed his wife out of the restaurant.

"Well well well," said Mrs. Chaipul. "It looks as if Jacob Schlemiel has finally found a good business partner. Can I get you some more tea?"

Composing himself, Reb Cantor shook his head, paid the bill, and stumbled home.

Chapter Thirty-Two

The Rider From Chelm

"So, the usual plan?" Bertie Zanuk asked. He smiled and petted his horse's nose.

"Right," said Alex Krabot. "The usual plan."

Vlad nodded. He was tightening the cinches on his horse's saddle.

"Umm, excuse me," Abraham Schlemiel said. "But what is the usual plan?"

"It's simple," Bertie said. "We ride into town, gather everybody together, and then rob them. If we have to, we shoot a couple. Then we ride away."

"Oh," Abraham said. He stared at his new donkey's face. The animal gave him an angry leer, and Abraham wondered whether it liked the plan better than he did.

He'd wanted to escape from Alex Krabot's gang, but the opportunity had never quite presented itself. Alex drove them at a furious pace, so Abraham was usually too exhausted to wake up in the middle of the night and slip away. The few times he had opened his eyes after midnight, he'd found Krabot or Bertie awake, stoking the fire or drawing maps in the dirt.

Three days ago, when they'd stolen the animals from a farm, Abraham had tried to argue that he couldn't ride a horse, so they should go on ahead without him. Instead, they'd taken the donkey and made him ride that.

"If nothing else, it'll make a good pack animal," Krabot had laughed.

Now that Abraham was riding a stolen donkey, it seemed too late to do anything, except go along. Was this how criminal careers started, by falling in with the wrong people and never managing to get out? The last thing Abraham wanted was to rob anyone, let alone shoot somebody. Maybe I'll get lucky, he thought, and I'll fall off the donkey and break my neck.

Then he had an idea. "Couldn't we just wait until dark, then break into their houses and steal everything while they're asleep?"

"That's not a bad plan," Vlad said. "It's a terrible plan. First, where do they hide their valuables? Some place difficult to find. Second, are they really asleep? Maybe not, and maybe they have a gun. Third, we can only do one house at a time, so it's too slow."

Whose side are you on? Abraham thought. Then he realized that he wasn't sure. Sometimes Vlad had almost seemed like a good man, and others he appeared just as wicked as Krabot. Even worse, Abraham found himself starting to like Bertie, who seemed like a very nice fellow, full of laughter. Of course Bertie had been one of Krabot's robbers for years, dating back to when they had come to rob Chelm when Abraham and Adam were just boys…

"Fine, fine," Abraham said. "Any last minute advice?"

Krabot smiled indulgently. "Relax and take your time. There's no rush. There aren't any soldiers for miles. We've done this many many times before, and there's nothing to worry about. Try to enjoy yourself."

Abraham nodded glumly. Maybe I should escape now and let them shoot me in the back.

"So, remind me," he said, "how do I get up onto this donkey?"

Bertie grinned and shook his head. "Just put your foot into that rope there and jump up."

Now he remembered. "Right." Abraham slipped his left foot into the loop on the right side of the donkey, jumped up, and landed with a sudden jolt.

The three other robbers burst into laughter. "You're facing backwards!" Bertie guffawed.

But Abraham didn't have time to find humor in this situation. The sharp landing startled the donkey, and it raced off at a gallop toward the village. Abraham had nothing to hold onto but the donkey's tail, which he grabbed tightly. That, of course, provoked the animal to run even faster.

A moment later, the donkey had galloped out of sight.

"I said take your time!" Alex Krabot shouted, before doubling over and clutching his side. "Haw haw hahahaa!"

The donkey covered the five miles to the village in a remarkably short period of time.

As it descended down the last hill, Abraham's right foot had fallen off, but the other was still trapped in the rope stirrup.

Fortunately, the exhausted donkey had slowed to a fast walk, but Abraham still had to hop along backwards on one leg.

"Stephan," the village barber said to his customer, "Something just came into town neither walking nor riding, facing both North and South."

"It's too early for riddles," said the customer, his face wrapped in a towel.

"No, look," said the barber.

By now, the donkey had stopped in the village square, and was drinking from the community horse trough. Abraham was gasping for breath, still hopping and trying to untangle his foot.

One of the village elders, who liked to sit in a chair under an old elm tree said, "That is an unusual way to ride a donkey."

"Quick," Abraham gasped. "Robbers. They're coming. Run. Hide. Aaagh!"

And then he fell on his face with one foot still tied to the donkey, which dragged him several more feet through the square to nibble on a patch of grass.

A crowd began to gather. Someone tried to help Abraham up, but he stopped them, saying, "Please no. Save yourselves. The robbers. They'll be here any minute."

"What did he say?" the elder asked. Someone told him, and the old man hobbled over to where Abraham was suspended upside down. The old man turned his face upside down to look in Abraham's eyes.

"Who are you?" the old man asked. "Where are you from?"

"It doesn't matter. I'm telling you. Please. Hurry. You have to flee."

"Of course it matters," the old man said. "Do you really expect me to believe something as preposterous as that, simply because an upside down and backwards young man says so?"

"My name doesn't matter. I'm from Chelm. I'm telling you…"

But the rest of Abraham's words were drowned out as the villagers all burst into laughter.

"He's from Chelm!"

"Of course!"

"Only a fool from Chelm would ride a donkey like that."

"Which is the donkey, and which is the fool?"

"Come now, you shouldn't insult the donkey."

And so on.

The crowd grew and grew, until everyone in the village who could walk was laughing, shouting, and pointing at Abraham.

And then, the robbers arrived.

"Quite a festival," Vlad said.

"It seems our clown has his uses," Krabot answered. He drew his pistol and fired it into the air.

Instantly there was silence.

"Hello, my name is Alex Krabot." He handed his gun to Bertie, who gave him another loaded pistol. "Is there anyone here who wants to be shot?"

Sad Sack

Everything of value gathered from the village only filled two empty potato sacks. These were tied shut, and thrown on the back of the donkey.

"What about him?" Vlad asked, poking Abraham's limp body with his toe. "If we leave him, the villagers will kill him."

Abraham groaned.

Alex Krabot ordered, "Bertie, Vlad, give him a hand up."

Together, Bertie Zanuk and Vlad bent down, picked Abraham up, and threw him on the back of the donkey.

"Oy!" Abraham's head hit a burlap-wrapped candlestick. But he was too weak to do or say more.

The bandits mounted their horses, then, as an afterthought, Krabot grabbed a little girl, and pulled her up onto his horse.

"Don't follow us," he said, as the girl's mother burst into hysterics. "If she's good, we'll let her go in an hour."

Then they rode away.

Abraham didn't know how long had passed, but when he opened his eyes they were riding through a thick forest. He squinted at Krabot's horse. The girl was gone. The sun was well past noon.

Vlad nudged his horse next to Abraham's mule.

"At last, you're awake" he said, quietly.

"What happened to the little village girl?" Abraham croaked.

"We let her go. But I had to insist. I pointed out that she'd only slow us down."

"How kind of you." Abraham closed his eyes.

When he next woke, it was dark. He found himself lying on the ground, with a book under his head for a pillow. A campfire was lit, and the sound of snores filled the woods.

Maybe now would be a good time to escape.

As he sat up, he moaned softly. Everything hurt.

"Ahh, you're still alive." Vlad, who was sitting beside him, handed him a tin cup. "Drink this."

Abraham lifted the cup to his lips, downed it in one draught, and then gasped.

"Slivovitz," Vlad laughed, "Plum brandy. One of the villagers made it. Good stuff."

Abraham coughed. "If this is good, I'd hate to see what the bad stuff is like."

Vlad laughed again. "I'm glad you're not dead."

"I wish I were." Abraham's voice was dry. He tried to give the cup back to Vlad, but the large man refilled it instead.

"You're feeling guilty, aren't you?"

"Guilty?" Abraham said. "Yes. I feel broken, bruised, nauseous, humiliated, and guilty."

"Come now," Vlad said. "You are not responsible. What you did back there was good, very very good."

"Oh, yes. I rounded them all up," Abraham whispered.

"No." Vlad shook his head. "You saved their lives. You probably tried to warn them. Am I right?"

Abraham nodded, his head spinning from the effort. "Yes."

"So, they didn't listen." Vlad shrugged. "Whose fault is that? Yours? I don't think so. You have managed, in your quiet way, to delay and stall these robbers for weeks now. You can't stop a thunderstorm, but at least the lightning only struck one tree instead of a whole forest."

"Wonderful," Abraham muttered. "I am so happy. If I asked you to kill me would that be suicide?"

"Don't be an idiot." Vlad looked around to make sure that the others weren't listening. "If you hadn't galloped in there like an idiot, you think those people would have given us everything they owned without a fight? Somebody would have been shot, maybe more. Families would be in mourning today, rather than just cursing you."

Abraham didn't say a word.

"You saved lives," Vlad said. "According to your own people, there is nothing more important than that."

"I owe them their money," Abraham said. "Guilt isn't something that I can banish on the say so of a thief. My people have spent centuries perfecting the art of long and lingering guilt. For us, guilt is always having to say you're sorry."

Then Abraham stopped and looked at Vlad. "I'm sorry."

Vlad snorted. "For what?"

"For calling you a thief."

Vlad shrugged. "Are you going to mistake me for a military police inspector? We are all at some times in our lives thieves and at others heroes. You, however, are the only person I've met that has managed to be both at the same time."

"I'm not a thief." Abraham whispered, his voice quiet but firm. "I am taking nothing from that village. I will find a way to pay them all back."

"You're already drinking their brandy," Vlad said.

Abraham turned his cup over, and poured the rest onto the ground.

"What a waste." Vlad shook his head. "You're a very strange man. So, how do you think you'll manage to pay them back? I can tell you that everything they owned came to about two, maybe three-thousand rubles. You have that much on you?"

Abraham shook his head. "I'll escape. I'll get a job. I'll work."

"Come now. It took those people, an entire village, their whole lives to save up three-thousand rubles. You think you can find a job that pays that much?"

"First I'll escape," Abraham said. "Then I'll do what I can."

"You'd better wait until you can walk," Vlad said. "Your legs are in pretty bad shape."

Abraham looked down at his feet. He'd been deliberately ignoring them, trying not to pay attention to the fact that every time he moved his knees, he felt stabs of pain. He flexed his toes. A little better. "Is anything broken?" he asked Vlad.

"I don't think so. You would have been screaming by now. In a day or two you'll be fine."

"So, in a day or two I'll escape."

"Where will you go?"

"Home. And then, maybe to America. My uncle is a rich man there. He owns a bridge in a place called Brooklyn."

Vlad raised his mug. "Good luck to you." He drank deeply.

"So," Abraham said, "where are we? What is Krabot's next big plan?"

"I asked him just that question," Vlad said. "All that waiting and risk for a few thousand rubles? He looked like he wanted to shoot me. Instead, he claimed that we were just practicing. I said, how is practicing going to make villagers give us more money? His hand went to his gun, but that's when he noticed I already had my knife in mine. He muttered something about revenge and patience. He's a coward. Pathetic isn't it?"

Abraham shook his head. "Don't underestimate him."

"Oh, I won't. Cowards can be very dangerous, because, like snakes, they'll kill you when you're not looking."

Abraham sniffed the air. It felt cool and good. "Where are we?"

"He said we are somewhere in the Black Forest. A few miles

north of a town called Smyrna. Naturally, I asked our glorious leader whether we were going to rob this Smyrna. He said it was too big, but he had another target. What? Abe, what's the matter with you? You look like you've seen a ghost."

Abraham's mouth was open and his eyes were wide.

"We're near Chelm, aren't we?" Vlad said, his voice dropping lower. "Your village?"

Abraham nodded.

Vlad extended the bottle, and filled Abraham's cup. This time, Abraham drank without saying a word.

Chapter Thirty-Three

Delirious

Rivka Schlemiel calmed her panting, and reluctantly poked her head into Mrs. Chaipul's restaurant. After looking around for a moment, satisfied that neither her father, father-in-law, nor anyone close to her family was eating, she stepped inside.

"Good afternoon." Mrs. Chaipul smiled. "Would you like some tea?"

"It's about my husband," Rivka said. "He's not well."

Mrs. Chaipul's brow creased, and she began untying her apron. "Tell me about it."

"It started yesterday as he was working in the shop. He began to dance and to twitch. His father said it was quite funny at first. He was hopping backwards with one foot in the air. Then he stood on his hands and began making faces, like a clown. After that, he just collapsed. We all assumed that it was overwork. We've been working day and night, ever since my father told us that we must have all of the five thousand, five hundred boxes made by tomorrow or the deal would be off."

Mrs. Chaipul nodded. She took her black bag, and they left the restaurant. Rebecca Schlemiel had worked out too good a deal with Reb Cantor. Even though Rivka was his daughter, the merchant would do whatever he could to save himself a few thousand rubles.

"So," Rivka continued, "we brought Mud back to our house, and he slept poorly. On and off he moaned and groaned. Sometimes he was delirious."

"Why didn't you come and get me last night?" Mrs. Chaipul said.

"It was late. You were asleep. He wasn't feverish."

The old woman, who was the closest thing in Chelm to a doctor, nodded her head. "Go on."

Rivka continued, "In the morning, he ate, he drank. I thought everything was going to be fine. He was ready to go back to work. You see, there wasn't such a problem."

"But then…"

"Then he tried to get out of bed, and he crumpled to the ground. I helped him up, and he began talking such horrible nonsense."

They stopped in front of Rivka and Abraham's house. Mrs. Chaipul frowned. "What kind of nonsense?"

"He said he was in the woods. There were robbers. A donkey. Then there was a girl. A little girl. He was babbling. You understand?" Rivka shook her head. "I can't remember any more."

"All right." Mrs. Chaipul was concerned. The last time one of the Schlemiel twins had babbled about robbers it had come true. "I'll find out for myself."

Rivka opened the door, and when they stepped in, Mrs. Chaipul smelled chicken soup simmering on the stove, and nodded approvingly.

The newlyweds house was small, like all houses in Chelm. You entered into one room that served as kitchen, dining room, living room, play room, and study room. This room was packed with everything one could possibly want, from a stove in one corner, to a small bath tub in another. In between were the table, chairs, bookshelves, and cabinets. To one side was a tiny pantry. Since this was a carpenter's house, there were no goats, and only a few chickens. Off from this common room were the bedrooms. Usually these were only added as necessary. One bedroom belonged to their adopted son, little Adam, and the other was Rivka and Abraham's. Its door was open, and Mrs. Chaipul saw Rebecca Schlemiel sitting at the bedside, holding her son's hand.

"Channah," Rebecca said. "He still has no fever. I can't find anything wrong."

Mrs. Chaipul smiled. "So, now you're a doctor as well as a businesswoman?"

Rebecca blushed. "No. I'm just worried."

"I understand. Rebecca, go back to the shop and finish with the boxes. I'll send for you if I need you."

Rebecca leaned over, and kissed her son's forehead. She stood, and kissed Rivka's cheek. "I'll be nearby," she said. Then she took her coat, and left.

"Mother-in-laws," said Mrs. Chaipul, "are wonderful resources and powerful friends. But you have to be careful about letting them take over your house."

"What?" Rivka said.

"Never mind. Let me look at him." She pulled a chair next to the bed. His face looked normal. Troubled, but neither flushed nor pale. He was frowning, clearly miserable, but not moaning in pain. She rested a hand on his forehead. Cool as a cucumber. "Abraham."

"Call me Mud," he muttered.

Mrs. Chaipul rolled her eyes. "All right, Mud. May I look at your legs?"

"Of course," he said. "I didn't realize you found me attractive."

Now Mrs. Chaipul blushed. A sense of humor, albeit warped, was usually a good sign. She peeled the covers back, and then pushed his pants legs up.

The young man twitched and moaned as she bumped and jostled his legs. But again, there was no blood, no bruises, no sign of a break, not even a scab.

She squinted at him, and then without any warning, she suddenly picked up his leg and bent it at the knee.

The young man screamed.

Mrs. Chaipul dropped his leg and jumped back.

In the kitchen, Rivka Schlemiel dropped a soup bowl, which shattered with a crash. "You're killing him!"

"Oy," Mrs. Chaipul shouted. "You're both going to give me a heart attack!"

"Ahh! My leg hurts!"

"It does not," Mrs. Chaipul insisted. "There's nothing wrong with it! You're faking."

"How can you say that?" Rivka hissed, rushing to her husband's side. "He's in agony."

"Hush, girl. Mud, tell me what's wrong."

"They're going to kill us."

"Delirious. I told you," Rivka said. "This is what he was babbling about this morning."

"Quiet. Who?"

"They're going to kill us!" Adam moaned.

"Rivka, quick," Mrs. Chaipul said, excitedly pointing out the window, "look over there."

Rivka's face turned to look out the window.

Immediately, Mrs. Chaipul slapped Mud squarely across the cheek.

"Ow!" he said, sitting up quickly.

Rivka said, "What did you do to him?"

"That was real pain," Mrs. Chaipul said, her voice firm. "The other is in your mind. Your legs are fine. Now, tell me what is going on in your mind."

"This is nonsense," Rivka said.

"Rivka, sha! Be quiet, or else I'll send you out," Mrs. Chaipul ordered. "Mud, tell me. Tell me what you saw. Tell me exactly."

"Rivka, don't go," he said, taking his wife's hand. "I'm all right."

He looked up at Mrs. Chaipul, then he closed his eyes.

"It was like a dream. I was riding a donkey. And the villagers were laughing. Then they all hated me. They wanted to kill me. But they took me away. And the girl. A young girl. But they let her go, and I was alone with them. They're in the woods. They're nearby."

Rivka's eyes were wide. Mud's face looked thin.

Mrs. Chaipul nodded. "So, was it a dream or not?"

"No," he said. "It's real. You're right. My brother. The mind-talking. It's started again."

"Mind-talking?" Rivka asked.

"Not now," Mrs. Chaipul said. "Tell me something. Who? Who are they? Think. Try to see…"

"The robbers," Mud whispered. His eyes shot open. "Krabot. He's coming. Again. With two men and my brother. They're going to kill us all. This time, they're going to kill us all."

"Oy," Mrs. Chaipul said. She steadied herself against the chair. "Oy."

Chapter Thirty-Four

Night Falls

"I am a wandering fellow.
My tale is too long to tell
Now give me every ruble
Or I'll send you straight to…"

The singing suddenly stopped with a crash and a yelp.

Abraham blinked his eyes and propped himself into a sitting position.

Bertie Zanuk was lying flat on the ground, sprawled face down in front of him. "Fooey on these tree roots," Bertie said, as he pushed himself up. "I wish Alex left us in a forest without any trees."

"Then it wouldn't be a forest," Abraham said, softly.

"Exactly my point." Bertie smiled. "You're awake. Good. One more day, and Alex was going to leave you for dead."

"Maybe I'd be better off."

"Don't say such things." Bertie dusted himself off. "As soon as Alex gets back, we'll have money, and after the next village, we'll probably be rich."

Abraham didn't answer.

"Look, I know you didn't have much fun last time, but you'll get the hang of it. Get it? You were hanging upside down from that donkey! Haw!" Bertie brayed. "No, really. Once you've done a few robberies, it gets to be fun. Lots of excitement. Never a dull moment. In between jobs, now that's where the boredom sets in. Me, I'm teaching myself to sing. And I'm writing an opera. It's about a thief who falls in love with a princess and steals her heart. Get it?"

Abraham nodded.

"Do you know how to write?" Bertie squatted down beside Abraham. "That's my biggest problem. I know how to sing. And I've made up some wonderful songs, but I don't know my letters well enough to write them down. Then I forget them and I have to start all over."

"I can write," Abraham said. "What language?"

"What language?" Bertie looked confused. "What do you mean?"

"What language is your opera in? Russian, Polish, Yiddish, Hebrew, English, German?"

Bertie's eyes widened. "You know all those languages?"

Abraham nodded. "And a little Spanish, a little French. And some Latvian. Also, I'm learning Romany."

"Romany?" Now Bertie's eyes narrowed. "You're not a Gypsy, are you?"

"Unfortunately, no. I'm Jewish."

"Oh, well, that's a relief. The Roma are thieves. No homes. They wander everywhere and take what they want. Your chickens, your daughters. Nothing's safe."

"Even assuming that's true," Abraham said, "how is that different from what you do?"

"Oh." Bertie thought for a moment. Then he smiled. "Well, I'm not a Gypsy. You see? Why are you learning Romany?"

"I'm in love with a Gypsy Princess," Abraham said softly.

"Really?" Bertie leaned closer. "She stole your heart?"

Abraham nodded.

Bertie slapped his thigh. "Just like in my opera. Except, of course, in your case it's the thief whose heart is stolen. That makes it a bit hard to understand, though. I think I like my version better."

"Mmm hmm." Abraham hoped his indifference would get the robber to shut up. Maybe he would get bored and take a nap, and Abraham could finally sneak away.

Bertie did not stop talking. He prattled on and on, explaining in great detail how his hero, a dashing thief, met a maiden at a well, fell in love with her, and only later learned that she was a princess.

Then, after escaping from her father's dungeon, he crept into the castle's tower and took the girl's heart from a magical box where it was kept.

Abraham made the mistake of asking why the girl's heart was kept in a box, and Bertie went on to say that a witch had promised that the girl would be beautiful and live forever as long as her heart was outside her body. So, when the thief stole her heart, the girl began to wither and die. Naturally, the thief had to return the heart and put it back in the box.

"So, he climbs the outside of the castle's tower, squeezes in through a window, returns the heart, and is about to escape when the King's guards burst in and shoot him full of arrows," Bertie explained. "The princess, recognizing the thief as her true love, rushes to his side, and is accidentally shot by the captain of the guard, who the King immediately kills. Then, seeing his daughter dead, the King kills himself."

"Not a bad story," Abraham admitted. "A rather sad ending."

"The lovers die in each other's arms," Bertie said. "It's very tragic. I couldn't think of anything better. Besides, crowds love bloodshed. It should sell out every performance."

"I suppose," Abraham said. "But I thought you said the girl couldn't die as long as her heart was out of her body."

"Hmm." Bertie scratched his head. "Well, the captain of the guard could shoot the heart instead of the girl... Or the thief could eat it!"

"Eat it? Ecch." Abraham made a face. "Why would he do that?"

"You're right." Bertie nodded. "It's too repulsive. I'll have the captain accidentally shoot the heart. Do you think you could write it down for me?"

"I suppose I could try. We'll need some paper, and we'll have to wait until tomorrow to start. It's getting dark."

At this, Bertie jumped to his feet. "Dark already?" He spun around, looking into the forest.

"What's wrong?" Abraham asked. "Did you hear something?"

"No. Nothing. Alex said that he and Vlad would be back by now. I've been in this forest before, and I don't like it after dark. I think it's haunted."

"Really?" A plan began to form in Abraham's mind. "Are you afraid of ghosts?"

"Of course. Aren't you?" Bertie glanced over his shoulder and began whispering. "Years ago, me and Alex and another fellow named Dimitri got lost in this forest, and we were harassed by ghosts. Alex said it was nonsense, that it was just a couple of kids, but I never saw them. What they did was impossible for humans."

"I know." Abraham nodded, a slight smile on his lips. "The ghost in this forest can do some amazing and terrible things. You don't want to be alone here after dark."

"I know," Bertie agreed. "That's why Alex assured me he'd be back before sunset."

"Well, he's late," Abraham said. "Maybe the ghost got him."

"You mean there really is a ghost in these woods?" Bertie's eyes were wide with terror.

"Absolutely." Abraham nodded. "It's a horrible story."

"Stop," Bertie said. "You're making me nervous. Besides, Alex isn't alone. Vlad's with him. And you're with me. So we're safe. Also, I've got this."

Bertie reached under his shirt and pulled out a large silver crucifix on a chain. "This will protect me."

"Not from this ghost," Abraham said, solemnly shaking his head. "Your cross won't do you any good."

"Why not?" Bertie said, still clutching the chain.

"Because," Abraham said softly, as Bertie leaned in closer. "It's a Jewish ghost…"

The Ghost in the Schvartzvald

"Once upon a time…"
"Wait," Bertie interrupted. "Was this recently?"

Abraham Schlemiel stared into Bertie Zanuk's eyes. The light in the forest was fading fast.

"Not long ago," Abraham said, "there was a merchant…"

"What did he sell?"

"It doesn't matter."

"Of course it matters," Bertie said. "A spice merchant travels through the Indies. A silk merchant goes to China."

"What if I don't know?" Abraham asked.

"Then how do you know that any of this is true?" Bertie insisted.

Abraham sighed. "My father-in-law told me this story, and he never lies. Can I go on?"

"All right."

Abraham continued…

Once upon a time, there was a fish merchant named Mottle, who lived in the village of Chelm, but traveled far and wide transporting fish – fresh fish, smoked fish, dried fish, pickled fish, oiled fish, caviar, whatever he could find. But not shellfish. He was known as a kind and honest man, one who could be relied upon to provide good quality at a fair price.

Often, he was gone for weeks at a time, but no matter how far from home he was, he always came back at the end of the month for three or four days. That was the arrangement he made with his wife. She would take care of the house while he took care of the business, and for at least three days at the end of every month, they would live together in happiness. It wasn't a difficult promise, because the merchant loved his wife. As his family grew and he prospered, he was careful to keep his part of the bargain.

At the end of every month, he returned home, and the family celebrated. Relatives and friends came to visit, and Mottle kept them awake late into the night telling stories of his travels and the strange places and people he had met along the way. Truth be told, as much as his wife enjoyed and needed to see him, when at last it was time for him to leave, she was relieved. The new month came, there were tearful good-byes, the house grew quiet, and again he was on his way.

One month, however, Mottle decided to make a quick trip to the Caspian Sea. He had heard that the caviar catch was good, so its cost would be low, and he would make a hefty profit. He had successfully made the journey dozens of times. This time, however, he got caught up in a drinking match, and accidentally spent three days in a tavern, and another two days recovering. By the time he remembered where he had left his horse and wagon, he was almost a week behind schedule.

The horse paid for its master's pleasure, though to be fair, the quick and bouncing journey nearly jogged the poor merchant's brains out of his skull. There wasn't time to make all the stops he had planned, so he sold all his caviar to a single distributor in Smyrna, with barely a haggle. Without all the bargaining and dickering his profit vanished. Still, it was the last day of the month, and returning to Chelm was more important to him than earning a few extra rubles...

Bertie interrupted, "Are you sure this is a merchant?"

"Yes," Abraham said. The sun was long down, and he could barely see the robber's face. "His smaller profit taught him a valuable lesson about avoiding contests in taverns."

"Oh." Bertie looked thoughtful. "I suppose."

"Now, shhh."

It was dark as he finally left Smyrna, and Mottle was so busy muttering and cursing his luck that his exhausted horse strayed from the road, and he became lost in the Schvartzvald.

As you know, the Black Forest is no place to wander around in during the day, let alone at night. There was no moon to guide him, and the stars were hidden in the black canopy of leaves. He heard hoots of owls, the yowl of a big cat, and then the howls of wolves.

Suddenly, the merchant grew worried and afraid.

Never had he missed returning to Chelm before the end of the month. His wife and family would be frantic with worry. His dinner would grow cold, and the children would huddle together in fear. He searched and searched for the road, but it was nowhere to be found.

At last, he decided to build a fire, eat a sardine sandwich, and wait until morning.

"It is getting very dark," Bertie said. "Maybe we should build a fire."

"No, no fire!" Abraham warned. "You see..."

Unfortunately, Mottle had forgotten the legend that if you build a fire in the Schvartzvald after dark, you may accidentally summon the Devil himself.

No sooner had the merchant kindled his blaze and begun to eat his dinner than out of the flames rose the Prince of Evil.

"Don't kill me!" Mottle cried. "I have a wife and family waiting for me in Chelm."

"You'd like to get back to them, wouldn't you?" the Devil asked.

"Right now," Mottle said, "I would give you my soul. Anything to have left for home before I even saw you."

"Done!" the Devil screamed. "That sardine in your hand is magical. It shall guide you home, and you will arrive before you ever met me. But, if you ever lose that sardine, you will meet me again, and this time you will not escape."

Then, Poof! The Devil was gone.

"Wait!" Mottle shouted. But except for the snorts of his terrified horse, the forest was dead quiet.

Mottle stared at the sardine, climbed on his wagon, and in no time he found himself back in Chelm warm in his own house.

That night, after the children were asleep, he told his wife and friends the story of his horrific journey, and everyone stared at the sardine in awe. Before he went to bed, he was careful to pack the sardine in oil, wrap it up tightly, and place it under his pillow for safekeeping.

Four days passed before the merchant again journeyed into the world. He put the sardine into his wallet, and made a solemn promise to his wife to stay out of taverns, and to return home in a month's time. The journey went smoothly, as did the one after that, and many more to follow.

Over the years, Mottle grew wealthy and happy.

The sardine, however, did not fare so well. As time passed, the oil began to leak from its wrapper, and the fish began to smell. Mottle's wife complained about the odor. She said that the stench of rotten fish had infested their bed, and was driving her half crazy.

"What can I do?" Mottle said. "If I lose the fish, the Devil will take my soul!"

He repacked the sardine in fresh oil, but his wife was not satisfied.

On the morning before his departure, she switched the packages under his pillow, substituting a new sardine for the old one, which she fed to the cat.

Unsuspecting, Mottle packed the new sardine into his wallet, kissed his wife and children, and rode away from Chelm.

The merchant was neither seen nor heard from again.

"What about the cat?" Bertie asked, rubbing his arms to get warm.

"The cat? Oy." Abraham rolled his eyes. "The cat lived a healthy and long life."

"But the merchant," Bertie asked, "do you think the Devil got him?"

"Some say the Devil got him," Abraham said. "Others say that Mottle the fish merchant is in the Schvartzvald, still lost. They say that if you hear strange sounds in the forest after dark, it is the decayed ghost of Mottle, the fish merchant searching, for his lost sardine…"

Just then, there was a thudding crash in the woods, and Bertie leaped to his feet screaming, "No sardines here! No sardines!"

They're Coming!

As soon as Bertie started screaming, Abraham was running. The forest was thick, so he couldn't go too fast. He ducked around trees, hopped over roots, and dodged branches. It was dark, but he was careful.

His biggest fear was that he would accidentally run straight into Alex Krabot.

Bertie's yelps were receding when Abraham heard a howl that stopped him dead in his tracks.

"Schlemieeeeel!" It was Krabot.

His voice sounded wild and inhuman.

"Abraham Schlemieeeel! I know who you are. I know where you live. And I will come for you."

Abraham felt his heart beating like an old woman pounding out decades of frustration on an old dusty carpet. The skin next to his ears tightened in fear. His teeth hurt, and his legs ached from their recent injuries.

Krabot knew.

It was only by an effort of will that Abraham kept going. One foot in front of the other, away from the robber's camp and toward Chelm. He hoped he was going in the right direction. He had to hurry. They were on horseback, but in the forest that wasn't an advantage. He had to trust that he knew the way better than they did.

How had Krabot found out? What slip had he made? Had Vlad told him?

The questions came and went without answers. None of them really mattered.

Alex Krabot was on his way back to Chelm, and Abraham Schlemiel had led him there.

It was an accident, he told himself. But what does that matter? Again, it's my fault. I should have run away sooner. I should have tried to get them into prison. The Curse of the Schlemiel.

-*Hssst!* said another voice in Abraham's head. *Just run.*

+*Adam? Adam is that you? Adam, can you hear me? They're coming. The robbers. They're coming now! Again! Please forgive me.*

+*Adam?*

"Mud's fever's burning up," Rivka told her mother-in-law. "I don't care what Mrs. Chaipul said, he's not well. He's hot. He's panting and sweating."

She dipped a cloth into a bowl of cool water, squeezed it, and lay it across Adam's forehead.

Rebecca Schlemiel frowned, then nodded. "Ahh," she said, softly. "He's giving Abraham his strength."

"What? What do you mean?"

Rebecca shrugged, and then struggled to explain. "They did it once before. Abraham or Adam. I don't remember which. They're very close. They're connected. They always have been. It's nothing I've ever understood. Rosa knew."

Rivka scowled. "Their so-called Gypsy Princess?"

"Hush. Don't say it like that. She's the mother of my grandson."

"What kind of a mother abandons her son into the hands of strangers?"

Rebecca didn't answer for a long time. She watched as Rivka again dipped the towel and wiped Adam's brow. "Do you love little Adam?"

Rivka nodded. "Yes. More than I thought possible. He is a sweet boy."

"Then," said Rebecca, "he is not in the hands of strangers. He is with his family."

"But…"

"Hush. Rosa's life, and her choices, are not for you to judge. Be thankful for the gift she has given you."

"I am," Rivka said quietly.

"Then say no more."

"Yes, Mother."

Rebecca allowed herself a proud smile. In the midst of a chaotic world, she had lived a truly blessed life. Her family was good and kind and loving. What more could one want?

Just then, Adam sat bolt upright in bed and moaned, "They're coming. The robbers. They're coming now!"

His eyes were wide. Rivka hugged him close.

Rebecca snorted. What more could one want? Peace and quiet would be nice. "Shemini," she called. "Shemini!"

Her daughter poked her head into her son's bedroom. "Yes, Mama?"

"Run and tell your father that the thieves are coming. There isn't much time."

The young girl nodded. "Is he all right?"

"We'll take good care of him," Rebecca said.

"Are you hungry?" Rivka asked her husband. "I've got chicken soup."

<u>Amoral Compass</u>

"Sardines?" Alex Krabot bellowed. The back of his hand struck Bertie Zanuk across the cheek, and Bertie fell backwards.

"Don't make fun of ghosts, Alex," the skinny thief said as he scrambled to his feet. "You don't want them to get angry."

"There is no such thing as ghosts!" Krabot screamed. "Schlemieeeel! Schlemieeel! Abraham Schlemieeeel! I know who you are now. I know where you live. And I will come for you."

"What?" Bertie said. "Schlemiel? Abe's one of those boys?"

"Yes!" Krabot struck Bertie and again the younger thief fell to the ground. "You really didn't know, did you?"

"Ow!"

"Where is that torch, Vlad?" Krabot hissed.

"You think I'm a wizard?" Vlad muttered. "Just because I have a grey beard I can start a fire with a spell? If you'd listened to me and allowed me to light the torches while it was still daylight we wouldn't have this problem."

Vlad's steel shot a spark into the oil-soaked rag. It caught instantly.

Krabot grabbed it. "Start packing," he ordered. "We move now."

"In the dark?" Bertie said. "Alex, remember what happened the last time we tried to go through these woods in the dark?"

Krabot's eyes glowed red with the reflected torch light. "Do you want me to hit you again? Then get packing."

Trembling, Bertie began rolling up his blanket and filling his pack. He tied these to the back of his horse's saddle. When he moved to Abraham's donkey blanket, Krabot snarled, "Leave it. He won't need it."

"Alex," Bertie protested, "this is a good blanket."

"Bring it along," Vlad said. "We can always use it for a burial shroud."

Bertie opened his mouth, and then closed it. He had rather liked Abe.

Within minutes, the campsite was cleared, and the men mounted on their horses.

"Which way is South?" Krabot said.

Vlad squinted, then pointed. "That way."

Without another word, Krabot kicked his horse, and with the torch held high began to ride through the forest.

"Are you really a wizard?" Bertie asked to Vlad as they trailed after Krabot.

"A wizard?" Vlad laughed. "It's more likely I'm a colonel in the Russian army."

"Then how do you know which way is South?"

Vlad opened his hand. "It's called a compass."

"Really?" Bertie laughed. "Sometimes I'm such an idiot. Everyone says so. That's a nice compass. Russian army issue, isn't it? It even looks like it might have belonged to a colonel."

"It did," Vlad nodded. "Now shut up, and ride. I don't want to lose sight of the torch. As long as we see it, we don't have to worry about the sardine ghost."

Bertie looked around nervously, gulped, said nothing, and snapped his horse's reins.

Then, a tree branch reached out, grabbed him, and threw him to the ground.

"Alex! Vlad!" Bertie hollered, as he began chasing after his horse. "Wait for me!"

Almost a Reunion

Abraham stared into the darkness of the Black Forest. His eyes darted left to right. He had heard something. Had he heard something? But it wasn't a ghost, was it? Couldn't be. Could it?

Then he laughed. He had done such a good job scaring Bertie that he'd almost scared himself half to death.

Wincing, he slowly rose to his feet.

At that moment, a hand from nowhere grabbed his face across his lips and pulled him back down to the leaves and dirt.

"gRph!" Abraham said, but his mouth was covered by the palm, so the word came out faint and muffled.

"Quiet, you fool," a soft voice whispered.

"gfeerpfGH!" Abraham answered, indignantly. He reached out to pull the hand away, but then, through his beard, he felt the smooth flat touch of a steel blade resting cold against his cheek.

"If I take my hand away, will you stay silent?"

"rkbfrl," Abraham said. He didn't dare nod. "Nrf, numr frummer."

"Shhh!!" The flat of the knife pressed closer.

He shushed.

Hours seemed to pass, but it was probably only a few minutes.

Still, it gave him time to think. Another bandit had found him, and was just waiting for the Krabot gang to disappear before slitting his throat. The Curse of the Schlemiels again.

His only chance was escape. At the first opportunity, he would run as fast as he could. It was a dark night, but if he could evade Krabot, Bertie, and Vlad, he could certainly get away from this new bandit.

"All right, I think they're gone." First the knife left his throat, and then the hand slowly released him.

Instantly, Abraham rolled away, rose stiffly to his feet, and ran straight into a tree.

The last he remembered were the sounds of laughter and the twirling stars visible through the leaves.

When Abraham finally awoke, it was nearly dawn. The sky was growing brighter and the forest looked a little less terrifying.

He felt his forehead. He had a bump the size of a duck egg. He winced. What was he doing sleeping in the Schvartzvald on such a cool autumn day...

And then everything came back.

Krabot and his gang were on their way to Chelm once again. He had to go and help!

He pulled himself up to his feet, and teetered back and forth.

"Be careful," a soft voice said, "or you'll slam your skull into another tree."

Wobbling, he turned. On a nearby stump sat the hooded shape of the other thief, the one who had stuck a knife to his throat.

"You won't stop me this time," Abraham said. "I have to go. By now, you know I have nothing to steal. If you still want to kill me, kill me. But I have to save Chelm."

"I still want to kill you." The thief chuckled. "But, we have to save Chelm. Again."

"What? We? Again? I don't understand. Who are you?"

"Really? You don't know?" The thief laughed louder. "You don't!"

Then she pulled back her coat's hood and a waterfall of auburn hair spilled free.

"Rosa!" Abraham whispered. He had found her at last.

Rosa Kalderash had grown up since he had last seen her. Gone was the smooth-faced young girl. Now she was a beautiful woman with lines of care and hardship etched into the skin next to her eyes. He had dreamed of her face, of her smile. He had imagined the laughter in her eyes when they met, but here in the woods there were too few lines of laughter. Still, he thought she looked lovely.

"Hello, Schlemiel," Rosa said. "I've been looking for you."

"I've been looking for you too."

"Really?" Rosa said. "It's been years. I shouldn't have been that hard to find."

"Perhaps if my family wasn't cursed, it would have been quicker."

"Which one are you?" she demanded.

"What?"

"Abraham or Adam?"

"Which do you think?"

"I don't know."

"I'm the one who loves you," he said. "I'm the one who always loved you."

She jumped to her feet and came closer. "I have to be sure."

He could smell her now, a sweet and mysterious scent, like sandalwood and orange and sage.

Without warning, Rosa leaned forward and kissed Abraham hard on the lips. She held him there, pressing her body against his.

He did not struggle. His breath was gone. There was no one else. They were alone in the world, enjoying the warm glow.

And then she jerked free and stepped back.

"What?" he said. "Rosa, don't stop."

"I can't tell!" Rosa moaned. Then, a sudden stream of unintelligible words spat from her mouth, and he realized she was cursing in her family's tongue. She seemed dangerous now, but if anything more beautiful.

Abraham began to move closer, but from nowhere her long knife appeared again and pressed into his chest.

"Again you threaten me with a knife?" he said. "Rosa. Rosa, please stop. There isn't time. Maybe it really is my brother you love. I don't care right now. My village is in trouble. You know this. You said you would help me save Chelm. Please. We must hurry."

She stood still and kept ranting, spewing curse after curse to the sky, to the dirt, at him.

It was hopeless, he realized. Just his luck. Rosa really was in love with Adam. He had been so wrong. He didn't know what he would do after, but for now, he would go on alone.

Abraham stepped back, turned away from her, and began hobbling south, toward Chelm.

"Wait," she said.

He stopped and looked back.

She spoke, quietly insistent. "I spent years running away from what I thought was the truth, only to learn that it was a lie. Then I spent years searching for the new truth. Our truth. We were both lost, wandering in circles, but I knew, if I stayed true to my stars, I would find the one I loved. We would find our truth together. He and I. Closer, further. I could feel him. Now. Close. Closer than ever. And I was certain that he was here, now. You. Not you. Do you understand?"

Abraham was silent for a moment, and then said, "No. Not really. But my brother is close. He's in Chelm. And he's in danger. We have to hurry."

"I know." She picked up her back pack, and stood next to him. "But I'll believe it when I see it. And even then, I'm not so sure."

"I know just what you mean," he said. "Are you sure you weren't born in Chelm?"

They both smiled, and began walking. From time to time he stumbled, and she helped him to his feet. Then, as he walked, the knots in his legs began to loosen. The pain began to fade. Soon they were able to move at a trot, and then at a run.

+*We're coming,* he said, trying to mind-talk...

+*Adam, we're coming!*

Chapter Thirty-Five

A Deal's a Deal

"Mama?" Shemini poked her head into Adam and Rivka's bedroom. "How is he?"

Adam lay in bed, his face pale. He was panting like a worn out racehorse. "Rosa…"

Rivka gritted her teeth as she patted her husband's forehead with a damp cloth.

"He's giving his brother strength," Rebecca said. Her voice was soothing and reassuring.

"Oh. Mama, Reb Cantor is here."

"My father?" said Rivka. "What does he want?"

Shemini said, "He asked to speak with Mama."

"To me?" Rebecca looked puzzled. "Are you sure?"

"Oh, yes. He was at Papa's shop, looking for you. Papa told him that you were here, and I ran on ahead."

"Go. Talk to him," Rivka said, waving her hand. "Be careful, though. I love my father, but when it comes to business, I don't always trust him."

Rebecca leaned over and kissed her son on the forehead. "Take care of your brother," she whispered. Then she turned and went into the kitchen.

"Rebecca," Reb Cantor said. He rose as she entered the room, a broad smile on his face. "It's so good to see you."

"Isaac, have you lost your mind?"

"No. I don't think so.

"My son is sick, and a band of robbers are about to descend on Chelm. You'll pardon me if I don't seem too cheerful."

"It's too bad," Reb Cantor said. "One of your smiles could still brighten my day."

Rebecca blushed, and a faint smile crossed her lips. "You always were a flirt."

Reb Cantor smiled back.

Shemini, who was sitting in a chair near a window coughed, and they both glanced over at her, nervously.

"Did you eat?" Rebecca said. "This isn't my house, but the least I can do is offer you some tea…"

"Nonsense," Reb Cantor said. "I'll only be a minute. I wanted to give you something."

He reached into the pocket of his coat, and removed a small black leather pouch. This, he dropped on the table. It landed with a soft clunk.

Rebecca and Shemini stared at the bag.

"How many jewelry boxes has your husband made?"

"Five thousand, five-hundred and twelve."

Reb Cantor nodded. "Our agreement was for fifty-five hundred boxes at seven and a quarter rubles each, plus materials, correct?"

Rebecca nodded. She couldn't take her eyes off the bag.

"That comes to a total of thirty-nine thousand, eight-hundred and seventy-five rubles, plus materials, which since Jacob gets his wood from the Black Forest is mostly nails, paint and so on, so we might estimate materials generously at a hundred and twenty-five rubles."

Rebecca nodded again. Her heart was beating fast.

"A total, I believe," said Reb Cantor, "Of forty-thousand rubles."

"Yes," Rebecca said, softly. "If you say so."

"Yes, Mama, that's right," Shemini said after quickly doing the sums in her head.

"All right," said Reb Cantor. "I'm going to stop beating around the bush. I don't have forty-thousand rubles."

"Whaat!" came a voice from the bedroom. Everyone in the kitchen jumped. Rivka stormed into the room, and advanced on her father. "Papa, how can you make an honest deal like that with my family and then break it? I know how much profit you make in your buying and selling. Didn't you tell me when I was just a little girl that as a merchant your most valuable possession was your word, and that you never ever broke your word. I can't believe that

you'd go back on your promise, especially since it's my husband you
are dealing with!"

Reb Cantor, who had been backing away from his furious
daughter, found himself pinned in a corner like a frightened mouse.
"Rivka Rivka Rivka!" he said. "Please!"

"No, Papa!" Rivka said. "No. You will pay these people. They
have spent years working for this. I know you have the diamonds."

Shemini and Rebecca Schlemiel inhaled sharply.

"Yes, yes, that's exactly my point," said Reb Cantor, inching
his way out of the corner. "I have diamonds, but not rubles. Do
you know how big a pile forty-thousand rubles is? It's the size of
a Torah. A big Torah! Do you think I keep that kind of cash in
my house in Chelm? No. Nonsense. But, as you say, I have the
diamonds.

"The question is this, what are they worth? Over the years, I
have bought them one at a time for a few thousand rubles here and
another five thousand there. The value of diamonds, however, is
flexible. It's not stable. That sack of diamonds may be worth forty-
thousand rubles, or it may only be worth thirty-thousand. Or it
may be worth fifty-thousand! I don't know.

"I made a promise to this good woman that I would pay her
forty-thousand rubles for all the work that her family has done –
your family as well, my dear – but I need to know if I can pay her
with these."

Reb Cantor looked at Rebecca. "You understand my problem?"

"Yes," Rebecca said, slowly.

"Papa," Rivka said, sternly, "are you being honest?"

The merchant put a hand on his heart. "So honest it hurts me.
Do we have a deal?"

Once again, Rebecca slowly nodded.

Reb Cantor spat on his palm, Rebecca on hers, and they shook.

"No hard feelings?" Reb Cantor asked.

"Hard feelings?" Rebecca smiled. "Isaac, why should I have hard
feelings? I'm stunned. What about you?"

"I'll get the boxes later," Reb Cantor said. He quickly began
buttoning his coat.

"Wait, Papa," Rivka said. She caught him by the elbow, and gave him a gentle kiss on the cheek. In his ear she whispered, "Please help them get a fair price from the diamond merchant."

Reb Cantor nodded, glancing nervously at the sack. "I'll do my best, daughter. I'll do my best."

And before Rebecca or Shemini could come to their senses, he was out the front door and gone.

"Diamonds," Rebecca said at last.

"Yes," Rivka said. "He's been collecting them for years."

"Mama, can I see?" asked Shemini.

Slowly, Rebecca reached out and picked up the bag.

"Don't worry," Rivka said, "They won't break."

"It's so light," Rebecca said, her voice barely a whisper. She untied the pouch strings, and pulled the bag open. "Get a napkin."

"A napkin? For diamonds?" Shemini giggled, but she found a clean cloth napkin and opened it on the table.

Then, Rebecca turned the bag over and poured the diamonds onto the cloth.

There were only twelve of them, but they sparkled and glittered like the sun glinting off water on a bright summer day.

"So few," Rebecca said. "So small."

"We're rich, Mama!"

Rebecca smiled, and Shemini and Rivka smiled back. The diamonds were lovely, but the women's smiles were human and warm.

"Here," Rebecca said. She took the smallest and gave it to Shemini. "Now you have a dowry."

"A dowry!" It was Shemini's turn to blush. She looked at the small stone, which felt cool in the palm of her hand. "Don't give it to me now, Mama. I'll just lose it."

"Yes," Rivka said, "let's put them away. I'd hate to see one fall off the table and get stuck in a crack in the floor."

Reluctantly, Rebecca agreed. One by one she picked up the diamonds and dropped them back into the pouch.

A loud shout came from Adam's bedroom.

"What?" Adam yelled. "Rosa, don't stop."

Rivka froze, a scowl on her face.

Rebecca dropped the pouch into a pocket on her dress, and then put a hand on her daughter-in-law's shoulder. "I'm sure it's not what you think."

Rivka shrugged and silently went to her husband's side.

"Mama," Shemini said, "I'm afraid."

Chapter Thirty-Six

The Unexpected Welcome

The three thieves came from the North. They rode out of the Schvartzvald, across the crest of East Hill, and down the gentle slope. They came at dawn, their shadows long, the sun peeking gold above the horizon. Fall leaves blew in the wind, and muffled the sounds of their horses' hooves.

The farm fields on the outskirts of Chelm were empty. The harvests were in, the winter rye planted, haystacks stood in tied bundles drying before the first snows.

The first houses they passed were dark. No sounds came from the streets save the cackles of hens and the brays of goats.

"It's so quiet, Alex," said Bertie Zanuk. "Do you think they know we're coming?"

"Yes, of course they know." Alex Krabot nodded. "I'm sure that worm Abraham Schlemiel warned them."

"Come now," Vlad said. "How is that possible? He was on foot. You worry too much."

Krabot stared at Vlad for a moment. "Be on your guard. These people seem simple, but they are not."

Up ahead, a little boy peeked from behind a house, and then vanished at a run.

"All right," Vlad said, chuckling softly. "I'm shaking in my boots."

The three horsemen turned the corner where the narrow dirt road opened up into the village square.

They reined their horses to a sudden stop.

There in the round square, dressed in their finest clothes, stood a hundred and fifty, perhaps two hundred villagers.

"They're here!" someone shouted. The thieves hands went to the guns in their belts as every eye in the square turned toward them.

And then all the faces in the crowd broke into broad smiles, and a cheer went up, "MAZEL TOV! Welcome! Hurrah!"

A klezmer band began playing a lively tune. Men, women, and children all surged forward to meet the robbers.

Dazed by the shouts and the music, startled by the good cheer, (a banner strung from roof-top to roof-top read, "Welcome Krabot Gang!") they found themselves pulled from their horses and ushered – with pats on the shoulder, claps on the back, and even a few hugs – to the middle of the square where a small platform had been erected.

The noise was incredible. Everyone was laughing and talking and cheering simultaneously. The invaders were hustled up the steps of the platform, and surrounded by a group of town elders who reached out and shook their hands firmly, while a few young boys darted in and around them with frightened glee.

One man, Rabbi Kibbitz, the oldest there, was standing at the front of the platform saying, "Shaa, shaa." But to little effect. At last, another man, young Rabbi Yohon Abrahms, the schoolteacher, stepped forward, put two fingers into his mouth, and blew a sharp whistle.

After a startled laugh, the villagers quieted.

"Thank you, thank you," said Rabbi Kibbitz. "It seems that my young associate has a knack for nonverbal communication."

Another laugh, until the Rabbi raised his hands.

"As you know," the Rabbi said, "we are honored today to welcome three of the most notorious thieves in all of Europe."

Another cheer went up.

"Alex," Bertie whispered, "what's going on?"

"Shh," Krabot hissed. "Pay attention."

When silence was restored, the Rabbi turned to the thieves.

"Mr. Krabot," he said. "There is a tradition of presenting the key to the city to honored guests. Chelm however, as you know, is a small village, and we don't lock our doors. So, we spent a good deal of time trying to decide exactly what to give to you."

"How about all your money and valuables?" Krabot said.

"Besides that," the Rabbi laughed. "Patience, please. Perhaps you didn't know this, but we've heard from our neighbors in Smyrna that Chelm is known far and wide for only one thing – our wisdom."

At this last, three visitors from Smyrna who happened to be in Chelm that day, and were hiding at the back of the crowd, burst into hysterical giggles.

"We in Chelm think this is undeserved praise," the Rabbi continued, "and yet the belief persists. We spent many hours trying to decide what words of wisdom to offer you, but none seemed quiet appropriate."

"I still like, 'Don't step in puddles!'" shouted a girl's voice. Everyone laughed.

"Wise words," Rabbi Kibbitz said, "but hardly sufficient for the occasion. So, instead, we would like to present you with these."

Just then, three beautiful young girls stepped forward and hung three wooden medals on ribbons around the thieves' necks.

Bertie glanced down at his, squinting. "What does it say?"

Vlad turned his around and answered. "It says we're honorary citizens of Chelm."

"That's right," Rabbi Kibbitz said. "Welcome home!"

Another cheer of "Mazel Tov!" rose, and once again the band began playing.

Alex Krabot stood still, his face frozen and impassive. He scanned the crowd with his eyes, and then from the corner of his mouth he told Bertie, "Shoot someone."

"What?" Bertie said. "Alex, they're being very nice."

"It's a trap. Shoot someone."

With a shrug, Bertie reached down to his belt for his gun, but found that it was missing.

Both Vlad and Krabot realized that their guns were gone as well.

The thieves now glanced from one to the other with a feeling of growing panic and unease.

Toward the back of the crowd, Krabot thought he spotted a little boy running away, hiding a small bundle under his shirt.

"It looks like you were right, Alex," Vlad said. "They're sneaky."

"What do we do now?" Bertie whispered.

"That Schlemiel," Krabot said through gritted teeth. "I'm going to kill him."

A Long Walk

Alex Krabot leaned his head back and shouted, "Schlemiel! Abraham Schlemiel!'"

Everyone on the platform jumped back a foot, except for Vlad, who blinked and then grinned.

Krabot turned toward the Rabbi, the merchant, the accountant, and the other assembled elders of Chelm.

"Where," he bellowed, "is Abraham Schlemiel?"

When the Chelmites hesitated, Bertie Zanuk added, "You heard him. Where is Abraham Schlemiel?"

"Abraham's not here?" Reb Shikker said. "I thought for sure he'd be here…"

"I think he's sick," Reb Cantor said. "He's home in bed."

"Bring him to me." Krabot's eyes were wide with rage. When no one moved, he roared, "Bring him now!"

"Uncle," young Abraham said, creeping into Adam's darkened bedroom. "Uncle, wake up. The robbers, they're here. They want you. You must hurry and hide. Uncle, please."

His uncle didn't move.

The boy was worried. He had run from the square to his grandfather's and then home as fast as he could. Where were Grandmother Rebecca and Tante Rivka? Probably they were in the village square standing around and wondering what to do. The villagers of Chelm didn't understand danger the way a Gypsy would. You needed to act fast. If you hesitated, you might be killed.

From under his shirt, Young Abraham removed the three pistols he had stolen from the thieves. He set them on the bedside table.

No, that was too obvious. If they came and found their guns they would probably use them. He knelt down and slid them under the bed.

"What are you doing?" came a weak voice.

"Uncle! You're awake?"

"Of course I'm awake. Who could sleep with a young boy rooting around under his bed like a giant rat. What are you doing down there?"

"Nothing, Uncle." Young Abraham stood up quickly. "I thought I dropped something."

Adam squinted at his nephew. He knew the boy was lying, but they would talk about it later. There wasn't time. "So? The robbers have come?"

The boy nodded. "Yes. They're calling for Abraham. They'll be here soon. You have to hide."

"No, I can't hide," Adam said, shaking his head. "They don't want me. They want my brother." Adam smiled. "Abraham must be nearby."

"My father?" young Abraham said, a note of surprise in his voice. "My father is here?" He looked around the room.

"No," Adam said. "Not yet. But soon." He pushed himself up to sitting. "Help me out of bed."

"You can hide from them in the basement of the shop. Or in the attic."

Adam laughed and slid his feet onto the floor. "You think I'll fit inside one of our jewelry boxes?"

"Maybe if you held your breath." The young boy grinned. "No. But Reb Cantor had me and Grandfather move the boxes out of the attic. The basement and the warehouse are empty, too. The boxes fill two wagons. I even swept the floors, so you won't get your trousers dirty."

Adam smiled. "You've been busy. No. I won't hide. They want Abraham. They'll get me."

"Uncle, no. You must not," young Abraham pleaded. "These men are killers. I can see it in their eyes."

Adam stood unsteadily. He put a hand on his nephew's shoulder.

"I faced them before, when I was a boy not much younger than you."

"Yes, yes. I've heard the story. But they weren't expecting you then. And you were younger. And they didn't know that you and my father were twins. And you weren't hurt."

"Ahh," Adam said, pulling on his coat, "but if I wasn't hurt they wouldn't be certain I was Abraham."

"I don't understand."

"You will. Come and help me to the square."

Adam opened the front door to the house just as Reb Cantor had begun knocking. Instead of knocking on the door, Reb Cantor rapped his knuckles on Adam's forehead.

"Oh, Abraham," Reb Cantor said. "There you are." Two dozen villagers stood behind him. Some of the children giggled, while others cried.

"Ouch," Adam said. "It's not enough my legs are on fire, you had to make sure that my head wasn't hollow?"

"Sorry," Reb Cantor said. "Our brilliant plan to welcome the robbers is not working. These men are unhappy. Krabot wants you, and I'm a little nervous about the whole situation."

"I understand," Adam said as he hobbled outside, squinting in the morning sun. "My brave nephew here told me. Come, let's go see what they want."

Reb Cantor tousled the boy's hair. "He runs so fast. Still, I'm not sure giving them what they want is such a good idea."

"My good father in-law, what else can we do? If we don't give them what they want, they'll take what they want and more. We're not strong enough to fight them. They are armed and we have no weapons."

"Uncle," the little boy said, "about their guns…"

"Shh," Adam said. "Even if we did have guns, I'm not sure I'd want to use them. Because, if we did, we'd be no better than they."

"But at least we'd be alive," Reb Cantor said. "Whenever someone tries to cheat me, I always make sure I cheat them back. That way, they'll learn a lesson and won't try it again."

"There's a difference between cheating a cheater and killing a killer," Adam said as they walked. "In one case you are only taking back through guile what already belongs to you. In the other, however, you are taking forever what belongs to the Almighty."

Reb Cantor shook his head. "I'm not a rabbi. I'm a practical man. I don't want my daughter to become a widow."

"But she is safe," Adam said.

Reb Cantor nodded. "Safer than you."

"Then don't worry." Adam patted his father in-law's broad shoulder. "In fact…" He stopped and turned to young Abraham. "You need to go and be with them."

"But Uncle, I can't leave you alone."

"Your cousin, your Tante, and your Grandmother need you to protect them."

The little boy's lips pursed as he considered whether it was an honest mission or if he was being sent to hide with the women.

"Please," Adam said. "As long as my family is hidden, the robbers can take nothing of value from me."

"Will you be able to walk?"

Adam shrugged. "I once walked half way to Pinsk. I think I can make it from my house to the village square."

At last, young Abraham nodded. "I need to get something from the house first."

Adam looked into his nephew's eyes and saw a fierce determination. "All right, but be quick."

Young Abraham gave his uncle a hug, and then raced off.

Without the boy's support Adam wobbled, until Reb Cantor steadied him. "You all right?"

"Yes," Adam said. "He's a good boy. I'm proud of him."

"Yes," Reb Cantor agreed, as they made their way slowly down the narrow dirt road. "But you didn't tell him that the robbers probably want to kill you."

"We all have to die," Adam said. "Usually it's for no reason. I can't think of a better reason than to give my life for my family. Besides, I don't think that's going to happen. It's too nice a day to die."

Reb Cantor smiled. "Now you're going to depend on the

weather to protect you? This is Chelm. It could start snowing at any moment."

They entered the edge of the round village square, and slowly and quietly the crowd parted, making a path to the front. Up ahead on the platform, Adam could see the three bandits standing next to the Rabbis of Chelm.

"Reb Cantor, you're being very pessimistic," Adam said, shaking his head, but smiling. "Besides, I happen to like snow."

A Final Offer

Adam Schlemiel had never felt such fear in his life. He stared up through the corridor of people at the robbers and found it a wonder that his legs still moved, taking him closer.

When he was a boy, he had faced these same men without quaking. He had been bold and forceful, a bit frightened, but certain of victory. He'd been stupid and immature, and lucky.

As a boy, when he knew nothing, it had been so easy to be a hero. Now Adam realized how much they all had to lose.

Still, he walked forward, limping but not showing the pain on his face.

On either side of him stood his friends and neighbors, wishing him luck and making signs against the evil eye. Not one of them would trade places with him, nor should they. If it were not for the Schlemiel brothers, the thieves would have robbed them years ago, realized that there was nothing to be stolen from Chelm, and never returned. Now the whole village was once again at risk.

And then, as he reached the steps at the bottom of the wooden platform, another thought entered his mind.

How dare they?

How dare these three pathetic excuses of men stand in front of an entire village and attempt to dictate terms? What right had they? Guns and strength and a willingness to kill, that was enough? That was it? That was all it would take to cow hundreds of people into submission?

What nonsense! It made him want to scream. Adam wondered what had happened to the pistol he had taken from Krabot so long ago. Perhaps he should have stopped and asked his father for it… But it was too late for that.

Rabbi Yohon Abrahms helped him up the last few steps, patted him on the back, whispered "Mazel Tov," and then edged quickly away, standing next to Rabbi Kibbitz off to one side.

"Abraham Schlemiel," Alex Krabot said, his voice calm, but loud enough for every one in the square to hear.

"Yes!" Adam squeaked, his voice cracking with tension. "That's me."

"How do I know it's you and not your brother?"

"You want to see the bruises on my ankles?"

"Yes," Krabot said. "Why not?" Bertie laughed. The other thief just stood there, silent.

Adam bent down and rolled up the legs of his trousers.

All the women in Chelm turned their heads. The men gasped. This made the women turn back, and gasp as well. Adam's legs were as black and blue as a thundercloud against an otherwise clear sky. It was a wonder he could stand, let alone walk.

Adam let the trouser legs fall. "Satisfied?"

"How did you get here so quickly?" Krabot demanded. "We were on horses and it took us hours."

"Maybe the ghost helped me," Adam said, grinning. Bertie jumped back as if he'd been poked with a stick and nearly fell off the platform. "I live here. I know all the short cuts. No matter how dangerous you are, you are still fools."

"Fools!" Krabot roared. "You dare call me a fool?"

"I think perhaps," Rabbi Kibbitz began, "he meant that…"

"Quiet old man," Adam said, altogether startling Rabbi Kibbitz. "Yes, I mean that you are fools. What kind of an idiot comes to Chelm expecting to get rich?"

(Down in the crowded square, Reb Cantor looked nervously from side to side. "What is he doing?")

("Shh," someone told him. "He's not talking about you, Reb Cantor.")

("Well," laughed a third, "I don't know about that…)

Adam continued, "What kind of numbskulls come to Chelm once, learn that we have absolutely nothing of value except to ourselves, and then return to rob us a second time? It's more than foolish, it's stupendously ignorant.

"You know, we were actually willing to let you go. That's right. We could have called the soldiers, but we didn't. Instead, we went out of our way to welcome you here. We made you honorary members of our community. We offered you everything we have and still you're not satisfied? You're like pigs who don't know when they've had enough slop and eat until their stomachs split open with pain!

"You may have thought we were being dishonest with our medals and our cheers and our band. They were not false. You don't understand the kind of people we are trying to be. Where else in Europe would a village, knowing who you are and what you have done, welcome you with open arms? Nowhere. You have no one. You have no home. You have no family. You have no friends.

"You have nothing. Nothing but money, and when you've spent that, all you have is poverty. What do you know about love? What do you know about family? What do you know about God? I'm not talking about a Jewish God or a Christian God. I'm talking about the Maker of the Universe. You think this is how your days ought to be spent? Fleeing from one pathetic village to another until someone shoots you or hangs you from a tree?

"Your pleasures are as fleeting as your rubles. You build nothing. Your legacy is pain and destruction, and you're not even good at it. Your companions are not friends. They're thieves and murderers and liars. Everyone else is your enemy.

"And yet we offer you a home. We say, 'Here is Chelm. Be part of our village. We don't have much, but what we have we will share so long as you live with us in peace.' We offer our hands, and our hearts, and you laugh in our faces.

"I pity you. I feel sorry for you. I would pray for you, but I don't think it would help.

"You can't steal anything from us. We give it to you. Again. It is all yours. You can take everything we own away, but you will still leave behind everything we value.

"Once more I say to you, put down your weapons and live with us. Join our community. In Hebrew one word, 'Shalom' means both hello and peace. Hello and peace is what we are offering. Give yourselves time to learn what it's like to have a home, to live without fear or violence. That is our gift."

No one in Chelm dared to breathe, except Rabbi Yohon Abrahms, who was about to explain that Shalom also meant goodbye, but Rabbi Kibbitz clapped a hand over the school teacher's mouth.

Bertie Zanuk looked nervous. Vlad's face was a mask. Alex Krabot's eyes narrowed.

"Are you done?" Krabot said.

"More or less," Adam said. "There are always details to be worked out."

"Where is your brother?" demanded Krabot.

"My brother?" Adam nodded his head. "He's right behind you."

In one smooth motion, Alex Krabot bent down, drew a small revolver pistol from his boot, stood up, turned, and fired.

The bullet sped through the air, passing through emptiness until it vanished in a field of rye.

Krabot spun around and aimed the revolver at Adam.

"So, I lied," Adam shrugged. "I suppose that was your answer?"

"Alex," Bertie whispered. "maybe we should consider their offer…"

"Shut up." Krabot backhanded Bertie Zanuk, who fell off the platform into the crowd.

Then, Krabot stepped forward and poked the pistol into Adam's stomach.

"I want the diamonds."

"What diamonds?"

"What diamonds?" Krabot grinned. "And you dare to call me dishonest? I didn't think you meant what you said, and now you've proved it. You liar. The merchant's diamonds. I want them. Then we will leave your little village of Chelm in Shalom."

Chapter Thirty-Seven

A Shot Rang Out

When he was asleep, Captain Boris Plotz often dreamed of leading troops to glorious victory. Never mind that, in his job as the captain in charge of conscripting troops into the Czar's army, he had been a complete and utter failure.

In his dreams, when they had finally assigned him to the Western Front, he had found his true purpose in life, and won medal after medal. Now he imagined himself brilliantly dressed in Cossack red, riding a white horse, and brandishing a sword, as his men charged bravely into battle.

In this dream, he hacked and slashed and laughed with joy at the carnage his soldiers inflicted on the enemy. There, up ahead on the crest of a hill was the German General. His capture or death would mean defeat for the Germans, and certain promotion for the Captain. Plotz considered riding up the well-defended hill and cutting his way to the General by himself, but then he realized that simply shooting the man would be much simpler – and much safer.

He drew his pistol, pulled the hammer back to cock it, and…

There was a loud gunshot!

Plotz was stunned. He hadn't fired yet. No. On the hill, the General had his own pistol out. Smoke was floating from its barrel.

Then Plotz felt the sudden impact from the General's bullet. It hit him in the shoulder, knocking him off his horse…

WHAM!

Captain Boris Plotz awoke suddenly with a sharp pain in his shoulder. He blinked and looked around in confusion. He had rolled out of bed and fallen on the tines of an old fork he had lost two weeks ago.

He sat up and, cursing, pulled the fork from his shoulder. Blood leaked through the holes in his night shirt.

So much for battle. He was still in the village of Chelm, still in his small room above Mrs. Chaipul's restaurant. He had been there for years now, first looking for Adam Schlemiel or any other recruits for the army. But as the months had passed, and he hadn't found Schlemiel or anyone else worth putting into the Czar's uniform, the spirit had gone out of him. He'd given up. And, after his second winter, he'd forgotten to send reports back to his commander, the Colonel. Now, if headquarters thought of him at all, they probably assumed he was dead or a deserter. And if he came back, they'd shoot him for dereliction of duty.

So, a few years ago Plotz had realized, he was stuck in Chelm, possibly forever. Still, it wasn't a bad life. As an officer, they gave him free food and lodging. He played chess with the Rabbi almost every day, and wandered around the countryside on long "recruiting expeditions." Life was boring, but at least he wasn't dead, starving, or frozen in Siberia.

Now at last, he'd been injured in battle. He smiled. When he went down to breakfast, he would ask Mrs. Chaipul to bandage him up. Of course he'd have to come up with a better excuse for the wounds. Maybe he would claim it was a rat's bite. He smiled again. The idea that a rat was living above her restaurant would drive the old woman crazy.

He yawned and rolled over. It had been such a sweet dream.

Retired Sergeant Vasilly Shnuck heard the distant gunshot and immediately dropped to the dirt. The last time he'd been in battle it had been a slaughter. Officers ordering men onward while the Poles sat behind barricades and shot them by the dozens. The only reason he'd escaped then was that he'd tripped, and his friend Misha the giant had taken a bullet through the throat and fallen on top of him. By the time Shnuck realized that he himself wasn't dead, the massed weight of the Russian army had overwhelmed the Poles. He'd actually gotten promoted to Sergeant because of his so-called heroism during that battle.

The Sergeant reached for his gun… and realized that it was a shovel. He didn't even have his rifle with him. Why would he? He had put in his retirement papers two years ago, and had been living in Chelm as a farmer ever since. There was no reason to carry a gun when you're digging up potatoes.

He would have to hide. Without a weapon, that was the only solution. So he quickly dug a fox hole six feet deep (finding thirty-four potatoes along the way), and jumped into it.

Panting hard, he wondered if he was safer now, or just more likely to be trapped. They couldn't get him in a crossfire, but if they had artillery, he was doomed. Shnuck wondered if he'd just dug his own grave.

He looked up at the sky.

It was becoming a beautiful day. The sky had been cloudy in the morning, which was good if you were planning on doing a lot of digging, because that meant it would be cooler. Now the clouds had turned white and the sky was blue. The dirt smelled good and fresh.

He hadn't heard any rumors of war. There were always skirmishes along the German and Polish borders, but that was all very far away. The last time he'd been in Smyrna, he'd heard rumors that a band of Cossacks was foraging to the North, but there was no reason for them to come to Chelm. Everyone knew that there was nothing of value here.

Still, there was no point in taking any chances. A sniper working his way ahead of an army could be just as deadly as a cavalry charge.

Enough was enough. He put his hat on the top of his shovel's handle and slowly raised it up above ground level. He waited, waved it around a bit, and waited some more.

Several minutes passed, and he began to wonder if he'd just imagined the whole thing. He knew old soldiers who had suddenly snapped and imagined themselves trapped once again in burning buildings or cowering in the trenches… Was he that old and decrepit?

Still, nothing.

Perhaps he had imagined the gunshot.

"Mordechai!" he shouted. "Did you hear a gunshot?"

Shnuck's potato patch was no more than a stone's throw from

Mordechai Blott's potato patch. The two of them had often shared lunch beneath Blott's Oak tree.

"Mordechai!" Perhaps the sniper had gotten him… If Blott wasn't dead, he might need help.

At last he decided that he'd had enough cowering in the dirt. If he was going to die today, so be it.

Shnuck pulled himself out of the fox hole and, ready to jump back in, looked around. The countryside was quiet. Too quiet.

"Mordechai! Did you hear a gunshot?"

Where was Mordechai? Where were the cows that were usually in the pasture to the West? Now that he thought about it, he hadn't seen either Mordechai or the women dairy farmers this morning…

Something was going on. If that noise was a gunshot, then Chelm was in danger.

Sergeant Shnuck realized that he had three choices. He could ignore it. He could run and hide. Or he could try to help.

If you'd asked him twenty years ago whether he'd risk his life to help a bunch of Jews, he'd have laughed.

Now, almost without thinking, he was on his way to the village square. A round square. The fools.

But first, he'd have to go back to his house and load his rifle.

Chapter Thirty-Eight

What Diamonds?

"Diamonds?" Adam said, laughing. "Where did you hear about these diamonds?"

The rest of the crowd took up the laughing question. "Diamonds? Ha! Whoever heard of diamonds in Chelm. Now potatoes. We have a lot of potatoes. And rocks. Heaven knows that whenever we plow a field we find more rocks. But diamonds? Ha!"

Krabot frowned. "I heard in Smyrna. From a very reliable source."

"Well, that explains it." Adam shrugged. "No offense, but you're known as a thief and a murderer."

Krabot shrugged back. "None taken. So?"

"So, if I was talking to you, I might lie about diamonds in any village that wasn't my own."

"You might lie about your own brother," Krabot said.

"Point taken." Adam nodded. "Still, you have to understand that the idea you could find diamonds in Chelm is like saying you could have a relaxing vacation in one of the Czar's Siberian Gulags. It's a possibility, but…"

"Bring the merchant here," Krabot insisted.

Adam raised his hands to calm him down. "My father-in-law, Reb Cantor…"

"You're related?" Krabot said. "No wonder you're lying. Bertie, Vlad, find Reb Cantor the merchant. Bring him here. You saw him before. He's the fattest one in Chelm, he can't have gotten far."

The two other thieves nodded at Krabot. They jumped off the platform and began working their way through the crowd.

"I'm telling you," Adam said. "You won't find any diamonds in Chelm."

"We shall see," Krabot said. "Would you care to wager your life on it?"

Adam blinked. "I'm not much of a betting man, but what would you stake?"

Krabot smiled. He'd forgotten how stupid these Schlemiel men could be. "Your life."

"That's not much of a deal. How about this? If you win, you can kill me. If I win, you work for me."

"Me work for you? HA HA HA HA!" Krabot began laughing so hard, he doubled over.

Adam nudged young Rabbi Yohon Abrahms, who was cowering behind Rabbi Kibbitz. "Do you think he's thinking it over?"

"I don't know," Rabbi Abrahms said. "I'm too busy wishing I was visiting my mother in Minsk."

"Adam," Rabbi Kibbitz whispered. "Be careful."

"Shh, Rebbe," Adam nodded, holding a finger to his lips. "I'm Abraham."

"All right," Krabot said, finally getting himself under control. "It's a bet. I'll work for you for a year." He giggled.

"No bet," Adam shook his head. "What makes you think that a year of your life is as valuable as the rest of mine?"

"Since I could kill you now," the thief said. "It sounds like a fair bargain to me."

"You have a point," Adam said. "All right. On one condition. You have to show me the diamonds before sunset."

Krabot squinted. Was this one up to something? It didn't matter. A little torture ought to produce the diamonds quickly enough.

"Done!" Krabot shouted. He spat into his palm.

Reluctantly, Adam spat into his, and they shook.

Reb Cantor had just about made it to the carpenter's shop to warn Rivka and Rebecca when Bertie Zanuk caught up with him.

"Excuse me, your fatness," Bertie said, putting a hand on the merchant's shoulder. "Aren't you Reb Cantor, the Merchant?"

For a moment, Reb Cantor thought about lying, but who else could he be?

"How would you like a job?" Reb Cantor said. "Good pay, short hours, lots of vacation time?"

Bertie smiled and said, "No thank you. I'm a thief. I work for myself."

"I thought you worked for Alex Krabot?"

"No, no," Bertie said. "We're partners. Alex has the brains, and I have the muscle."

"Really?" Reb Cantor said. "I always thought you were much smarter than him."

Bertie blushed. "Come on. Alex wants to speak with you about the diamonds."

Reb Cantor shrugged, turned around, and began walking slowly back toward the center of Chelm.

"How many diamonds do you think there are?" he asked the skinny thief.

"Me?" Bertie said. "This is the first I've heard of any diamonds."

"Really?" Reb Cantor nodded. "You mean he didn't trust you enough to tell you sooner?"

"Please, Reb Cantor, stop. I know what you're trying to do, and it won't work. Alex and I are like brothers."

"You have a brother who beats you, and does not trust you," Reb Cantor said. "Keep that in mind."

Bertie did not answer.

"Did you know?" Reb Cantor said after a moment, "there's also a legend about gold in Chelm. That if you dig in just the right spot in the Uherka River you will find a wealth of gold? When I was a young man I spent many days searching. Do you know what I found?"

Bertie shook his head.

"Mud. Lots of mud. My hands were covered with it. My arms were covered with it. My face was covered with it. I washed it off, and my skin, which had been callused and blistered from digging, was as smooth as a baby's tuchas. You know what a tuchas is?"

Bertie grinned. "A baby's bum?"

"Yes, yes," Reb Cantor said, as they reached the edge of the village square, where everyone in Chelm was waiting around nervously, "That mud made me a fortune..."

"How did it do that?" Bertie asked.

"I packed the mud into jars, and I sold it in England as skin softener."

Bertie shook his head. "What nonsense."

"True," Reb Cantor said, raising his palm to heaven. "As true as there are diamonds in Chelm. Let me go. I'll make it worth your while."

Bertie shook his head again. "I can't. You have to talk to Alex. You tell him about the mud." Then Bertie shouted, "Coming through!" and the crowd parted. "Right this way."

Reb Cantor sighed and walked slowly toward what was certainly his doom.

"Is that your father-in-law?" Krabot asked, as soon as he saw the fat merchant waddling through the crowd.

Adam nodded. The smile on Reb Cantor's face did not cheer him. He had seen that frozen smile before. It meant that Reb Cantor was putting up a good front in the face of imminent bad news.

"Merchant," Krabot shouted, not waiting for Reb Cantor to climb the platform, "tell your son here about the diamonds."

Isaac Cantor stopped, and looked up. The village square was silent around him. The only sound he heard was his own rapidly beating heart. He wondered whether it was a sin to hope to die before he had a chance to reveal the truth. Probably. He waited another moment to catch his breath, and decided that he wasn't going to keel over just yet. There was only one thing to do. When all else fails, stall for time, and negotiate.

"Even assuming there are any so-called diamonds," he said, "why would I tell you?"

Krabot smiled. "Because if you don't, I'll burn down your whole village."

Everyone stared at Reb Cantor. "Good reason," he mumbled. Then he raised his voice. "So, what do you want to know?"

"The usual," Krabot said. "How many are there, what are they worth, and where are they?"

Reb Cantor nodded. "All right, I'll tell you. There were a dozen diamonds. They were worth somewhere between twenty and fifty-thousand rubles."

A gasp of shock shuddered through the crowd. Adam Schlemiel felt the blood drain from his cheeks.

"I knew it!" Krabot laughed. "Where are they?"

"I don't have them."

"Where are they?"

"I don't know."

"Tell me," Krabot drew his pistol and aimed it at the Merchant, "where are they?"

Reb Cantor looked at the pistol. Then he spoke directly to Adam. "I traded them. I traded them to the carpenter's wife for fifty-five hundred jewelry boxes. I'm sorry." Tears began rolling down Isaac Cantor's cheeks. He looked at his son-in-law. "Please forgive me."

Krabot looked at Adam and shook his head sadly. "You bet me your life? I didn't even have to torture him."

"I knew nothing about any diamonds," Adam said.

"Too bad," Krabot said. "A bet's a bet." He nodded to Vlad and Bertie and then prodded Adam with his gun. "Come on boys. Now, let's go find them. If I remember correctly, your father is the carpenter. Why don't you take me to his shop?"

Jacob Schlemiel peered out of the carpenter shop's small attic window and wondered what was going on in the village square.

Why wasn't he afraid? He only knew that this was the place he had to be. His wife, daughter-in-law, and grandson were hiding in the basement.

Perhaps from here, somehow, he could protect his family...

Now, just behind one of the wagons piled high with the jewelry boxes, he saw that someone was coming. He could see a crowd of heads bobbing closer.

Jacob picked up the gun that Adam had stolen from the thieves so many years before. It was old and rusted, and probably wouldn't fire, but it was all that he had. His hands were trembling as he aimed it out the window.

"Who is it?" Jacob shouted down. "Stop or I'll shoot!"

"Father, don't shoot! It's me, Abraham!"

"I thought you were in bed. Why aren't you? Who is that with you?"

"I'm fine. This is Rosa. Rosa Kalderash. You remember her."

Jacob quickly put down the gun and said a prayer. Then he scrambled down the ladder.

Before Jacob's feet reached the floor, his grandson's head popped up through the trap door that led from the cellar, and an instant later the boy was rushing outside to hug his mother.

Abraham only glanced curiously at the boy hugging Rosa, and then strode past them into the shop. "Mama?"

"She's back here," Rivka said from behind the counter. She was helping Rebecca up through the trap door.

"Abraham," Jacob said. "What happened?"

"Thieves, Father. There's no time to explain."

"But, your clothes…"

At last, Rebecca appeared, pale and panting. "Is everything all right?" She stopped in her tracks. "Adam? Is that you?"

"No." He smiled, but shook his head firmly. "Where are the diamonds?"

"They're in my jewelry box."

"Diamonds?" Rosa Kalderash said as she entered the shop.

"What is she doing here?" Rivka said, frowning.

"Tante Rivka," the little boy said, "this is my mother. You remember her."

Rivka nodded.

"Father, give me the diamonds, quickly," Abraham said.

"Son," Jacob said. "What's going on?"

"The robbers are coming here! Now! Quickly. They can't find the diamonds or they'll kill my brother. Now, quickly! Where are they?"

"What diamonds?" Jacob said.

Rebecca reached into one of her dress's deep pockets and removed a small seven-sided box.

"Wait, Omama," the little boy said. "You can't give them that box!"

"Shhh," Rosa said, hugging the boy tightly. "Your father's life is at stake."

"It is?" The boy looked at his mother, who nodded. "But still…"

"Shhh."

"Take it," Rebecca said. "We have lived our whole lives without diamonds. What do we need them for now?"

Abraham took the box and stared at it. "This is a beautiful box."

Jacob nodded. "It ought to be. We made so many of them. We just sold five thousand to Reb Cantor."

"Those boxes outside? In the wagons?"

"Yes, of course," his father said. "Abraham, are you all right?"

"I'll be fine. I just need to…" He nodded, and then smiled. "Yes, yes. This is a brilliant idea… Is there time?" He spun on his heels and headed for the door.

"What? What is going on?" Rivka asked. "Please, tell me!"

Everyone arrived outside the carpenter's shop at the same time.

From the round square came the parade, with Adam and Reb Cantor in the front, prodded on by the three robbers and followed by the entire village of Chelm, and the few people from Smyrna.

From inside the shop came the rest of the Schlemiel family.

As the two brothers saw each other, they stopped. Everyone stopped.

"The twins." A whisper rushed through the village. "The twins!"

"I knew both of you were here," Krabot said, baring his teeth. "I could tell. Now, give me the diamonds."

"They're right here, in this box."

"Throw them to me. Now!"

The brothers looked at each other, and nodded as one.

The box with the diamonds flew into the air.

Krabot's grin of satisfaction grew wider as the seven-sided jewelry box spun and twirled high, higher… And then his smile flipped upside down into a scowl of proportionate rage.

The box fell on top of one of the wagons piled so high with identical boxes. But it did not settle there. It's impact nudged the precarious pile, and like a row of dominos, both cartloads of jewelry boxes spilled onto the ground with a loud clatter, until at last they all came to rest in a gigantic heap.

"Fool!" Krabot shouted through gritted teeth. He aimed his revolver and fired.

Moments

It happened all at once.
The bullet.
The screams.
The push.
The second bullet.
The rush. The confusion.
Everyone in Chelm had a different story.
This is what really happened.
The villagers saw the shadow of the angel of death swoop into their midst, and they felt terror.

As Krabot aimed and fired, Adam lurched forward and rammed into him. It was too late to stop the bullet. The hammer had fallen and it was on its way down the barrel, but its path was deflected, diverted by no more than seven inches, so instead of punching a hole through Abraham's heart, it struck him in the shoulder and spun him around wildly, like a broken toy ballerina.

From the attic of his carpenter's shop, Jacob Schlemiel had his gun aimed directly at his son's killer's head. He felt the anger rising in him, and only just stopped himself from shooting, as his other son lurched into the line of fire.

At the door to the shop, Rebecca Schlemiel, her grandson and daughter-in-law, watched, first with amusement as the jewelry box filled with diamonds dropped into the wagon filled with identical jewelry boxes and vanished, but then the twinkles in their eyes turned to wide-eyed panic as they saw the gun, heard the explosion, and watched the horrifying dance begin.

Abraham was content, holding his ground, standing weaponless against a murderer, protecting his family with his body. The sudden pain in his shoulder took him by surprise. He watched the world swoop and swirl. He stumbled. As he fell, he looked up and saw the face of the woman he loved.

Rosa Kalderash saw his eyes widen and melt into hers, and she knew at once who he was and that he was hers. She felt a sudden icy fear that the Curse of the Schlemiels had brought them together only to rip them apart. "Abraham!" she screamed.

Vlad and Bertie, two steps behind Alex Krabot, were drawing their hidden pistols as the women's screams began, and men pushed their children and wives down to the ground and threw themselves on top of them.

From the north, on a small rise at the edge of the road, just where the village began to turn to farmland, retired Sergeant Vasilly Shnuck saw the crowd surge, watched the bandit's gun spit, raised his rifle and aimed at the thief.

The young half-Gypsy half-Jewish boy watched in stunned disbelief as his mother rushed toward the man who he'd thought was his uncle, but must be his father. He felt his heart harden and stop as he reached into his coat pocket and lifted one of the heavy revolvers he'd stolen from the thieves.

In horror, Rivka watched the man she thought was her husband fall, and saw the Gypsy woman run like lightning to his side where she cradled his head like a lover in mourning.

Rabbi Kibbitz closed his eyes and prayed for peace, hoping that for once the Almighty might break with thousands of years of tradition and habit, reach down with a heavenly finger and put a stop to the disaster that was unfolding before him.

The second gunshot came as Krabot caught his balance and began aiming his pistol at Adam.

It took him in the chest, and knocked him backwards. His arms opened wide, as if he was asking for a hug, and then he fell back hard in the dirt.

Bertie's jaw dropped open.

Vlad's head turned, his eyes first scanning the crowd and then the horizon.

In his attic, Jacob Schlemiel blinked.

Rivka saw her nephew holding a pistol and without thinking snatched it from his hands.

Down the road, Vasilly Shnuck ejected the spent shell, and loaded another into his still-smoking rifle.

"No one moves!" came the voice of Captain Boris Plotz, buttoning his collar as he ran through the terrified crowd. "You're all under arrest!"

"Under arrest?" Bertie said, turning white as a sheet.

"Nonsense, don't worry," Vlad said, putting his hand on Bertie's shoulder. "This captain is a fool."

Boris Plotz straightened his shoulders. "I am Captain Boris Plotz, of the army of his majesty the Czar. Who are you?"

Vlad allowed himself a sly grin. "I am Colonel Vladimir Estrogonovitch, of the Czar's personal guard. I am on a special secret assignment, scouting the borders and identifying deserters."

Now it was Captain Plotz's turn to totter and collapse.

Vlad rolled his eyes and shook his head. Then he continued in his best loud Colonel's voice. "I am also required to tell you that this village has been restored to Polish territory. Did you know? It was a wedding present from the Czar to the King of Poland's youngest daughter."

Retired Sergeant Shnuck, who had arrived just in time to watch his former superior officer fall to the ground in a faint, pumped his fist in the air, and shouted, "Huzzah!"

Colonel Vlad's eyes widened. "Vasilly? Vasilly Shnuck, is that you? My Sergeant Cousin!"

Shnuck grinned. "My Colonel Cousin, good to see you!"

The two large Russians laughed and embraced warmly.

In the chaos, Krabot tried to raise his pistol, but the blackness was closing in. He saw one of the Schlemiel's faces leaning close to his and with a last smile whispered, "I guess you win the bet. But at least this way, I'll never have to work for you."

Then, Krabot spat. And missed.

For a moment everything stopped. There was silence and

stillness, no breeze, as the thief known as Alex Krabot stole his last breath, was caught, and passed from this world to the next.

Adam left the corpse and hurried to his brother. He knelt down and stared into his brother's eyes, which were so blue, so like his own. The blood seeping from Abraham's shoulder was bright red.

"Abraham," Adam said.

"Are you sure?" Abraham said. "I thought you were supposed to be Abraham."

"No." Adam couldn't help himself. He laughed. "I'm Adam. Finally, Adam."

"Really? Then I must be Abraham."

"Stop it, you two," Rosa Kalderash said, tears flowing freely down her cheeks. "Stop!"

"Which one of you is Adam?" Rivka shrieked. She looked at the two of them, one kneeling, one lying. She didn't realize that she still had the gun in her hand, that it was aiming back and forth between one brother and the other. "Tell me!"

"He is!" Everyone in the entire village pointed at once to Adam, who quickly but calmly stood up.

"Tell me your name," Rivka demanded. "Who are you? Tell me the truth. Now!" Her finger whitened on the trigger.

"I am your husband," he said. "You can call me Mud. Rivka. Put down the gun, please."

"Adam?" she asked.

He nodded.

The gun fell from her fingers, and she ran into his arms.

"Mother?" the little boy's voice was quiet, and filled with fear. "Which one is my father?"

Rosa saw her son standing close, and nodded her chin to Abraham.

Abraham's eyes turned and for a moment it was as if he was looking into a mirror and seeing himself as a boy. "Is he your son?"

"Yours, too. He's ours." Her hand stroked the boy's hair.

"I have a son?" Abraham whispered. "Really? You never told me."

"When did I have the chance?" Rosa said, suppressing a sob.

"What is your name?" he asked the boy.

"I'm..." the boy began, but then stopped.

"What? Speak louder. I can't hear you."

"I don't know." There was a catch in the boy's throat. "I'm not sure what I should say anymore."

"It's Abraham," his grandmother said to the boy. "Your name is Abraham. We don't have to lie any more."

Abraham looked at Rosa. "You named him after me?"

Again, Rosa nodded.

By now, Mrs. Chaipul, her black bag in hand, had made her way to Abraham's side.

"Excuse me," she said. "Please move back."

"No," Abraham said softly, but firmly. "I have to see my son."

"Fine, look at your son," Mrs. Chaipul said. "I have work to do. The rest of you, give me some room."

Abraham stared at the boy, who looked at the ground.

"Are my boys all right?" Jacob said, limping and panting. He would have been there faster, but as he tried to climb down from the attic, the ladder had fallen, so he'd had to lower himself, and then jump onto the counter. "Please, Mrs. Chaipul, tell me."

"I don't know yet." The old woman shook her head. "You'll all have to wait."

Chapter Thirty-Nine

Heavy Lifting

Adam Schlemiel lifted the tack hammer, tapped it gently on
the brass nail, and watched in frustration as the nail bent. "Fooey!"
That was the thirteenth nail he'd twisted since breakfast. He found
it nearly impossible to concentrate.

The bullet had gone clean through Abraham's shoulder. Mrs.
Chaipul had assured them all that it was a miracle it hadn't hit any
bones or nicked an artery. She had sewn him back up, and sent him
back to his parents house, where he had lain in bed for three weeks.

Abraham still had not fully reawakened. For three weeks he had
been in and out of consciousness, growing weaker and thinner.

Adam had tried sending his brother strength, but the bond that
they'd had since children seemed thin or broken by the gunshot.

Perhaps for the first time, Adam felt truly afraid. Abraham
looked so small, lying on their old bed in their parents' house. His
brother's cheeks had felt cool, almost cold.

The bleeding had stopped. The wounds were closing. But
Abraham still did not wake up.

Adam whispered a prayer, then went back to work in the
carpenter's shop.

There were too many people in his parents' house. His mother
and father were sick with worry. Shemini was always bursting into
tears. Rosa Kalderash refused to leave Abraham's side. And, now
that his real father had returned, young Abraham treated Adam like
a stranger. The boy was resentful, angry that he had spent so much
time with someone who only looked like his father.

And in his own house, it was worse. Everything that should have
been better wasn't. Rivka seemed distant and shaken. She had been
deeply embarrassed by her father's behavior. None of Reb Cantor's

explanations (about how he had given Rebecca Schlemiel the diamonds to protect everyone) held water with his daughter. She accused her father of being a liar, a thief, and a cheat, and refused to listen. She also missed the little boy, who she'd grown to think of as her own son. Worst of all, Rivka had seen her husband get shot, and thought she'd lost her love. Even now she wasn't completely sure.

Adam had tried to comfort Rivka, but she would not have his arms around her. She had watched the work as the pile of jewelry boxes were searched for the diamonds. One box after another was opened. But the diamonds were never found. All the boxes were empty, save one which was filled with dead bugs. At the end of the day, Rivka had turned away from her father and her husband, and walked back to her house alone.

The rumor was that Captain Plotz and Vlad, the mysterious bandit who turned out to be a colonel, had somehow found the jewels and fled Chelm for good.

Retired Sergeant Vasilly Shnuck did his best to defend his cousin's reputation. Vlad, he believed, never would have done such a thing. But neither the Colonel, nor the Captain, nor the diamonds were ever found. With all of his former superior officers gone for good, and Chelm restored to Poland, the retired sergeant breathed a sigh of relief, and returned to tend his potato farm during the days, and drink with his friend Mordechai Blott in the evenings.

The Curse of the Schlemiels

Adam raised his hammer, and smashed it down on the jewelry box. The thin wood shattered with a satisfying crunch.

No more jewelry boxes. Not now. Not ever. Fifty-five hundred jewelry boxes without a single ruble of pay was more than enough wasted effort for a lifetime.

In the end, Reb Cantor had taken the two cartloads of boxes west toward England, and paid Bertie Zanuk handsomely to ride along as an armed guard. He had promised the Schlemiels a percentage of the profits, if he could recoup his own losses.

Before he left, Reb Cantor had tried to visit his daughter. With his eyes filled with tears, he'd hammered on the door, but Rivka refused to open it to say good-bye. She had said she'd rather vomit, and then she did.

Adam looked at the broken pieces of wood in his hand, and all the bent nails, and began to sob.

Clunk-Clank! The carpenter shop's door knocker startled him, and he raised the hammer in self-defense.

"Ahh," said Rabbi Kibbitz, "you're in. I'm glad you have your hammer. You may also need a saw. My favorite chair broke, and I'm having a difficult time studying on the school children's benches."

Silently, Adam nodded, put the hammer into his tool tray, and followed the rabbi.

Repairing the chair took only a moment. One of the support struts had broken, and the back left leg bent under the Rabbi's weight. Adam straightened the leg and found a dowel at the bottom of the tool tray. He cut it to length, and with two nails, hammered it back.

"All better," he said, quietly. He used a cloth to wipe the sawdust off the Rabbi's study's floor.

"You're sure?" Rabbi Kibbitz said. "Mrs. Chaipul says that I've been gaining weight. When the chair broke, I thought for sure she might be right…"

"It will be fine," Adam said. He stood.

"What do I owe you?"

Adam waved his hand. "Nothing."

"Nonsense," Rabbi Kibbitz said. "Let me give you a blessing at least."

Adam bowed his head, and nodded.

"All right…" The Rabbi raised his hands, fingers open. "Abraham, I…"

Adam's eyes snapped open. "I'm Adam."

Rabbi Kibbitz looked confused. "But you're the carpenter. Adam left Chelm. Abraham is the carpenter."

"No. He's not."

"But you're married to Rivka," the Rabbi insisted. "Abraham is married to Rivka."

"No, Rebbe, Adam is married to Rivka."

Now, the old man looked angry. "Don't you keep playing tricks on me. I remember when you were a mischievous little boy. I also remember signing the ketubah. Abraham married Rivka."

Adam's cheeks grew red. "Rabbi, I lied. The Russians were going to draft me into the army. I told everyone that I was Abraham. "

"Ahh. Well, that explains it. Does your wife know who you are?"

"She does," Adam said, softly. "At least I think so…"

Rabbi Kibbitz nodded. Then he raised his hands, and spread his fingers.

"So, Adam, I…"

This time, Adam's hands shot up and grabbed the Rabbi's wrists. "Wait. Rabbi. The Curse. Can you lift a curse?"

"Of course," Rabbi Kibbitz said. "I don't mean to be modest, but I've never met a curse so heavy I couldn't lift it."

"Please," Adam said. "I beg you. Make it go away."

"All right. Fine. But, I'll need you to let go of my hands."

Adam's fingers let go. "I'm sorry."

"It's all right. Shh."

For the third time, Rabbi Kibbitz raised his hands to heaven, and spread his fingers. This time, his voice was quiet, the softly chanted words almost inaudible. Afternoon turned into twilight, and at last, when the North Star was high in the sky, Rabbi Kibbitz dropped his arms. He slumped into his chair.

"Whew," he sighed. "Who knew that curse would be so tricky?" Then his eyes opened, and he jumped up. "Oy, I'm late for dinner." And rubbing his sore arms, the great rabbi hurried out the door.

"Rabbi!" Adam shouted after him. "Wait. Is it true? Is it gone? Is it really gone?"

But Rabbi Kibbitz was gone. That much was certain. As for the Curse, was such a thing possible? Could it be true? Had the Curse of the Schlemiels finally been lifted?

Adam sighed and shook his head sadly.

But then he realized that his head felt lighter. He shook it again. Yes, it definitely felt lighter. He shook his head so hard that he bumped against a wall. And he wasn't hurt! Not even a bruise. His head did feel lighter. His whole body felt lighter.

Adam stood in the doorway of the Rabbi's study, and for the first time in weeks a smile grew across his face.

He threw his tools into their tray and ran home. He banged through the front door "Rivka! Good news! The Curse is lifted."

Rivka, who was stirring a pot on the stove, didn't even look up. "You're late for dinner."

"The Rabbi," Adam explained. "He lifted the Curse! It took a lot longer than we expected, but it's gone. Isn't that wonderful?"

"I don't love you," she said.

"What?"

She shook her head. "I don't think I do. I'm not sure. I thought I loved you. And then I thought I loved Abraham. And then I thought I loved somebody named Mud. And then I thought I loved you. And now I'm not sure."

Adam's head spun. How could it be? Perhaps the lifting of the Curse had not yet reached Rivka.

"Rivka." He put his hands on her shoulders, and felt her silently sobbing. "Rivka. What?" He turned her toward him. "What?"

"I'm pregnant!" she said, tears running down her cheeks.

Adam felt as if his heart would burst with joy. "Why that's wonderful news!"

"No," she sobbed, "because I don't know who the father is."

That stopped him cold. "Have you been with somebody besides me?"

"I'm not sure," she said. "I don't know. I'm so confused."

She looked so sad, and afraid.

Adam reached his finger under her chin and raised her eyes to his.

"Rivka," he said, "I don't care. I don't care. I love you, and the baby is yours. That is all I need."

"Really?" she said. "Because I don't think I slept with anybody else, but…"

"Shh. Yes. Really."

"I love you," she said. "I don't want anyone else. Who are you?"

"I'm your husband." He hugged her close. "And I always will be."

<u>Chapter Forty</u>

<u>Fools on the Hill</u>

Adam held Rivka in his arms for a long time. Her hair smelled sweet, like nutmeg.

"I love you," he whispered.

She smiled, and held him tighter.

Just then, the front door to the house slammed open, and Shemini stumbled in, nearly out of breath.

"Adam..." Shemini panted. "Abraham..."

Adam let go of his wife, and helped his sister into a chair. "What?" he said. "Is he all right?"

"Leaving," Shemini gasped. "Now."

Adam turned to Rivka, who said, "Go. Hurry. I'll take care of her."

He blew her a kiss, and ran as he had never run before.

The carpenter's house was filled with an odd blend of tears and laughter.

Rebecca Schlemiel was following her son around the house, trying to convince him to wait, at least until Mrs. Chaipul could come and check his wounds.

"Mother," Abraham said, "for the tenth time, they're healed. I feel fine. I feel better than fine. It's like a great weight has been lifted from my chest."

"But Mrs. Chaipul should examine you."

"What's she going to say? Either she's going to say I should lie back down, in which case she's wrong, or she'll say that I should hurry up and go already, which I already know." He laughed and gave his mother a kiss on the cheek. "You should be happy I'm all right."

"Don't tell me you're all right." Rebecca stamped her feet. "You were shot. I haven't seen you in years. And now you're rushing off before we can even talk! Now that you feel well, you can't stay? This I don't understand."

"Mother, Rosa's father is up for re-election as King of the Gypsies. Rosa told me that my father-in-law will need every vote. If we hurry, we can just make it to the grand gathering."

"Now you're a Gypsy? What about your family here?"

"No." He shook his head. "Don't make this hard like that. I can't vote, but Rosa and my son, young Abraham, can vote."

"I still say that Mrs. Chaipul should be consulted."

"Mother, for the eleventh time…"

In another corner, Jacob Schlemiel was sharing a few private moments with his grandson.

"I made you a tool kit," he said, his voice cracking. He had heard Rosa whispering to Abraham, making their plans. "It's got a hammer, pliers, screw driver, a hand drill, and this."

He held up something that looked like a block of wood with a wide slit in the middle and handles on top. "My grandfather was a wise man, but when I told him that I wanted to be a carpenter, he gave me this plane. It is used to smooth pieces of wood. Look underneath. You see that blade? That is Damascus steel. I'm told that it was taken from a sword that was broken in Jerusalem. You could take the blade out and sharpen it, but I've never had to."

"Opapa," the little boy said, "I can't take this."

"Feh." Jacob pressed it into his hands. "My grandfather gave it to me, and I promised I'd give it to my grandson. Long ago, I met your grandfather, because one of their wagons was broken. Your people need good carpenters, and one thing that makes a good carpenter is good tools."

Young Abraham nodded solemnly, slipped the plane into his backpack, and gave his grandfather a hug.

Jacob felt the tears rolling down his cheeks. He patted the boy's head. "You're such a good boy."

"Yes, yes," Rosa Kalderash said. "I know this is very sad and very sudden, but we'll be back."

Both grandparents shot the Gypsy princess a look that could have been a curse, except Rosa waved it away with a small hand-sign.

"To catch the train in the morning, we'll have to take the shortcut through the Schvartzvald tonight. The sky is clear, the moon is full. The only ghosts are in stories. And the walking will do us all good."

"Staying one more day wouldn't kill you," Rebecca muttered.

"Now Mother," Abraham began.

"But," she interrupted, "leaving now, I just might kill you!"

"Mother…"

"Rebecca," Jacob interrupted. "He's made up his mind. Our twins are twice as stubborn as any other child in Chelm."

"Children," Rebecca muttered. "That's just what they're acting like. Impatient children."

"Are you ready?" Rosa reached for Abraham's hand. "Come."

Abraham gave his mother a kiss on the forehead, and then nodded. "Yes. Let's go. Come along, son." He smiled. A feeling of deep pride filled his heart when he saw the boy's eyes brighten.

"Wait," Rebecca said. "You're not going to leave without food." She turned and dragged a heavy sack from under the kitchen table.

Rosa picked it up, staggering momentarily under the weight. "What's in this?"

"Salamis, potatoes, pickles, some black bread, and a fruit cake. Just a few things. In case you get hungry."

Rosa smiled. "Thank you, Mother."

Rebecca raised a finger. "Don't call me mother until you marry him. And this I'm not holding my breath for. You be good to him. Don't hurt him. Don't leave him."

"I won't," Rosa said. "I just found him. We're staying together."

"What more could a mother wish for her son," Rebecca said, "except that his family stays in Chelm instead of wandering all over creation…"

"Mother!"

They were out the door, and turning north, just as Adam dashed into sight.

"Wait!" he gasped.

"It's about time," Abraham said. "I thought you would have been here hours ago."

"How," panted Adam, "was I to know?"

"You didn't hear me mind-talking to you?"

Adam shook his head, and Abraham shrugged.

"Walk with us," Abraham said. "A little way at least."

"Mama," young Abraham said, "I need to speak with Grandmother before we go."

"Now?" Rosa frowned. "There wasn't enough time before?"

"I need to talk with her in private," the boy insisted.

Rosa looked at Abraham who said, "You wait here for him. I'll walk ahead with Adam. We'll meet you at the top of East Hill."

Rosa nodded, and watched, first as her son ran back to his Grandmother's open arms, and then as her husband meandered off with his brother.

"Grandmother," young Abraham whispered.

"I didn't think you'd forget me." Rebecca smiled.

The boy brought his mouth next to his grandmother's ear and whispered, "The diamonds."

"I know," she whispered back.

"I have them," he said.

"I know."

"You do?" He pulled his head back and stared. The old lady nodded. "Well, I'm not a thief. I took them from you by accident. I have to give them back."

"No," Rebecca shook her head. "You keep them. What would we do in Chelm with diamonds? Someone else would come for them and try to kill us."

"But what will I do with them?"

"Bubbeleh," Rebecca said, running her fingers softly on his cheek, "your people are poor, and they have no home but the road. As you get older you will see opportunities where a bit of money could save a life. Use it then. Hire teachers so they can learn how to read. Now that he has found your mother and you, your father has dreams for the future. Help him. And save a bit, so that if you ever settle down, you will have something to start with."

"But what if somebody tries to steal it from me?"

"So, give it to them. Bits of rock are not worth losing your life." The little boy, not so little any more, nodded.

"Here," he said. He reached into the bag and gave Rebecca a single diamond. "This is for Shemini's dowry."

Rebecca took the small stone from the boy's hand, and put it in the locket that Isaac Cantor had made for her so long ago.

Then Young Abraham kissed his grandmother on the cheek one last time, left his grandparents' house, and he ran to catch up with his mother, as they followed Abraham and Adam's footsteps out of Chelm.

"They're gone," Rebecca said, as Jacob stepped beside her.

"Shemini still lives at home," Jacob said. "And Adam will be back soon enough."

"Nothing's the same."

"It never is." Jacob nodded. "If Reb Shikker hadn't sworn off liquor, I'd ask him to get drunk with me."

"We should both celebrate." Rivka turned her husband's face toward hers and smiled. It was her famous smile, glowing with warmth and love. "Let's go inside. Quickly, before Shemini comes home."

"Really?" Jacob said, his voice squeaking a little.

"Really."

The Village Twins walked together in silence. No longer could they share each other's thoughts, but they took comfort in the closeness.

As they reached the summit of East Hill, and the circle of fallen logs, they sat together, looking south to Chelm.

The moon was bright. The village looked small and perfect, a few streets, a synagogue, a community. Families.

At last, Abraham broke the silence. "Do you remember when Father brought us up here to tell us about the Curse?" He laughed. "And we didn't believe him."

"I almost forgot!" Adam smacked his forehead. "Rabbi Kibbitz told me that he'd lifted the Curse."

"Really? When? How?"

"He started around noon. It took all afternoon. He only finished this evening, around sunset. He told me that he could have removed the curse years ago, but nobody had bothered to tell him about it."

"Oh, Papa!" Abraham shook his head and laughed. Then he sighed. "Sunset was when I started to feel better. You think it's really gone?"

"I don't know," Adam said. "I hope so. Rivka's pregnant, and the last thing I want is to give my son is the kind of troubles we've had."

"Adam, Mazel tov!"

"Your own son, Abraham, is a wonderful boy," Adam said.

"He doesn't know me," Abraham said, sadly.

"He will. Give him time."

"I meant to thank you for taking such good care of him."

"Nonsense." Adam shrugged. "It was a pleasure. Now it's your turn. Talk to him. You will be a magnificent father."

Abraham shook his head and said, softly, "I'm afraid he won't love me as much as he loves you."

"Fooey. You're his real father. As alike as you and I are, he's always known that. Have patience, talk with him, and try to listen to him before you get angry."

"Good advice," Abraham said. "When did you become so wise?"

"What, you thought you were the only one who was smart?"

They both laughed.

"I hear them coming," Adam said. He stood. "I have to go."

"Say goodbye to the boy first."

"No. I can't. It's breaking my heart to let him go. I'd just want him to stay here with me. It's better if he's angry with me. You tell him I love him."

"Adam, don't be foolish."

"One minute I'm wise, and the next I'm foolish? I can't. Just bring him back to Chelm when you visit. You're coming back, right?"

Abraham paused. "I hope to."

Under the moonlight, the brothers embraced, and thumped each other soundly on the back.

They let go and stepped away.

"It's been good knowing you." They both said it as one.

Then they parted.

Abraham Schlemiel waited on the hilltop for his family, and then headed north through the Schvartzvald along the Smyrna Road and into the world beyond.

Adam Schlemiel slipped into the shadows and watched as Rosa, his nephew, and his brother began their journey.

"It's been good knowing you, too," he said softly.

He turned and half walked, half ran back down the hill toward his village, his home, and his family.

The End

About the Author

    Izzy Abrahmson is the pen name for Mark Binder, a professional storyteller, and the author of more than two dozen books and audio books for families and adults. He has toured the world delighting readers and listeners of all ages with his stories, interspersed with his unique klezmer harmonica sounds.

    Under his "real" name, Mark began writing about The Village as the editor of *The Rhode Island Jewish Herald*. These stories were so popular that they have been published in newspapers and magazines around the world. His epic *Loki Ragnarok* was nominated for an Audie Audiobook Award for Best Original Work, and *Transmit Joy* won a Parents' Choice Gold Award for Audio Storytelling. Mark is also a playwright, and the founder of the American Story Theater. In his spare time he bakes bread and makes pizza. He lives in Providence with his wife, who is a brilliant ceramic artist.

For tour dates, news, and bonus material visit:
izzyabe.com or **markbinderbooks.com**

Thank you

We hope you've enjoyed this book.

Please consider telling your friends
and writing a review.

May we send you a bonus story as a gift?
Subscribe to our email newsletter at
izzyabe.com

You'll also find tour dates, podcast and blog posts

You can also tag us on social media
#TheVillageLife
@IzzyAbrahmson

We value your readership.
Have an excellent day.

A Village Glossary

"A word clearly spoken is like a pattern of golden apples on a silver mosaic." –Proverbs 25: 11

Yiddish is a language of sound and subtlety. Hebrew is an ancient tongue. These are the villagers' interpretations of words you may, or may not know.

Chelm: The Village. The place where most of the people in this book live. A traditional source of Jewish humor. The "ch" in Chelm (and most Yiddish and Hebrew transliteration) is pronounced like you've got something stuck in your throat. "Ch-elm."

Chelmener: the people who live in The Village. Often known as the wisefolk of Chelm. Sometimes called Chelmites. Sometimes called, "The Fools of Chelm".

babka: a delicious cake. Usually served with coffee, tea and gossip

bar mitzvah: the Jewish coming-of-age ceremony for boys. Celebrated at 13. Almost always catered.

bimah: the platform at the front of the synagogue where the rabbi stands so that everyone can hear him.

bris: a ritual circumcision ceremony. Usually catered.

cantor: a person who leads a religious service with song. Not to be confused with Reb Cantor the merchant.

challah: a braided egg bread. In English, the plural of challah is challah.

Chanukah: the festival of lights. Celebrated in the winter, it commemorates the victory of the Maccabees over King Antiochus. The miracle of Chanukah was that one day's measure of oil burned in the Temple for eight days. Sometimes spelled Hanukkah. Or Hanukah.

chanukia: the Chanukah menorah. A lamp or candelabra with room for nine candles: one for each night of Chanukah, plus another, called the shammos.

cheder: the school for young people. Not cheesy. See also yeshiva.

cholent: a slow-cooked stew usually prepared on Friday and left to simmer for Saturday's dinner. Delicious… unless it's burnt.

chometz: all sorts of delicious baked goods that aren't matzah. Only obsessed about during Passover.

chuppah: the wedding canopy.

daven: to rock back and forth in prayer.

dreidel: a four-sided top spun in a children's game during Chanukah. The game of dreidel is usually played for high stakes, like raisins or nuts. Although immortalized in song, rarely are dreidels made out of clay, because clay tops are very difficult to spin. The Hebrew letters on the dreidel are Nun, Gimmel, Hay, and Shin. They signify the words, "Nes Gadol Haya Sham" or "A great miracle happened there." In Chelm, where Yiddish is spoken when the game is played, the Shin, means "stell" or put one back. Hay is "halb," so you would take half. But, Gimmel, instead of getting the pot means "gib" or give everything back into the pot. And Nun, instead of nothing means "nimm," or take everything. Confusing, isn't it?

erev: the evening that begins a holiday. Jewish holidays start at sunset and end after sunset.

gelt: money. In the old days, Chanukah gelt was given to teachers. Today gelt means foil-wrapped pieces of chocolate shaped like money.

goyishe: something that is not Jewish.

goob (English): when something is so delicious that you can't pronounce the letter "d" because you're too busy eating, it's "goob."

hamotzi: blessing over the bread – or matzah.

kafratzed: Completely messed up. Incapable of working.

kabalah: Jewish mysticism, often numerological. It's secret: shhh!

kasha varnishkas: buckwheat groats with noodles. Serve it with brisket and gravy. Mmm.

kiggel/kugel/keugel: a baked pudding. Mmmm.

klezmer: Jewish jazz. Very danceable!

knaidel (or, if you're in a spelling bee, kneydl): a matzah ball dumpling, usually found in chicken soup. Often served during Passover. The plural of knaidel is knaidlach. After lead, one of the densest materials known to Chelmener.

knish: dough stuffed with meat or potatoes. Sort of a Jewish calzone.

kreplach: Jewish wontons. Yiddish ravioli. Filled dumplings that are sometimes boiled, sometimes pan fried.

kugel: an incredibly rich pudding. Sometimes savory, sometimes sweet. Often made with noodles. Mmmm.

kvell: to glow with pride.

kvetch: 1. To complain. 2. To really really complain. 3. A complaint. 4. The complainer.

latke: a pancake fried in oil. At Passover, latkes are made with matzah meal. At Chanukah they are made with potatoes.

mandlebread: a twice-baked cookie, Jewish biscotti.

mashgiach: the rabbi in charge of making sure everything's kosher.

matzah/matzoh: unleavened bread made from flour and water with no salt or yeast. Sometimes spelled "matzoh." Eaten during Passover, the holiday celebrating the Israelites' exodus from Egypt. Also known as the bread of affliction, perhaps because it is tasteless, bland and often binding.

matzah brie: fried matzah. Mix damp matzah with eggs and salt and fry it to make matzah brie. Yum!

menorah: a candelabra. Usually with seven branches, but on Chanukah it has eight (plus another one for the shammos) and is called a chanukiah.

mensch: a good man. A nice fellah. Charitable, wise, intelligent, kind-hearted. The sort of man who, if he had a little money as well, you'd want your sister to marry.

mishugas: craziness.

mikveh: the ritual bath.

mitzvah: a commandment, often a good deed. Not to be confused with a Bar Mitzvah, which is the coming of age ceremony for boys.

nachas: joy, pride, and happiness. Especially something you get from good children.

Omama/Opapa: Grandma/Grandpa.

oy: an expression of excitement and often pain. "Oy! My back!" or "Oy, I can't believe you're wearing that to a wedding!"

Passover/Pesach: the celebration of the Exodus from Egypt. Celebrated for eight days in the diaspora or seven day, depending on where you live and what you believe.

plotz: to explode. As in, "I ate so much matzah brie I nearly plotzed."

Purim: another holiday involving survival and food. The original gift-giving holiday. Nowadays, presents of food and treats may be given on Purim.

Rabbi: a scholar, a teacher, a leader in the community.

Reb: a wise man. And, since everyone in Chelm is wise, the men are all called Reb… as in Reb Stein, Reb Cantor, and so on.

Rebbetzin: The rabbi's wife.

Rosh Hashanah: the Jewish New Year.

schlep/shlep 1. To walk, but not a happy joy-filled walk, more like a burden. 2. To carry a burden. 3. Someone who is a burden.

Seder: the Passover feast. A huge meal with lots of prayers, songs and stories. No leavened bread. No challah. Just matzah. Followed by seemingly endless days of matzah. Oy.

Shabbas/Shabbat/Shabbos: the Jewish Sabbath. Starts Friday at sundown and ends Saturday after sunset.

shalom: Sometimes hello, sometimes goodbye, but especially peace.

shammos: the candle used to light other candles on the Chanukah menorah.

shmaltz: chicken fat. Used in cooking and spread on bread. Source of many heart attacks.

shmear: a big hunk of cream cheese usually spread on a bagel, but during Passover you can shmear matzah.

shemini: Hebrew for eighth. Shemini Schlemiel was born on the eighth day of both Chanukah and her mother's labor.

shmootz/shmuts: dust, dirt, those little brown flecks of stuff that you find here and there.

shmooze/shmoozing/shmoozed/shmoozer: to chat at length about nothing or everything. A shmoozer shmoozes, shmoozing until shmoozed out.

Shmura Matzah: a special round matzah made from carefully guarded wheat. Often burned. Don't use it for matzah brie.

Shul: the synagogue.

shvitz: to perspire.

Shul: the synagogue.

simches: joy. See also *nachas*.

Smyrna: the town nearest to Chelm. Lots of nice people and a few practical jokers live there.

tallis: is a fringed prayer shawl. (plural: tallisim or tallit)

Tante: aunt.

Torah: The Five Books of Moses. The first five books of the Hebrew Bible, which is frequently called the Old Testament.

tsedaka: a gift of charity.

tsuris: woe, trouble, aggravation. Especially something you get from rotten children.

tuchas: the posterior. The behind. The bottom. The part of the body you sit with. The southern end of a north-going Chelmener. Clear enough?

yad: a pointer. You're not supposed to touch the Torah Scroll as you read, so instead of pointing with your finger, you use a yad. The word means hand, so it often looks just like a tiny hand with its index finger outstretched.

yarmulke: the skull cap worn during prayers. Often abbreviated as **kippah**, which is not to be confused with the fish.

yenta: a gossip, a busybody.

yeshiva: the religious school. In Chelm, the yeshiva is the only school.

Yom Kippur: The Day of Atonement. No one eats or drinks. No kiggle, knaidel, babke, challah, or shmaltz or even matzah. Always followed by the break-fast, a sumptuous meal served after dark. All the food at the break-fast is eaten in a matter of moments.

zaftig: plump, but in a good way. Rubenesque.

Acknowledgements

Books are a journey. This one has been particularly long and winding. Thanks to Vicki Samuels at the *Jewish Herald Voice,* Rena Potok at Jewish Publications Society, the Pucker Family, Nora Gerad and Susan Bronson at the National Yiddish Book Center. Thanks to Marc Chagal for the inspiration with his painting The Blue House. Thanks to the initial subscribers to the digital version of *The Brothers Schlemiel,* and to all my fans and listeners over the years. Thanks to the Little Rest Storytellers, especially Carolyn Martino and Jeanne Donato, who heard many of the first drafts, and gave me the nudge to become a performing storyteller. Thanks to Fishel Bresler for both his music and his teaching me how to play a bit of klezmer harmonica. Any flat notes are mine, not his. Thanks to George Dussault for working with me on my audio books, starting with *The Brothers Schlemiel From Birth to Bar Mitzvah.* Thanks to my "pitch" listeners Max Binder, Simon Brooks, David Fishman (one of my oldest and dearest friends), Robb Cutler, and Gayle Turner. Thanks to Jessica Everette, Nina Rooks Cast, Margie Beller, and Elaine Binder for their careful line by line, word by word, comma by comma editing. Thanks to Callie Beaulieu for her advice on the audiobook. Thanks to my staff: Beth Hellman, Stephen Brendan and Lou Pop. Without you, everybody would blame me for everything. Thanks always to Heather, for her love and keeping me sane.

If I missed thanking anyone, I apologize. Let me know and we'll add it to the next edition…

The Village Life Series

"The Village is snuggled in an indeterminate past that never was but certainly should have been, a past filled with love, humor, adventures and more than occasional misadventures. And when you go, be sure to bring the kids." – *The Times of Israel*

The Village Twins - a novel for adults

When the seventh daughter of a seventh daughter has twins, you know there will be trouble. Abraham and Adam Schlemiel star in this warm comedy that blends ordinary life with adventure and epic confusion.

"In the spirit of Sholem Aleichem… identical twins, confused from birth, will charm with their simplicity and sincerity." – *AudioFile*

A Village Romance - a short and sweet book

He's the wisest man in the village. She runs the only restaurant. They are both widowed…. What could possibly go wrong?

"engaging tales… Village stories that deftly lift a curtain on a world of friendly humor and touching details of Jewish life." – *Kirkus Reviews*

Winter Blessings

National Jewish Book Award for Family Literature Finalist!
Eleven funny and heart-warming Chanukah stories and a novella.

"Parents and grandparents will enjoy reading selections aloud and retelling the stories." – *AJL Newsletter*

The Village Feasts

Ten tasty Passover tales for adults and children of all ages. Delightful and amusing.

The Council of Wise Women - a novel for adults – Coming Soon!

Another set of twins? Oy! The birth of Rachel and Yakov Cohen bring new blessings and challenges to The Village.

books, ebooks, and audiobooks available at your favorite retailer and at IzzyAbe.com

Made in the USA
Middletown, DE
29 July 2022

69986923R10250